# WAKING
# DARK

Also by Robin Wasserman

*The Book of Blood and Shadow*

# THE
# WAKING
# DARK

## ROBIN WASSERMAN

www.atombooks.net

ATOM

First published in the United States in 2013 by Random House Children's Books
First published in Great Britain in 2013 by Atom

Copyright © 2013 by Robin Wasserman

The moral right of the author has been asserted.

A CIP catalogue record for this book
is available from the British Library.

ISBN 978-1-907411-45-8

Printed and bound in Great Britain by
Clay Ltd, St Ives plc

Papers used by Atom are from well-managed forests
and other responsible sources.

MIX
Paper from
responsible sources
FSC® C104740

Atom
An imprint of
Little, Brown Book Group
100 Victoria Embankment
London EC4Y 0DY

An Hachette UK Company
www.hachette.co.uk

www.atombooks.net

*For anyone who needs a little courage*

*This is your hour—when darkness reigns.*

Luke 22:52

*Oh, this is a state to be proud of! We are a people who can hold up our heads!*

William Allen White

## 1

## THE CALM BEFORE

Later, after he'd trashed his bloody clothes, and stood under the cold shower long enough that the water circling the drain had gone from red to pink to clear, Daniel Ghent would wonder if some part of him had known what was to come—or should have. If there had been something false, something crafty, in Gathers' crookedly welcoming smile, or some too-still quality in the air, like the pressure drop before a storm. He would wonder if there was some reason he had walked into the store on exactly that day, at precisely that time, if despite all previous indications to the contrary, he had been meant to be a hero and save the day. He would wonder whether, if he had seen it coming, he could have done something to stop it, or whether he would simply have backed out of the store and run away. But that was later.

That afternoon, that sticky, sweaty Tuesday in the dog days of summer, he'd seen nothing but heat waves shimmering from pockmarked concrete and a long walk home. He'd known only that it was hot, and that Gathers Drugs on the corner of Ashton and Main was the closest place to buy a Coke or maybe, because there was something about the sun and the sweat and the smell of scorched cement that made him feel like a kid again, one of the sodden ice cream sandwiches Mr. Gathers kept in a tank behind the register.

So he went inside.

The door chimed with his entrance and Gathers took the time to grin a hello before turning back to filling a prescription for Eugenia Wooden. The self-described spinster lived down the street from Daniel and spent half her life in the doctor's office cheerfully complaining of coughs and wheezes and stomach pains and all manner of imagined infirmity until the doctor wrote her a scrip for something or other just to get her to leave. She was nice enough, at least now that Daniel was too old to trample her flower garden with his bicycle or break her windows with an errant baseball. She believed in the healing powers of chamomile tea, strict rules about wearing white after Labor Day, the Republican Party ("after they booted the criminals out" and "before the kooks took over"), civil rights ("within reason"), the wisdom of the Lord and the foolishness of His self-assigned deputies, and, on occasion, a stiff shot of whiskey.

She had approximately ten minutes left to live.

They all did: Sally, the waitress at D'Angelo's who gave free breadsticks to anyone who knew enough to flirt with her. Kathleen Hanrahan, who had babysat for Daniel's little brother until the night Daniel's father stumbled home drunk enough to mistake her for his dead wife. Happy Jerry, a thirty-year-old who couldn't read past a third-grade level but loved comic books and spent every afternoon browsing through the drugstore racks. All of them, dead in ten minutes, except Old Winston, who'd been kicked out of the bar next door and had slumped down by the ladies' hosiery shelf rather than go home and face his wife. He survived for nearly half an hour—though if his desperate prayers to *Please, God, just let me die already* were any indication, he didn't exactly welcome the delay.

They all—except a snoring Winston—greeted Daniel by name, exchanging the standard pleasantries about the weather (too hot), the day (too long), and the town (waning). There were no polite inquiries about his father; there was no need. Anyone interested in Daniel Ghent Sr.'s well-being could take a field trip down to the church square, where the Preacher, as he preferred to be called, had set up camp. He'd fester in the plaza for a few weeks, shoving his wrinkled End of Days pamphlets at passersby until the spirit—or the Jack Daniel's— moved him to try somewhere new. Daniel, who'd overdosed on humiliation back in grade school, when the whistled chorus of "Son of a Preacher Man" followed him everywhere, was officially no longer bothered by his father's extracurricular activities. But he still kept track of the wandering ministry—if only to ensure he stayed, at all times, on the opposite side of town.

"You bringing someone pretty to the church picnic this weekend?" Gathers asked. Daniel didn't bother to wonder at the glaze in the old man's eyes or the perfunctory note in his voice. Nor did he spot anything unusual about the way Gathers kept fiddling with something beneath the counter, sneaking quick, nervous glances at whatever lay below. "Supposed to be a fine, fine day."

"Not going to the picnic," Daniel mumbled. Daniel never went to the picnics. Or the ice cream socials or the potlucks or the bingo nights or the theme dances that featured Reverend Willet dressing up as a pirate or a biblical forefather or, on one memorable occasion, a feather-headed, war-painted Navajo brave.

A damp, meaty hand landed on his shoulder. Every muscle went on alert. His fingers, of their own accord, twitched and balled themselves into a ready fist.

But it was only Happy Jerry, smiling and defenseless and meaning no harm.

"For Milo," Jerry said, shoving a sticky comic book into Daniel's hand.

"Thanks, Jerry—he'll love it." Daniel flipped through the wrinkled pages, past caped heroes who never arrived too late and punches that never left a bruise. He couldn't remember ever being young enough to believe in that kind of world; he didn't want to imagine his little brother ever being old enough to stop.

He was thinking about Milo as he picked out the least squashed of the ice cream sandwiches and dropped a wad of crumpled bills on Gathers' counter. About the things he'd overheard the kids screaming on the playground, the claims that Milo stank, that he was dirty and unwashed and probably diseased. He was thinking about the foot-thick layer of worn and reworn clothing that covered both their bedroom floors, and the broken washing machine and the empty refrigerator and the housekeeper, paid for by his father's disability checks, who had quit two weeks before.

But that was well-worn mental territory, and, as if his life were the scene of an accident, replete with mangled bodies and gasoline fires, he forced himself to look away. By the time he stuffed his wallet back into his jeans, cracked open his Coke, and murmured agreement with Eugenia Wooden that, yes, it was an excellent thing that flu-shot distribution had begun so early this year, you could never be too careful, he was instead thinking about *her*. Cassandra Porter, again, still, always, Cass Porter and those damn short skirts that tended to ride up on her long, tan legs when she bent to adjust her strappy sandals or with self-conscious whimsy pluck a dandelion for her hair. Cass Porter, who'd spent the first eight years of her life at his side—and barely looked at him in the nine years since. Any illusions he nurtured that they could pick up where they left off—if with a little less playing alien explorer in the backyard and a little more groping in the dark—were swiftly dispatched every time he set eyes on the real thing. There was only room in the family for one delusional Ghent, and his father had already laid claim to the role.

His father. There Daniel's thoughts finally landed, just before Gathers, with a bland smile, drew the secret thing from beneath the counter and the secret thing revealed itself to be a shotgun. Whether his father was getting worse. Whether Daniel would care if his father left one morning and never came back. Whether somewhere, in the deep recesses of Daniel's brain, rested a time bomb that would eventually explode and launch him into a dream world as bad as his father's, or worse. Whether he could, for one more day and then one more day after that, stop himself from leaving his father and his house and his brother behind, in hopes that even the nowhere he had to go would be better than the somewhere he longed to escape.

The first blast screamed past his shoulder. Behind him, a

wall of ketchup exploded and showered him with a gush of sugary red. He didn't think. He dropped. Face down, arms sprawled, eyes closed. Playing possum. Playing dead. He tried not to move.

He tried not to hear the screams.

Breaking glass.

Footsteps.

The heavy thud of bodies hitting the floor.

The scraping, scrabbling of useless limbs.

Screams and screams and screams.

Rasping.

Moaning.

Again, again, the thunder of the gun.

And then nothing.

After a long moment of silence, he opened his eyes, fully expecting to see Gathers standing over him with the gun the old man had bought years before to scare off tweakers on a Sudafed rampage.

But Gathers had a hole where his face used to be. Daniel didn't want to touch the gun.

Sally was dead. Jerry was dead. Winston's eyes were open but his body was more blood and exposed organs than skin. Eugenia Wooden was beyond prescriptions.

Daniel thought he must be dead, too—that he was one of those pathetic TV ghosts, clueless until someone shoved his corpse in his face. As he crawled across the linoleum, palms and knees tearing on a carpet of broken glass, he was nearly convinced that if he turned back, he would see himself, ventilated and still and already starting to rot.

It occurred to him that it might be best to stop thinking anything at all.

He gave up on checking the bodies, and lay down again, oblivious to the pool of blood, Gathers' blood, beneath him. He closed his eyes.

Later, alone, locked in his room, ashamed and afraid, he would cry.

But there, in the corner drugstore that would soon be boarded up and skirted by children who whispered of vengeful ghosts, lying facedown in the mingled blood of a murderer and his victims, waiting for the cops to come, waiting to discover he was dead after all, Daniel did something he would never confess to anyone and would soon convince himself to forget.

He closed his eyes. He let go.


The girl standing in the doorway was altogether too happy, not to mention too pink. She looked like a crayon and smelled like stale corsage. Jule should never have opened the door. Hadn't they warned her that often enough? *Stranger danger*, that was the mantra every Oleander child learned to recite. Except that at school, you were taught to flee the danger by seeking a uniform, a cop, a fireman—even a mailman would do in a pinch. At school, she'd dutifully colored in the pictures of Officer Friendly, but even at that age she'd known enough to throw them out on the way home, before her uncles could see. At home, uniforms were the danger. At home, strangers were everywhere, and their strangeness ran deep. It lived in their mouths of rotting teeth and the twitchy hands that carved mysterious trails through the air as if sculpting with invisible clay, and eyes that were all at once too bright and too empty. Jule knew better than to open the door.

But this girl, this crayon, could not possibly be a customer.

She chirped, "Hi there! I'm here to spread the Word!"

"The word is *bullshit,* and we already have enough of that. Thanks anyway."

It felt good. But as soon as she slammed the trailer door in the girl's now slightly less perky pink face, Jule realized her mistake. She recognized the girl from school, one of the interchangeable church girls who twitted in distress about all the sinners in their midst, the smokers and the swearers and—they loved nothing more than an excuse to be *shocked!* and *horrified!* by these—the sluts. Jule was beneath their notice. Or had been, until she'd let her frustration with the clogged toilet and the broken stove and her mother's latest parasite erode her common sense. She'd opened the door. She'd opened her mouth. Now who knew what stories the girl would run home and tell her saintly friends about the Prevette compound, with its browning weeds and its heaps of junk and its triple-locked double-wides and the sad, ragged girl who lived among them.

"You got more beer?" The parasite's voice filtered out of the closet space with the cardboard door that her mother called a bedroom. Most nights the couch was fine with Jule, but nights when the parasite stayed over, and the noises began, thumps and gasps and the occasional muffled scream, she preferred to spend sitting outside the trailer, chugging Red Bull and waiting for dawn.

It had been one of those nights. There'd been time for a

lumpy catnap in the early hours of morning, curled up on the couch, half asleep and half alert for any stirring from the happy couple, but all too soon had come the knock at the door. Now *he* was up.

"You drank it all last night." Her mother sounded annoyed, but not annoyed enough to do anything about it. In Jule's experience, this level of irritation suggested another month or so before she rid herself of the parasite—or until he sucked her dry and left her with a black eye and a broken heart. She was a country-western song writ large and loud, and Jule had given up trying to save her.

"I was *thirsty*," the parasite said, and then there was a pause and, from her mother, a disgusting giggle.

"Jule!" she shouted. "You out there?"

Jule said nothing.

"We need more beer!"

Jule said nothing.

"I hear you breathing," the parasite called. "You want me to come out there and teach you to listen to your mother?"

"Be nice to Jule," her mother said, which was almost good enough. But then she giggled again.

This time when Jule opened the door, she was smart enough to go through it.

Jule hated her name—*the only thing your father ever gave you*, her mother liked to say. Juliet, the most beautiful name he'd ever heard, or so he told Jule's mother while they lay naked and hungover in the flatbed of a friend's pickup. Not beautiful for a daughter, per se, since the trucker had been halfway to California before an endless bout of puking proved itself to be morning sickness. The name was all-purpose, suitable for baby, pet Rottweiler, naked woman on a grease-stained tarp—*it's just pretty*, he'd said, and then kissed Jule's mother again, not wanting to waste his last night in town. *Like you.*

Jule didn't know his name. She didn't know if he was Mexican (as her mother guessed) or "good old-fashioned Indian, the scalping kind" (as her uncles claimed). Her mother wasn't stingy about the details, at least those she could remember. But what she remembered—the heat of his body, the palm-sized birthmark on his thigh, the scratches he'd carved in the heat of passion—Jule wished she would forget. As she'd forgotten his name. But Juliet, that she remembered. When the baby came, her skin the color of weak tea and her eyes as dark as her father's, the choice was simple: Juliet Prevette. A name for something beautiful.

It didn't fit; it didn't last.

She was, had always been, Jule, an ugly sound that twisted the mouth into an ugly shape, and easily attached itself to other, more important things: Jule-do-the-dishes, Jule-get-the-laundry, Jule-stop-whining, Jule-find-us-some-beer.

They were names that hadn't always defined her, not when defiance was safe because Uncle Scott was there to protect her. Her mother's bloodsuckers could say what they liked, but let them even think about raising a hand against Scott Prevette's darling niece, and they would reap the consequences. Jule was the family's only child, and Scott the family's only authority. That made her safe, but that was before: Before he'd started sampling his own merchandise, before he'd started seeing enemies everywhere—in the bushes, in the bedroom, in the bloodline. Before Jule had stopped being cute and started talking back.

She was still his favorite—but that wasn't worth nearly as much as it once had been. Which meant if the parasite wanted beer, she'd better get him beer. Though the options on that front were limited. Scott's younger brothers, Teddy and Axe, were locked in the trailer at the edge of the compound, brewing up another batch of the "stuff" that Jule—presumed to be a moron—wasn't supposed to know about. Their women, usually high and always temporary, saw Jule as a threat. When her uncles weren't around to impress, they competed among themselves for who could humiliate her the most efficiently. (Scott's latest, a strung-out redhead with cigarette burns running up and down her arms, was currently in the lead.) But her uncle James, the youngest of her mother's brothers, was likely to be awake, unoccupied, and sober. His girlfriend—an actual girlfriend, with a name and a sock drawer of her very own— had once given Jule a manicure, just for the hell of it, and since then seemed to consider them girlfriends.

Jule kept her eyes open as she crossed the compound, but there was no sign of the crayon. James and Gloria lived on the southern edge of the barren grounds that had been marked out as Prevette territory, as far from the meth labs as they could get. James preferred pot to speed. James preferred pot to pretty much everything.

She knocked at his trailer. There was no answer.

"James? Gloria?" She paused, listening. "Mom wants some beer."

Nothing. But she could hear them, behind the door, and

that was strange, because neither James nor Gloria was the yelling type. They were yelling now. Not even yelling, but yowling, like the cats did when Scott seized them by the tail and swung them over his head. She eased open the door.

Even though she knew better.

She really should have known better.

James was . . . *leaking*. At first, her brain scrabbling for purchase on the situation, that was the only word she could muster. He was sitting on the floor of the trailer, leaking glops of something dark and red and—

*No*, she told herself, some dim animal sense of self-preservation jerking her gaze away from the hole in James's stomach and the things sliding out of it. But she couldn't look away from the sounds he was making. The feline screams had stopped, and now there was only a soft, wet noise, a whimpering snuffle moistened by sprays of blood.

*Stranger danger*, she thought, moving in slow motion, out of the trailer, away from the quivering, leaking thing that had been her uncle James. She stumbled backward, but not quickly enough. Gloria lurched out of the bathroom, a matching hole in her stomach, a bloody hunting knife in her hand, a knife she noticed as if for the first time and then threw against the wall with what must have been her last burst of strength, because in the same motion her legs gave out. When they did, it was Jule's neck she slung her slippery arms around and Jule's shuddering body she dragged to the floor. "I did that," Gloria said, blood bubbling from her lips with every word. "Why did I do that?"

Jule threw up.

Gloria died before James, though she had stabbed him first.

The knife had been Uncle Scott's favorite, and later, after making his new woman wash off the blood, he reclaimed it as his own.

*The Lord will raise me up.*

*The Lord will raise me up.*

*Raise me up, Lord.*

*Raise me* up*!*

The Lord was silent.

The Lord was disappointed.

Ellie prayed for His forgiveness.

Ellie prayed for His suffrage.

Ellie prayed.

The Church of the Word was empty at this hour, as the faithful fanned across town to Spread His Word. Fortunately, Ellie had the key to the youth ministry office, for Ellie had been indispensable in rallying troops for the annual Spread His Word Day. Ellie had worked tirelessly on promotion and organization, Ellie had sacrificed her summer to the Lord, and about that Ellie had no regrets.

But Ellie had failed.

She'd tasked herself with the most difficult and least desirable of assignments, because He said whatever you did not do for the least among you, you did not do for Me. The Prevettes were, by any measure, the least. Reverend Willet had warned her away, but Reverend Willet was soft. That's what Deacon Barnes always said, though never to the assistant minister's face. Ellie liked Reverend Willet, but she *listened* to Deacon Barnes. His was the voice that had brought her to God, and this voice tolerated no weakness.

Clair and Morgan, her youth co-leaders, praised the Lord for her bold sacrifice, but she knew they thought she was showing off. They hated her for it, as she'd hated Clair for baking twelve batches of cookies for the bake sale, and she and Clair had together hated Morgan for spending all day in the rain, helping to build the Noah's Ark float for the Fourth of July parade, despite having the flu. (She called it the flu; her doctor called it mono. They all politely ignored the fact that Andrew Chadwick—with whom the virginal Morgan had *certainly* exchanged no fluids, how dare you?—was down with the same thing.)

But Ellie wasn't showing off, not this time. She was testing herself.

And she had failed.

She'd failed from the first moment she set foot on the compound, her heart thumping rabbit-fast, and she'd spotted a blond giant who could only be Scott Prevette lurching toward her. He was perhaps the town's most infamous sinner, his prison stints, his war with the cartel runners, and his subsequent appropriation of the county's meth distribution all common lore. *The least of us,* Ellie had thought, crouching ignobly behind a rusting Buick. *The very least.* But it was only after Scott Prevette had wandered off with his unsteady toddler's gait that she dared rise to her feet. With a silent prayer for strength and forbearance, she'd passed one trailer after the next, this one guarded by a loosely chained Doberman, this one padlocked, this one occupied by someone screaming what her mother would have called bloody murder. Finally, she'd found it within herself to approach one of the sad excuses for a house, and smile inanely at the girl who opened the door, who had blasphemed and slammed the door in her face. It was all the excuse Ellie needed to burst into tears and run away.

She wasn't delusional. She knew Scott Prevette lay beyond her powers of redemption. But Jule was just a girl, probably a sad and lonely one, if the glimpses Ellie caught of her at school were any indication. She needed help. And instead of delivering it, Ellie had fled.

Because the trailers frightened her, yes. But also because she'd been looking for an excuse. The compound was dirty. The compound smelled. *Jule* smelled, or at least her trailer did, an unsettling mix of mold, dish soap, and sewage. People weren't supposed to live like that. Facing Jule, with her ratty, skintight jeans and combat boots, her tangle of black hair that had surely never seen the inside of the Cut-N-Edge, her dark skin that everyone was supposed to ignore because of course educated people knew better than to care, Ellie had been seized by a powerful revulsion. It was the same wave of disgust that had washed over her in the soup kitchen and the cancer ward and on the day she'd accidentally stumbled into a Narcotics Anonymous meeting and taken—meaning *touched,* meaning *drunk from*—one of the rapidly cooling cups of coffee. Those other times, she'd been in public, surrounded by people with certain expectations of sweet, kind Eleanor King. So she'd stroked damp foreheads and shaken callused hands and drunk that entire cup of weak coffee, and smiled throughout, because people were watching. At the Prevette compound, no one was watching, and Ellie's true nature had revealed itself.

*Raise me up, Lord,* she begged, but the Lord wasn't listening, and who could blame Him.

She'd let herself into the office thinking to bury herself in work, but the work was done. Today there was only the Work, and sitting in the office, surrounded by her lists and maps and happy-face-dotted Post-its, reminded her too much of failure. She would retreat to the nave, she decided, where there would be less to distract her from prayer.

The nave, too, should have been empty, but when Ellie slipped into the dark, hushed chamber, she could hear someone breathing. They were high, rapid breaths, air whistling through a clenched throat, and Ellie's heartbeat sped to match the rhythm. On sunny afternoons, the soaring stained-glass windows showered the pews with rainbows, but this day the deep summer haze had bleached the sky white, and there was little sunlight to filter through the glassy scenes of sorrow and retribution. It took Ellie's eyes a moment to adjust, and a moment more to place the man who'd intruded on her solitude. She had entered at the back of the nave; he was all the way at the front, up in the sanctuary. But as she approached, shuffling down the aisle even though everything in her screamed that she should be heading in the other direction, she was sure. It was Henry Pierce, who did odd jobs around the church, repairing drywall, plugging leaks, uncrossing wires, all for what he claimed was a churchly discount but what Deacon Barnes referred to, not always under his breath, as extortion. He was widowed and mustached, and more than occasionally smelled of whiskey.

He was nailed to the cross.

Ellie rarely had lurid dreams, and never nightmares. But surely this was an exception, because surely Henry Pierce was not in the church sanctuary, stripped naked and hanging from a wooden cross by stakes driven through his bloody wrists and ankles. Even more surely, Eleanor King was not standing before his spread-eagled figure, her fingertips approaching, then touching—*touching!*—the cross of blood that anointed his forehead. His face was slick with sweat. His eyes were closed.

And then they were open.

Ellie screamed.

"Go," he whispered. "You have to go."

The dreamlike detachment collapsed in on itself, and suddenly the sticky blood and the fetid sweat smell and the pain in his voice and the fear in his eyes were all too real. She screamed again, and began tugging first at the thick spikes pinning him to the cross and then at his arm itself, trying to ignore his choked moans every time his torn flesh ground against the iron. She tugged, and his lips flapped, and no sound came out until, again, every word a labor, "You have to go."

"But I have to help you," she said, fumbling for her phone, staining her dress and purse with blood.

Henry Pierce swallowed. His bare chest heaved as he drew in a mighty breath, readying himself to speak again.

The words came slowly, and softer than before. "He's. Coming. Back."

For one slow, stupid moment, Ellie thought he was referring to the Lord.

"*Run.*"

The pieces fell into place, and already she was moving, her legs smarter than her foggy brain. Henry Pierce was nailed to a cross.

*Someone* had nailed Henry Pierce to a cross.

*Someone* was coming back.

She did as Henry said and she ran, reaching the doorway just as Reverend Willet emerged from the passage behind the sanctuary. She was about to scream in panic and joy and sheer relief—until she noticed that Reverend Willet was carrying a can of gasoline in one hand and a lighter in the other. Reverend Willet was coated with blood.

Crouched on the safe side of the door, Ellie peered through the crack and dialed 911, but she couldn't speak. She could only watch as Reverend Willet—who had helped her memorize her first psalm, who took any excuse to don a costume, who played hymns and, in trusted company, Beatles songs on his ukulele, who was too kind, too tolerant, and all too soft—poured gasoline over Henry Pierce, and the altar, and the pews, and himself. He flicked his lighter, and she watched the fire spark. She watched them burn.

And something within her sparked, too.

The flames burned away her fear. She swung the door open wide. "I see you!" she shouted at Reverend Willet, at the burning thing he had become. As the fire devoured the men and their cross, Ellie understood with a blazing clarity that the tests she had set for herself had been nothing but a child's game.

She saw her purpose now.

She saw, even across the burning sanctuary, the reverend's

eyes, which held something she understood and was finally prepared to fight.

She saw evil.

The street was deserted, but it was daytime, and you could never be too careful. So they would not hold hands. No matter how much West might have wanted to.

They walked slowly, ostensibly to accommodate Nick's limp but also, by unstated agreement, to draw out the trip back to town as long as possible. They couldn't stay in the cornfields forever, lying on their backs and naming the clouds, tall stalks bending in the wind, their linked fingers and tangled legs hidden by waves of golden green. They could, if they dawdled, delay the inevitable return.

"I found a new one," Nick said. "*Jupiter 5050*—a bunch of astronauts accidentally travel to the future and end up the main exhibit in some kind of alien zoo." Their current obsession was bad sci-fi movies from the fifties, the cheesier the better. (Extra points when the special effects involved alien spaceships dangling from visible strings.) "You want to come over and watch Sunday?"

West didn't answer.

"We don't have to watch the whole thing," Nick said. "We could just . . ." He cleared his throat. "My parents are out of town."

"Can't."

Nick looked alarmed. "I didn't mean— I mean, we don't have to . . ."

"It's not that. I just . . . can't."

"Oh."

"I'm going to that picnic thing," West said. "With Cass."

"Oh."

"It's no big deal," he said quickly. He didn't know how this worked. He didn't even know if he *wanted* it to work.

No, that was a lie. He wanted it.

"It's just a thing." He shrugged. "It's nothing."

"It's fine," Nick said. His pace quickened, and West pretended not to notice him wince each time his weight landed on the bad leg. Nick wouldn't say where the limp had come from. Rather, he said plenty, fantastical explanations about skydiving crashes and circus calamities, until West gave up asking. He knew only that in fifth grade, Nick had been perfect, one of those golden-haloed kids that the others knew instinctively to follow, as if the shine would rub off on them. Maybe too much of it had, because Nick had appeared on the first day of sixth grade with long hair that nearly covered his permanent scowl and a leg that moved like a block of wood. At unpredictable intervals, it gave out beneath him, pitching him into pratfalls that the old Nick would have known how to turn into a joke. The new Nick only lay there, rubbing his leg and scowling harder, as if daring someone to kick him while he was down.

The limp had improved over the years, but it always marked him as different. West sometimes wondered whether that made the rest of it easier for him, not having a choice.

"I can tell her I can't go," West said, hating himself for how little he wanted to do that. Cass was like armor. As long as he wore her on his arm every few weeks, he was safe. Or, at least, safer—nothing about this was safe. "I will. I'll just tell her."

"I said it's fine."

"It's obviously not fine."

Nick reached for him, then remembered himself, and pulled back just in time. He shook his head.

"I'm sorry," West said. "I really am."

"It's a movie. We'll watch another time."

"I know what you want me to do, but . . . I can't."

"Jeremiah." This time, checking first to make sure there were no cars in sight, Nick did take his hand. Only briefly, long enough to give it a single, quick squeeze. Nick was the only one who called him Jeremiah. Even his mother had been trained out of the habit. "I don't want you to do anything. The way things are now, it's fine. It's good."

"Now is when you say *'But . . .'*" It stunned West how well he had learned to read Nick's face, the crinkle of concern in his pale forehead or the way he bit the inside of his cheek when he was nervous. As he did now.

"*But* it's going to be different, once school starts."

"I told you—"

Nick held up a hand to stop him. "I meant what I said. I don't want you to do *anything.* I'm just . . . sorry it's ending."

"You mean summer."

"Yeah. Summer."

They had reached the fork in the road where they habitually parted, one path leading to Nick's house at the heart of town, the other to West's family farm on its outskirts. The narrow highway was lined with cottonwood trees, one of them thick enough to provide cover. West took a deep breath, then took Nick's hand. They secreted themselves behind the tree. West leaned into the trunk, savoring the roughness of the bark on the back of his neck. It came to him that these were the kinds of details he would want to remember.

When it ended.

"We shouldn't risk it," Nick said, but he didn't mean it.

"I want to," West said, and he did.

Nick had never asked anything of him. Not even at the beginning, when they were near strangers to each other, just polite acquaintances sharing an exile from phys ed. Nick had his limp; West had a football injury he'd exacerbated at the start of baseball season, enough so that his season soon ended for good. Nick never pressed, never hurried. It was West who had to suggest they continue their long talks over warm beers in Nick's backyard, their shirts in a heap beside them, the sun blazing down, the sweat pooling between their shoulder blades. For endless afternoons, they rehashed old Super Bowl plays and debated whether their math teacher's chin mole was grosser than their Spanish teacher's werewolf knuckles and circled around the thing neither of them was willing to name. Eventually the conversation ran out, and then there was only the two of them, and an empty house, and a soft bed of grass, and sweaty skin, and want.

When it happened, it was West who moved first.

The guys had understood West keeping to himself as long as he was sidelined by an injury. But his arm had healed, and in the fall, the team would be waiting. Watching. Nick believed it was the team he was worried about—and the girls who worshipped him, the almost-ran guys who wanted to be him, the teachers who turned a blind eye and passed him, the full cast of characters who'd long accepted the myth of Jeremiah West. Nick believed that West cared, and it was easier to let him.

"You're insatiable," Nick said, offering his first real smile since they'd left the cornfield.

"Perks of dating a jock," West said, aware of the word that had slipped out, the one they'd both been conscious never to use. "Plenty of stamina."

"Let's not forget conditioning." Nick ran an appraising hand across West's defined torso. "Also much appreciated."

West kissed him.

They clung to each other, bodies mashed together, and Nick's hands found West's waist, his shoulders, his neck, then cradled his head, pulling him closer, and closer still. Before Nick, there had been girls, and that had been pleasant enough. But with them, West had never felt this kind of hunger, this need that consumed him now for pale, freckled skin, for wiry muscles, for hands and lips and tongue.

It was the hunger that had, finally, been impossible to ignore.

It was safer to emerge separately from their flimsy hiding spot, and so Nick set out first, reluctantly. "I'll miss you," he said, with excessive melodrama, so West wouldn't mistake it for what it obviously was: true.

West laughed. "You'll see me *tomorrow*."

"Excellent point. I take it back—I'm sick of you."

"Not as sick as I am of you." West wanted to grab him again, to drag him back behind the tree, to kiss him, to swallow him whole. But he didn't.

He let Nick go.

Down the road, limping, slowly, oblivious to the black Chevrolet that suddenly roared up behind him—oblivious until West shouted, and then too slow, too awkward, to get out of the way. Spinning around to face the oncoming car, Nick shuffled backward and then, as he hadn't in years, pitched into one of his awkward falls. The car kept coming. The chrome bumper caught him at the waist and lifted him off his feet and carried him like a hood ornament and West ran and ran and no feet had ever been so slow. He ran, and the car slammed Nick into a tree, another cottonwood, sturdy and unyielding. The car backed up and rammed him again, and again, and again, until the bark was bloody and Nick was a broken rag hanging from the dented bumper. With a final gunning of the engine, the driver shot through the windshield and landed on top of him, and only then did the car finally rest. Only then did West reach the bodies, an eternity past too late.

Nick was in the grass, his limbs jutting at all the wrong angles, metal and glass and gravel embedded in his fair, perfect skin. The driver lay across him, the blood that gushed from his chest splashing on Nick's face and pooling in the hollow of his neck. It was Paul Caster, West's assistant coach, a man who'd once led West's Pee Wee football team to a league championship.

Neither of the bloody heaps was moving.

West knelt. He wiped the blood from Nick's forehead and pressed his lips to the ruined skin. It was still warm, and, in some dim, calm place miles beneath his panic, West supposed it took some time before a person turned into a corpse. He dug into Nick's pocket and found his phone, mysteriously intact, and used it to call 911. An accident, he reported, though it had not been that. Come quickly, he begged, though there was now no hurry.

He kissed Nick's lips, hungry, even now, now more than ever, for more.

And now the hunger, he realized, would never go away.

Now there would be only want and need. There would be no Nick.

West was the one who felt cold.

He folded the phone into Nick's limp fingers. And then, because there was nothing left he could do, because Nick was gone, and because he was a coward, he ran away.

No one knew how much Cassandra Porter hated children. Except perhaps the children, who seemed to sense the hostility that leaked from her pores. The timid ones smiled politely and stayed close to their mothers. The bold ones kicked her shins or shouted things like "Not the ugly lady!"—which failed to help their cause.

It wasn't an abnormally strong aversion; it wasn't even hate, precisely, so much as disinterest verging on mild distaste. She could admit that giggling babies and dimpled kindergarteners were cute; she just wanted nothing to do with them. It wasn't her fault that in the eyes of the child-adoring world, that translated as hate. So she kept it to herself, and no one was the wiser, except the children, who could always tell.

It made babysitting a bit of a chore.

Gracie Tuck stood up from the table, her untouched pizza cooling on her plate. "I'm going to my room," she said.

"Okay."

"No big plans for the night."

"I wouldn't expect so."

"Probably I'll just smoke and drink a little and maybe play with some matches if I get bored."

"Don't burn the house down."

Gracie was twelve, a blond waif with an elfin smile, which she deployed now. She was, by far, Cass's favorite babysitting charge, self-sufficient, jaded beyond her years, and clearly embittered by the fact that her parents still felt she needed a babysitter. Hence the polite fiction that Cass was only there to supervise the baby now miraculously asleep upstairs. As far as Cass could tell, Gracie hated children even more than she did, and seemed to reserve a particular animosity for her baby brother. Or, as Gracie liked to call him, the Accident.

She wasn't the type of child most people found adorable, but Cass appreciated her peculiar charms. Usually. Tonight there was something unsettling about the appraising way she looked at her babysitter, as if weighing whether it would be safe to leave her downstairs, alone. There was something about her tonight . . . something that made Cass wonder whether she really did have big plans of some sort, whatever would constitute big plans for a twelve-year-old whose best friend was a pet chameleon. For a moment, she toyed with the idea of following Gracie up the spiral staircase, inviting herself into the girl's bedroom for a round of Monopoly, or Truth or Dare, or whatever it was normal twelve-year-olds spent their time doing. But then the baby cried, and in the subsequent flurry of rocking and feeding and diaper changing, Cass forgot her concerns. An hour later, settled in front of the TV, she closed her eyes and promptly fell asleep.

She dreamed that Jeremiah West was gnawing at her arm, his teeth tearing through flesh and muscle and sending a hot pain radiating through her shoulder. When she jerked awake, the pain was still present, sharp and real. She gasped and searched around wildly for the source of attack—until the dream faded. She remembered that the throbbing in her arm was courtesy of that afternoon's flu shot; West would no sooner tear into her arm than he would tear off her clothing. She hated needles even more than she hated babysitting, which made it all the worse that the latter necessitated the former. The Tucks insisted on a flu shot for anyone who came within ten feet of their precious Accident. Since every dollar earned dragged the out-of-state-tuition dream a little closer to reality, Cass had consigned herself to a Saturday of needles and diapers and pain. Her arm only really hurt when she rubbed it, which she did now out of sheer spite.

The TV had somehow shut itself off; the house was dark and quiet. But Cass was suddenly convinced that something had woken her. Some noise, some instinct. Something wrong.

"Gracie?" she called, softly, not wanting to wake the baby.

There was no answer.

*I don't want to go up there.* The thought came unbidden as she stood at the base of the stairs.

*Don't make me go up there.*

She shouldn't even be babysitting. She should be at Hayley Patchett's party, toasting the dregs of summer or getting toasted by the Patchetts' sorry excuse for a pool. But she hadn't been invited. Not really, not until Hayley's best friend, Emily, had accidentally-on-purpose asked Cass what she would be wearing to the big party that, oops, she wasn't even invited to. Hayley had played it off like of course she'd just assumed Cass would hear about the party and realize she was wanted. She wasn't. Not that she cared. Here was another secret that Cass had resolved never to reveal: She was better than them—and she knew it. Better than Hayley and Emily and Kaitlin (who had inanely dubbed herself Kaitly to fit in with the others). Better than the idiot jocks and the ignorant teachers and the drug cases and the head cases. Better even than her parents, who'd proved their inferiority by growing up in Oleander and then, against all reason, *staying*. She didn't hold it against them, any of them. But she gave herself credit for an insight that few people seemed to grasp. The town was rotten; the town was dying. There were only two more years to endure, and then there would be college, somewhere so far away she could be excused for never coming back.

But that meant finding the money to make her escape, which meant, at least tonight, playing the dutiful babysitter. She mounted the stairs slowly, and crept down the dark hallway, telling herself she was only staying quiet so as not to disturb the children. Not because it felt like there was something lurking in the shadows, something around which it was best to make no sudden moves, lest it stir, lest it strike. The ceiling fan sighed overhead, stirring up a hot breeze. Just the fan, she told herself. Not someone's warm breath, misting against her neck in the dark.

She was too old to be afraid of the dark.

She did not believe in gut instincts, in premonitions, in the body's ability to sense danger and plead, as it did now, *Turn back.*

*Get out.*

*Save yourself.*

She thought she'd left the door to the baby's room open,

but it was closed now. Probably just Gracie, paying a visit to her baby brother. Except that Gracie hated her baby brother, and treated the room as if it carried the plague.

She was trembling.

Feeling abundantly foolish, she twisted the knob—slowly, silently—and eased open the door.

Cass laughed.

The room was intact, and empty, but for the baby in his crib. He lay there gurgling, with a small smile, and for a moment Cass felt a rush of what she realized other people must always feel when they see a baby. She lifted the tiny package of warm, wriggling flesh, breathing in the fresh, sweet smell and pressing her lips to his pale dusting of blond hair.

"Turns out you're pretty cute after all, aren't you?" she whispered.

Silly of her to suddenly panic because of a bad dream and a dark house and a noise it turned out she hadn't even heard.

Nothing was wrong.

Everything was fine.

She smiled, and patted the baby's head, and that was when the darkness claimed her.

Grace woke up from the dream and knew it had not been a dream.

Grace ran down the hall.

Grace blew through the door.

Grace tore the pillow out of the babysitter's hands.

Grace lifted the baby, the blue baby, the cold baby, and pressed her lips to the baby's lips and tried to make him breathe.

Grace screamed, and the babysitter gave her a blank look, then pushed her to the floor, then opened the window, then began to climb through.

Grace didn't know whether to grab her leg and drag her back into the room or give her a push and watch her fall, but she delayed too long. And maybe it didn't matter, because Grace was just a kid, that's how everyone treated her and that's what she suddenly realized she wanted to be, because a little kid couldn't be expected to know what to do. A little kid could just lie on the floor, watch the baby turn blue and the babysitter climb out the window, and cry.

Grace cried.

Grace saw, through her tears, the babysitter's face as she turned back one last time before launching herself into the air. She looked at Grace as if to say *You always claimed you were old enough to take care of yourself, now see how you like it.*

Grace ran to the window and looked down, just in time to see the babysitter land, and to watch her writhe on her back like an overturned hermit crab, and to hear her screaming in pain.

Grace picked up the baby, who she had not liked, but had no choice but to love. He was her brother.

Grace vowed: the babysitter would pay, the babysitter would be punished, the babysitter would die, because her brother was dead.

Grace would, if necessary, see to it herself.

The killing day.

The day the devil came to Oleander.

*That* day.

Whatever they called it, through the months to come—through the funerals and the potluck dinners and the sermons and the sidelong glances between formerly trusting neighbors—it was all anyone could talk about. It seemed safe to assume it was all anyone would *ever* talk about, as it was assumed that Oleander had been changed forever, and that, once buried, the bodies would stay in the ground.

But then the storm came.

## 2

### TO EVERYTHING THERE IS A SEASON

One year in Oleander.

One typical year, as those were the only kind Oleander dealt in, even the year of the killing day. In blood as in drought or in poverty or in flame, Oleander was Oleander, and there were still crops to be sown and meth to be harvested, pies to be baked and pigs to be prized, bargains to be hunted and farms to be foreclosed, cherries to be popped and hearts to be broken, worship to be offered and sinners to be shamed. There was still the promise of a warm night on a covered porch or a sledding trip on a snowy afternoon; there was, flickering on the periphery, like the shy fireflies that danced around Potawamie Lake on late-summer nights, still a glimmer of hope. There was gossip and tradition, for these were the fumes on which Oleander ran, chugging steadily along with its needle wobbling on empty, and would until it faded to a dried-up husk, with only a broken and rusted WELCOME TO OLEANDER, HEART OF THE REAL AM ERICA! sign to mark what had once been a town.

Tradition: In early October, once the funerals had been endured and the mourners' houses purged of dying flowers, frozen lasagnas, and baskets of corn muffins long gone stale, the veil of solemnity lifted, and business—what little business the town had left—continued as usual. In the liminal days between summer and fall, this meant the annual Harvest Festival, capped off by the Main Street parade. The recently departed Sally Gunther, who, thanks to the flask of Jack Daniel's stashed in her bra, could always be counted on to mount the D'Angelo's float and strip with Mardi Gras–worthy aplomb, was sorely missed. Kathleen Hanrahan, who'd been favored to win that year's Miss Oleander banner and wax-flower crown, was not. At least, not by Laura Tanner, third-grade teacher, two-time divorcée, and four-year reigning Miss Oleander, who was more than happy to continue her streak. The parade route was altered for the first time in memory, stopping three blocks short so as to avoid the empty drugstore, with its boarded-up windows, faded police tape, and, if you believed in such things, bad juju.

The rest of the month was dominated, as per usual, by election drama, which this year culminated in a mayoral victory by local businessman and walking comb-over Mickey Richards. Known to the satisfied customers who drove off his car lot as Mouse—and to the former football players who'd shared his high school locker room as Mouse Dick—the new mayor had coasted to an easy victory. It didn't hurt that, a couple of years before, he'd recruited a corporate tenant to inhabit the refurbished power plant on the edge of town—a white elephant into which a previous mayoral regime had sunk millions the town didn't have. But Mayor Mouse's real selling points were one: his financial involvement in the reconstruction of the Church of the Word, which had burned down on the day of killing. And two: his key campaign promise, the firing of Oleander's long-serving chief of police, Richard B. Hayes.

The almost total absence of surviving murderers to imprison had left behind a free-floating lynch mob's worth of blame. It had, unsurprisingly, settled on the town's top cop. In his decade in office, Hayes had established a long and undistinguished record of crosswalk management, the occasional meth-lab bust, and the quiet fixing of parking tickets for any teacher willing to give his kid an A. The killing day had overwhelmed his mediocre investigative abilities, and his final conclusions were best summed up as: "A lot of people had a bad day." Occasionally, when pressed for more, Hayes suggested, "Must've been something in the air."

November meant the annual all-church bake sale, its funds buying Thanksgiving dinners for indigents all across eastern Kansas, its participants vying eagerly for bragging rights that would last well through Easter. This year's sale, in honor of the recent church groundbreaking, was co-chaired by Ellie King, who everyone agreed had, of late, gone a bit spooky around the eyes. Something about the way she looked *through* you, as if aiming for your soul but coming out clear the other side.

November meant football and cheerleaders and a warm beer on a cold night rooting for a team that had not a chance in hell of winning, and a rote moment of silence for the lost soul Nick Shay and the assistant coach who'd killed him. The moment was briefer than intended, broken as it was by the howls of the marching band, who'd just discovered the feces that certain thuggish members of the team had secreted in their instruments. This, too, or at least some crude and beastly act like it, was tradition. The participation of Jeremiah West—about whom the thuggish branch of the team had harbored its suspicions until he'd turned up at practice this season a new and brutish man—was not.

By November, Daniel Ghent was finally sleeping through the night. Though he still had nightmares of bullets and blood, he no longer jerked awake at two a.m. in a puddle of his own sweat, and he never remembered them in the morning.

There was no Founders' Day tradition in Oleander, no bunting-bowed ceremony of child-chanted couplets and paeans to hometown pride. It was an odd absence in the communal calendar, odder still in a town that had been founded twice. The first settlers arrived in the fall of 1855, Boston abolitionists determined to ensure Kansas's entrance to the Union as a free state.

There are towns in the Midwest where residents can trace their heritage back to Civil War days—where even the meth-addled Dumpster divers can map out the exact boundaries of their forebears' ancestral homestead. But not in Oleander. Here history stretched back no further than 1899, because here, while the rest of the country celebrated the birth of their Lord and awaited the birth of a new century, Oleander died. It was a Christmas Day fire. That much was known, but nothing more—not how it began, or why, or how it happened that not a single resident survived. On Christmas Eve, there had been 1,123 souls living in the town. By sundown the next day, there were none.

There were charred bones and piles of ash, and that was all.

They founded a new town on Oleander's mass grave, and gave it the same name. They never spoke of the dead; they spotted no ghosts. The new town filled up with strangers who saw the possibilities of cheap property and ripe fields rather than the outlines of buildings that no longer stood and the gray dust of a cremated world. The new Oleander bustled and shone, its determined noise drowning out any echoes of the past. Grass and flowers and trees sprang from fallow ground. The scents of corn and life drove out the lingering smoke, and finally, the fire and its carpet of bones could be safely buried in the past and allowed to slip through the cracks of collective memory. But the earth had memory of its own.

Christmas in Oleander now was a twinkling wonderland, complete with an unexpected Christmas Eve snowfall. No one but Grace Tuck and her parents remembered that little Owen had been meant to play baby Jesus in the winter pageant. The Tucks skipped Christmas that year. Grace—no one called her Gracie anymore—had frozen pizza in front of the TV, trying not to look at the corner where the tree should have been. Her mother had not come out of her room since the night before, while her father had been drunk since Thanksgiving.

They weren't the only family in town to bypass the festivities: Ellie King gave herself up to a marathon prayer session in the skeleton of the half-rebuilt church. While she was out, her father packed up the last of his belongings and carted them over to the Sunflower, a sad apartment complex for a sad assemblage of men whose families had moved on without them. The daughter who'd once been his secret favorite, back before she turned into a bigger zealot than her mother, promised she'd come visit the next morning. She never got around to it.

The remaining Prevette brothers sought salvation in the

form of hammers and spray paint, laying midnight waste to the town crèche. They broke every window at town hall before graffitiing giant red genitalia across its century-old stone face. Scott signed his name at the bottom.

Daniel Ghent was alone. The Preacher had taken to the road; the Preacher had not been home in three days; the Preacher had developed a habit of sleeping on the street, in small lean-tos improvised from cardboard and plastic wrap, the better to stay close to his flock. The Preacher had been claimed by God, and Milo had been claimed first by social services, then by his mother. Giuliana Larkin had materialized in the Preacher's life a few years after Daniel's mother died, and dematerialized before Milo was on solid food. For good, they'd all thought. But then came the killing day and Daniel's turn in the media spotlight, and she'd spotted Milo on the evening news. A week later, she was back and settled into a house on the luckier side of town. She'd needed only one efficient hour to pack a small red suitcase for Milo, then pack Milo into a small red Civic. One hour to dissolve any illusions Daniel might have had of a family. This year there would be no reason to feign a belief in Santa and no need to hastily wrap an old stuffed animal from the bottom of Milo's toy chest with a card attached reading "Love, Dad." Around the Ghent house, there lately didn't seem to be much reason for anything.

Jeremiah West's Christmas was picture-perfect, at least judging from the family portrait that topped the family's annual Christmas letter. The West patriarch, it was reported, had posted record earnings in farm-equipment repair. Mother West intended to spend the winter perfecting her pie recipe in time for the spring bake-off. This year nothing would stop her from taking home the blue ribbon, not even her "dear neighbor" Maddie Thomas's "white-knuckle grip on the trophy" thanks to her "thoroughly reliable pumpkin pie." (The letter's careful breeziness here could not disguise the bitter determination underlying this upcoming grudge match.) The letter detailed Jeremiah's record-breaking rushing and receiving stats, but not the joyriding escapade for which he'd spent a night in jail.

Winter passed, cold and barren, with hearty meals and stoked fires, empty streets and packed bars. Down at the Yellowbird, where Old Winston had been a constant fixture, beers were hoisted in his honor, their departed patron saint of lost weekends. The regulars lived for that time of night when the door would swing open and a sullen Jule Prevette—always in those mannish combat boots and distinctly unmannish fishnets—would arrive to escort her new stepfather home.

Oleander thawed, snow melted, crops sprouted, and the Preacher prepared for the end. He saw the angels of death shadowing their prey; he saw Satan's handmaidens digging their pit to hell. Oleander thawed, but the chill lingered in the shadow that was cast over the town, promise of dark days to come. Only the Preacher saw the signs. Only the Preacher knew what lay beneath the earth, the darkness stirred up by the misguided creatures above. Only the Preacher heard the song whispered by the budding branches, *the end the end the end of days*. The Preacher warned them, though they would not heed. So be it. When the time came, they would be lost to the shadows. When the pit opened and loosed its demons upon the world, he would be prepared.

He would take care of his own.

\* \* \*

The year passed from Sunday to Sunday, the churches vying for souls with brimstone sermons, potluck dinners, bingo nights, and the ever-shifting tiles on the welcome signs that hung by their doors:

FREE COFFEE. EVERLASTING LIFE. M EM B ERSHIP HAS ITS P RIVILEGES.
STAYING IN B ED SHOUTING "OH GOD!" DOES NOT CONSTITUTE GOING
TO CHURCH.
YOU HAVE ONE NEW FRIEND REQUEST FROM JESUS: ACCEP T OR DENY.
DO NOT W AIT FOR THE HEARSE TO TAKE YOU TO CHURCH.
EVEN SATAN B ELIEVES IN GOD.
IT'S THE TEN COM M ANDM ENTS, NOT THE TEN SUGGESTIONS.
SEVEN DAYS W ITHOUT GOD M AKES ONE W EAK.
DOW N IN THE M OUTH? TRY A FAITH LIFT.
SANTA CLAUS NEVER DIED FOR ANYONE.
SIGN B ROKEN. M ESSAGE INSIDE.
GOD SHOW S NO FAVORITISM , B UT W E DO—GO ROYALS!
THINK IT'S HOT HERE? IM AGINE HELL.

Eventually, though it never seemed possible through the days of clouds and frost, the sun returned, and with it the birds and the leaves and a planting festival as exuberant as the harvest extravaganza. Amanda West took second prize in the bake-off; the 4-H club showed off its wares, its hand-churned butter and free-range goats; the high school's ag class staged the annual slaughter and barbecue of its chickens. Grace Tuck rode the rickety Ferris wheel and threw up behind the custard stand. Daniel Ghent watched Milo's Cub Scout troop perform a knot-tying demonstration; he watched from a distance, and left before the parents crowded the muddy field to congratulate their precocious offspring.

Eventually, though it never seemed possible, Eisenhower High School emptied its hallways for the summer and a lucky few, with a fanfare of halfhearted speeches and tossed caps, got to leave it for good. Jeremiah West was not among them, but—small consolation—at least got to join the rest of the team's rising seniors in the ritual streaking across the stage.

Summer was, traditionally, too hot for traditions. Summer was for sitting on porches sipping lemonade—or talking wistfully of a time when summer meant sitting on porches sipping lemonade, when there were fewer bills to pay and no DVDs to watch, and of how in this mythical past, this rustic paradise of outhouses and unlocked doors, life had been good. Summer was when the gossip that had been fermenting all year was finally ready to pour. Tempers rose with the heat; grudges defrosted; things got interesting. This summer was no different, except that as August approached and blanched the town with its white heat and its memories of the killing day, the rumors took on a new intensity. It was as if the murders themselves had become Oleander tradition. Any argument, any lovers' quarrel, any innocent encounter in the new drugstore, cattycorner to the old, carried the seeds of potential violence. Surely it was only a matter of time before one would bloom. People waited; people watched. People whispered: about the source of Mayor Mouse's campaign funding, about the Tucks' failing marriage and the way that girl of theirs wandered with no apparent supervision, turning up in the strangest places at all hours of day and night. They noted, with their communal eye, the way *that man* looked at his stepdaughter Jule, who seemed always to be by his side. They knew the King girl had turned into a bigger Jesus nut than ever, as they knew about the restraining order Milo Ghent's mother had taken out against his father and half brother—and about the way Daniel had taken to lurking in bushes, just to catch a forbidden glimpse.

They never stopped talking about the murders, but by the time summer had fully settled itself over the town, they'd learned to once again talk of other things, the pettier the better. Somehow, the town talked itself back to life.

They never talked of Cassandra Porter.

There had been no trial for the sole surviving Oleander killer. Cassandra Porter, who could not remember her crime, pleaded not guilty by reason of mental disease or defect. The DA offered a deal: conviction with a sentence of twenty years to life, to be served not in a maximum-security prison but the slightly cushier state mental hospital.

She supposed she should have wanted to fight. Her lawyer had explained: If it was true she'd lapsed into some kind of fugue state, an insanity with the life span of a fruit fly, then she was innocent. At least in the eyes of the law. (If, on the other hand, she'd purposefully squeezed the air out of Owen Tuck's lungs . . . if she, Cassandra Porter, being of sound mind and body, had held the boy in her hands and ended him, with malice aforethought, for reasons her brain now contrived not to remember? She was, as they say, guilty as sin.) These were the issues her lawyer walked her through as she lay in a hospital bed recovering from the leap she couldn't remember taking.

Floating on a morphine cloud, dizzy with the pain of twelve broken bones, she nodded along, pretended to listen, and let her parents decide for her.

They had, in short order, decided to deliver her up to the criminal justice system, then pack their belongings and skip town. The Porters had settled with relatives in a faraway coastal city where they could pretend to whoever asked that their smart, successful daughter was off at boarding school—or perhaps that she'd never existed at all. Cass knew this because of the emails they sent, in lieu of calling or visiting or sending the packages of cookies and clean underwear the lawyer had repeatedly told them they were allowed. She knew this, but not the city to which they'd moved, the relatives with whom they were staying, or the address where they could be found.

No one told her what had happened to the house. She preferred to imagine it intact, her belongings stored away in the bedroom she'd lived in since she was three years old, each scrapbook, homework assignment, stuffed animal, memory filed in its proper place. Gathering dust, maybe. But still, somehow, *hers.* Impossible to imagine the house given over to strangers, the kitchen where she'd been planning to bake cupcakes for the student-council election given over to someone else's TV dinners. The dining room where she would have filled out her neat stack of college applications crowded with someone else's awkward Thanksgivings. The living room couch where she'd spent more than a few nights waiting, in vain, for Jeremiah West to take off her clothes or in any way indicate he hoped she would do so—cushioning some other, happier daughter, one with a future rather than just a past.

She tried not to think about that. As she tried not to think about the baby.

What she did to the baby.

After, she jumped out the window. That's what they told her, and when she refused to believe them, they showed her the video. The nanny cam captured life in a fuzzy black and white, but the sequence of events was clear. There she was, like the distressed damsel in a D-grade horror movie, creeping into the baby's room as the audience shrieked at her to stop. She'd shrieked, too, when the lawyer first showed her the video, and she'd watched herself lift the baby from his crib. But the figure on-screen continued with silent determination no matter how loudly the real Cassandra screamed. She pushed Gracie Tuck out of the way, moved calmly to the window, and, with no visible hesitation on her dim face, flung herself into the night. Cass remembered none of it. Nothing but waking in the dirt, in pain, staring up at the police, the flashing lights, and Gracie Tuck's empty eyes.

That was what she saw, every night, when she waited for sleep to rescue her. Gracie's dead eyes.

The broken bones had eventually healed. It was the infection that followed that left her floating for months in blissful oblivion. In that timeless time of fever haze, she would close her eyes in one impersonal room and wake up in another, always surrounded by strangers. There was something wrong with her blood. That was what they told her, when they told her anything, which wasn't often. She was a possession of the state now, like a sewage pipe or a garbage compactor. She was broken, and so they would fix her. But you didn't tell a sewage pipe what was wrong with it, and you didn't hold its hand when the pain kept it awake all night, writhing in sweaty sheets, begging for help. You didn't explain to a garbage compactor why you were performing this test or that one, or which ones would hurt.

Later, when she was healthy again, and the questions came one after another after another, she would realize how good she'd had it. There was an ease and simplicity to being an object, to lying still and letting the world exert its will.

When she was healthy again, they'd locked her in the cell. It had no bars, just a bed, a desk, a sink, a toilet, and softly padded walls. They allowed her books, but no newspapers or magazines, nothing that would tether her to the outside world. Emails from her parents were printed out and delivered to her room, until the day the emails stopped. Cass had seen plenty of movies set in mental hospitals. All of them played variations on a theme: moon-eyed inmates drifting about a sterile hospital lounge, playing checkers and shouting at shadows; inmates forced to bare their souls in a group-therapy circle of trust; dazed and cooperative inmates lining up for meds; rebellious inmates flattened by linebacker orderlies. But there were no inmates here, as far as Cass could tell, and no orderlies, either. There were no lounges or corridors or electroshock laboratories. No checkers games. There was only Cass, and her room, and the doctor.

The doctor, old enough to be Cass's mother but with an angular, birdlike, distinctly unmaternal edge to her, came every day. And every day, she took a sample of Cass's blood. She brought food and watched Cass eat it. She pulled up a chair to Cass's bed and asked her questions. It didn't seem much like therapy. The questions never strayed from the past—and not the distant past, either, the Freudian depths of potty training and father-daughter dances. They dwelled only on, as the doctor put it, "the night in question." She wanted every detail of how Cass had felt in the moments before and after the blackout, what she had been thinking, what she had been *wanting*, as if any of that could matter with Owen Tuck's body moldering six feet underground. Cass had nothing to offer but a stream of *nothing special, nothing much, nothing out of the ordinary*. And then, always, when her memories gave out and she ran smack into that featureless mental wall, *I don't know.*

*I don't know.*

*I don't know.*

She didn't know if she wanted to.

The doctor only asked questions, never answered them. In all those months of daily visits, Cass never succeeded in learning her name.

Then came the day the doctor didn't show up.

Cass had thought nothing could be worse than reliving "the night in question," over and over again. But then the doctor didn't come, and didn't come.

And never came back.

That was worse.

There were no windows in the cell; the lights never went out. She slept when she could; she woke when she was hungry, or when she needed to pee, or when nightmares tossed her from sleep. Sometimes a slot in the door would open, and food would appear: she ate. And then she would read, and then she would try to remember, and then try not to, and then, again, she would sleep, and this she called a day.

There was no mirror in the cell. The most reflective surface was the metal basin of the sink, which offered only the shadow of a reflection. She was forgetting what she looked like; she was imagining a monster.

She supposed she was going crazy. There was a part of her rooting for madness; there was a part of her, bigger every day, that wanted to fall into the black. It was her only remaining hope of escape.

She hoped she was already crazy, as the lawyer had suggested. Not guilty, not *responsible*, by reason of mental disease or defect.

She clung to that, until she couldn't anymore.

She couldn't.

*Guilty.* It was the one thing she did know; it was the answer she couldn't avoid. That was why she didn't throw herself against the walls or slice herself open with one of the toilet tank's rusty screws. This was hell—and where else did she belong?

This was home. So she tried to forget the girl she had been, the future that girl was meant to have. This was torture, and this was right.

And in this way, a year passed.

# 3

## ANY WAY THE WIND BLOWS

The door had a bell on it that jingled with every customer. Daniel heard that bell in his dreams. There'd been no bell on the door of Gathers Drugs—it would have offended the old man's shop-owner pride to suggest he needed an alarm, no matter how festive, to signal that someone had walked through the door. "Customers aren't cows," Gathers liked to say. "No need to hang a bell around their neck."

Of course, in the end, it hadn't been Gathers who needed to watch out for his customers, but vice versa, and so there was a new store, with a new regime. The bell ensured that its employees—mostly shift-shirking teenagers and disgruntled ex-farmers—noted every person who entered the store. It was cheaper than a security camera—and just as useless at fending off crime.

There had been three robberies in Daniel's tenure at Jacobs & Colton Drugs, two of them armed. The J&C had cash and cold medicine, irresistible temptations for a certain meth-addled demographic. Standing behind the counter, a stupid yellow apron tied around his waist, the cash register chirping and humming merrily along, the bell jingling, Daniel couldn't shake the certainty that he was the new Gathers, destined for a bad end.

He'd taken the job anyway. It's not like there were other options. The town's farms and businesses were failing, and enough had already done so that half the town's population was looking for work; it didn't make for much of a job market. Daniel vaguely remembered a period of optimism a couple of years back, when a corporate tenant had finally picked up the lease on the old power plant and the town went breathless, waiting for the job offers to rain down upon them. But the new company shipped in its employees from out of town, employees who never crossed the barbed wire surrounding the property and certainly never contemplated hiring a native. Which meant no revenue for local businesses and no jobs for anyone. Daniel had been lucky to score this one when he did, and he was determined to make the luck hold out for another nine months. Nine months till he turned eighteen and could apply for custody of Milo. Nine months to acquire a high school diploma and a savings account, and with them some chance of getting his brother back. The thought of which kept him from fleeing the J&C, even on hot, humid summer afternoons that reminded him of all the wrong things. It was the hottest day of the summer so far, sticky and ominously still, the sky holding its breath and waiting for something to happen. Murderously hot, the old folks said to each other, with a glimmer of malicious humor. The kind of day that could drive a man insane. Not the kind of day you'd want to set foot in a drugstore, not if you knew your history.

But here he was, history repeating itself, because jobs were scarce and he was desperate. A coincidence, maybe. Behind that counter, it seemed like fate. And if living in Oleander had taught him anything, it was that there was no point in trying to weasel out of your fate. On the prairie, you could see a bad end coming from miles away. Knowing something's coming didn't mean you could outrun it.

So every time the bell jingled, Daniel waited for a gun.

The girl, dark and hollowed out, seemed unlikely to have one. But she was a Prevette, and with them, you never knew. He recognized this one from school. Jule skittered through the aisles, furtive as it was possible to be in combat boots. He watched her in the ceiling mirror as she clomped past the cleaning supplies and hesitated by the hair dyes—her hair, this week, had a rich purple sheen, and Daniel had a sudden weird urge to tell her she should stick with it a bit longer. She moved on without taking anything, turning into the feminine-products aisle. He looked away and began resolutely restocking the bagging area. So he didn't see her approach.

"Can I pay, or what?"

She slammed a box of tampons down on the counter and thrust a few limp bills in his general direction. Her scowl was stained a purple-black that nearly matched her hair, and her eyelids wore a raccoon mask of smeared mascara. Her eyes themselves, such a deep, dark brown that the iris shaded into the pupil, had a glossy sheen. Daniel wondered if she was high.

The Sudafed was behind the register, along with all the other prized substances over which he was to stand guard.

He told himself, not for the first time, that he needed to quit this job.

"What?" she said. Her voice was husky, like she gargled with gravel just to ensure it matched the rest of her.

"What?"

"You're *staring*."

He shook his head, and shoved the rumpled bills into the register.

"Never seen tampons before?" she said.

He wondered again if she was high. She had a reckless look to her, and these were more words than he'd ever heard her say in a row. Daniel offered her a fistful of change, fumbling the handoff. Coins scattered everywhere.

She laughed. Not meanly, but not kindly, either. "We don't have cooties, you know. Girls."

"I know that."

"But we do have girl parts." She shook the box of tampons in his face. "It's not like your little sister's Barbie doll."

The words came unbidden, and too angry: "I don't have a little sister."

She gave him a sharp look.

There were no secrets in this town. He knew that.

She shrugged. "Whatever."

He scooped the last of her change off the counter and, this time, pressed it firmly into her warm palm.

"But you *were* staring," she said.

"Look, I just . . ."

"Yeah? You just . . . ?"

Better she think he was freaked out by her purchase—which, to be honest, wasn't his favorite thing to be ringing up, especially when it was a customer whose girl parts he preferred not to be thinking about—than realize that he'd marked her as a potential threat.

"I'm sorry. For staring. Have a nice day."

She snorted. "Unlikely."

Maybe it was the defeat in her voice that made him say it. "I like the purple. Your hair, I mean. It's pretty good."

And so it was out there, sitting between them, too late to take back.

She seemed no happier about it than he was. But before she could respond, the door jingled and the two of them became instant allies with a glance at the threshold and a single, simultaneously muttered response to what appeared there: "Shit."

The football thugs came in a couple of times a week, pawing at the merchandise and contriving clumsy distractions as if Daniel didn't notice them shoving beef jerky into their pockets and Red Bull into their bags.

Jule groaned. "I'm out of here."

Daniel envied her easy escape right up until the moment they formed a human blockade and barred her from the door. Baz Demming and Matt Crosby, the latter a foot taller than her and twice as wide, sandwiched Jule between their muscled bulk. Jeremiah West stood to their side, focusing hard on the greeting-card spinner, like a getaway man already figuring whether nonparticipation would cut down on his eventual jail time. He did nothing when the quarterback yanked the tampons from Jule's hand and used his vaunted passing arm to toss them to Matt, saying, "I never got these things—maybe you wanna give us a little private demonstration on how they work?"

Of course, Daniel did nothing, either.

Jule grabbed for the box, fruitlessly. "If you're looking to stick something up your ass, surely you've got a better option." She looked pointedly between the quarterback and his linebacker.

"You got a big mouth all the sudden." Baz flicked the collar of her pleather jacket, letting his hand stray all too close to her face. "Doesn't she have a big mouth all the sudden?"

"Sounds like it," Matt said.

"Seems like there's plenty better things you could do with that mouth," Baz said.

He was known for his fast hands. It was smooth as any of his moves on the field, the sudden, graceful quarterback cradle, Jule efficiently locked into place against his chest.

*Say something,* Daniel told himself. *Do something.* She wasn't looking at him, but surely she was thinking it, too.

West cleared his throat. "Leave it, Baz. If Coach hears about this . . ."

"Coach can suck it," Matt said, but Baz let go.

For a moment, Jule froze in place. Daniel could see the battle play out across her face: Fight or flight. Pride or cowardice. Vengeance or survival. The store itself seemed to hold its breath waiting to see which way she would fall. Daniel, who'd never been to an Eisenhower Bulldogs game, suspected the quarterback's expression looked much like this when he hunched over the field, waiting for the snap—tense, watchful, dangerously still. Jule's lip curled into a snarl, hinting at a pounce—but it was a fake. With a final, fierce hiss of *"Assholes,"* she abandoned the tampons and the door and fled to the opposite end of the empty store. She disappeared into the back storeroom, either not realizing it had no exit to the street or not caring.

No one followed her. The thugs returned to the business at hand, pawing through merchandise, arguing about which tabloid celebrity they'd rather screw, and presumably inventorying all the potential treasures to claim—at the low, low cost of $0.00.

Daniel cleared his throat. "We're closing soon. And I have to clean up first, so . . ."

This was a disastrously wrong tack to take. He knew it even before he heard Baz's nasty chuckle, before he caught the look tossed from quarterback to linebacker, and well before Matt took his cue and, with one wide sweep of his beefy arm, flung an entire shelf of sauce jars to the floor. Then, for good measure, opened the refrigerated cabinet, pulled out a carton of eggs, and, one by one, slammed them into the floor, atop the pooling sauce.

"It does look like you got a lot to clean," Baz said, with a sorrowful shake of his head. "You're right, you better get started."

The bell jangled—once, twice, three times—and they were gone.

It could have been worse.

This Daniel reminded himself as he tried to summon the will to clean. The constellation of broken glass, the splashes of red on the counters and wall, the rising odor, fetid and sweet—it was more of a reminder than he needed.

It could have been worse.

"You got any mops?" Jule had successfully snuck up on him again. "Other than that pissy disposable crap in the cleaning section, I mean?"

And instead of calling him a coward, or abandoning him to

his karmic reward, she took the mop he found her, neither disposable nor pissy, and together, silent, they cleaned. They kept their heads down; they didn't look at each other. And neither of them looked up when the door opened yet again.

"Hey."

It was West's voice. Daniel forced himself to raise his head: at least he was alone. "Hey."

"Sorry about . . . all this." West nodded at the soapy pink smear. "Those other guys are sorry, too."

Jule snorted.

"So. Yeah," the Bulldog muttered. "I just thought I should . . ."

"Mops are in the closet on your right," Jule said. West's face lit, as if, in the prospect of manual labor, he'd glimpsed salvation.

Working together, they erased the spill in less than half an hour. None of them spoke, and when West deposited the mops back in the closet and Jule retrieved her box of tampons, neither of them said goodbye. Nor did they make it out the door. They froze on the threshold, side by side, Jule comically short beside West, who'd had to bend his head to avoid the dangling bell.

"Daniel," West said, in a strange, choked voice. Daniel hadn't even thought the football player knew his name. "Daniel, look."

He joined them in the doorway. He looked.

All light had drained from the day. The flap of leftover Fourth of July flags beat a steady thunder in the gusting wind. And in the distance . . .

Daniel had to remind himself to breathe.

In the distance, something that looked very much like Mayor Mouse's vintage Chevrolet was spiraling thirty feet above Main Street, silver fins glinting as it spun in the wind.

And in the distance, farther, but not far enough, not nearly, an ink-black funnel cloud swallowed the sky.

*Drive.*

West flattened the gas pedal to the floor. He cursed the battered engine, the useless wipers, the pickup itself, a rusted bruiser solid enough to barrel through snow and mud but now too solid, too big a target for the battering rams of wind and the gravel torpedoing across the road. The wheel jerked and bucked in his hands. The truck shuddered beneath him. The road ahead was nearly invisible beyond the curtain of driving rain. Somehow, West kept the tires on the concrete as he left the heart of Oleander behind and sped, as fast as he could yet still maddeningly slow, for home.

They'd thought him crazy for leaving the drugstore: maybe. And maybe a year ago, he'd have agreed to stay, and huddled under a table, pretending a fear he didn't feel. Assuming, as the building shook in the storm and the funnel tore up the town, that all would be well, because it always was. He knew better now, and he knew crazy. He'd seen it on that road, in that car, mowing down Nick. He'd seen it in the mirror, the days and weeks after, in his own eyes.

He had muffled it—and tamed it—by driving. Everywhere. Nowhere in particular. The Wests were rooted in Oleander: four generations on the same homestead, tending the land, tending each other. Staying in one place ran in their blood. But after the killing day, West found himself in motion.

Before, it had been place that held him upright—*his* town, *his* land, *his* home; after, it was only constant movement that kept him steady. He preferred the long, straight two-lane highways that cut through the prairie, nothing but grass in all directions and an unthinkably wide sky above. He liked the sameness of it, the ribbon of blacktop, the steady rhythm of rubber on concrete and gravel between, the radio turned up high as it would go, skipping from rap to gospel to rock to pop and back to rap again, surfing the static that hid in the gaps.

That was where he lived now, after Nick. In the static. In the gap.

At some point, he'd replaced driving with football. There was a mindless repetitiveness to it—and, as an added bonus, it gave him something to hit and permission to hit hard. Hanging with Baz and Matt served the same function. He laughed, he partied, he steered them away from felonies, and he let the fog fill him up and hide what needed to be hidden. It frightened him sometimes, how easy it was to pretend.

He'd never been to Nick's grave.

Now there was a funnel in the sky, and it cut through the fog. Something was coming, and he wasn't about to ride it out with strangers while his mind turned over images of tractors, horses, parents spinning into the sky. If he was going to lose something else—like the only two people left who meant anything at all—better to lose himself with them. And maybe this time, if the damn truck would go faster, he would get there in time to save the day. It was stupid and reckless, and he didn't much care.

West had never imagined himself living anywhere other than Oleander—had never conceived of himself as separate from the place and people that shaped his life. But after Nick, there had been times when he wanted to aim the car at the horizon, gun the engine, and *go.* The impulse was still there. The impulse was strong.

Maybe the crazy was still there, too, much as he'd thought he'd numbed it into submission. Because part of him wanted to turn the truck around. To arrow into the spinning black and let it lift him away.

If you live in Kansas, you know how to handle yourself in a tornado. Get to the basement, preferably the northeast corner, though there are those who believe that a myth. If without a basement, get to the lowest point in the house. Protect yourself beneath something heavy and hard: a desk, a table, an overturned bathtub. If outside, get out of your car, stay clear of overpasses. Lie flat in a ditch. Pray.

Oleander was prepared—as prepared as it was possible to be for two-hundred-mile-per-hour torquing winds. There were protocols, instructional pamphlets, emergency kits, backup generators; there were warning systems and sirens and storm cellars. There were advance warnings from the local weather station, and warnings from the weather itself, at least for those who knew what it meant when the air went still, the pressure dropped, the birds stopped singing, and the sky turned a funny yellow-green. But some months there were warnings nearly every day. You could set your clock by them. You couldn't duck down to the cellar every time some waxy-haired forecaster warned you bad luck *might* be on the way.

You waited. For the rains to come, the winds to pick up, the black clouds to roll in, the sirens to blare. The average tornado moves across the land at thirty miles per hour. Which means a funnel spotted from a mile away offered two minutes for life-saving measures. If you're lucky enough to have any on hand.

But not everyone had a storm cellar to flee to.

Not everyone could get to it in time.

Not everyone wanted to.

*This is my time.*

*This is my calling.*

Ellie heard her name on the wind, and Ellie was afraid.

That was all right. Abraham had feared what would come of taking Isaac up the mountain; Daniel had feared the lion, the wild hunger, the teeth that awaited him in the dark.

She raised her face to black sky. The rain hurt, but it washed away her tears. The streets had emptied themselves of life, and in the windblown darkness, Oleander turned alien. A barren and hostile landscape; a town at the end of the world. It seemed to take hours to traverse the six blocks between her house and the Church of the Word, but there it was, stony and unbowed by the storm. A single ray of sunlight poked through the dark and glinted off the stained-glass windows, as if to confirm her calling.

The doors were unlocked: she went inside.

The church had been rebuilt bigger and better, with a soaring arched ceiling ringed by biblical scenes in a rainbow of stained glass. The windows were even grander than those in the original church, twice as high and twice as colorful. But today the windows all seemed the same shade of black. She flicked the lights, but nothing happened. The power had blown, and the nave would bear the storm in the dark. So would Ellie.

She'd spent years waiting for God to answer, wondering how it would come if, when, it did. A voice in the darkness; a burning bush; a vision; a sign. Perhaps something subtle she'd been too lazy or too vain to see, missing her chance forever. But when it came, it came without intermediaries. There was no voice. Just a truth, a *knowing*, as soon as the storm began. The church needed her; He needed her. Tonight, neither of them would be alone.

The pews were made of burnished red oak. She chose a bench midway between the doors and the sanctuary, and watched the cross. Remembering.

Only Ellie knew what had happened that day in the church, why it had caught fire when it did. Only Ellie knew evil had made its way into the old church. She would not let it cross this threshold.

Wind battered stone. Above, a window shattered, and glass showered the nave. Ellie felt a hot pain on her cheek, and the trickle of blood, but then the water came and washed this away, as it had her tears.

She was allowed to be afraid, she reminded herself, feeling very small in the dark.

She was not allowed to crawl under the pew, curl into a ball, cradle her head in her arms, and try, in some small, useless way, to save herself. The Lord would spare her, or He wouldn't. It was His choice, as He had chosen this as her place.

Unless she was wrong.

And she was nuts.

The ground shuddered; the air smothered her; a deep sonic

boom rattled her bones. And then, from above, there was a great tearing sound, as if the universe were rending itself in two. She forced herself to stay in her seat, to tip her head toward the arching roof, the stained-glass windows, the dome of stone.

It was gone. All of it neatly sheared away. There was nothing above her but a swirling tunnel of cloud and debris.

Ellie screamed.

But she would not look away from the face of God.

Grace Tuck knew better. Hadn't her parents drilled her on storm-survival strategy since she was five years old? *Get to the cellar, Gracie. Ride out the storm.*

She no longer went by Gracie. That was a child's name—and she was old enough now to do the right thing in case of emergency. It was only because thirteen was old enough to know better that her parents left her alone overnight. Not because they didn't care what happened to her, definitely not that. But because they trusted she could take care of herself.

She imagined them driving through the storm, rushing home to protect their remaining child. The wind blowing their car from one lane to the other, their headlights useless in the curtain of rain. They would be arguing—they were always arguing. And maybe her mother would take her eyes off the road for just a second, or maybe the sky would reach down, close them into its cloudy fist, and carry them away. Grace supposed the idea should worry her. Instead, she turned it over in her head with a clinical fascination: What if they never came back? Would anything change?

People assumed she was still grieving her brother. That

Owen was the reason she never smiled. It didn't occur to them that when Owen left, he'd taken her parents with him. They were the ones she wanted back: The father who woke her up by tickling her feet and teased her with riddles over the dinner table and swung her upside down until she stopped complaining she was too old for such things and started to laugh. The mother who insisted she make her bed and put potato chips on her pizza and read to her every night—Judy Blume and Jane Austen and Shakespeare, with a sprinkling of Dr. Seuss. When Owen was born, Grace had worried the baby might wreck everything. But she hadn't known what broken meant. Not then. Nor had she known what it would be like when the people who were supposed to care about you more than anyone in the world no longer cared about anything.

Somewhere above her, the windows rattled in the wind. She wasn't worried about broken glass. That was no threat to her hiding spot, the narrow space beneath Owen's overturned crib. Even if a branch were to poke through the window, or some poor idiot's coffee mug came hurtling into the room, the expensive maple frame and plush mattress would protect her. And if the tornado ripped the house off its foundations and sent it spiraling into space? Well, it had worked for Dorothy. There was a temptation to extricate herself from her hiding place and press her face to the windows, to see for herself exactly how bad things could get. Maybe it would be like the movie, houses and horses and tractors flying past, in transit to another world. Maybe she would even spot the Wicked Witch, pedaling toward a hell of her own making. If she opened the window, if she leaned out and let go . . . would she fly?

\* \* \*

Inside her windowless room, Cass heard no wind, no sirens, no rain. But, even through the thick padded walls, she heard the screams. And the sharp reports of something that could have been gunfire.

She climbed onto the bed and tucked her knees to her chest, as if the old rules of childhood still applied: stay on the bed, and the monsters hiding in the shadows can't get you. Somewhere beyond her walls, there was a small series of pops, and then an explosion. The bed rattled beneath her.

The lock on the door was supposed to protect the people out there from her, from the monster. She doubted it would protect her from them. They were the ones with the key.

She focused on the door, and overlooked the crack beneath it, only a few centimeters high. It had never been wide enough to reveal anything when she'd lain on the ground and peered out, longing for a glimpse of something new, even if it was just the rubber tread of a passing set of shoes—but it was wide enough for smoke.

It seeped in, slowly enough that at first the faint, acrid smell could have been her imagination, the wistful remnant of all those cigarettes she'd been too conscientious to try. But it got stronger, and it got thicker, enough to cast the room in a gray haze, enough that it burned when she drew a breath. It scraped her throat and constricted her lungs, choking her voice so that there was nothing left but sad, hoarse whimpers by the time she thought to pound her fists against the door and scream.

The day had been shit to start with, and things had only gotten worse from there. The parasite had woken her up when he'd stumbled into the trailer a couple of hours before dawn, reeking of beer and cheap perfume. Since the idiot was too piss drunk or too lazy to find his way without knocking over a stack of dirty dishes and cursing as he crunched through the broken glass, the sun had risen over yet another scene of domestic bliss. Jule's mother and the parasite screamed at each other until they got bored, then turned on Jule. Somehow, the fight became her fault, and it didn't help that she had to endure it in a pair of boxers, all too conscious of the parasite's gaze playing across her bare thighs. She knew better, but had suffered enough summer nights beneath thick, baggy sweats. That night, the hottest of the summer, it had seemed worth the risk.

He hadn't raised a hand against her mother yet, which was unusual, and maybe why Annie Prevette had taken the even more unusual step of marrying this one. She talked of having another kid. "A sister for you, baby," she told Jule, with an embarrassing giggle. "Like you always wanted." Annie was fond of making up things that Jule had always wanted, especially when they complemented the things that Annie herself desired. On this latest wedding day, decked out in a yellowing dress made all the dingier by the fluorescent lighting of the county clerk's office, she had squeezed Jule into a lily-scented hug and whispered, "I finally did it, baby. I found you a dad."

She hadn't noticed the way the parasite looked at Jule.

For most of the year, Jule showered in the school locker room, sliding in and out of the cold spray before the jocks rolled in from morning practice. But in the summer, she was pretty much stuck with the trailer's privacy-free stall, unless she wanted to tote her soap and towel down to the swampy lakes that lay just beyond the edge of the trailer camp. Most mornings, she did. The water was cold and left a gloss of slime on her skin, but it was worth it for the privacy. The swamps and surrounding wood were considered Prevette territory. The only people who ventured into them with any regularity were the Prevette brothers themselves, and then only during hunting season, when they'd worked themselves into enough of a frenzy to lay down their test tubes and load up their arms. Turkey season was over, deer season was yet to start, and though squirrels were fair game year-round, the Prevettes considered rodents beneath them. (Or maybe, as was whispered around town, they didn't think it right to shoot their own.)

She'd forgotten discovery was possible . . . until, about to rinse the shampoo from her hair, she heard them. Tires crunching gravel, roaring diesel engine, the hoots of drunken morons. She made it into the bushes just as the pickup skidded to a stop and the guys piled out of the truck. Five of them, all football thugs. They'd spent nearly an hour laughing and shoving and farting and trying to light empty beer cans on fire while she cowered, dripping and naked behind a beautyberry bush, all too clear on what would happen if they found her there, too angry to be afraid. Imagine their faces if she rose from the bush like a miracle, five foot two inches of bare skin, daring them to do anything but get the hell out of her swamp.

She hadn't done it. And when they finally drove away, the rage lingered. When three of the thugs appeared in the drugstore that afternoon, it was almost a gift. A second chance. Except that once again, all she'd done was run away.

Now here she was, hiding for the third time, in a cramped closet with this boy Daniel's scrawny body wrapped around her, as if his lean arms and brittle bones would somehow protect her own. And she let him do it, play protector, imagine that he could stop the wind.

She had to get out of this town. That was her prime directive, the necessity that drove her through every day. Jule had a lifetime of reasons to hate Kansas, but topping her list was its landscape, its *sameness*, the way the yellow-green prairie droned on and on as if to bully the eye into accepting that there was and could be nothing else. A world of flatness and corn, a life of leaky trailers and arrest records: all resistance futile. Bad enough she had to live in Oleander; she refused to die here.

The closet was tiny and crowded with cleaning supplies. Not enough space for one person, much less two. A mop handle jabbed her back, and everything smelled like bleach. Outside, it sounded like the world was coming to an end. They stayed put.

"It'll be okay," Daniel said, sounding unconvinced.

"How do you know?"

"I don't *know*, but—"

"But you thought if you said it out loud like you did, that would, what? Make it true?" She didn't know why she felt such an urge to be a bitch. It probably had something to do with the prospect of getting blown out of existence—and doing so like *this*, in a closet, with a stranger and a mop.

"I thought I should comfort you."

She laughed. And the blessed dark meant he wouldn't see the flush that crept across her face. *Comfort* her. When was the last time someone had dared try that?

"So what if it's not?" she said.

"Not comforting?"

"Not okay. Let's say we die here. Right now."

"That's not going to—"

"The roof caves in and I get hit in the head and die, like, instantly. But you're trapped under the debris, and your legs are crushed, and—"

"Can you please stop?"

"—you just have to *lie* there, next to my corpse, waiting." She didn't want to stop. She wanted to push him and push him until the ridiculous Dudley Do-Right facade broke and something real came through. "And you can hear them above you, search and rescue, but you're too weak to scream, and you lie there day after day until the oxygen runs out and you—"

"Enough." There was no anger, only exhaustion. Like he expected her crap, everyone's crap, and had long ago decided to roll over and take it. "Please."

"What do you think would be the worst thing?"

Silence.

"I'd guess dying a virgin."

Nothing.

"You *are* a virgin, right?" Sometimes she hated herself.

But it won her a sigh. "What are you trying to do?"

"Comfort you," she said.

And, to her surprise, he laughed. He had a nice one. It was lighter than the rest of him. It made her hate herself just a little less.

It seemed like they were done talking then. His breathing was quiet, like the rest of him.

"I've done that, you know," he said. "Lie next to a corpse."

"I know that," she said, because everyone did.

"It's not like you imagine it. Not like in the movies or

anything. Dead people. Bodies. They're . . . it's not like the movies."

"Yeah. I know that, too."

Unlike Daniel, Jule was not famous for her role in the killing day. The trailer park's murder-suicide of James Prevette and Gloria No Last Name wasn't a secret so much as it was a nonevent, compared to the deaths of all those upstanding citizens in other parts of town. As far as Oleander was concerned, a sordid business like "whatever that man did to his wife" (it was rarely remembered that Gloria had been the one with the knife) was just Prevette business as usual. Translation: no one cared.

"Your aunt and uncle?" Daniel said, almost as if he did.

"She wasn't my aunt."

"Okay," he said.

"Okay."

There was a bone-rattling boom overhead, and then a crash that sounded like it might have been the storefront window blowing in. They clung to each other. It was the first time in a long time that someone's body had been pressed so close to her own. There was primal comfort in his touch, in his warm breath and the rise and fall of his chest against hers—something prerational in her response to the visceral pleasure of flesh on flesh. She wondered at that, the delusion that seemed programmed into the DNA: that no matter how flimsy a shield the human body made, the simple act of embrace, of feeble arms wrapped around narrow chest, signaled protection. It seemed counterproductive to the survival of the species that something so useless, and dangerous more often than not, could feel so safe.

\* \* \*

The emergency lighting, powered by the Wests' backup generator, cast the storm cellar in a dim blue light. It glimmered off the jars that lined the walls, cranberry, raspberry, and strawberry preserves all carefully shelved and ripening for winter.

West's mother was crying.

She always did that when tornadoes passed through town. She hugged her son, and he let her, thinking that this was his father's job. But his father was fiddling with the generator, his back to his wife and son, his mind on more important things than comfort.

"What if it's all gone?" his mother whimpered. "The house, the barn, everything?"

"It's not." As many times as he'd found himself in this position, West still didn't quite know how to get the job done. When girls cried, you stroked their hair and rubbed their back and touched your foreheads together to reassure them, eye to eye, lip to lip, that all would be fine. But this wasn't a girl; it was his mother. He liked that she trusted him to comfort her. It suggested she saw him as solid and reliable. As a man. He just wished he were better at playing the part. "Our Father in heaven, hallowed be your name," he added, because he knew the words would buoy her; because she wasn't the only one who needed something to hold on to.

"Your kingdom come, your will be done," they murmured together as the winds gusted and the ceiling shook. "On earth as it is in heaven. Give us today our daily bread. And forgive us our debts, as we also have forgiven our debtors. And lead us not into temptation, but deliver us from evil."

The words warmed him, as they did every night, an incantation against the darkness.

"You're a good son, you know that?" his mother said. "A good man." Even in the dim light, he couldn't face her. He'd never been able to stand the way her eyes looked all filled up with tears. The way she pinned him with a stare that said her happiness rested on his shoulders. There was supposed to be a house full of sons—rowdy, filthy boys that would have eaten her out of house and home, she said, often, to convince him and herself how pleased she was with just the one. Instead, there were trips to the hospital and antidepressants and tiny grave markers and, in the end, one son, who would never be enough, and had no right to stop trying.

"Tell your son how proud you are of him," she called to his father.

"I'm proud of you, West." He finally gave up on the generator and took over, encircling both of them in his wide embrace.

"And we love you, sweetie," West's mother said, squeezing tighter.

His father grunted agreement.

"Love you guys, too." West reminded himself they only wanted what was best for him. That's what parents were for.

Cass was on the floor, a sheet dampened with toilet water plastered over her nose and mouth. It wouldn't buy her much time. Her eyes burned in the smoke; tears streamed down her cheeks.

Her chest hurt. She didn't want to die without remembering what she'd done.

She didn't want to die.

She closed her eyes. Thinking: *Maybe it'll be better.*

Tough to be worse.

She heard a woman's voice speak her name.

Between its five churches, Oleander had several hundred God-fearing Christian congregants, and none of them had ever raised the suggestion that the Lord might be a woman. Despite this, Cass let herself entertain the idea that she might already be dead. Then soft hands closed over hers and pulled her to her feet. A mask was slipped over her face, and cool, pure oxygen streamed into her lungs. Cass opened her burning eyes, squinting through the haze. The doctor whose name she had never learned yanked her toward the doorway. She said something incomprehensible, her face muzzled by a respiration mask of her own. Her meaning was clear: Time to get the hell out.

They ran down a long corridor. Flames licked the walls. They passed no open doors. They rescued no other patients.

But the facility wasn't empty. They rounded a corner, pushed through a pair of double steel doors, left the fire mercifully behind, and emerged into a large, high-ceilinged room. It was about twice the size of the high school cafeteria. It was filled with dead bodies.

And some that weren't quite dead, not yet, despite having holes in them, with fluids and things leaking out.

There were doctors, marked by their white coats.

There were soldiers. Lots of soldiers. Lots of guns.

The doctor, Cass's doctor, snatched one from the hand of a soldier who had no more face, just a fleshy crater atop a blood-spattered uniform. "Don't look," she shouted to Cass. "We can't stop. We can't help them."

Cass didn't want to help them; she wanted to throw up.

There was a siren blaring. Some of the bodies were

writhing and twitching, their mouths working, fishlike, to breathe or to pray. Cass suspected the noise of the alarm was covering up other noises, final gasps whistling through broken lungs, moans and whimpers, pleas for help. She was glad of it.

She was, though the smoke hadn't yet penetrated this room, still crying.

"What happened to them?" she asked, but there was no answer, and no choice but to pick her way through the bodies, not so delicately that she didn't crush a finger here or a belly there under her feet. Surely, a good person would try to save these people, whatever harm it might mean to herself.

Cass had given up on thinking of herself as a good person.

There was so much blood.

From behind the double doors, there was a crack of gunfire, and then another. Cass took the doctor's hand. They ran away.

They made it to the parking lot and the doctor shoved her into a black SUV, then jumped behind the wheel. The wind was blowing fiercely, and it was only when the swirling clouds parted enough to let through a sliver of sunlight that Cass realized it was daytime. The doctor gunned the engine and floored it, and the SUV rocketed across the parking lot, barreling straight through the wooden gate at a deserted guard post. It had started to rain, water gushing down with the force of her parents' superpowered showerhead. The SUV skidded down a muddy bank, tipping precariously as the doctor took the turn onto the main road far too quickly. Then tires gripped concrete, and they were on their way . . . somewhere. Cass twisted around for her first and final look at her home for the last year, barely able to make out the outlines of the complex through the mud-spattered back window and the sheets of rain. Nothing about it screamed hospital, or even prison. The three massive buildings were windowless concrete, rising into smokestacks as wide as her house. A gaping chasm stretched between them, and within it a complicated network of piping and drills ripped something from the earth.

She was trying to imagine what its purpose could be when the black funnel glanced off the complex, ripping straight through its steel and concrete exoskeleton, the fleet of SUVs scattering into the sky like a murder of crows. But when, only minutes later, an explosion tore the complex apart, they were miles away, too far to see anything but the fireball that rose into the clouds, and the billowing crimson smoke.

"What the hell was that place?" Cass asked.

Then, because the doctor showed no inclination to respond: "Where are we going?"

No answer.

"What was I doing there?" she said. "Why aren't we dead?"

"I'll explain everything later," the doctor said. "We have to get you somewhere safe."

"Why? Why not just leave me there?"

"Because you're the only one left."

Any follow-up questions might as well have been cast into the void. The nameless doctor kept her eyes fixed on the windshield, not that there was anything to see. Sheets of rain hid the road ahead; wind buffeted the SUV from lane to lane; the doctor drove faster and faster, far too fast. Her fingers were white and trembling on the wheel, her head shaking, violently, no. And when she did speak, it was as if she were alone.

"It's not our fault," she said, more than once. "It wasn't supposed to be this way."

"We should get off the road," Cass told her. There was no safe place to be in a tornado, but some things were *less* safe, and some things were plain stupid. "We should stop. *Now.*"

The doctor seemed to suddenly remember Cass was in the car. She turned toward the passenger seat, her eyes wide. "It was necessary," she said softly. "But I'm sorry we did this to you."

"Did what to me?" Cass asked.

"All of you," she said, which was no answer at all. Cass held her gaze, and so neither of them saw the uprooted tree until it slammed into the SUV and sent it tumbling off the road.

Beneath the crib, hidden from the storm, Grace slept. Her pale lids twitched. Her head rested on her brother's yellow blanket, folded neatly and soft beneath her cheek. Her hands curled into fists. She dreamed of blood.

When Cass woke, she was upside down. Still strapped into her seat belt, hanging before a broken windshield. The doctor hung beside her, blood trickling from a slash on her forehead. Cass hurt, everywhere.

Some time had passed; she knew that because the rain had stopped.

The doctor's eyes opened and, with a grunt of pain, she twisted her head toward Cass. "My arm . . . ," she croaked. It was pinned by the crumpled door.

Carefully Cass tested each of her limbs: all present and accounted for.

"Help me," the doctor whispered as Cass released herself from the seat belt and climbed out of the SUV, trying her best to avoid the shards of glass. Her head and neck throbbed, and her face stung in a hundred places, but she could stand, and she could walk.

Cass had no phone, but probably the doctor did, somewhere, and Cass could call for help. She could do her best, in the meantime, to tend to the doctor's wounds. And then whoever came would summon the police, and they would recognize her, and take her back to a cell, and lock the door, and she would be alone again, forever. *Or.* She could get away, find somewhere to hide until it was safe. The hospital, or whatever it had been, was gone. And for all anyone knew—anyone but this doctor, trapped in a wreck of her own making—Cass was gone with it. No one would be searching for her. Not for some time, at least.

She looked up, and there was the sky, right where she'd left it all those months ago.

There were trees, and grass, and road, and mud.

She could not go back.

"I'm sorry," she told the doctor, who knew better than anyone about the bad thing hidden inside of Cass. It was the universal imperative, right? *To thine own self be true.*

"Don't go," the doctor said. "Please."

But she had also said: *We did this to you.*

*This:* Something Cass didn't understand. Something that had made her this person who could stand by this wreckage and look at this woman trapped inside, helpless and bleeding— and walk away.

## 4

## OUT OF THE RUINS

The majority of tornadoes to strike the country register a zero on the Enhanced Fujita scale, meaning the rotating columns of wind spin no faster than a breezy 85 miles per hour and tear off the occasional tree branch or picnic blanket. Most of the rest qualify as EF-1 tornadoes, with winds between 86 and 110 miles per hour, gusts that can shove a car off the road. The tornado that touched down in the southwest corner of Oleander, Kansas, at 2:31 that Thursday afternoon, cutting a diagonal swath across the town before curving slightly to the north, jumping the Nanimwe River, and dissipating into the atmosphere about twenty miles down the road, rated an EF-5. To qualify for that category—which only one or two storms a year manage to do—wind speeds must exceed 200 miles per hour. At that speed, a funnel of wind can lift a car, strip the bark off a tree, or atomize a house. As the inventor of the scale put it, when a Category 5 storm strikes, *incredible phenomena will occur.*

By 2:45 that afternoon, more than forty of Oleander's houses had been ripped from their foundations and turned to dust. Four of the town's five churches were rubble. The north wing of the town hall, built in 1907, collapsed. The town green, which had been home to a gazebo, a playground, and a small pond perfect for duck feeding in the daytime and old-fashioned necking at night, was now a debris field, littered with concrete, broken telephone poles, tree limbs, flat tires, and roof lumber shot out by the storm. The tornado had sliced straight through the graveyard, spitting up bodies in its wake and distributing them as far as a mile away. For several days, it was not unusual to find a rotting face peering out from the trees. Mayor Mouse's car was found, in nearly perfect working order, on the firehouse roof. Much of Main Street was spared, but Elmo's Luncheonette, the Hardware Shack, the Cut-N-Edge, and everything else between Fourth Street and Seventh Street were a lost cause.

Tornadoes, unlike hurricanes, do not get named. A hurricane is an unwelcome houseguest, one you see coming. You can watch it from afar, learning its habits and its nature. The hurricane is the enemy you know well enough to hate, the lover who inevitably betrays. The tornado is the stranger at the door with a knife. It has no features, no habits, no face.

Names have power; to name something is to domesticate it, or to try. Naming a tornado would be like naming a shadow. What happened in Oleander that day was simply *the storm.* A cloud that faded back into sky before it had a chance to enjoy what it had wrought.

The power was still out when Jule made her way to the trailer park, trudging along deserted roads, stepping over downed power lines, and avoiding eye contact with the dazed survivors who'd ventured out to see what remained of the town. Sparking live wires snaked across the street, and several of the houses that weren't yet burning emitted a strong natural-gas smell that didn't bode well. Broken *things* littered the concrete, torn notebook pages scribbled with homework, a smashed picture frame, half of a bed frame, a large red valentine heart carefully inscribed with a child's "I love you." Shredded American flags dangled from broken branches. One car had been wrapped so tightly around a tree trunk that its fender and bumper kissed. People staggered past her, caked with mud or plaster or blood. One man had a fork embedded in his cheek.

She never forgot the smell. It was the smell of nature gone wrong: grass and leaves and manure churned up by the wind, animal entrails and unearthed corpses, wet wood, must and mold from the heart of demolished buildings, lake water flung too far ashore and trees stripped of their bark. And beneath it all, a breath of the unnameable, with the metallic tang of blood and earth—as if something ancient had been violently dredged up from below.

It took Jule an hour to make it back to the compound and discover what the storm had left behind: nothing. The handful of trailers that remained were toppled from their concrete blocks, some crushed like tin cans. The triple-padlocked door of her uncles' secret lair had torn from its hinges and embedded itself in the trunk of a poplar tree. Near the edge of the woods, a fire burned, puffing up noxious clouds of smoke. The cops were reluctant to bust meth labs, Uncle Scott had once told her. The chemicals were both highly flammable and highly toxic, and more than one inexpert bust had ended in conflagration.

She stayed clear of the flames and tried not to inhale too deeply.

Overhead, her frayed underwear dangled from a tree.

"Mom?" Her thin, wavering voice couldn't have traveled far. Maybe, she told herself, that was why it got no response. "Uncle . . . Scott?" A little louder this time. Scott would have taken charge, as he always did. He would know what to do. But no answer came from the smoking ruins.

Jule sank to the muddy ground, and surveyed the broken land that was her only home. She stayed there in the gathering dark, steeling herself, until finally, there was no delaying it anymore. She rose, approached the nearest pile of twisted aluminum wreckage, and began the search for bodies.

Of the town's churches, there was only one whose interior remained intact and whose sanctuary and wooden cross were unharmed, which was strange—for the roof had been neatly sheared off. Left open to the elements for nearly the entire duration of the storm, the church below bore no scars of what had raged overhead.

This is what Deacon Wally Barnes found when he set out to investigate his masterwork. A church watched over by open sky, and beneath it, a girl, sitting poker straight in a wooden pew, hands clasped and eyes fixed on the sanctuary as if waiting for the sermon of her life. The deacon spoke her name. When there was no response, he sat beside her. The crown of broken glass in her hair glinted in the twilight sun. But, except for a narrow cut on her pale cheek, she appeared unharmed. A trail of dried blood traced a line down her face.

"Eleanor," he said again. "Ellie." She looked no older now than the day she'd been delivered to his doorstep three years before in dire need of guidance and cleansing. They had struggled then, but he had eventually delivered her from need. He had shown her the way.

She blinked once, slowly, like a princess stirring from a trance.

He pressed his lips to her forehead in benediction, and she awoke.

She looked at him strangely, as if she could see *into* him, including and especially the parts no one was ever meant to see. She peered straight through him with those strange, muddy eyes, and a smile played on her lips. "Yes," she said, as if in answer—and the deacon, who before taking on the cloth had killed a man bare-handed, a man who'd been drunk, surly, and nearly twice his size, looked at this skinny, wet seventeen-year-old girl, and was afraid.

"Yes what?"

She blinked again, and the strange look was gone. "Is it over?" she said.

"The storm? Yes, it's over."

She looked around, and smiled. "Then it worked. The church is safe."

"Well . . ." He tipped his head toward the nonexistent ceiling. "In a matter of speaking."

Ellie stood. "Then I guess I can go." She sounded foggy, half asleep.

"Did you get trapped here, when it started?"

"I came here to watch over it through the storm, as He told me to."

"Who did?"

Ellie glanced to the missing roof—no, to the sky. "*He* did."

The deacon cleared his throat. "You're telling me . . . *God* called on you to watch over the church?"

She nodded.

He surveyed the damage above, and the lack thereof below. Maybe just some trick of the shifting wind. Or maybe the Lord had stopped turning a deaf ear and finally taken notice of this festering town. He wanted to believe that—it should have been easy for him to believe that. But it would also mean believing that the Lord had passed him over, and put His faith in this girl. Offered this girl the gift Wally Barnes had waited so long, and so desperately, to receive.

Envy was not his only sin, but it was his ugliest.

And yet . . . he had prayed for a sign. Pleaded for some confirmation, no matter how slight, that his work wasn't in vain. That he had not been abandoned. If he could believe that God had whispered in this girl's ear—and he *had* to believe it—then wasn't it possible to believe He'd meant the whisper to spread? As the deacon so often told his flock, signs came in many forms.

He took Ellie's hand in his own.

"You aren't the only one with a mission from the Lord today, Ellie."

"He sent you here, too?"

"Yes. But not for the church." He waited.

"He sent you . . . for me."

"As He sent you to me." The deacon stood with her, still holding her hand, in the church he had built with his will and his craft, and he looked up, and saw no limit.

* * *

Reports had the Preacher wandering into the storm, raising his arms to the rain, and furiously chanting lines from *King Lear*. The latter was probably poetic license on the part of witnesses eager for a good story, even in the face of calamity. But Daniel knew his father, and the rhetorical extravagance had a ring of truth. Not that it mattered. Shakespeare spouting or not, the Preacher had been consumed by the wind, and Daniel didn't have time to care, because the Preacher wasn't the only Ghent unaccounted for.

No one had seen Milo—not his camp counselors, who'd sent the kids home early, and not his mother, who'd belatedly shown up to claim him.

"I thought he'd be with you," Giuliana told Daniel, with a wild-eyed despair that left him nearly sick with fear.

They had promised him it would be best for Milo: a nice home, with a nice woman, who had the added credential of being his mother. Even though she'd done crap to show it over the last eight years. When Milo was six months old, she'd dumped him in the Preacher's arms and taken off to find herself. No one had asked her to find her way back.

After Giuliana's, Daniel went home, because that's where Milo always went. There was no sign of him. At the day camp, Laura Tanner was of no help, and he had to restrain himself from shaking her when she offered some thinly veiled observations about children from broken homes. He checked the empty school and, doorstep by doorstep, the houses of Milo's few friends. When that, too, came up empty, he tried Giuliana's neighbors at random, most of whom failed to open the door, although he saw more than a few pairs of eyes peering out from behind lace curtains. Everyone on the block knew better than to speak to a Ghent.

Only Grace Tuck answered her door, sizing him up with those cold, narrow eyes.

"I'm here alone," she said. "So if you're a roving ax murderer, you should really pick someone who would be more of a challenge."

He nearly told her she shouldn't answer the door to strangers, then reminded himself she was someone else's problem.

"I'm looking for my little brother," he said. "Milo? He's eight. Maybe you've seen him around?"

"I know Milo." She softened. "You can't find him?"

He shook his head, swallowing the fear. The Christmas before last, he and Milo had spent the night watching *The Wizard of Oz*. The flying monkeys had given the poor kid nightmares for a month, but that didn't stop him from demanding to see the movie again and again, until he knew all the lyrics and could do a fair impression of Dorothy shrieking for her Auntie Em when the twister was a-comin'. He'd always wanted to see a "twister."

"I'm sure he's fine," Daniel said tightly.

"Yeah."

"I just need to find him."

"Yeah. You do."

The roads were largely impassable by car, so he walked, calling his brother's name, trying to ignore the heaps of wreckage, overturned cars, vacant lots where houses used to be, men scrabbling with their bare hands to pry up collapsed beams and crushed walls and extricate whoever lay beneath. He didn't let his mind stray to the question of what he would do if Milo was gone.

In the scrabble of weeds behind the Ghent house lay an old shed that Daniel's father had used as a workroom in better times. Its wood beams and floorboards had rotted at approximately the same rate his father had, until its walls sagged alarmingly, its door rusted shut, and a hive of wasps took up residence under its eaves. There was a loose floorboard in the back corner, which, for a couple of years, Daniel had used as a hiding spot for things he didn't want his father to find—candy, books, a Victoria's Secret catalog that seemed to qualify as porn. But the last time he'd pried up the bent wooden board, a clutter of spiders had spilled out of it, the largest the size of his thumb. As he'd knelt there, mesmerized by the swarm, they had reached him, and crawled over his sneakers, into his hands, up his pant legs, his back, his neck, everywhere, until he broke from his stupor and screamed and screamed and screamed. It was weeks before they stopped skittering over his dreams. Lesson learned: don't go looking in dark places, because dark things live there. And hidden beneath the prospect of Milo's death were the real spiders. The truth, buried deep enough that ignoring it was unconscious as breathing: Without Milo, things would be easier. There'd be nothing to hold him to his father, to Oleander, to his small and hateful life. He had known it even at age nine, when the baby had appeared on the doorstep like a fairy-tale changeling. He'd known it, without letting himself know it, every day since. Sometimes he woke up in the night, from a disguised wish of a dream that would have made Freud proud, feeling guilty and ashamed. He never let himself remember why.

Daniel looked for Milo until the sun set, and then stole a flashlight from the drugstore and continued his search.

They would tell no stories of that night. Stories of the storm itself, yes, the *Where were you when . . .* and *If I'd been a little less lucky . . .* Stories of the dark days that followed. But not that night. The day's adrenaline surge cast the night into shadow. Energy ebbed away, and with it, the capacity to remember, to mark the moments, narrating for some future self, *This matters. This is how it happened.* They moved through the night in a fog. They searched the wreckage and collected their belongings and taped up windows and hugged their children, and in the morning, they remembered only that they had survived, and then, sometime later, shaky with relief, they had slept.

Two people died in the hospital that night; three more died under the wreckage of their houses before help could reach them. Oleander had an all-volunteer fire squad, a five-man police department, and a handful of utilities employees charged with righting the water, gas, and power. But that night, anyone with an able body ventured into the darkness, flashlights and supplies in hand. Gas and water mains were mended; blankets and coffee were distributed to the shattered and wounded; cots were provided to the newly homeless. Plumbers joined electricians and handymen to jury-rig the town's infrastructure while friends and neighbors dug through piles of rubble, searching for keepsakes and loved ones. Even among the sturdiest of old-fashioned farming stoics, there were more embraces than handshakes, and more tears than either.

The hospital overflowed with bleeders, people pressing shirts and tissues and rags to dirty wounds. While the nurses tended to the critical cases, the rest tended to each other, fetching washcloths and rubbing shoulders and doing the kind of banding together and communal rallying that played well on the evening news. In the homes without emergency generators, candles were lit. Families played cards and told scary stories of scarier days. Some stayed in the storm cellar all night, waiting.

Many looked to the sky. The night had cooled, and a soft breeze rustled what few leaves remained on branches. The storms were gone, the skies clear from Wichita to Topeka. But they weren't clear over Oleander, where a thick layer of clouds blotted out the sky. A strange trick of the moonlight had stained them red. And when people remembered anything about that night, it was this: there were no stars.

What Daniel saw was so close to what he wanted to see that for a moment, he didn't trust it: a small, lithe figure creeping out of the shed and shutting the door firmly behind him, darting a look over his shoulder to make sure no one was watching. It was too dark to see the boy's face, but he could easily make out the baseball cap perched cockeyed on a mess of curly hair. Daniel's legs, which had nearly given out after hours of walking the town, felt new again, capable of leaping small buildings in a single bound, more than capable of sprinting across the yard in seconds, and then he was close enough to reach out and grab Milo, who was no desperate hallucination, who was solid, and whole, and alive.

"I will *kill* you," Daniel promised, his face buried in his brother's shoulder. He squeezed Milo tight enough to pop him. "You run off like that again, you're dead, get it?"

Milo wiggled out of his grip and looked up at his brother. Daniel aimed the flashlight at his face.

"Hey, watch it!" He jerked away from the beam, but Daniel didn't let up.

"You listening to me? No more wandering away from grown-ups, no more running home. You . . ." Daniel swallowed hard. "You have to listen to your mom. She's in charge."

"She hates you," Milo said, sullen now.

"But she loves you." Maybe it was even true. "Promise," Daniel said.

Milo shrugged.

"Say it."

"I promise I'll listen to her."

"And do what she says."

"Danny!"

"And *do what she says.*"

"And do what she says."

"What are you doing here, anyway?" Daniel said.

"I just needed to . . . get something."

"In the middle of a *tornado*?"

"I waited till it was over," Milo said, in a tone that indicated he didn't appreciate Daniel calling him an idiot. He paused. "Dad's not here."

"No, he's not."

"You think he's out saving people?"

Daniel rolled his eyes in the dark. This was a kid who'd seen through the Santa sham from day one, but somehow he still believed their father was a superhero, out to save the souls of the world. "Sure, Milo. That's what he does, right?"

Milo grinned. It faded quickly. "You're gonna take me back there, aren't you. To her house."

"To *your* house," Daniel said. He flicked off the flashlight, preferring not to see his brother's face. "Yeah. I am."

"But we don't have to go now, right? Can we eat first, or something? I'm hungry."

The dark gave him no protection against Milo's high, eager voice.

"And tired," Milo added quickly. The kid knew what he was doing.

"It's pretty late. Your mom's probably already asleep," he said, knowing better. "No reason to wake her up. But first thing in the morning, you're going right back. Got it?"

"Got it." Milo took his hand, and together they crossed the dark. "Danny?" Milo sounded younger than usual.

"Yeah?"

"Missed you."

"Yeah."

They dined on cold pizza and warm pop, and then Daniel tucked his brother in and stayed by his side until he fell asleep. It didn't occur to him—not that night or the next, not until it was too late—to wonder what Milo was hiding in the shed.

## 5

## EVERYBODY KNOWS

After.

After the bodies were zipped into body bags and returned to their graves.

After the newly dead were buried beside the old.

After the windows were taped up and the caution tape taken down.

After the sun came up and the tanks rolled in.

After the men in uniforms blockaded the road.

After the food ran out.

After one day passed, and then two and then three, and the power came back but the phones, the Internet, the outside world never did.

After that, things were different.

But maybe not different enough.

There were three main routes out of Oleander: State Street to Route 8 ran along the southern edge of the town, skirting Potawamie Lake to the east and tracing the woods in the west before winding into the prairie. Route 72 cut through the farmland in the east and crossed a set of disused railroad tracks on its way to the horizon. The Nanimwe River bordered the town on the north, but crossing Asylum Bridge would take you only to the old power plant or an endless field of corn—in other words, nowhere you'd ever want to go.

All three were blocked by a cluster of tanks and soldiers, each carrying some this-means-business weaponry. The soldiers wore surgical masks. Barbed-wire fences had been erected along the highway lines, while floodlights swept over the lake. Word soon spread of the ATVs that cut back and forth across the farmland by Route 72, hunting for anyone who'd made an ill-advised trek into the wild.

It took a couple of days, and more than a handful of border skirmishes, for anyone to find the time and energy to care. Those first forty-eight hours were about digging out and rebuilding, patching wounds and wiping tears. The lack of access to the outside world via phone, computer, or car was expected. The crimson smoke that still billowed overhead, blocking the stars and staining the sun? That was not.

Nor was the absence of media vultures, eager volunteers, photographers, FEMA paper pushers, politicians, the complete cast of characters who could be counted on to descend after any communal tragedy. The town had waited: for the Good Samaritans who would drive cross-country with bags of ice and racks of barbecue, for the charity groups who would apply their overpriced tool kits and rudimentary carpentry skills to the rubble, for the medical volunteers who would supplement the overrun hospital, for the politicians who would pose with the sad and brokenhearted, for the camera crews who would capture it all on film for *News at 11*. But the federal disaster workers were the first and last to arrive. And whatever work they were doing beyond the borders, these strange nonsoldiers with their soldier-like bearing, it didn't include restoring television and phone reception, constructing temporary housing, or bolstering the mental health of the town, the last of which was decaying by the day.

The police department had a staff of five, including two patrolmen who served part-time and devoted most of their energies to buying and selling antique guns online. Oleander considered itself a *nice* town, full of *good* people, and there wasn't, in those first two days, much looting or vandalism. But there was more than the police were equipped to stop. Especially since one officer was tasked to spend most of his days driving through town, piping announcements through his rooftop megaphone that were intended to calm the populace. *Do not panic. The water is safe to drink. The air is safe to breathe. The soldiers are here for your safety. Do not panic. Do not panic.*

It was a phrase that tended to have the opposite effect.

Those who had an in-case-of-emergency bottled-water supply drank only from that. Those who trusted neither the police nor the air donned masks or wrapped T-shirts around their faces when they went outside. Those who depended on constant access to the Internet went a little nuts.

And everyone had a theory:

The tornado had caused a nuclear-reactor leak (though there was no nuclear reactor within a hundred miles of Oleander—"as far as we *know*").

The country was under attack.

The government wanted to erase Oleander from the map, just because it could.

They were all unwitting subjects of a psychology experiment.

Possibly an experiment run by aliens.

On Saturday afternoon, two days after the storm, the megaphone message changed, announcing a town meeting. Every household was requested to send at least one representative. There would be free coffee.

There would be answers.

They crammed into the school gymnasium, downed their weak coffee, and waited to be convinced that their world wasn't broken beyond repair. No one was in much of a hurry to sit down, not before they'd exhausted all possibilities for hugging and weeping and retelling the story of how they'd made it through. It would hurt less once it became a story, something to be remembered and rehashed in a neat linear form. Some tottered on crutches; others brought pillows on which to rest plaster-encased limbs. Almost everyone bore bandages, stitches, burns, or scratches, some badge of honor from the storm. Even Ellie, though the shallow slash on her face had nearly healed.

She and her parents—temporarily reunited by crisis—squeezed into the fourth row. To their left sat Chip Gordon, the high school chemistry teacher known to bump up his salary by making and selling illegal fireworks out of the chem lab all summer. On their right was Rosemary Wooden, older sister of the departed Eugenia, who had always been (in her own estimation) the smarter and (in everyone's estimation) meaner sibling. Her disposition had not improved with the slaughter of her sister in a drugstore massacre.

Ellie had come to the meeting only because her mother requested it, and when it came to her mother, saying yes was easier. She would have preferred to stay at home, in her room, staring. It was how she'd spent the last two days, staring at the ceiling, trying and failing to regain her purchase on the world. Since the storm, she'd felt like she was living underwater, everything blurry and muffled and slow. Everything except the voice in her head.

Unlike the rest of the world, the voice felt real.

And it knew her sins.

The mayor took the stage. Ellie wondered if everyone else could see that he was trembling, or if it was just her. She'd started to think a lot of things were just her.

He welcomed the town, offered his sympathies for their struggles, promised them that Oleander would band together in this time of trouble. He recited these sentiments in a monotone, reading verbatim from his notes, never once raising his eyes to meet the crowd. He called a line of football players onto the stage, introducing them as the Watchdogs, an impromptu neighborhood watch that would ensure the continuing security and tranquility of the town. Special commendation went to Baz Demming, police lieutenant's son and star quarterback, whose brainstorm this had been.

The sight of Baz penetrated Ellie's haze. She could feel his eyes searching the crowd—surely not for her. It had been years since she'd had to worry about that. But they could easily fall on her accidentally, and if they did, she felt as if her skin might literally burn.

*That time is over,* she told herself.

*That me is gone.*

The voice knew better.

A screen was unfurled. It lit up, revealing a middle-aged middleman, graying and paunchy and dressed in civilian clothes. He introduced himself as Colonel Matthew Franklin. He didn't bother to explain how he'd managed to appear before them with all phone and Internet lines down; when it came to its own needs, the government always had its ways.

"I apologize that I couldn't join you in person," he said, smiling avuncularly into the camera, "but rest assured that a joint task force of National Guard and FEMA personnel is doing everything in its power to restore . . . Oleander to the life it once knew." There was a noticeable pause before he spoke the name of the town, as if he'd needed a whispered reminder from someone off camera. "I'm sure you have many questions about the quarantine" that's been erected at the town borders—"

It was the first time anyone official had used the term *quarantine*. Murmurs rippled through the crowd.

"—but I assure you that all measures taken have been for your own safety. We've had a bit of an . . . incident at a facility several miles from your borders, but I assure you *no harm will come to you*. I repeat, as long as you remain *within the town borders*, you will be *perfectly safe*. As soon as the situation has been contained, we'll restore full freedom of movement. In the meantime, our top priority is *your safety*. On that you have my word, and the word of the United States government."

The screen went black. The murmurs rose to a dull roar.

"If it's so safe, why ain't he settin' foot in it?" someone

shouted from the back. Someone else cursed the tornado, and several more cursed the government. The surging anger was palpable, and bubbling beneath it was a dangerous current of fear.

"People, people, stay calm," Mayor Mouse pleaded with the crowd. "You heard the man. Something spilled out there, or exploded, or what have you—nothing those men can't handle." He was off his written notes, and out of his depth. "Let them worry about fixing whatever mess they made out there, and what say we worry about fixing our town?"

"How 'bout you fix the damn phone lines!"

"And how much longer am I supposed to go without my TV?"

"My kids are out there—they don't even know if I'm dead or alive!"

"They're liars," said a deep voice on the far right of the room. Scott Prevette rose to his feet, fist in the air. "You don't clue into that soon, they'll see us all dead."

The audience fell silent, hesitant to give its fury full release if it meant siding with a Prevette. But Scott saved them the trouble, striding out of the room, the rest of the family falling in behind him, single file. Jule wasn't with them, Ellie noticed. She hoped the girl had made it safely through the storm.

The mayor was losing his audience. That might have been the end of it, right there, the death of law and order and the trappings of civility that keep the many subordinated to the will of the few, had the deacon not seized the moment—and the stage. Ellie sat up straighter. She hadn't spoken to him since the night of the storm. In his presence, there'd been a peace, a sureness, that she had not found since. The town felt it, too; she could tell by the way they shifted in their chairs, stilling their restless mutterings, waiting for him to speak.

"The wages of sin is death," he boomed, joining the mayor at the microphone. "But the gift of God is eternal life in Christ Jesus our Lord." Then, astoundingly—especially for a man who believed humor to be the devil's favorite trick—he laughed. "I don't know about you, but I'm not quite ready to meet my Maker."

More astoundingly, the audience laughed with him.

"The government has forsaken us. Nature has forsaken us. I'll admit, I've asked myself: Has the Lord forsaken us?" He hesitated, giving the question time to settle over the crowd. Or maybe giving himself time to worry the answer. That wasn't like him. "I'll admit, I was angry at Him. I'll admit, I doubted." From him, it was the ultimate admission of weakness. That wasn't like him, either. "But then I thought: What if the storm wasn't a punishment? What if it was a warning? What if this quarantine is a gift? The wolves are at the door, friends. We know this. But maybe the Lord just installed a dead bolt. Oleander belongs to us now. Imagine it: no meddling outsiders, no East Coast politicians telling us how to teach our children, how to love our wives, how to live. Imagine if we could remake this town into what the Lord knows it can be, a shining city on the hill."

There were a few scattered *amen*s from the crowd, and more than a few hushed dismissals.

"Never forget, our Lord is a just Lord. And He listens to His people. When God called Abraham in the desert, and warned him that Sodom and Gomorrah would be destroyed, did Abraham let this pass? Did he turn his back on the cities of sin and wish them farewell?"

The *no*s were cautious at first, then—maybe because it was a good day for shouting—less so.

"He did not!" the deacon boomed. "He pleaded with the Lord: *Please, my God, spare these cities for the sake of the righteous yet dwelling within.* Why do I remind you of this story? Because Sodom and Gomorrah were beyond redemption—but we are not. Because it takes a brave soul to argue with the Lord, and a truly fierce soul to argue and win. You here, Ellie King? How about you come on up here for a moment?"

Ellie started in her seat, unable to believe she'd actually heard her name. But heads were swiveling toward her, and her mother was poking her, urging her to rise. She climbed the stairs to the stage and took her place beside the deacon. With the weight of his hand on her shoulder, she felt steadier than she'd been in days, rooted to the earth and to the world.

"Three nights ago," the deacon began, "while all of us were hiding fearfully beneath the earth, awaiting the Lord's judgment, this young, defenseless girl strode into the storm. She entered the house of the Lord, and there she prayed. Not just for the preservation of her own life. Not for the humble building in which she sat. She prayed for the soul of Oleander. *Please, Lord*, she cried, *do not smite the righteous along with the sinners. Have mercy, Jesus, and allow me to lead my people to salvation.*"

Is that what she had done? Ellie wondered. Was that the prayer in her heart as the lightning cracked and the sky fell?

"And the Lord listened. You think it's a coincidence that

of all the churches, only hers was spared? You think it's an *accident* that the roof was torn away but the building, and the pure soul within it, were left intact? He removed the roof of His own house, and now that it's gone, now, *now,* we look up and we can see. *I* see a Lord who will reward us for our righteousness, as he punished us for our trespasses. I see a merciful Lord who wants us to repent, and quickly. I see a divine opportunity."

"I see a fraud and a blowhard," came a shout from the front row, where, as editor in chief of the local paper, Howard Schwarz had brandished a hastily improvised press pass in order to claim a seat. "You think praying is going to rebuild our houses? Or protect us from whatever's bubbling up out there? You think it's ever a *good* sign when the government cuts off all access to the media?"

"Well, now, I don't know about that," the deacon said jovially. "We still have the good old *Oleander Post,* so things can't be *too* dire."

It punctured the tension in the room and scored him another laugh. Schwarz had taken over the paper three years before, turning what had once been a tired but dignified reporting of Little League scores and pie recipes into a weekly screed against small-town life. He didn't have many friends left.

"He's not lying!" a woman shouted from the back of the room. "I saw that girl walking through the storm like a crazy person."

"I saw her, too!" another cried. "Headed to that church like she was on a mission."

"A mission from the Lord," the deacon said. "A mission to save the church, in which she succeeded. And a mission to save the town, in which . . . well, time will tell, won't it? Ellie, perhaps you'd like to lead us in prayer?"

She'd never spoken before this many people, and she expected her voice to tremble. But it did not. As if some other voice was channeling through her, the words flowed, steady and clear.

"Lighten our darkness, we beseech Thee, O Lord. And by Thy great mercy defend us from all perils and dangers of this night, for the love of Thy only Son, our Savior, Jesus Christ. Amen."

They listened to her in silence. Most crossed their hands and bowed their heads, but a few stared with naked curiosity, as if she were a strange museum piece—or a holy relic.

The deacon believed that she could hear the word of God, and these people believed it, too. She knew it, the way she knew things now, deep within herself, clear and certain.

Maybe they were right. Maybe the voice knocking around her skull was neither a sign of madness nor the devil's tease, but the Lord, with her before, with her still. If it taunted her, if it reminded her of all her stumbles and her great fall, then perhaps that was only God's way of redeeming her inner Gomorrah, reminding her of that which must be destroyed.

As usual, the real action happened in the meeting before the meeting. Mayor Mouse and Deacon Barnes—habitual enemies who could each recognize a situation that required allies—hovered before the computer screen side by side, waiting for the duly appointed representative of the United States government to explain exactly what the hell was going on.

Mouse was already starting to consider resignation, and

specifically what effect it might have on car sales. This wasn't the job he'd campaigned for; this wasn't the town he'd determined to lead. And he had no doubt the deacon would be more than happy to take the reins in his absence. It was the one thing they had in common: they were both ambitious, not just for themselves, but for Oleander. Sure, the deacon had a stick up his ass and was always harping on some lunatic cause or another, waging his endless wars against science textbooks and drugstore condoms. But at least he understood that the town could be something more. And no one agreed more than Mouse. Why else had he persuaded the previous mayor to lease the old power plant to a nameless consortium that, given its deep pockets and paranoia, was almost certainly a front for the military? Why else had he, as mayor, asked no follow-up questions and granted any permit requested of him? Because his reward was an influx of cash: payments for land use and taxes far higher than they should have been. His reward was a new Oleander, soon flush with prosperity. That was the dream, at least.

This was the reality: a "containment breach." A quarantine. And only Mouse to blame.

Colonel Matthew Franklin explained nothing. Yes, there was a "situation." Yes, communications lines would be restored when the government deemed it prudent. In the meantime, deliveries of food and emergency supplies would continue to appear at the border . . . as long as the mayor kept his people in line.

"And if I don't?" Mouse said, striving for a boldness he didn't feel.

"You have two choices, Mayor," the colonel said. "You can

keep your people in line, or I can have my men do the job. I'd rather you save us the trouble. In return, I'm happy to offer you complete autonomy."

"Complete autonomy?" the deacon put in. "In what sense?"

"In all senses. Think of this as an opportunity. A gift from the United States government to you. Comply with our regulations—which, I should note, you *will* do, one way or another—and for the duration of the quarantine period, Oleander belongs to you."

# 6

## SOMETHING WICKED THIS WAY

There was a rhythm to life in Oleander in this time, syncopated but steady. Even for those untouched by the storm, there was no business as usual, only business in spite of. Despite house-guests taking refuge on couches, despite downed phone lines and severed supply lines, there were still cows to be milked and fields to be mowed. The business of nature continued apace, as did the business of those whose job it was to keep the town in business, the mayor and the cops and the doctors and the carpenters and the plumbers all working overtime, as if to compensate for the rest—shopkeepers with no goods to sell, gas-station attendants with no gas to pump, farmers whose herds had taken flight. And then there was the business of re-covery: cleaning up wreckage, tending to injuries of body and soul. They were two towns in one: those who bore only a faint battle scar living side by side with those who had been cut down where they stood and now struggled to rise.

It had been four days, but Jule could not get used to the house. Though she had, for the moment, stopped expecting the tap of a police baton against the solid oak door, the place showed no signs of becoming a home. Or rather, with its procession of family portraits marching up the stairs, its height chart carved into the kitchen doorway, its bookshelves cluttered with dried flowers and porcelain cats, it was very much a home—just not hers. For the first time in her life, Jule had a real bedroom, complete with solid walls, a full-sized mattress, and a door that locked. But she couldn't sleep. Vaguely familiar faces grinned down at her from photo collages; a diary chronicled someone else's dull, effortless life. Whenever she flicked the light switch, a neon sign on top of the bookshelf flared to life: CASSANDRA, in glowing curlicues of pink and blue. Jule was no stranger to labels; at home, her cramped scrawl marked half the items in the fridge, yogurt and soy milk and frozen pizza that she'd bought with her own cash. She had a feeling that Cassandra hadn't needed labels any more than she'd needed that lock on her door. The fact that the diary was just tucked under the pillow for anyone to find—the fact there was a diary at all—suggested a girl who took walls for granted. That was why Jule wouldn't let herself feel guilty about squatting in Cassandra's bedroom. Well, that, and the whole baby-killer thing.

There were more than a few empty houses in Oleander this week. Some people had left town and been unable to get back with the roads blocked; some people had died. Some fled a couple of broken windows and the inconvenience of a leaky roof in favor of a neighbor's couch or a room at the town's only motel. The Porters were in a category of their own. Jule had heard that they left town soon after their daughter was sentenced to life in the loony bin, but who left town without taking a sliver of their life with them, or at least a couple of pictures off the wall? Who kept paying the electric bill for a house they never intended to see again? The place was eerie in its intactness, as if the Porters had walked up the stairs one night and never come down again, and Jule wondered how long her uncles had had their eye on the place. The Prevettes weren't the only squatters, not this week, but somehow they'd managed to get their hands on the best vacant property in town. It probably didn't hurt that they'd set up camp as the first clouds were still gathering in the sky—not that any of them had bothered to tell Jule.

That morning, she woke up to the smell of coffee and eggs, which was strange enough. Stranger still was discovering, when she padded downstairs, her mother pouring coffee for her uncles Teddy and Axe. The three of them sat around the kitchen table stuffing their faces while Scott, of all people, stood at the stove on frying-pan duty.

"We got peppers, onions, and tomatoes," Scott said, bent nearly in half over the stove, which had not been built for someone of his height. "Take your pick, Jaybird."

It was what he'd called her when she was small and he was still Uncle Scott, the big man who'd swung her in loop-the-loops like a stunt plane and promised to protect her from the big bad world. Over the years, both of them had gotten harder—with the world, and with each other. Maybe, Jule thought, the house was haunted by the ghosts of domesticity past, and even the fearsome Prevette brothers were unable to resist. She nearly smiled, and then she noticed Scott's thick leather belt. Hanging from it, in a makeshift holster, was his favorite knife.

"Just tomatoes," she said quietly. "Please."

Her mother shifted to make room for her at the table. "Where's the—" Jule swallowed the word *parasite*. "Billy?"

"Don't you worry about that," her mother said. "He's doing some work for your uncles."

"Billy? *Work?*"

"You'd be surprised how useful your stepfather is making himself around here."

Axe scowled. "Shut up about that, Annie."

"Useful as a human garbage disposal, maybe," Jule said. "Or if you've got a burning need to turn beer into piss. But I'm not sure that qualifies as work."

An uncomfortable glance passed between Teddy and Axe, and then a plate slammed down in front of her. *"Eat,"* Scott said.

She asked no follow-up questions.

After invading the house, Scott had claimed the master bedroom. It meant Jule's mother and the parasite were consigned to the pullout couch in the office, while Teddy and Axe and the girl they shared got stuck in the guest bedroom, with its two twin beds. Jule had no idea how she'd scored a room of her own, and the not knowing didn't sit easy with her. It was like the omelets, and the specter of Scott Prevette with a red-checked apron tied around his waist—pieces that fit together into a puzzle she couldn't quite solve.

Scott's latest woman, another dishwater blonde whose name Jule always forgot, had not made the move with them, and it seemed wisest not to ask where she'd gone. As a rule, Scott was almost never without female companionship, but lately, his interest seemed to have waned. His interest in everything had waned, except for his hunting knife. Even the business fell mostly to Axe and Teddy these days. Of course, that was before the trailer camp had been wiped out, and with it, the padlocked trailer and whatever was secreted inside. Now it was the basement that had been declared off-limits. Jule didn't want to know. Not that it mattered what they were making down there, if they couldn't move their product—so Axe and Teddy had spent the last several days hunting for a way out of town. But the government cordon was tight, and enforced with more firepower than the Prevettes were willing to take on. Frontal assault wasn't Scott's style: he liked to stay a shadow, slipping through the gaps. They'd yet to find him one. Jule suspected they were starting to get a little desperate.

After four days stuck in Oleander with no phones, no Internet, tanks at the borders, and an expanse of toxic *something* lurking just beyond, a lot of people were getting desperate.

"Those FEMA people are shipping in more food this afternoon," Jule's mother said. "I'll see what I can get."

"Get more eggs," Axe mumbled around a runny mouthful of omelet. He scraped a last bit off his own plate before scooping a forkful off his younger brother's. Teddy whacked his knuckles, which were tattooed HATE and PUNCH, the C and H crammed together on his pinkie—Axe was better at fighting than counting. Axe was, in fact, better at fighting than he was at anything. He claimed that the red devil flames he'd had tattooed across his face and shaved head were intended as a warning, but he loved nothing more than when people failed to heed it.

"FEMA." Scott snorted. "Some people will believe anything."

Scott's world was a web of conspiracy. His catalog of nefarious plots against the common man expanded every year, and currently included: driver's licenses, fluoride, taxes, email, flu shots, parking tickets, and pretty much every governmental program and department, from the EPA to UNICEF. Sometimes his caution was warranted—it's not generally a good idea to declare meth-generated income to the IRS. Other times—as when he'd spent several weeks hiding in the swamp, convinced that defense contractor Gold Mountain Trust had teamed up with the FBI to assassinate him with a fleet of robotic drones—it was less than productive.

Jule's mother rolled her eyes. She was the only one who dared poke fun at his "theories." "Your uncle here thinks we've all been duped, and the army's taking over."

"What the hell would the army want with Oleander?" Jule said.

"Whatever they want, they'll get it." Scott drew his knife and laid it flat on the table. "'Less someone stops them." His eyes were redder than usual, his motions fluttery, with a telltale twitch. Teddy and Axe were nearly bouncing in their seats. There'd been a time when Scott was good about keeping himself and his brothers to a low level of consumption—enough to enjoy the party, not enough to crash it, he liked to say. It was a long time ago.

"Scotty says they're why the phones still don't work." Teddy looked to his big brother for approval. He was no good at thinking for himself, and so more than willing to let anyone else do the thinking for him. It made him everyone's favorite, at least now that James was gone. "And the computers."

"Scotty probably also thinks the government fascists made the storm in the first place," Jule's mother said. "All part of their evil plan. Go ahead, tell them."

"I never said that." Scott rubbed the knife handle between his palms. For a moment, the silver blade looked to be coated in blood. Jule blinked, and the crimson stain faded—just a trick of the light. "But I wouldn't put it past 'em."

Before he could elaborate on Uncle Sam's dark intentions, there was a squeal outside and then a loud crash. Everyone froze.

Scott jerked his head at Axe. "Check it out."

Axe shrugged. "Sounds like raccoons getting into the garbage."

"How about you go see for yourself?"

Axe nodded at his plate, which was now heaped with left-overs from Jule's and her mother's plates. "Can't it wait till I'm done?"

Scott snatched the plate and flung it against the wall. Omelet and ketchup spattered against the beige paint. "You're done."

No one spoke as Axe trudged toward the back door to investigate the noises, and no one made a move to clean up the mess. Scott played with his knife. A few minutes later, Axe reappeared. Dangling from his hand, like a kitten wriggling from its mother's jaw, was a child. Scruffy and gap-toothed and certainly no more than seven or eight, he didn't look nearly as frightened as he should be.

Axe dumped the boy on the floor. "He was looking in the window. Trying to spy on us."

"Was not!" The kid scrambled to his feet, but couldn't get very far with Axe's meaty hand locked on his collar. "Let go of me."

"How about you tell us what you're doing here," Scott said. "Someone send you here to spy on me? You working for someone?"

"He's seven," Jule snapped. "He's not working for anyone. He's probably just lost."

"I'm eight," the kid said, like out of everyone in the room, she had now caused him the greatest offense. "And I'm not lost."

"Not too smart, either, apparently," Jule's mother said wearily. "Axe, let go of the boy."

Axe looked to Scott, who nodded. He let go.

"Boy, what is your name?" she asked.

He pressed his lips together.

Scott lumbered over to the child, and looked down at him from what must have seemed a great distance.

"My sister asked you a question," Scott said. It was not the voice he used on children he liked.

It turned out, the kid had the capacity for fear after all. He'd gone pale and shaky. "Milo. Ghent."

"Son of a Preacher Man!" Teddy laughed. "That's who we got here, Scotty. Son of a Preacher Man!"

Of course, that was why the kid looked so familiar, Jule realized. Daniel had the same scruff of hair and the same crooked nose. This was the little brother he'd been so keen to find the day of the storm—the one with, as Daniel had put it, an inconvenient urge to wander.

"Your daddy send you over here?" Scott favored the boy

with a lopsided grin that revealed his blackened teeth. "He want you to tell me I'm going to burn in hell? Because he's passed that message along already, loud and clear."

"No one sent me," Milo said. "I, uh . . ."

"You, uh, what?"

"I guess I'm lost."

"You guess you're lost."

"Yeah. I guess."

Scott's smile widened hideously. "You're not planning to tell anyone what you saw here," he said. "Or who?"

Milo shook his head solemnly.

"I'll take him home," Jule said quickly.

"He goes home when I say he can," Scott said. "And I don't recall saying that yet."

"You didn't say it yet," Teddy said.

Scott glared down at Milo. "You know what we do to spies around here?"

Milo shook his head again.

Scott drew his knife and ran the blade along his index finger.

Jule gripped the edge of the table. Scott just wanted to scare the kid, that was all. That's what she told herself. But Scott was high, and when Scott got high, he got dangerous.

And, crazy as it sounded, there were times when she thought the knife might have ideas of its own.

"I'm taking him home." Jule grabbed Milo's hand and pulled him out of the kitchen before anyone could argue. "Now."

"You do what you need to, Jaybird," Scott called after her. It was the voice of the knife. "That's our only job on this earth, ain't it? But you remember who'll always be here waiting for you when the doing's done."

Jule shoved Milo onto the doorstep and rang the bell. Daniel opened the door with murder in his eyes. "You have *got* to be kidding me," he said.

"He was poking around places he shouldn't be."

"And that's my fault?"

"Did I say that?"

"You were thinking it," Daniel muttered. But when he turned to his brother, the fury washed out of his face. Jule could see him struggle with trying to keep some vestige of anger there, just to put enough fear into the kid that he wouldn't do it again—but he wasn't doing a great job of it. "What gives, Milo? We talked about this."

"I needed to get something for a friend," Milo said.

"What friend?" Daniel asked, sounding suspicious enough to make Jule suspect the kid might not have any.

"Doesn't matter."

"Well, did you get it?" Jule asked, wondering what he could possibly have been looking for in some bushes on the opposite side of town. Probably the kid had been on some quest for magic beans or whatever it was that kids decided their invisible buddies couldn't live without.

Milo shook his head.

"You should have brought him to his mother's house," Daniel said. "He's not supposed to be here."

"She's not home," Milo said.

"So where is she?"

Milo shrugged. "She left somewhere. She didn't tell me."

"She left you *alone*?" Now, instead of faking fury, Daniel was trying to mask it. Again, it was a poor job. "Does she do that a lot?"

"I guess," Milo said.

"Is that why you're always coming over here?"

"It's why she doesn't *know* I come over here," Milo clarified, not so dumb for an eight-year-old after all. Then he mumbled something else.

"What?" Daniel said.

"Nothing."

But to Jule, it had sounded like *You don't always know, either.*

Daniel sighed. "What did you promise me?"

"Don't remember."

"I think you do."

Milo grinned. "Prove it."

"That's it," Daniel said. "Come on." He shut and locked the door behind him.

"Where are we going?" Milo said.

"Church."

Jule jerked in surprise. She knew the father was a religion nut, but Daniel had shown no signs—until now. Dragging your little brother off to church on a Monday afternoon to repent for the sin of being eight seemed extreme enough to qualify.

"No way," Milo said. "No. Uh-huh. Not there."

"They set up this day-camp thing," Daniel told Jule, as if knowing exactly what she'd been thinking. "So there's someone to watch the kids while their parents are cleaning up and . . . you know."

She did know: planning funerals, sitting by hospital beds, cursing unpaid insurance premiums, searching through wreckage, throwing useless cell phones against the wall, shouting at border patrols, doing whatever had led Milo's mother to leave her son alone.

"I got stuff to do here, Danny," Milo said.

"Yeah? What?"

"It's private."

"Then I guess it's not getting done."

Milo crossed his arms and sat on the ground, and Jule wondered if she was going to witness her first-ever full-blown temper tantrum. "Not going," he said. "Not there."

"You don't think I can *make* you go?"

Jule tensed. If she'd tried this when she was a kid, Uncle Scott would have scooped her up and thrown her over his shoulder—that's if she was lucky. Any of her mother's boyfriends would have done worse, and some of them had. Daniel wasn't much taller than she was, and he looked like he'd have trouble bench-pressing a beach ball. But compared to Milo, he was big.

Daniel lunged for Milo and started tickling the crap out of him. Squirming in his grip, the boy shrieked with laughter. "Let goooooooo." But the torture continued until one of Milo's involuntary leg spasms caught Daniel in the balls, and both boys rolled to separate corners, moaning and gasping for different reasons.

"Okay," Daniel said when he'd caught his breath. "You win."

"I can stay?"

"No . . . but how about we get you some new comics on the way?"

Milo's eyes widened. "You gonna *steal* them?" The drugstore, after all, was still closed for repairs.

"Borrow," Daniel said firmly. "I work there. I can do that."

Milo looked dubious, but stuck out his hand for a shake. "Deal."

"Deal."

They set off for the road, pausing only when they realized Jule wasn't with them. "Well, you coming?" Milo called back, as if it were a foregone conclusion.

"I guess." Jule started after them, keeping her head down and wishing her hair were long enough to cover her face. She wasn't about to let either boy see that, for whatever stupid reason, she was trying very hard not to cry.

Daniel had the feeling that if she caught him looking at her legs, she'd beat him up. But then, he reasoned, sneaking another glance, why would you wear fishnets if you didn't want people looking at your legs? They weren't even particularly special, as far as legs went—neither long nor slender—but somehow the inky web that carved her legs into diamonds of smooth skin cued his brain to mark them as tantalizing and slightly forbidden. Though not so forbidden he wasn't justified in taking a peek.

"What?" Jule said, almost catching him at it.

"Nothing." If he'd been a religious person, he might have taken it as a sign that, at that moment, they reached the church.

The lobby was ordinarily papered with flyers about

tutoring and yard sales and various substance-abusers Anonymous meetings. But the detritus of ordinary life had been replaced by a wall of government notices, support-group ads, requests for short-term labor and short-term employment, volunteering opportunities, and, in red, a row of handmade wanted posters featuring Cassandra Porter's junior prom photo. She'd been spotted in the storm, impossibly free and headed for Oleander.

Daniel couldn't suppress the wave of sympathy that washed over him at any mention of Cass Porter, as he couldn't help appreciating the curl of her lips and the bounce of her hair in the grainy picture. And, as always, the wave was quickly followed by a tsunami of guilt. All the hours and years he'd spent drooling over her every move . . . surely there'd been some kind of sign, a dog whistle of a signal that he'd subconsciously ignored, and what kind of a person falls for a future murderer?

Probably the same kind of person who feels sorry for her after the deed is done.

With its roof stripped off and its nave exposed to the elements, the church was starting to show some wear. Birds nested behind pillars and flitted beneath tables scavenging for crumbs. Scritch-scratches in the shadows suggested that the rodents of Oleander had also found themselves a hospitable home. The pews were still slick with morning dew, and it seemed only a matter of time before a layer of moss would creep over the hardwood that stretched to the altar. Daniel had heard that the day before, a sparrow had objected to a particularly boring stretch of sermon by crapping on the deacon's head. The thought of it happening again was the only thing that could tempt Daniel to a service.

Pink day-care signs directed them to the basement, but to get there, they had to muscle through the crowded nave. Oleander's only remaining church had quickly become a default meeting place and distribution center for food, clothes, or any kind of assistance, spiritual or otherwise. There were cots for those with nowhere else to sleep, and a rotating staff of volunteers handed out blankets and soup at all hours of the day. Here, as everywhere, people had cell phones attached to their hands, redialing every few seconds in a useless attempt to get a signal. Here, as everywhere, stories flew about desperate attempts to make it across the border, and the uniformed men with guns who lurked in the prairie grass, determined to turn them back. It was the same all over town, but on the streets, you could feel a rising desperation, the claustrophobic's wild-eyed need to *get the hell out*. In here, there was only quiet acceptance, and despair. It was a mishmash of people—young mothers, elderly women leaning on canes and rolling in chairs, a handful of kids Daniel recognized from school, a man in his Sunday-best suit who reeked of whiskey, a couple of red-eyed tweakers—all of them wearing the same expression, a mixture of loss and hope; all of them tracking Deacon Barnes as he glad-handed his way across the room. He kept one arm at all times tightly around the shoulders of a willowy blonde a third his age.

"Crap," Jule said suddenly. "I gotta go."

"Because of her?" Daniel asked just as the blond girl spotted them. Her face lit up at the sight. "Is that Ellie King?"

"It's Saint Ellie now. Or haven't you heard?"

He'd heard the rumors: that she emitted, under the right light, a saintly glow; that she knew things about you she should never have known; that beneath her fingers pain dissipated and twisted muscles regained their use. These stories were mostly on the order of something a friend of a friend who heard from a neighbor said. It was impossible to pin down anyone who'd seen the miracle worker in action. In fact, as far as Daniel could tell, what Ellie King mostly seemed to do was stand by the deacon's side looking beatific and nodding sympathetically at the shattered masses.

Now she was heading toward them and waving frantically, the deacon on her heels. People kept reaching out to touch her as she passed.

"I have to get out of here," Jule said, but she made no motion to leave.

"God saved her," Milo said, in a low voice that sounded eerily like their father's. "He called her to the church, and he saved them both."

Daniel wanted to shake him. "Who told you that?"

Milo gave him the you're-a-moron look that only an eight-year-old can truly pull off. "*Everyone* knows that."

"He's right," Jule said. "Everyone's saying it. Guess that makes it true."

"Jule!" Ellie King threw her arms around Jule, who stiffly endured. "I knew you'd be safe. He's not done with you yet."

Jule shoved her away. "Apparently, neither are you."

Daniel didn't know what was going on between the two girls, nor did he want to. Not as much as he wanted to get Milo away.

The deacon nodded politely to the new arrivals, then whispered something in Ellie's ear. She shook her head. "He can wait."

"This is important, Ellie."

"*This* is important," she said softly. "Five minutes."

He obviously wasn't happy about it, but he left her to it. "Five minutes."

Once they were alone, Ellie took Jule's hand. "I know what you've said before—"

"Which?" Jule asked. "Leave me alone, or leave me the hell alone, or leave me the—"

"Do you know my dad?" Milo said suddenly.

Ellie started, like she hadn't realized he was there. "Who's your father?" she asked.

"It doesn't matter." Daniel tugged at his brother. But Milo was an immovable object when he wanted to be, and the last thing they needed was a kicking and screaming fit in the middle of a crowded church.

"The Preacher," Milo said. "That's what people call him. He talks to God, just like you."

Jule snorted.

From Ellie's expression, it was clear she knew exactly who the Preacher was and didn't much appreciate the comparison. At least, not as much as Jule did.

"I'm not sure it's exactly the same," Ellie said.

"No, it is," Milo told her. "And God talks back to him, too. Like he talks to you. Doesn't he?"

"He does . . ."

"See? Same thing. So, can you ask him something for me when you talk to him?"

"Your father?"

"No, God. Can you ask him where my dad is? And give him a message for me?"

Daniel swallowed. It had been four days, and the Preacher still wasn't back.

It had been four days, and it was time to accept that the Preacher probably wasn't coming back. But no one had explained that to Milo yet.

"I will do that, Milo," Ellie said, with an unruffled assurance that suggested it was as simple as picking up the phone. "And remember, the Lord has a reason for all He does. I'm sure your father's safe, whether on earth or in the bosom of—"

"Milo!" Daniel barked. "Go wait for me by the stairs."

"But I haven't given her the message."

"Milo. *Go.*"

Milo went. Daniel stepped closer to Ellie, close enough that her wispy bangs nearly brushed his forehead. "I don't care what you tell the rest of the idiots in this town. But you don't tell my brother God has his reasons, and you don't tell him God has the inside line on his dead father. In fact . . ." He didn't want to leave Milo here. He wanted to take his brother home, back to his real home, dingy as it was, and watch him every second of every day until he could be trusted to protect himself. But storm damage meant repairs, and repairs meant money—there were weeks' worth of odd jobs awaiting him all over town, enough hammering, towing, cleaning, and plumbing to be worth a year of shifts at the J&C. He could make enough to get them both out of town . . . if he could get Milo squared away. And if he could stay awake.

He wasn't sleeping. The dreams were back, ever since the

storm. And they were worse than before. The screams were no louder, the moans no more gut-wrenching, the current of blood no stronger. But in this version of the dream, Gathers died first, gut-shot on the wrong side of the register, a stack of comic books in his gnarled hand. In this dream, Daniel was the one holding the gun.

He wondered what Ellie's chatty God would make of that.

"Just don't tell my brother anything," he said finally. "Period. Stay away from him."

She was silent, and he wondered if she had even heard him, or if Bible quotes ran through her head on a permanent loop, crowding out everything else.

"Do you understand me?" he said.

She nodded, letting her hair fall forward across her face. "I'm sorry about your father. And I'll . . . I'll stay away."

"From me, too," Jule put in.

"I'm sorry," Ellie said again, and then she was gone.

Daniel felt like he'd stepped on a kitten.

"Impressive," Jule said. "I haven't managed to get rid of her all year, and you get it done in five seconds?"

His righteous disdain had drained away. "I guess she wasn't hurting anything. . . ."

"You guess wrong."

They herded Milo downstairs. The volunteers tending to the children were mostly church ladies he didn't know but who, he could tell from their freshly pressed blouses and starched hair, were from the "right" part of town. Definitely the type to snitch on him to Milo's mother. This wasn't because they took her as an equal—perish the thought—but because any adult was to be trusted over a teenager from the west side, especially one descended from the town drunk. None of them was a likely candidate to watch out for his brother.

Then he spotted the one person who might be right for the job.

"Grace!" he called. She handed off the infant she was holding to an older woman and carefully threaded her way through the children. "You volunteering here?" he asked, surprised, and not just because with her twin braids and delicate features she didn't look much older than her charges.

She offered him a sour smile. "Suffer the little children, right?"

"They certainly seem to suffer you," Jule said as a toddler wandered up to Grace's leg and gifted her knee with a kiss. It almost seemed like Grace was tempted to kick the child away, but instead she patted him on the head and gently disentangled herself.

"I see you found your brother," she said.

"I know you," Milo said.

"And I know you. Your brother went to a lot of trouble to find you—and now he's dumping you here?"

Milo grinned. "That's what I said!"

Daniel shook his head. "You're perfect for each other. Enjoy."

"I got some new comics," Milo told her. "We stole them."

Daniel cleared his throat. "Borrowed them."

"Whatever. Wanna see?"

"Desperately," Grace said in a flat voice. "Make my day."

Daniel dared another glance at Jule, though this time at her face. She looked like she wanted to adopt Grace for her own.

"Your parents make it back?" Daniel asked the girl. "You're not still alone in the house, are you?"

"Now, why would I give out that kind of sensitive information to a stranger?"

"If you're staying there by yourself—"

"It's taken care of," she said.

Daniel shrugged, reminding himself it was her business, not his. You developed a knack for that, living in a town this size. "Just don't let him out of here until I get back, okay?"

Grace took hold of Milo's shoulder. "Nothing happens to this kid on my watch."

She was smiling when she said it, in a tone that suggested a lighthearted joke, or tried to, but there was nothing light about the girl, and nothing warm about the smile. Whether in spite or because of it, Daniel decided to believe her.

Ellie hovered in the doorway of the deacon's office, cursing herself for thinking that she knew better than he did. It was Jule Prevette. Something about the girl made her lose perspective. It had been a year, and Ellie was no closer to convincing her to come to the Lord than she'd been that first day at the trailer park. But she couldn't let go. Even now, when she had so many more important things to do.

"We can't hesitate," the deacon was saying, hands waving expansively as they did when he had particularly warmed to his topic. "Don't tell me there aren't changes you've been wanting to make around here, Mouse."

"I told you not to call me that." The mayor rose to his feet.

"The Lord knows you by all your names, Mouse. You can't hide from Him, and you can't hide from this moment." The deacon stood, too, slapping his hands flat on his broad desk, and as he did, he caught sight of Ellie in the doorway. He beckoned her inside. "Here she is, sir, the main attraction."

Ellie allowed herself to be introduced to the mayor and inspected like a show pony, smiling and shaking hands as she tried not to consider the phrase *main attraction*. It all too easily called to mind the circus that passed through town every other summer with its carnival freaks in tow, the bearded lady and the strong man and the mermaid. Fakes, all of them, but content enough to sit on their stools and bear Oleander's curious gaze. That was how the town looked at her now. Even her mother stared when she thought Ellie wasn't paying attention.

No one was more surprised by Ellie's newfound divinity than the woman who had borne her.

All children were filthy little beasts. That's what Charlotte King believed, and that's what she taught her girls, from the moment they were old enough to speak (and to smear pudding on the walls and spaghetti on the floor and snot on their mother's face, among other unforgivable transgressions). Be clean, stay clean, never associate with anyone who shows signs of not being clean—that was the prime directive. Home-schooled and raised on a steady diet of chores, Sunday services, and Christian pop, the King girls were allowed three hours of supervised television a week. Their mother selected the shows. They could read any book they chose, as long as it came from their mother's library. They dressed first in clothes their mother picked out for them, and later in clothes she carefully vetted, occasionally bringing out the measuring tape when a hemline crept close to a knee. At age fourteen, each daughter slipped on a purity ring, to signify her promise to God that she would keep her body and soul clean. Henry King, who'd wanted sons and didn't understand daughters, suffered this with the same mixture of bemusement and impatience with which he endured all of his wife's decisions. But he occasionally took his youngest on illicit movie dates and, when his wife was out, let her poke around online, "our little secret." He couldn't disguise his pride when she developed a rebellious streak of her own.

Ellie could still remember how she'd felt, fourteen and lawless, capable of anything but getting caught, so proud of her shoplifted mascara and the PG-13 DVDs tucked beneath her mattress. She'd felt invincible, and if her mother hadn't opened her eyes to her sin, she didn't know where she'd be now.

Probably dead.

Now word had gotten around: Ellie King, handpicked by the Lord to watch over His house. Ellie King, unscathed by the storm. Ellie King, who had stared unafraid into the eye of the tornado, and been spared. They really believed it—she could feel that in the weight of their stares—and so it must be true.

There were pleasantries exchanged and nothing of substance discussed and, after the mayor thanked her for her service to the town, the deacon maneuvered him out the door with a final, meaningful look whose meaning Ellie couldn't penetrate. Then they were alone. They sat together on the couch. They always did. He said it made things less business-like between them, and after all, their business wasn't business, but the work of the Lord. She knew it was vain, but she couldn't help it: she liked feeling special.

*You're no one special*, said the voice that was partly in her head but partly not.

*You're no one.*

*No one but a filthy whore.*

In the days since the storm, she had given up hoping that anyone else would hear the voice, but she still watched the deacon carefully, silently begging him to react. Because the voice wasn't just in her head, it was in her *ears*. Which meant either it was a hallucination, of the kind no sane person should have, or it was real. A voice that spoke only to her, the way she had always dreamed that His voice would speak only to her, but the things it said . . .

The voice was not, could not be, of the Lord.

*He can smell it on you,* the voice said as the deacon rested his hand on hers and told her he was proud of her.

*You can't clean a filthy soul,* the voice said as the deacon told her how, together, they would clean up the town; how they would seize this moment to bring not just God's word but God's law to at least one small corner of a lawless world; how desperate people needed a leader to tell them what to do, and she would be that leader "with me by your side, of course—we're in this together now."

*You want him to shove it in you,* the voice said as the deacon suggested that perhaps they should order in a pizza to discuss their plans in more detail, or perhaps, if she liked, they should pray on their future, and the future of the town.

*You want to get on your knees.*

*And show him what you're good for.*

*Because that's all you're good for.*

"I'm sorry," Ellie managed as the bile rose up her throat. "I have to—" She flew off the couch and somehow made it to the small sink by the custodian's closet before the gush of hot vomit forced itself out of her. She bent over the sink, gasping, the rich, sour stench making her sick all over again, and then someone was pulling her hair away from her face and rubbing her back and the deacon was saying that he would take care of her and it would be all right.

*You want to ruin him with your garbage soul like you ruin everything you touch.*

*Because you're a disease.*

*And there is no cure.*

She heaved again, but there was nothing left to come out.

"Remember, men, you're the future of this town. All those little kids who look up to you? All those fans who cheer you every Friday night? All those girls who drop their panties after the game? You think that's because they care about football? You think football matters?" The coach paused to give the team space to hoot and stomp. They didn't disappoint. "Damn right, football matters," he continued as the noise died down. "But it's not all that matters. Your *families* matter. Your *town* matters. And at a time like this, they're looking to you to show them the way. So go get 'em!"

The speech was out of character for Coach Hart, who favored monosyllabic grunting over soaring rhetoric. West supposed it was possible that communal crisis had awakened the man's poetic side. But it seemed more likely that, as often happened around homecoming time, he'd overdosed on a marathon of inspirational sports movies and decided to fulfill his cinematically ordained duty as a molder of men. As the team charged out of the gymnasium and into the dark, broken streets of Oleander, flashlights deployed and testosterone surging, West couldn't help wondering what the coach believed they would find as they entered the breach. What challenge it was they—the future of midwestern civilization—were so uniquely qualified to face. He'd spent the previous night's patrol picking up litter and helping a woman nearly his mother's age and obviously stoned out of her head search for her dead sister's cat. (Which, the woman remembered about an hour into the search, was dead, too.) That night, he'd been on his own. Tonight he was paired up with Baz and one of his linebacker lackeys, and it was clear from their swagger that they had a different kind of evening in mind.

The improvised neighborhood watch had been Baz's idea. His father was a cop, and the tiny department had eagerly embraced the opportunity to spread the crap work around. So the Bulldogs became the Watchdogs, equipped with heavy flashlights they swung like police batons, deputized to scout the streets and keep the peace. Baz had even tacked one of the department's spare badges to his jersey.

He'd claimed prime territory for their night's beat: the north end of Main. It had been left nearly untouched by the storms, and so instead of ferrying stray branches out of the road, they would have little to do but protect the scatter of stores from looters who seemed unlikely to appear. West had to admit, it was a relief to stroll down the intact street, past Hot Buns (the coffee shop/gym), past the junk shop and the health clinic, the old-fashioned barbershop and the vintage-everything store Rags to Riches, and pretend Oleander was exactly like it used to be. To escape, for at least a few hours, the heaps of rubble, the flattened fields, the overturned trucks, the uprooted stumps, the still-gaping wounds of the homes and landmarks that used to be. Worse than the ruins were the people who wandered among them, even at night, dazed and confused and, in some invisible and incurable way, wounded. They said they were searching—but had no answer when you asked them *Searching for what?* Two nights before, West had found a man he dimly recognized from his dentist's office slumped against a crushed Honda on the side of Third Street. West had tried to help him up and walk him home—and gotten a punch in the jaw for his trouble. For all he knew, the guy was still there.

It was inescapable, even at home, where the Thomases had taken up permanent residence in their neighbors' guest room. The storm had skirted the West property and flattened the Thomas farm that lay a couple of acres due east. Their house was rubble, their crops uprooted, their cattle lifted by the wind and scattered across Route 72. And so they haunted their borrowed home, drifting from room to room with the expression of people so lost they couldn't even muster the desire to be found.

Pointless patrolling or not, West was in no hurry to get home.

Hayley Patchett and Emily Dunster were leaning against the darkened window of Hot Buns, clearly waiting for the players to arrive. Baz slipped an arm around Hayley. Her slightly less blond and significantly less pretty friend nestled into Matt's bulk.

"You should have told me West was coming," Hayley said, with a giggle. She said everything with a giggle. "We wouldn't have blown off Kaitly."

"Probably we would have anyway," Emily said.

"Okay, yeah, probably. But we could have found *someone* for him."

Baz elbowed West. "Our boy's not into the ladies, is he?"

*Smile*, West told himself. *Grit teeth, laugh, go along, get along.* It was his formula for survival, and it had always worked.

Nick had thought him a coward, though he'd been too kind to say so. West let him think it. That was easier than explaining something he still couldn't explain to himself. *Someday, I'll tell Nick the real story.* So he'd promised himself. Someday, in this infinite future they'd pretended they would have together, he would explain that Nick wasn't the first.

First had come Miles Stoddard, fullback on West's Pee Wee football team. West, who'd still gone by Jeremiah back then, had been thirteen, a halfback, and just old enough to know better. That hadn't stopped him, as it hadn't stopped Miles. They were, after all, thirteen, well practiced at the fine art of getting themselves off but less skilled at suppressing the flagpole when it deemed the most inopportune moments—bus rides, gym class, Sunday dinner with Grandma—a good time to rise. They could, perhaps, be forgiven for experimenting. It was only a few feverish fumbles in the Stoddards' rec room or behind Jeremiah's locked bedroom door: harmless. Miles had been a freckled redhead, fond of farting the alphabet and telling jokes about dead cats. He hadn't yet discovered deodorant. West suspected that the whole thing would have petered out on its own after a few weeks, and then maybe everything would have been different. But instead, Mrs. Stoddard came home "sick" so she could catch a pivotal wedding on her soap—only to discover her half-dressed son with his hands down another boy's pants.

West had been sent home, and that night, Miles downed the full supply of his mother's antidepressants. He lived, and was promptly shipped off to his grandfather's farm in Kentucky. Within a few weeks, the rest of the Stoddard family followed, never to be seen in Oleander again.

Things hadn't been so stark at the West household. Everyone knew what happened; no one spoke of it. There'd been a private conference with their minister, who'd preached tolerance and understanding and so been informed by the Wests, in no uncertain terms, that he should stick to the Lord's business and stay out of theirs.

There'd been weekly doctor's appointments, ostensibly to treat West for the "shock" of his sort of best friend's sort of suicide attempt. The doctor spoke at first in veiled terms of *hormones* and *control,* and then in horrifyingly less veiled terms of *masturbatory reconditioning.* These were accompanied by supervised viewings of healthily heterosexual porn.

His parents never asked about the appointments. They didn't speak to West at all, unless it was absolutely necessary. When he dared speak to them, they generally made an excuse and left the room.

More than once, he came home to find his mother weeping.

And then, just when it seemed the cold war would last forever: a thaw.

A Sunday hunting trip, father and son, just like they'd

done in the time he had come to think of as a gone-forever Before. Everything had been normal as they trekked into the woods, set up camp in their favorite clearing, and waited for unlucky deer. It was only once they rested their faces against the sights of their rifles, and there was no chance their eyes would meet, that his father spoke.

"Do you like being a member of this family, Jeremiah? Do you value being a West?"

"Of course, sir."

There was a silence as his father took that in. Then, "When your mother was pregnant with you, she always told people she didn't care if you were a boy or a girl, as long as you were healthy. But I cared. I wanted a son. You know why?"

"No, sir."

"I wanted someone who would grow up just like me. To play football for the Bulldogs. To take my place as head of the household. To run the business when I'm gone. To uphold the West name in Oleander for another generation." He laughed. "Selfish dreams of a selfish man."

West thought it might be the longest speech of his father's life.

"I was mistaken," he added.

"No, Dad, I—"

"You're a man yourself now, Jeremiah, or at least you're getting there. And a man gets to choose who he wants to be." His father paused, and even now, five years later, West could still remember how that moment had felt, the sliver of hope between one sentence and the next. He'd lived an entire life in that pause for breath, a different life of possibilities he'd never let himself imagine. It was an impossibly short time to possess something; even now, five years later, he still felt the loss.

"So you need to choose," his father continued. "Do you want to be a member of this family? Do you want to be the kind of man who follows in his father's footsteps? Do you *want* to be a West?"

After that day, he'd stopped going by Jeremiah. The new nickname was a persistent reminder of his choice, and the reasons behind it. He'd vowed not to let himself forget—and then he had, and there had been consequences.

It didn't seem fair that Nick was the one who'd had to bear them.

"Admit it, West," Hayley said now, with a pointed wink. "If the *right* girl came along . . ."

Baz gave her shoulder a warning squeeze. That was territory he'd already marked, which made it definitionally the wrong girl for anyone else.

"Not my man West. He's holding out for a conjugal visit, am I right?" Baz said. "After a year behind bars, even Cass Porter might get desperate enough to let someone in her pants."

Hayley's giggle took on a tinge of faux shock. "You're terrible!"

"The only thing getting into Cass's pants is that perma-stick up her ass," Emily said. Then, as if realizing she might have overstepped the Hayley-laid lines of propriety, not to mention committed the worse crime of being surpassingly clever, she giggled herself. "I mean, not that it matters. You wouldn't *really* . . . with a *murderer.* Would you, West?"

"We don't know what really happened," West said. The baby killer's boyfriend, that's who he'd been after the killing day. If he seemed to be acting strangely, a little distant, a little *not there*, it was easy enough to ascribe it to the shock of discovering that the girl he'd dated on and off for the last two years, hypothetically scrabbling at her virginal defenses, was a cold-blooded killer.

"It could have been an accident," the girls chorused with him.

"Well, it could have," he said, but it was halfhearted. Everyone knew she'd done it. He supposed it indicated some defect of personality that he couldn't bring himself to hate her for it. They'd never been close, even in those early months when he'd done all he could to push things forward, proving something to them both. It wasn't until she was gone—or, maybe more to the point, Nick was gone—that he realized the shallow relationship was more honest than anything he had left.

"If she's so innocent, why did she run?" Hayley said. "Innocent people don't try to escape prison."

"Or nuthouses," Emily added.

"Who cares where she was?" Hayley said. "What matters is she's *back*. Jamie Meriden's mom saw her crossing Fourth Street during the storm."

Baz snorted. "Jamie Meriden's mom snarfs so much Percodan she probably sees *elephants* crossing Fourth Street on a regular basis."

"Chris Tapper saw her, too, when he was trying to get off the road," Emily said. "He saw her heading into the woods."

"I heard that old lady who lives by the cemetery saw her

heading *out* of the woods," Matt said. "And since when do you talk to Chris Tapper?"

Emily cleared her throat. "I'm just saying, she's back. Everyone knows it."

"So what?" West said, hoping it wasn't true, that Cass wouldn't be that bold or that stupid.

Emily gave a dramatic shudder. "So it freaks me out, thinking about her lurking around somewhere. I mean, she *killed a baby.* All those times we hung out with her, like she was totally normal or something. A week before it happened, she slept over! What if she'd . . . ?"

Matt gave her a hug. "I'll protect you, babe."

Emily kissed him on the cheek. "Thanks, babe."

Hayley rolled her eyes.

"What?" Emily said. "It's creepy, okay? And why would she even come back? Do you think she has, like, some kind of plan?"

"If she did come back, we'll make her regret it," Baz said. "Don't you worry about that."

"Can we get back to business?" West said.

"Aw, Jeremiah wants us to shut up about his killer girl-friend," Baz said. West tried not to wince. At some point in the spring, Baz had started calling him by his first name—always with a twisted smile suggesting he knew exactly how uncomfortable it made West and would keep poking until he could figure out why. "Don't worry, buddy, for your sake, we'll go easy on her."

Hayley laughed. "Not *too* easy, I hope."

"No. Not too easy." Baz wasn't laughing.

They "patrolled." This meant they meandered up and

down the street, flashlight beams dancing on the concrete, girls whining that they'd been promised a more engaging evening, boys exchanging boasts about beer consumption and who would do what with whose mother. West trailed them by a distance that widened with every lap of the block, lost not in his own thoughts, but in the effort to avoid them. The wind had picked up, and thrummed in his ears.

It sounded like West's name—his real one.

It sounded like Nick's voice.

It had been happening a lot lately. Ever since the storm.

*Jeremiah.* Just a whisper, easily imagined, if you were the kind of loser who imagined the wind whispering your name in the voice of your dead lover. It was a kind of loser West resolutely willed himself not to be.

But: *Jeremiah.*

*Jeremiah, I'm waiting.*

*Waiting in the dark.*

He'd never had much of an imagination. West hadn't been able to imagine the two of them together, not until the very moment that he'd pressed his lips to Nick's for the first time and slipped his hands under Nick's shirt and tasted sweat and sweet and felt muscle flex beneath slick flesh. Even then, he'd lacked the vision to see what to do next. To see how they could be what they needed to be to each other. To imagine his life as anything other than what it was.

And then Nick was gone, and West couldn't have imagined what that would be like, either. The worst of it—the worst of the black despair that sucked him down and down and down—was that he now couldn't imagine escaping it.

He certainly couldn't imagine Nick back to life.

But: The wind. The whispers.

*I'm cold here.*

*I'm alone here.*

*Here in the dark.*

*Waiting for you.*

There was a crash of broken glass, and West swallowed a scream. But it wasn't a vengeful ghost. It was just an idiot punching his fist through a window. "What the hell?"

Matt had, at least, been smart enough to wrap his T-shirt around his fist before slamming it into the rainbow display window of Green's Old-Fashioned Ice Cream Shoppe. He shrugged. "Emily said she wanted ice cream."

"I *said* I wished it was open," she gasped through her laughter.

"Now it is." Baz widened the hole in the glass enough to reach through and unlatch the door. The consummate gentleman, he held it open for Hayley.

"I thought the whole point of this was to *stop* looters," West said.

"Do you see any looters?" Baz said, looking up and down the street. "Then job well done. Seems like we deserve our just desserts."

But the freezer was empty—and the store wasn't. A scrawny guy with black glasses and hair gelled into the approximation of a miniature Mohawk emerged from the back room, shouting and threatening to call the police.

West knew him: Jason Green. Everyone knew him, just like everyone knew Bob and Jesse who ran the gourmet sandwich place and Popeye Pete who ran the tattoo parlor and Ellen Choi who served coffee at the luncheonette and taught knitting on the weekends and Farah and Kitty who'd been "roommates" for more than sixty years. What people guessed about Nick, they knew about Jason, who made sure they didn't forget it. He was fearless. This year he'd tried to start a gay-straight alliance at the high school, but the only person who showed up to the meeting was an English teacher who'd been ordered to under penalty of firing.

Or so West had heard. He averted his eyes from people like Jason, for fear anyone might notice him noticing.

"I'll do it!" Jason shouted. "I'll call the cops!"

"Good luck," Baz said. "Last time I checked, no phones. But if you do get through"—he tapped his badge proudly—"tell my dad Deputy Demming says hi."

"You have to leave here. Now."

"Why should we? *You're* here."

"This is my store!"

"Your dad's store, you mean," Matt said. "He even know you're here?"

"He's on his way," Jason said. "And he's been going around with his hunting rifle lately. Just so you know."

"I don't know, guys," Emily said, "maybe we should go—"

"Not until we get something out of this," Hayley snapped. "If there's no ice cream, I want something better. I was promised an entertaining night, Baz. So far: not."

Events were taking on a tinge of inevitability. And West did nothing to stop them.

*But you could.*

Just the wind, he told himself.

*You could stop them all.*

"Emily's right, we should go," Baz said, and Hayley looked

wounded until she got a telltale wink. "All of us," Baz added, and nodded to Matt, who grabbed Jason by the scruff of the neck and tossed him out the door. He landed on his knees, grunting with pain, and scrambled to his feet just in time for Matt to give him a sharp poke in the gut that knocked him back on his ass.

Hayley and Emily's laughter had an animal sound to it, rising higher and higher until the night seemed to fill with their screams. Jason was silent. His accusing eyes fell not on his tormentors, but on West.

"Jeremiah," he said. "Come on."

West tensed, and didn't allow himself to check on whether Baz was giving him a weird look, or furrowing his meathead brow in an effort to put the pieces together. More power to him if he could. West had no idea why this freak would call him by a name no one was supposed to use, or why he'd think that West, of all people, could be called upon for help.

*Come on, Jeremiah.*

He shook it off.

"I think you want to apologize for being so rude back there," Baz said, standing over Jason and toeing his shoulder when it looked like he might be trying to rise. "Perhaps you'd like to reconsider. You could invite us in and offer the ladies some ice cream."

"There *is* no ice cream, asshole."

Bad idea. Baz, who was slim for a quarterback but still had at least fifty pounds on Jason, most of it muscle, grabbed his collar and yanked his head forward. "I must've heard you wrong. Want to try that again?"

"Jeremiah, please tell them to stop it." Jason sounded

neither desperate nor afraid. It was an oddly polite request, as if they were having the discussion over coffee and he simply wanted West to have his friends turn down their music.

West steeled himself. It would be over soon. Baz preferred intimidation and humiliation to actual violence, which he was smart enough to know could have actual repercussions. The girls would soon get bored or nervous or both, and they'd all leave the kid whimpering in the street and go off somewhere to get drunk or stoned or both.

Except that instead, Baz slammed Jason's head against the concrete, hard.

And the girls laughed.

While Jason moaned and cradled his head, Matt kicked him in the stomach.

The girls laughed harder.

"Enough!" West said sharply. "You don't even know this kid. What's he done to you?"

"What's he done?" Baz said, his foot casually resting on the kid's chest. "Jason here used to have gym class same period as me. And I'm pretty sure I caught him looking at my dick. That right, Jason?" Baz dug in his heel. "You like to look at my dick?"

Jason shook his head.

"Word on the street is our friend Jason *likes* dick. What do you have to say about that, Jason?"

"Yeah, I like dick," he said evenly. "But trust me, I wouldn't touch your disease-rotten mini-peen for a million bucks, so you're going to have to get one of these morons to jerk you off instead."

West willed him to shut up. His flashlight caught Baz's face, which had gone slack, his eyes as empty as any West had ever seen. He was suddenly sure that Baz was going to murder this kid, right here in the dark street, with all of them watching, Matt and the girls maybe cheering him on as Baz pounded Jason's head into the cement again and again and again until the kid's stoicism slipped and he screamed and then, not much longer after that, he stopped. West could already hear the sick sound of skull on blacktop; he could smell the blood.

West was bigger; Baz was crazier. He'd never given much thought to which mattered more in hand-to-hand combat. He didn't have to think about whose side Matt would take, which meant two against one, and Matt was the size of a refrigerator.

Before he could decide what to do—decide *whether* to do—footsteps approached at a fast clip. Without a word, the girls took flight, willing enough to cheer on the bloodlust but not to get caught doing it. Baz hastily pulled his foot off Jason, who stumbled to his feet and scuttled away. He was gone by the time the owner of the footsteps emerged from the shadows.

Rosemary Wooden was unintimidating under normal circumstances—hunched to a height of five feet, all ninety pounds of her swimming in a flowing caftan, fringes of white hair artfully arranged to poof over bald spots. In the dark of night, she looked like a kitten wandering blithely into a lion's den. She smiled tightly at them, clutching her lacquered purse to her side.

"Warm night," she said, limboed between *friendly* and *un*.

"They're all warm this time of year, ma'am." Baz offered a

smarmy smile, betraying very little of the disappointment he must have felt in letting go of his prey. "Can we help you home?"

Rosemary looked at the darkened storefront, taking in the shattered window. Both arms now curled protectively around the purse. She shook her head. "Such strange times. I thought a walk might do me good."

"Okay, so . . . have a great night."

Baz waved her away, but she didn't move.

West realized he'd tensed all his muscles. He reminded himself that Baz wouldn't do anything stupid here. No eighty-year-old woman could come to harm on Main Street at the hands of a couple of varsity football players, even in the middle of the night, even on a night like this. Still, surely Rosemary Wooden hadn't lived in Oleander this long without knowing when it was best to be on her way. Quickly.

Instead, she took a step closer to the football players, peering at them through thick lenses.

"I know you," she said, not sounding pleased about it.

"Well, I am the Bulldog quarterback," Baz preened.

"No, not you. *You.*" She was now close enough to poke Matt in the chest, which she did. Hard.

"Matt Crosby. I live down the street from you?"

"Yes, you do." She pursed her lips. "I believe you and some of your friends festooned my front yard with several rolls of toilet paper last fall."

"Oh, no, that wasn't me, ma'am."

Accurate, technically: it had been more of an *us* than a *me.* Half the team, high on winning and several fully tapped kegs, repaying an old lady for some slight from Matt's childhood, some tongue-lashing he'd chosen that night to avenge.

"And the bag of feces on my doorstep? Not you, either, I take it?"

There had, West recalled, been many slights to avenge over the last season. Matt had a small brain, but a large capacity for grudges.

Matt shook his head. "Now, why would I do something like that?"

*Walk away,* West thought, gripped with the sudden certainty that something terrible was about to happen. *Now.* "Ma'am, I'm happy to walk you home—the long way, if you'd like."

"I believe I've already said that I would *not* like."

Her hands shifted around in her purse, and when she pulled one out, it was holding a tiny pearl-handled revolver. Before West had time to register that the sweet old lady was aiming a gun at them, it fired. There was a sharp report. And then, with equally little fanfare or fuss, Matt was on the ground, a neat hole in the middle of his forehead, his mouth open in familiar slack-jawed confusion, his sightless eyes popped wide.

Rosemary Wooden shook her head, chuckling. "Hmm, that *was* nice," she said, as if satisfactorily confirming a theory. Then, to West and Baz, "Remember, good boys don't give dog doody to their neighbors. You have a nice night now."

"Will do, ma'am," Baz said, and both boys stood there, looking neither at each other nor at Matt's body lying between them until she slipped the gun into her purse and, like nothing had happened, primped her hair poof, turned on her practical heels, and walked away.

West dropped to his knees by the body. Matt was dead. Not moving. Not breathing. Heart—when he finally willed himself to lift a hand and feel for a pulse—not beating.

Dead. Just like that.

A strange calm had settled over him, a numb acceptance of the bloody scene that some part of him knew, with the same clinical disinterest, must be shock.

"So that was weird," Baz said, his own nonchalance slicing through West's stupor.

"*Weird?*"

"You don't think so?"

"We've got to get him to a hospital"—it was too late for that—"or call the cops. Or something."

"We pretty much *are* the cops." Baz tapped his stupid badge. "And what do you think that bitch would tell people about us, if anyone asked? You think she'd say we're just a few nice boys hanging out in the road in the middle of the night, knitting or something? You think anyone would buy that we weren't about to do anything to her, and she just thought it'd be a nifty idea to . . ."

"Shoot him," West said. "She *shot* him."

"You noticed."

"So what do you suggest we do?"

"Go home," Baz said. "Forget this happened. Oh, and don't leave dog doody on old ladies' doorsteps. I'm going to remember that one." Incredibly, he laughed.

West wanted to throw up. Or punch him. Or both.

More than anything, he did not want to leave Matt Crosby

lying in the middle of the street with a hole in his head. How many corpses could one coward be expected to abandon?

"We can't help him now," Baz said. "And we didn't do anything. There's nothing to feel guilty about."

"Nothing to feel anything about, is that right?"

"Bingo."

West bent his head over Matt, feeling like he should say a prayer. Say *something,* no matter how little he'd liked the guy or how much he felt like running home and forgetting the entire night had ever happened. A quiet *sorry* was all he could manage, unsure what he was apologizing for.

When he looked up, Baz was already gone.

By the next morning, the corpse had been disposed of, and the street cleaned. West didn't know what, if anything, Baz had told his father, but no questions were asked.


Every night, when it was safe, although it was never truly safe, Cass slipped out of the shed and searched for stars. For three nights, a thick, reddish cloud cover had blotted out the sky. But not tonight. Tonight, the clouds were gone, the moon was a sliver, and the night was alive with stars.

She couldn't allow herself the sun. Even after a year in a windowless room, she couldn't take the risk. She would settle for the stars.

Cass lay on her back in the dirt. Dew seeped through her thin cotton shirt. Weeds tickled her face. Wind stirred her hair. She sighed, deeply, breathing in the night, the smells of fresh-cut grass and damp bark, the whispers of bugs and birds, the bright canopy of sparkling lights.

*This majestical roof fretted with golden fire.* The words drifted back to her from a soliloquy she'd learned for her sophomore English class, in the time before.

All of this, an echo of before, when she could afford not to notice the infinite diversity of a world that was more than four featureless walls and a cracked ceiling. Even the shed, with its mildew and rust and spiders, was pure pleasure, simply for being new. She could entertain herself for hours probing its dark corners, tracing her fingers along the variety of textures, losing herself in the sharp, sloping curves of a rusting shovel or the intricate operations of an ant brigade on the march. She could lie here happily, in the weeds, listening to the night songs, counting the stars, and waiting for dawn.

These were pleasures she didn't deserve; they were pleasures she couldn't deny herself.

She lay shivering in the dew, willing time to stop, dreaming of other suns, until a small figure crept toward her, crouched beside her, and reminded her, "You shouldn't be out here."

"And you shouldn't even be awake," she said. Then, because she knew he was right, "Just a little longer."

"That's what I always say to Danny." The kid laughed merrily. "It works, too. He's such a sucker."

Milo was a sucker, too, because they stayed outside. Just a little longer.

The first couple of times, the kid had snuck into the shed as if he were auditioning for a Bond film, tiptoeing with his collar up around his chin and his cap brim shadowing his baby fat cheeks. He'd hovered in the doorway, and Cass had pressed herself up against the back wall, both of them afraid to get too close. The kid had chattered nervously while Cass tried to remember what it meant to have a conversation, to ask questions that were answered, to talk to someone who didn't lock the door when they left you behind. Gradually she'd let herself get comfortable. So had he.

Four days had passed since she'd gotten lost in the storm and stumbled into the Ghents' backyard; four days since she'd set up camp in the town she'd meant to leave behind. She'd spent every day hating herself for staying there even though she couldn't trust herself around a child, didn't know what she was capable of. But she couldn't leave. Not yet. Not that the shed made for luxurious living quarters, with its bowing, mold-infested walls, its fertilizer stink, and the nest of spiders she was pretty sure lived beneath the folded tarp she'd used that first night as mattress, pillow, and sheet. Now she had the kid's old sleeping bag, one of his father's old pillows, and an eclectic collection of scrounged food—a bag of Doritos, a box of crackers, two useless cans of soup. It was dry, and relatively safe. He'd told her about the soldiers on the edge of town, and about the signs with her face on them. She would leave eventually—once the danger had passed. Find a way out of town and into another life.

And in the meantime, she would not hurt this kid. She promised herself that.

But if she didn't know why she'd done it the last time, how was she supposed to make sure she didn't do it again?

They sat cross-legged in the grass, close enough to the shed to duck inside if anyone came near. But it was the middle of the night, and they were alone.

"I brought you these." With great care and pride, Milo placed a stack of comic books in her lap. "I read 'em already. And I just got some new ones. So you can keep these."

It was strange to be back on the Ghent property after so many years. She'd spent half her childhood here, playing flashlight tag, splashing under sprinklers, begging Daniel's mother to make more lemonade. Cass hadn't been back since his mother died, and it seemed like the grounds hadn't weathered the storm any better than the family. When Milo first found her and proudly introduced himself, she'd searched his face carefully, trying to find traces of little Danny Ghent. But Milo must have taken after his own mother, and quickly, Cass stopped looking. It hurt too much. The way he smiled, the way he laughed, it was what Owen Tuck might have been like when he'd grown up. If he'd grown up.

"Thanks, Milo, but you really shouldn't—"

"And I went to your house."

She stopped breathing.

"I don't think your parents live there anymore," he added. "There were these other people there. Big guys. This one had fire all over his face." He dropped his voice to a whisper. "Like the *devil*."

Everyone in town knew about the man with a face like the devil.

"And the other guys?" she said. "Was one of them kind of tall, like a giant? With a weird walk?"

He nodded excitedly. "You know them?"

No one knew the Prevettes; everyone knew about them. And now they were living in her *house*.

"You can never go back there again," she said. "Promise me." What might they have done to him, if they'd caught him sneaking around there? Given their reputation, anything. Although, going by reputations, it's not like he was any better off with her. At least the Prevette with the devil paint wore his evil right on his face, so everyone knew to stay away.

"You don't get to tell me what to do."

"I don't think your parents would want you going over there anymore, either."

"My mom doesn't care where I go. And my dad's with God."

"Oh. I, uh, didn't know. I'm sorry."

The kid seemed unfazed. "It's okay, he'll be back soon."

"O . . . kay." Cass was totally lost. "Just trust me, then, you do not want to go back to that house. Or anywhere near those guys. They're bad guys. You know about that, right?" She tapped the stack of comics. "You've got to leave the bad guys to the superheroes."

"What about you?" he said.

"What about me?"

"Those posters with your face on them. They say *you're* a bad guy."

"Oh. Well, I guess . . . I am. But I already told you to stay away from me. You didn't listen."

"So what kind are you?" he asked.

"What kind of what?"

"Bad guy."

She wasn't about to walk him through the gory details. "I didn't know there were *kinds*."

He grabbed two of the comic books, an X-Men and a Batman. "See, there are two kinds: wrong guys and evil guys. The wrong guys do bad stuff by accident. Like Magneto, you know? They think they're doing the right thing. They rob a bank because they need money for their sick kid. Or to get revenge on a scientist that turned them into a giant lobster. Or because they think they can save the world. Stuff like that."

"Right. Stuff like that. And the evil guys?"

"They just do bad stuff because they like doing bad stuff. Like the Joker. Or the Riddler. Or—yeah, most of those Batman guys, actually. See, wrong guys think they're *good*. Evil guys don't think at all. They're just evil. And kind of lame." He tossed the Batman back on the pile. "So which are you?"

"Good question." It had begun to rain. She'd missed rain. "Let me know if you figure it out."

Cass resolved not to give him the chance.

Daniel was sleeping when the front door crashed open, and for a bleary-eyed moment his dreams intruded on waking life. He heard the clatter from downstairs as gunfire, and saw, in the moony dark, blood streaking his bare arms, pooling on his mattress, dripping to the floor. But the blood proved only a play of shadows and, as he blinked the sleep out of his eyes, he realized the noise could only be his father.

Boots stomped up the stairs, rotting wood creaking beneath the weight, and then the Preacher himself appeared in his bedroom doorway.

Daniel sat up. "So you're not dead."

The Preacher's hair was matted and ratty and his face wore several days' worth of stubble. He smelled like a sewer. "Disappointed?"

"Where have you been, then?"

"I've been wandering the desert for forty days and forty nights—"

"It's been a week."

"—and God has spoken to me—"

"What else is new?"

The Preacher chuckled, and somewhere in there Daniel heard an echo of the father he dimly remembered, the one who'd charmed Milo's mother into bed and every so often played parent to his sons. "Smart talk won't save you from the day of reckoning. We're running out of time to prepare for the battle that is to come."

"What battle?"

"The battle between the righteous and the sinners. This will be our fortress, and we'll need supplies. Food, medicine, enough to last through the dark times. I'll handle the weaponry."

That did not sound good.

"How about we talk about it in the morning?" Daniel said. "When's the last time you slept?"

"You think the devil sleeps?" But the Preacher wiped a hand across bloodshot eyes and, all at once, the fight went out of him. "You have no idea how hard it is to wage this fight alone, son. If I had your mother—"

"Well, you don't."

"The devil's bringing death to our world, death and darkness. I saw it with my own eyes, spilling out of the pit. Satan's crawling into all of us. I'm trying to fight him off, for you and your brother, but if I can't do that . . ." He choked back a sob.

Daniel stood up, hating himself for falling for this, again. It wasn't unlike his father to get weepy after a few too many bottles, especially when the subject of his mother came up. But when it came to Satan, it was unlike his father to admit the possibility of defeat. And it was unlike him to speak of it in such an empty voice, with such despair in his hollow eyes.

He took the Preacher's arm. "Let's get you to sleep, Dad. And in the morning, maybe some fresh clothes, even a shower? That'd be something new and exciting, right?"

The Preacher gripped his shoulders. "You know I'd kill for you, right? I'd slay the devil himself before I'd let him touch you or your brother."

"No one's asking you to."

"Tell me you know," the Preacher insisted.

"I know, Dad. I know you would." Daniel slung his father's arms around his shoulders, tried not to inhale the sour whiskey breath, and got the Preacher to his room, heaving him onto the bed. He dropped to the mattress with a grunt, and as Daniel pulled off his shirt, he spotted a smear of dried blood and purpling bruises across his shoulder. "You're hurt."

The Preacher touched his shoulder, winced, shook his head. "Wrestling with the angels. It's not for the weak."

By now, Daniel knew better than to argue with crazy. Instead, he ducked into the hall bathroom and doused a hand towel with warm water.

"I'm glad you're not dead," Daniel said as he returned.

The Preacher was already snoring.

"Nice talking to you, too," Daniel muttered. "I do love these father-son chats." He brushed a hand across his father's sweaty forehead. It wasn't supposed to be like this, the son putting the father to bed. The son hating the father.

Trying so hard to hate the father.

He pressed the towel to his father's wound, dabbing at the

dried blood, gently exposing the scabbed skin. Hoping it didn't hurt.

It wasn't just the drinking, and it wasn't just the grief. People got sad all the time, and sad people got drunk, and none of them ended up marching around town singing about Judgment Day. Daniel's father had taught history, read Shakespeare, played gin, cooked stir-fry, laughed, hugged, *fathered* . . . and then his wife died, and something in him had broken. And Daniel had learned how easy it was to break. How breaking was in his blood. That was the last real lesson his father had ever taught him: how to look inside yourself and be afraid. Because maybe you couldn't know how much weight you could bear until you snapped beneath it.

The Preacher's eyes opened, and Daniel quickly drew his hand away.

"There's still time, Daniel." Had there always been such a void in his eyes?

"Time for what, Dad?"

"Time to repent. Before the day is upon us and we lead the Lord's army into the Promised Land."

"*You* think *I* need to repent?"

"That's my blood running through your veins," the Preacher said, in a cracked voice.

"That's what I'm afraid of."

"Righteous blood. You can still be righteous. Doesn't matter what you're doing with her. Doesn't matter what you've done, long as you get rid of her now, one way or another."

"Who?"

"That girl you're keeping in the shed."

## 7

## OF THEIR SHADOWS DEEP

Daniel recognized the legs first, poking out from beneath Milo's Batman sleeping bag.

It was the sleeping bag that made him suck in a sharp, noisy breath as he realized who must have given it to her, and clumsily pieced it together: the shed, the unscheduled escapes to the Ghent homestead, the death-defying visit to the Porters' abandoned home. Daniel would kill him for being so stupid.

Or she would do it first, he thought.

Cass Porter, the baby killer.

That was what he thought as he made the noise that woke her, but when her lids flew open and in one fluid move she leapt to a crouch in the back corner of the shed, her hair slashing through a city of spiderwebs, the sleeping bag held before her like a shield, he was still staring at her bare legs.

Cass Porter, in his shed.

"The kid told me I could stay here," she said.

Cass Porter, whose long, silky blond hair was now a matted dirty brown. The color it had been when they were kids, before she'd started wrangling sun-kissed locks from a bottle. Either way, she was beautiful.

*Baby killer*, he reminded himself.

"Milo," he said. "The kid's name is Milo." She'd stopped coming around before Milo was born. They all had. With his father gone off the deep end and his mother gone for good, who could blame them?

"I know."

"You can't be here," he said.

Despite the wet-blanket heat of the night, she was shivering.

"I know that, too." She was already gathering her belongings—or rather, he spotted quickly, Milo's belongings (and a few of Daniel's). An eclectic assortment of granola bars, bags of chips, comic books, a brush that he thought he'd lost, and a Spider-Man toothbrush was shoved clumsily into the sleeping bag. All she needed was a stick to tie it around and sling over her shoulder and she would make the perfect storybook tramp. Or orphan runaway. She'd always seemed taller to him, but now Daniel realized he had a couple of inches on her. She flinched when he approached.

"Where will you go?"

She shrugged.

"I'm sorry, you just . . . you can't stay here. I don't know what you told my brother, or what you—"

Her eyes flared. "I didn't touch him."

"I'm not saying that."

"You're thinking it." She let the bag drop and straightened to face him. He recognized the look on her face, though he hadn't seen it since they were children and he'd accused her of cheating at whatever board game she'd just won. For a moment, he forgot what she'd done and why she was here, forgot even the years he'd spent watching her from afar, waiting for her to remember he existed. He went back to the beginning. "Say it. Go ahead. You don't want me here because you're afraid I'll do it again."

"The cops are looking for you," he said. "It's probably illegal for us to even be having this conversation. That's the reason."

"And."

"And . . . I don't know what you did. That night. I don't know what happened. Maybe . . ." He didn't want to say what he'd been thinking all year, that maybe events had been misconstrued, maybe the endlessly replayed video had been tampered with, and there was some crucial explain-it-all-away fact no one else knew. That anything was possible, except that Cass Porter, of all people, had fallen apart.

"You think I'm innocent, Daniel?"

Anyone could break.

"I don't know what happened," he said. "I wasn't there."

"I was."

"Well, yeah. Obviously."

"I don't know what happened, either."

He didn't know how he was supposed to answer that. She saved him the trouble, adding, in the voice of this new Cassandra who was both harder and softer than the old one, "But I'm not innocent." She hefted the bag again, clumsily trying to keep its collection of junk from spilling out. "I'll get out of here. Just please don't tell anyone you saw me." She shook her head. Her hair, ratted and greasy as it now was, still splashed about her face in the same rippling waves he'd always admired. "Scratch that. You don't owe me anything. Tell anyone you want."

"I need to ask you something," Daniel said. "And you have to tell me the truth."

"I don't owe you anything, either."

"The truth," he said.

She nodded, leaving her head bowed, her hair curtaining her face.

"My brother."

"Milo."

"Would you ever hurt him?"

She didn't speak. There was silence between them, and somewhere beyond, the chirping of cicadas and the sizzle of kamikaze mosquitoes dive-bombing the bug zapper, the whistle of wind through the gaps in the shed's rotting boards.

"Look at me," he said.

She did.

"Would you hurt him?"

"I don't know what I would do," she said, and he finally understood that the terror pooling in her eyes had nothing to do with him. "But I don't want to. I don't. That's why I have to go."

He told himself it wasn't her bare, coltish legs that made him say it, or the glimpse of thigh where her shorts were riding up, or whatever dark intentions the Preacher had intuited. He didn't know why he said it.

"Stay."

She didn't ask Daniel to go back to her house and gather some of her belongings, but he heard the need in her voice. She hadn't said outright that it was killing her to imagine the Prevettes nesting in the house still filled with the gathered debris of her life, but she didn't have to. She hadn't said much at all, actually. Not at first. But as they talked into the night, her answers had gotten longer and her muscles less tensed for flight, until finally, just before the sun rose, she had told him what happened that killing night, at least what little she knew. She'd told him about the gap in her memory, and the part of the video they never showed on the news, the important part.

He told her about that day in the drugstore. He told her, as he hadn't told anyone, about his nightmares. She told him what it was to feel guilty every second, to wish for judgment even as you were desperate to escape it. He didn't know why it was so easy for him to understand how she felt. But when he closed his eyes that night and saw the drugstore bodies lying beside him, and smelled the blood, he felt it, too.

It felt strange to talk to her like he still knew her; she admitted it felt strange for her to talk to anyone at all.

She asked him for some of his father's whiskey, to make it all go away; she said they could share, and that way they could both forget. He said no, because he knew where that kind of forgetting led; she pretended not to be angry, then she pretended not to be crying. He pretended not to pity her, and cursed whatever law of the universe dictated that everything good turn to ruin.

When the sun rose, he sat with her and watched her tip her face to the dawn, and told her she could stay as long as she needed. Milo could obviously be trusted to keep his mouth shut, and the Preacher didn't talk to outsiders . . . or at least, when he did, they knew better than to listen. She'd be safe. Daniel promised her that, then gave Milo a stern lecture on the right way and wrong way to keep a secret, and dropped him off at day care. And then, without giving himself time to over-think it, he went to see the Prevettes. He rang the doorbell with no plan whatsoever for talking himself inside.

"You again," Jule said, opening the door. "Does everyone in your family have a death wish?"

"The drugstore's closed, and Milo's at day care, so I, uh, I didn't have anything to do. I thought maybe you'd want to hang out." He cursed himself for sounding so lame.

"What, you don't have any friends?" Despite the fact that it was even hotter inside than out, ten a.m. and already an egg fryer of a day, she wore baggy sweatpants and a sweatshirt three sizes too big. The pants were gray but the shirt was a pale blue. It was, as far as Daniel could remember, the first time he'd seen her in a color.

"I guess . . . not really?" He could feel his cheeks warming.

She swung the door wide and jerked her head in an awkward imitation of a welcome. "Lucky for you, neither do I."

He stepped over the threshold, trying not to make it obvious that he was eyes peeled for knife-wielding giants.

"They're in the basement," she said. "Don't ask why."

He hadn't planned on it.

Everything was as Cass had described, down to the photos climbing the staircase and the lace runners spanning every table. He assumed the dirty dishes, the half-empty pizza boxes, and the six-foot bong were more recent additions. Jule led him upstairs to her bedroom—Cass's bedroom.

"You can stop staring—none of it's mine," she said as he took in the wrought-iron bedposts, the Christmas lights artfully arranged into a peace sign, the photo-studded vanity mirror, and, feeling like a sleaze, the black bras draped over the desk chair. "Well, those are," she added, stuffing the bras into a black duffel. "Perv."

He forced a laugh.

"I hope you know I didn't bring you up here to screw you."

This time the laugh came unprompted. "Excuse me?"

She pointed at the bed. "You. Me. There. Not happening. Got it?"

"Got it." Then, aware it might be pushing his luck, he cocked his head at the bathroom. "So does that mean shower sex is still on the table?"

Instead of a kick in the ass on his way out the door, this earned him a curious smile. She pointed to the floor. "Sit."

It was awkward at first. They were not friends, and their potential areas of common ground—teachers in classes that Jule never attended, students at a school where neither of them spoke—amounted to little more than a trickle of small talk. Fortunately, there was a more obvious topic of conversation at hand.

"Scott thinks it's some kind of conspiracy," Jule said. "Of course, Scott thinks everything's a conspiracy. He's convinced everyone's out to get him."

"Aren't they?"

"Fair point."

"What does he think it's a conspiracy to *do*?" Daniel asked.

"Take over." She curled finger quotes around the words, then laughed. "Destroy the common man, steal all his money, ruin his life. You know, the usual." She wadded up a pamphlet and tossed it at his head. "Some literature on the subject, in case you'd like further enlightenment. Scott's got the rest of them convinced this is just the first step—that all that junk in the air is some kind of chemical warfare. I think he's raising an army, just in case."

Daniel snorted. "I guess all the cool kids are doing it."

"What?"

"Nothing. Inside joke with myself."

"Shocking that you have no friends," she said.

"Whereas all the girls at school must be begging you to let them come over and hang out with the meth militia."

Her expression never flickered, but something about her went taut, and he realized he'd gone too far.

"Sorry," he said.

"Trust me, it's not the family I would have picked, but . . ." But who got to pick? "Yeah."

They watched each other in not-quite-comfortable silence. "So do you believe him?" Daniel said, trying to steer the conversation onto a safer track. "You think there's a conspiracy?"

"I think anyone who thinks keeping us trapped in this town is 'for our own good' has never actually been here."

"You seem to be doing all right," Daniel said, and they both knew he was talking about this room, which couldn't be more mismatched to the girl currently living in it.

"You think this was *my* idea?"

"Is it that bad?"

"It's . . ."

He waited.

"I've never had my own bedroom before," she said. "I've never had a door."

It was a plain-enough admission, but he could tell there was too much behind it that he wasn't supposed to know about, and she was wondering why she'd said it and what she'd do if he was stupid enough to follow up.

"Why are you here, Daniel?"

For a moment, he was tempted to admit it: one half confession for another. But before he could decide to trust her based on nothing but guilt, the door eased open. Daniel had never been this close to Scott Prevette. Even if he were a normal-sized man, his aura of pure menace would have been more than enough to strike fear in the hearts of scrawny teenage boys everywhere. And Scott Prevette was basically a giant. Each of his fists looked powerful enough to crush Daniel's head like a tomato. It was the aura that suggested he'd have a good time doing it.

Scott jerked his head. "You. Outside. Now."

For a heart-stopping moment, Daniel thought the order was meant for him, and quickly debated the merits of defenestration. Then Jule rose and left the room with her uncle, and Daniel could breathe again. Of course, the reprieve wouldn't last long if Scott caught Daniel going through his niece's underwear drawer. So he would hurry. As a bonus: the faster he plowed through her drawers, the less time he'd have to spend feeling like a pervert.

Scott wanted to know what she was doing with a boy in her room. Biting back all the more tempting responses—these days Scott was even less a person to mess with than usual—she muttered an insistent "Just a friend." He looked so pleasantly surprised she wasn't sure whether to be touched or offended.

"I do have friends," Jule said.

He was kind enough not to argue, and then the dark shadows returned to his face. "You want to keep him, you keep him away from the basement."

"He's not some lost puppy off his leash."

Scott grunted, and that was to be the end of it.

She couldn't blame Daniel for looking nervous when she came back into the room. Scott tended to have that effect. But she'd figured that Daniel, of all people, would be willing to cut her a break on the demented home-life front—instead of jumping to his feet, avoiding her eyes, and muttering something awkward and unconvincing about having other places to be. If one not-so-harsh look from Scott Prevette was enough to scare him off, then she shouldn't be so disappointed to see him go. Let him.

But the words were out of her mouth before he could. "Have you been down to Route 8 yet?"

"The main checkpoint?" he said, sounding surprised. "No. I heard it's pointless. You?"

There were protesters crowded at each of the government checkpoints surrounding the town, but word had it the biggest group was massed on Route 8, where high schoolers, hippies, housewives, and hunters had set aside their differences for a 24/7 vigil protesting the government quarantine. Howard Schwarz, who'd appointed himself and his press mouthpiece for the Free Oleander! movement, made periodic rounds to rally the troops.

"I don't think it's the way to get out." Jule didn't have any more faith than Scott did in frontal assaults, especially the kind made with placards and protest chants. There had been rumors of people making it across the border via bribes, nepotism, sexual favors . . . but nothing that could be verified. "But I've been wrong before."

Daniel mimed his shock and awe.

"Okay, rarely," she allowed. "Still. It's been five days, and *nothing*. Aren't you going crazy here? Figured I'd at least check it out. You . . . you want to come with?"

She was sure he'd say yes, sure she'd marked him accurately as someone who wanted to get out as desperately as she did, so sure he'd give in to the temptation painted across his face that it took her a moment to process his actual answer.

"I'm sorry," he said, sounding it. "I can't. I've got to—Yeah. I have to go. Now. So, anyway."

He wasn't the smoothest of operators. He wasn't much of anything, really, except awkward and decent and, for whatever reason, under her skin.

"See you around?" he said, edging for the door, probably sorry he'd thought to come in the first place.

"Better hurry," she said. "I don't plan to be here for long."

There were two kinds of people in Oleander these days: the kind content to stay put and rebuild their lives, and the kind desperate to leave. The former rallied behind Mayor Mouse and Deacon Barnes, busying themselves with carpentry or Christ, kneeling at the dual altars of Uncle Sam and Ellie King. The latter had better things to do. An intrepid handful—determined or drunk—set out to test the government quarantine on their own, picking through the woods that bordered Route 8, driving pickups into the prairie grass, even tackling the lake with dinghies or inner tubes, propelling themselves with paddles, oars, and in one (very drunk) case, a shovel and a broom. They were all turned back: by floodlights and tanks, by barbed wire and electrified fences, by men in uniforms and their very large guns.

Five days since the storm; five days trapped in Oleander. Five days plus the previous seventeen years of Jule's life, but it was those final five days that had pushed her over the edge. She'd always dismissed Scott's paranoid ramblings about government conspiracies—mostly under the theory that no one in the government seemed quite sharp enough to pull one off—but there were armed soldiers circling the most boring town in the Midwest. Distrusting their motives wasn't exactly the same as lying to a census taker or refusing a flu shot.

Not that Jule cared about their motives for keeping her in. She only cared about getting out.

Like her uncles—though not with them, never *with* them—she spent her days prowling the borders and exploring her options, which were narrowing down to none. She was tired of sneaking around and tired of failing and, after Daniel's hasty departure, unexpectedly tired of being on her own. So on this day, the fifth day, she took a vacation from lonely and fruitless prowling and joined the masses gathered at the Route 8 checkpoint. It wouldn't be a way out. But she was in the mood to shout at something, and it seemed as good a place as any to do it.

The protest had begun with just a handful of discontents. They tried to beg and plead and bribe their way across the border, and when that didn't work, they threw produce and cow shit at the soldiers and made timid charges across the line, turned back by volleys of gunfire into the sky. A fist-shaking

Howard Schwarz distributed hastily made flyers about abuse of power, and there were murmurings of the Second Amendment and local militias, though no one had yet been dumb enough to flash a gun. By the time Jule arrived, the scattering of people had swelled to a crowd, and the atmosphere had turned carnival-like. The prospect of escape ruled out, the protest was the thing, and the remaining true believers—some furious, some hyperventilating, some weeping—were subsumed by a mass of people who, despite their handmade signs and piss-filled water balloons, seemed almost to have forgotten why they were there. There were couples making out, children running wild, anarchists ranting; there were town gossips who poked their noses in for an hour and then slipped away again; there were spies for Mayor Mouse; there were tents inhabited by people who by the smell of things hadn't showered in days. There were the occasional unified chants—*Let us out! Let us out! Let us out!*—and at least two drum circles. There was an impassive line of soldiers, weapons at the ready, who refused to speak or flinch or allow anyone to approach within a ten-yard radius. There was, at the center of things, Howard Schwarz, standing atop a milk crate and shouting about how the mayor's craven obeisance to his government puppet masters would be the end of them all. There was a *lot* of beer. Given the sermonizing and the drinking, it felt like a cross between a church picnic and the world's most pointless tailgate, and Jule regretted coming anywhere near it. Especially when she spotted Baz Demming and a couple of his idiot friends lounging in the back of a pickup, drowning themselves in beer. Even more when he saw her.

"Tampon girl!" he shouted across the crowd, waving

wildly. "Yo, tampon girl!" His buddies took up the cry. Every-one was staring.

She thought: At least, Daniel's not here to see this happen again.

She thought: If Daniel had come along, she wouldn't have to deal with this crap alone.

She thought: Why the hell was she thinking about Daniel?

She yelled: "Yo yourself, brain-dead! How's your syphilis?"

Baz was laughing. Baz was climbing off the pickup truck and coming toward her.

Jule was not running away, would not run away.

"Clearing right up," he said as he approached. "So if you're asking because you want to take me out on a test-drive . . ."

"I would rather screw Howard Schwarz," she said, grop-ing for a suitably disgusting alternative to hammer the point home. "I would rather have one of those soldiers shove his gun up my—"

"Got it," Baz said. "Thanks for the visual."

"I aim to please."

Now he was close enough to touch her. "You know, you could be kind of hot if you weren't such a bitch."

"I'll take that under advisement."

"Though the bitch thing can be hot sometimes."

"Great."

"But not in your case."

"Bummer."

"Just trying to help."

"What are you even doing here?" Jule said. "Does the mayor know his little lackey's sniffing around the dark side?"

"Just keeping an eye on things. Helps to know who's loyal and who's not, if you know what I mean."

"J. Edgar Hoover would be so proud."

He flashed a smile. "I'll pretend I never saw you, though. Special favor. For a special friend, right?"

"I'm out of here," Jule said.

"You're wasting your time," Baz said. "There's no way out."

She forced her voice not to betray her. "What makes you think I'm looking for a way out?"

"Keeping an eye on things, remember? Things like hot little girls who think they're smarter than everyone else. Smart enough to find a way out."

Screw him and his smug face; screw the soldiers; screw the town. "So maybe I am," she said.

Baz laughed. There was something in the sound of it, something so unnerving that Jule backed away and, without another word, got the hell out of there.

"Never gonna happen!" he shouted after her. "No one's getting out."

The Preacher was drunk. But not so drunk that he couldn't recognize a demon when he saw one. She wore a different face than the others, but her clothes were the same, and bore the sign of the devil. She was of *them*, the plague that had beset his town.

The Lord had taken after her, that was clear. The demon's face was scarred and scratched and smeared with blood. The demon limped and hugged her arm to her chest and leaned against the trees as if God's green world would give succor to the likes of her.

And so the Preacher rose before her, rose from the dirt and the bushes, rose in her path like an avenging angel, like an emissary of the Lord, like a large, drunk man waving a loaded gun, and commanded her to leave.

"These are my woods," he intoned. "Begone, creature of the dark."

The demon stumbled backward and issued a pitiful, almost human cry, and asked for help.

"I know what you and yours have done," the Preacher said. "I know what you raised from the pit. Begone!"

She went.

He liked the woods, his woods. He liked the smell of wet bark and the taste of whiskey and dirt. Beyond these trees, the army of the apocalypse had mustered, awaiting the dark times. But in the canopy of green, all was peaceful. All was quiet. The Preacher liked the quiet now. It helped dampen the noise in his head.

No more noise. No more people. No more warnings issued to strangers who laughed and hurried their way to hell. So much time wasted, prying open their eyes.

That time was over now. The demon's trespass had proved it.

The new era was dawning. The time to reclaim that which belonged to him. To save that which could be saved, and leave the rest to burn.

By the time Cass heard the footsteps pounding toward her and recognized the voices they belonged to, it was too late to flee. She considered her dubious options: The shed was filled with crap, none of it large enough to disguise a full-sized human.

Milo's sleeping bag was made for a child. It would cover her feet or her face, but not both, not unless she curled herself into a ball with her cheek pressed to the gritty, mildewed floor, hugged her ankles, and tried not to breathe. So that was what she did.

They were just outside the door. She recognized Baz's voice. Daniel had warned her about the Watchdogs. It had been no surprise to hear that Baz had appointed himself their leader. It hadn't occurred to her that West would have gotten himself involved with them. Or that he would be taking orders from a thug like Baz. But there was no mistaking his voice, either.

"We got a tip she was in this area," Baz said.

"And how is that your problem?" Daniel's voice.

"You don't think it's everyone's problem?" Baz said. "A killer on the loose? Don't let the hot thing fool you. She's dangerous."

Cass wasn't sure which was stranger: to hear Baz describe her as dangerous, or as hot. The last time she'd seen him, a year before on a strained triple date to the movies, he'd barely spoken to her. But she'd overheard him needling West in the parking lot, assuring him that he could do better.

It hadn't been easy, this past year, to shut the door on her old life. But she'd somehow managed it, accepting that her parents were gone, her future was gone, the Cass Porter she'd seen in the mirror for seventeen years was, effectively, gone. It hadn't *seemed* easy, at least, but now she realized how much harder it could have been. It was one thing to accept the end of her old life while she was locked in a cell at a remote facility, everything familiar an impossible distance away. It was different back in Oleander, so close to home. It was one thing to hear a nameless doctor or guard or judge call her a murderer. It was different hearing it from the senior quarterback, the guy who'd asked her to dance at their eighth-grade formal, tried to cheat off her tests all through pre-calc, and once pantsed her at a kindergarten picnic.

It was one thing to imagine the people you'd grown up with calling you a monster. It was different to actually hear them.

"She's not here," Daniel said. "But my father is, and I've got to warn you, he doesn't like strangers snooping around the house."

"That guy spooks me," whined someone she didn't recognize. "Maybe we should skip . . ."

"I'm shaking." Baz raised his voice to a high, flighty register. "Oh, please, bad preacher man, don't thump me with your Bible. I'll be a good boy, I promise." He snorted. "Come on, let's go."

"You take the house, I'll take the grounds and the shed," West said.

She was suddenly certain: he knew. Maybe from Daniel's bluster or from whatever expression was perched on his transparent face, maybe because the "tip" had been more specific than Baz let on and they were just playing with her. Somehow, he knew.

"Whatever." The footsteps departed, Baz's light and sure, a rhythmic goose step thumping after him.

She curled tighter beneath the sleeping bag and squeezed her eyes shut.

"I'm telling you, I haven't seen her in a year," Daniel said.

The door creaked open.

Footsteps.

*Please,* she thought, though maybe she was praying for the wrong thing. Maybe it would be good for them to find her and drag her away, to jail or to a lynch mob or, if her suspicions about Baz were right, simply off to some secluded cornfield where she would scream in the moonlight, be used and then discarded, and lie in the corn and cover herself and cry. She couldn't stay here forever, waiting for Daniel to realize his mistake, waiting to be discovered, waiting for life to magically right itself.

Still: *Please.*

The sleeping bag shifted, slightly, as someone pulled it away from her face. She felt the night breeze on her skin, and opened her eyes. West looked back, his face impassive. Was he thinking about their nights together on her parents' couch, avoiding all discussion of why they were the only couple home alone that Saturday night actually *watching* the movie? About the sophomore formal, back when she'd thought that his asking her actually meant something, and she'd spent all her money on that shimmery silver dress and wasted an hour puzzling out her mother's makeup and another gathering her newly blond hair into some kind of upsweep she'd found step-by-step instructions for online? They'd danced cheek to cheek with his palm warm on her exposed back, and he'd kissed her on her front step, just like in the movies, her first real kiss, not with tongue, but with mingled breath and starry eyes and hands cupping her cheeks, and for a few feverish weeks she'd decided she was in love. But he probably didn't want to remember that—who she'd been, who they'd been.

She'd been sort of prettyish, once. Not beautiful, not ugly, but officially "not bad." Passable enough to score a fake boyfriend and a free pass to the extreme outer fringe of the popular crowd. That was then. Now, after a year of no mirrors, after a week of no showers and a literal bed of filth, she suspected even the sort-of-pretty was gone.

That wasn't why she couldn't stand for West to look at her.

The sleeping bag dropped back over her face. Maybe he couldn't stand it, either.

"Guess she's not here after all," West said. "I'll get the rest of them out of here."

"Uh . . . yeah." Daniel sounded uncertain. "Do that."

Cass didn't understand.

"She was a good friend," West said.

Daniel made a noncommittal noise.

"She was. A good person. I don't know what she did, but . . . she was always good. To me, at least." He cleared his throat. "You don't have to worry. We won't be back."

West didn't trust them with Cass. Not after that night at the ice cream parlor, and the look in Baz's eyes as he'd slammed Jason's head into the ground. Worse, the look in his eyes as he'd watched his putative best friend die. It was the *non*look that bothered West, the emptiness. Anything was permissible, that look said. Anything that Baz deemed fun. And so when it came to Cass, West watched the Watchdogs. He would protect Cass, because she'd protected him. But beyond that, he was out. No more nightly patrols, no more looter hunts. So after the Ghent house, West ignored Baz's entreaties and insults. He went home.

Broken dishes littered the front entryway and kitchen. He found his mother on her knees, sweeping the porcelain shards into a dustpan. Maddie Thomas lounged on the living-room couch, a bag of frozen ravioli lying across a swollen face.

"What happened? Where's Dad?"

"Nothing happened," his mother said, in a curiously flat voice. "Mrs. Thomas and I just had a small disagreement over sugar proportions, didn't we?"

"Just a small one," Maddie said wearily.

"Then what's with all the broken dishes? And with Mrs. Thomas . . ." He lowered his voice. "Mom, did you . . . did you *punch* her?"

"And your father, since you asked, went out hunting."

"At night? What the hell is going on?"

"You won't use that language in this house," she said.

"Oh, right. Because we have certain standards of behavior to maintain."

"Nor will you use that sarcastic tone with me."

"Mom." He took her shoulders and raised her to her feet. Amanda West was stout but small, and normally nothing roused her from a bad mood like her oversized son manhandling her into a waltz around the kitchen. But this was more than a bad mood. He looked down at her, thinking how strange it was to have a foot of height on his mother, to look down on the person to whom he was most supposed to look up. "What is it? What's wrong?"

"I told you, dear," she said, still in that same frostily polite tone. "Nothing's wrong." She shot a sharp look at Maddie Thomas. "Not now."

"Nothing's wrong. You're punching out the neighbors.

Dad's hunting. In the dark. Where's Mr. Thomas? Chained up in the basement?"

"Your father took him along."

"Mr. Thomas doesn't believe in hunting."

"Then why ever would he have gone?"

It was an excellent question, one West suddenly didn't want the answer to.

"Enough, dear. It's late and I'm tired."

"But . . ."

She pressed a finger to his lips. "You don't see me prying into your dirty little secrets, do you?"

When Johnson West told the story of how he'd courted and won his wife, it always began with the tale of how he'd asked her to the prom. Appalled by the thought of attending the dance on the arm of (in Amanda's words) "a cross-eyed farm boy," she'd laughed in his face. Amanda always denied it, and West, unable to imagine his stout, ruddy-cheeked mother as a svelte mean girl, believed her. But there was a nasty note in her laughter now that made him reconsider.

She was his mother, only and always the person who loved him best.

But he was afraid.

"Don't ask, don't tell, dear," she said, and he stopped breathing. "Speaking of which, you have a visitor waiting for you in the den."

She left him alone. It was surreal; it was crazy; it was, just maybe, the end of the world.

And in the den, it was Jason, the kid from the ice cream store. Jason, who called him Jeremiah, though they'd never even met.

"What did you say to my parents?" The rising tide of panic had to be suppressed, could not reveal itself to any stranger, much less this one.

"Pretty much 'Hello, is Jeremiah here?'"

"That's it?"

"Other than the part where I told them I was a serial killer waiting here to set you on fire? Pretty much. Then your mom beat that other lady up. And gave me some cookies."

"You didn't say anything else?" Everything was jumbled in his head. He couldn't worry about Jason now, not when his mother might have punched out the neighbor. But on the other hand, how could he worry about recipe tiffs when Jason was here running his mouth off to anyone who would listen? He had to get this guy out of the house.

"I said thank you for the cookies. Though between you and me, they were kind of stale."

West assured himself that his parents couldn't know. They believed that the episode from his youth—that's how they'd referred to it, before they erased it from their communal memory—was behind them. He was already on his second chance. They'd been clear: he wouldn't get a third.

The whole night was just a misunderstanding, he told himself. His mother did not give people black eyes. His father did not drag people into the woods at midnight, with a gun. "What are you doing here?" he said.

"Where were you all night?" Jason countered. "Out with your lovely friends?"

He was too tired for this. He wanted to climb into bed and wake up six months from now or, better, six years from now. Sleep through the hard part. Why not? Right now he felt like he could sleep through the rest of his life. "What do you want from me?"

"What are you doing with them, Jeremiah?"

The bent wire of tension snapped. "Why do you *keep calling me that*?"

"Why does it bother you?" Jason smirked. "You don't want to play the question game with me. I can keep it up all night. Ask my older brother."

"That's it." West took a step toward him.

"Big, tough football player's going to toss me out?" Jason waved his arms in mock terror. "Oh, no, please. Don't."

"Get out of my house. *Now.*"

Jason rose to his feet. "Look, I'm sorry. I'll stop. You've got to understand, I've been playing this conversation in my head for so long, I've been so freaking curious about you, and now here you are, in the big slab of flesh, and you're just . . ." He shook his head. "From everything he said, I was picturing Superman. But you're . . . a little disappointing."

"Everything who said?" He was afraid he knew.

"Not physically, of course. I see where he was coming from on that. I always have. But everything else? The whole package? You know what they say, lust is blind."

The door was shut; the den was soundproof. Could his mother hear anyway? Did she need to?

"Shut up and get out," West said.

"You really don't know who I am?"

"Jason, whose father owns the ice cream store. And who apparently doesn't hear very well. I asked you to leave."

"Jason, Nick Shay's best friend. Or former best friend. Ex–best friend? I don't know the official term for it."

"Nick Shay." West hoped he looked sufficiently incurious. "The dead kid."

"Really? 'The dead kid'? Nice."

"Look, I'm sorry that your friend died—"

"Ex-friend."

"Right, I'm sorry—"

"See, we were best friends for years, did everything together. I even watched these stupid sci-fi movies as a favor to him—he was into that kind of stuff, did you know that?"

West shook his head. His mouth was dry. "Why would I know that?"

"Best friends, and then we got in a fight. Seems like a stupid fight now—well, especially *now*. See, he started dating someone that, okay, I didn't particularly like the sound of, but I'd like to think I can rise above my own preconceptions for the happiness of my friends. This guy, though? This guy was obviously a nightmare, closet case, head case, and Nick wasn't happy, not really. Any idiot could see that. Well . . ." Again, that nasty smirk. "Maybe not *any* idiot. So I told him what I thought, and he told me what he thought, and that was the end of it. I take it this story doesn't seem familiar to you?"

"Should it?" Of course, it made sense that the two of them had been friends. It even made sense that West hadn't noticed, because he'd turned not noticing what people like Jason and Nick did into an art form. But that was before he and Nick were together. After, he was supposed to know things. Nick was supposed to tell him.

"I thought he'd come crawling back in tears," Jason said. "I mean, it's not that I was hoping for it. . . . Well, maybe I was, sort of. I like being right. I thought he'd end up miserable. Not dead."

"That was an accident," West snapped. "I mean, I heard."

"Who said it wasn't? But you know how it is: Unfinished business. Regrets. Things you wish you could have said. Like maybe I should have been easier on him and on this guy of his."

"Sounds like it."

"That's what I thought, until I figured out that you had no idea who I was."

"Look, I'm telling you, I barely knew Nick—" It was supposed to be a lie.

"That he never talked about me at all. Never . . ." Jason gnawed at the edge of his thumbnail. "So either he didn't care enough about this guy to tell him what was really going on, or . . . Well, the alternative is obvious, right? Even to an idiot."

It wasn't just Jason he'd never said anything about. It was his parents, it was his limp, it was his entire life. West had never questioned it, because it hadn't seemed important, not as important as the two of them in their secret world, together.

"I don't know what you want from me," West said.

"Before, I wanted to see you. Meet you. See what the big deal was. But it didn't seem like a good idea."

"And yet here you are."

"The other night, with your buddies—"

"They're not my buddies and they're not going to bother you again."

"Actually, I think they will, and I'm done asking you to stop them, because you obviously don't have that in you."

"Don't pretend to know anything about me."

"Yeah, yeah, and don't tell anyone what I totally don't know, and don't say anything to your parents, et cetera. I had all year, Jeremiah. I had more than that. You think if I wanted to ruin your life, I wouldn't have done it already?"

"Then why are you here?" West asked, suppressing an insane impulse to drop the act and just cop to the truth. Jason already knew the whole story, probably all the dirty details Nick had passed along before the two of them had split; probably they'd sat together watching bad movies on Nick's ratty couch, talking about West or, worse, not talking about him, talking about whatever esoterica lay between them. Maybe they'd done more than talk. West knew he hadn't been the first, but he'd never let himself think about the others, about someone else's hands finding their way to places soft and secret, about Nick pressing his lips to someone else's skin, fixing them with his goofy, besotted gaze.

What would happen if he asked the question? Just said it: *I loved him. Did you?*

Wasn't it worth the risk, if it meant he could set down what he was carrying, if only for the duration of the conversation? Maybe, that night, he would sleep.

"I want to get out of here, do you understand that?" Jason said. "I need to get *out* of this town."

"Well, yeah, we all do. But I'm sure it'll only be a couple more days, and then—"

"No, not in a couple of days—*now.*" There was a wild edge to his voice. "But I can't get out, can I? I'm trapped here. We're all trapped. We're all going freaking nuts. So why shouldn't I? Why should I bother to stay away from you, if I don't want to?

Why shouldn't I just do whatever the hell I want? Like your buddy Baz. Maybe he's got the right idea."

"Last night . . . I wouldn't have let anything happen. You know that, right?"

Jason laughed harshly. "You let *everything* happen."

"I would have stopped it."

He waved away the excuse. "Doesn't matter. He's going to do what he wants. And you know what he wants? He wants me hurt. Bad."

So Jason didn't know everything after all. Baz, West was pretty sure, wanted him dead.

"And you know what I want?" Jason said.

"I told you, I'm not going to let him—"

"I don't want to hurt him. That's not good enough. What I want? Is to *stop* him. For good. Maybe that's why I came here, Jeremiah." His fierce expression mirrored the one he'd worn on the ground, pinned by Baz's boot, the not-so-helpless prey daring the predator to go further, to cross the line, to give him an excuse. "For Nick's sake—to warn you. Stay out of my way."

That night, trying to fall asleep, he listened for Nick's voice in the wind. It wasn't there. But something was.

Not a voice.

A touch.

The weight of a hand on his chest.

The brush of lips against his neck.

A mist of breath warming his cheek.

It was like an echo.

Or a reward.

* * *

Jule dreamed of the knife.

These days, Jule always dreamed of the knife.

In the dream, it still wore James's blood. And she knew, with irrefutable dream logic, that it had gotten a taste, and that had awakened its hunger. It wanted more.

In the dream, she knew it wanted her.

It hunted her.

In the dream, Uncle Scott held the knife, caressed the blade against his meaty palm, drew it, in the way of a starving man delaying gratification, against his lips. It was Uncle Scott who prowled the halls, feet shuffling along unfamiliar floorboards, shadow advancing along fading walls, creeping down a long corridor that wasn't long enough, because at the end lay her bedroom door. Behind it, lying in bed but not asleep, she waited for him, listening for his steps, waiting for his hand on the knob, knowing, in the dream, that it was not him who wanted her. It was the knife. She could hear it, keening its hunger, whispering her name.

In the dream, when she cried out, there was only a silent scream.

Sometimes she bolted awake as the door opened, the echo of the knife fading from her ears as she blinked in the dark. But sometimes, as it did that night, the dream pressed on, and Scott, with madness in his eyes and the knife in his hand, slipped across the threshold, and the knife found its home in her chest, and sliced through flesh and vein, and fed.

When she woke up, gasping and feeling for a wound that wasn't there, it wasn't Scott in her doorway, but the parasite. He lounged against the frame, ankles crossed, hands in his pockets, lizard eyes on her. She was certain she'd locked the door.

"Have a nightmare?" He gave no indication of moving now that he'd been caught. It was unlike him. He was usually more subtle, or at least more abashed.

"Still am," she said. He looked to be considering it, the possibility that this was her dream, that he was her monster. While he weighed the possibilities, she scrambled out of bed and closed the door in his face.

The bedroom window opened onto a narrow ledge. It formed the top of latticework that climbed down the side of the house. Jule exchanged her sweatpants for jeans, and in a few moments, she was out and down and free.

She couldn't walk all night. Jule circled the town twice, but when she came upon the darkened church, and spotted the slender girl stooped on its front steps, she was just tired enough to drop down beside her.

"God's got long hours," Jule said. "Hope you're getting overtime."

Ellie turned to face her but, miraculously, didn't light up and start outlining the ways in which Jule, if she would only make the effort, could save her soul. Jule found herself strangely disappointed. Maybe she wasn't just tired. Maybe she wanted someone to talk at her. Or just wanted someone.

Hell, maybe she wanted to save her soul. But business hours were evidently done for the day.

Ellie's eyes were red.

"You okay?" Jule asked.

Ellie nodded. "You?"

"No worse than usual."

Ellie didn't ask what she was doing there, so Jule repaid the favor.

"So okay, since it's just us—you don't really talk to God, right? Or, I mean, you don't hear him *talking back.*"

"Yes, I do."

"Right, sure, I know that's what the deacon's telling people, and they're stupid enough to believe that because you went out in the middle of a tornado, *on purpose,* and didn't get blown away, that means you've got a halo, but you can tell me the truth. Who am I going to tell? It's a scam, right? Look godly, get some donations for the church or an award from the pope or whatever?"

"I don't have a halo," Ellie said. "And if people knew . . ."

"What?"

"It doesn't matter. But I do. Hear it."

*Don't laugh,* Jule reminded herself. "The voice of God."

She hesitated. "Sometimes."

It was too late at night for niceties, and that had never exactly been a hallmark of their relationship. "You do know how that sounds, right?"

"Crazy. I know."

"So how can you be sure it's God and not . . ."

"Schizophrenia?" Ellie straightened up a little. "You know, a lot of the great mystics and saints of the past would have been diagnosed as mentally ill today. Saint Teresa. Saint Bernadette. Margery Kemp. Joan of Arc. They'd all be doped up. Probably locked up. People are always asking why God doesn't talk directly to us anymore, the way He does in the Bible. Maybe they should ask why we stopped listening."

"But some people *are* just crazy. You can't be saying that everyone who thinks God talks to them is right."

"God talks to all of us," Ellie said. "In our own way. And His."

"Okay . . . but some guy who thinks God told him to murder his neighbor and bury him in the backyard? You're saying we don't lock that guy up, we elect him to sainthood?"

"I think most of the time, voices in your head are just voices in your head," Ellie admitted. "But there's a difference. True faith reveals it."

"And yours reveals to you that you're not crazy."

She didn't answer.

Instead, her gaze snagging on something over Jule's shoulder, she went rigid, her fingers knotting together so tightly that all blood leached out of them.

"Ladies," Baz said, giving Jule a jaunty salute as she turned to face him. "What a happy surprise."

Not again.

Ellie was shivering.

Jule put a hand on the girl's shoulder. "Not tonight," she told Baz. "In fact, how about not ever."

"But it's been such a *good* night," he whined, approaching the steps. Ellie jumped to her feet. Jule joined her. "And I've been a pretty damn good boy. Surely I deserve my godly reward."

"Stand with the Lord or stand with the sinners," Ellie murmured. "That's the choice. That's the only choice. The Lord or the sin. The sin or the Lord."

"You got it, Mother Teresa," Baz said. "And we all know which side you're on. At least, I do."

Ellie shook her head. "I reject the sin," she said, this time loud and clear. "I reject the sinners."

"Uh-huh." He turned to Jule. "And how about you? You've always got something to say."

"Don't talk to me," Jule said. "And don't even look at her."

He smiled, and it was the same forty-watt grin that had charmed more than one cheerleader into his bed, the mouthful of white brights and the crinkle of skin around the edges that said *This is all for you, not just the face and the muscles, but the* real *Baz, the guy who's better than his reputation, the guy who will buy you flowers and compliment your hair and worship at your pedestal and prove to you he's worth the trouble.* Jule was unimpressed.

"You can't still be mad about the tampon-girl thing," he said. "We were just having some fun."

"Oh, were we? I hadn't noticed."

"Please stop," Ellie whispered. "Go away. Go away."

"You don't strike me as the Team God type."

"And yet you know nothing about me," Jule said.

"I know you'd have more fun with Team Sinner. We win all the championships."

Ellie was losing it. Jule could spot the tears pooling at the corners of her eyes. Baz didn't deserve to see that.

"You're not scoring tonight," she said. "Not here, at least. Trust me."

He shrugged. "Your loss."

"Hopefully, someday I'll be able to forgive myself."

"I really was just kidding around before," he said, as his parting shot. "Sorry if I went too far. It won't happen again."

It seemed so out of character she thought she must have misheard.

"Some stains never wash out," Ellie said, watching him fade into the shadows.

"It's okay, he's gone. Are *you* okay?"

"You can't wash off a filthy soul," she said.

"Excuse me?"

"I know what he wants."

"Well, he made it pretty clear."

"Only a whore would let him look like that. Knowing what he wants. Knowing that he's always watching. Asking for it."

"Did you just call me a whore?" Somehow, Jule didn't think they were talking about Baz anymore.

"The sinner senses sin. He smells it. He's drawn to it. The taint. The filth. You can't wash it off."

Jule wanted to kick herself—or Ellie—for stupidly thinking it would be possible to shelve the God stuff for a night and talk like normal people. Ellie obviously had problems of her own, but that didn't mean she got to call Jule a filthy whore. Or suggest that Jule liked it. When he looked. She knew what most people in town thought about the Prevettes, and the parasite, and her.

Animals slept in their own filth; animals couldn't be expected to control their urges.

"If this means you're done trying to recruit me for Team God, don't expect me to get all broken up about it," she said. "I hear Team Sinner has an opening."

She was still tired—too tired to stop herself from leaving Ellie alone on the steps.

And running after Baz.

Ellie, who had long ago forgotten her presence, didn't notice she was gone.

* * *

"So, you wanna have some fun?" Baz asked her, flashing a startlingly genuine, or at least genuine-seeming, grin when she caught up with him. There was no leer, no insinuation, no roaming hands, nothing but open surprise. Running on the fumes of Ellie's insults, Jule told him that she'd changed her mind, that she was in the mood for trouble, that he was the closest with a ready supply. "Good enough," he said. "Trouble it is."

It was a mistake, she knew that.

But the other thing, the shameful thing: it was fun.

Jule, her mind ever on the prize, suggested they try sneaking across the border. But in the end, Baz had a better idea. No one would catch them, he assured her. No one would dare. This was a special mission from the mayor himself. This was righteous. Even at two a.m., even in the shadows, this was allowed.

She didn't care.

She simply liked it, the splash of gasoline against the cheap aluminum siding, the sick-sweet smell that pressed down on them, driving away that other smell, of storm and poison and death. She liked dancing in the darkness. Carving up the night with ribbons of fuel, coating first the outer walls of the building and then, after a satisfying shower of broken glass, the space within. She didn't let herself think about how her uncles would approve. She did, as Baz let her paint the trail of gasoline away from the newspaper office, think about the words the *Post* used to describe her family: *Animals. Beasts. Menaces. Parasites.* Maybe this was justice rightfully distributed; maybe it was, as Baz said, a service to the town. Neither seemed important. What mattered was that it was *bad*.

It was destruction, pure and simple. The sound of a lighter sparking; the whoosh as her trail of gasoline burst into light.

*A menace*, Jule thought, and it felt good, for a night, to be exactly the girl everyone believed her to be.

It wasn't like the movies. There was no explosion. Just a slow, steady build, hungry fire licking the walls and slithering under the doors, smoke chugging from the windows and collapsing the roof. It was mesmerizing. Baz stood behind her, his hands around her waist, and that felt right, too. His hands, large and sure, wrapping her up. His heart thumping in her ear and, when she twisted back to look at him, a little-boy grin on his face. He could have kissed her then, and maybe she would have let him. But he was fixed on the flames. "Team Sinner," he whispered.

You can't fight Mother Nature, Scott liked to tell her.

It was easier, sometimes, not to fight.

The street was deserted; no fire engines appeared. The fire burned on. They watched, proud as parents gazing on the child they had made.

And then a figure stumbled out of the flames, hunched over and shuddering with coughs, and all the euphoria drained away.

"You said there'd be no one in there!"

"Shit. Think he saw us?"

But Jule was already running toward the person, who turned out to be a she, and looped an arm around her shoulder, holding her up. The woman was middle-aged, with dried blood smearing her face and clothing. She limped on a mangled foot, and her left arm hung against her chest in a makeshift sling. She smelled like she hadn't showered in a week.

*What I did to her,* Jule thought, incoherently, shouting for Baz to help shoulder the weight, trying not to cry. *What I almost did to her.*

"Are you okay?" she asked stupidly. The woman looked at her, dazed, eyebrows knitting as if she were trying to figure something out. "Where are you hurt?" *No burns,* Jule thought, trying to calm herself, trying to weasel out of it. Old injuries. Broken, not burned.

The woman said something in a hoarse croak, too soft for Jule to hear. Jule bent toward her lips. "What?"

"I said, don't trust them, Juliet."

"How do you know my name?"

"You're not like them."

"Not like who? What are you talking about? *What?*"

But before she could answer, Baz was there. The woman's eyes widened and she shied away, but she was too weak to stand on her own, and collapsed in Baz's arms. She reached out for Jule, clamping down on her wrist. "This is my fault," she whispered. "I'm sorry."

"Why's she apologizing to us for setting her on fire?" Baz asked.

"Does it matter?" Jule said. She never wanted to think about the fire, or what might have happened, again. "We've got to get her help."

"There wasn't supposed to be anyone in there," he said.

"Well, there *was.* And she needs a doctor."

The woman blinked rapidly. "Yes. I'm a doctor. Call

Colonel Franklin. He'll tell you I . . ." Her eyes drifted shut, and she sagged in Baz's arms.

"Did you hear that?" he said.

"She's a doctor. So what?"

"She's with the government. We've got to take her to Mouse."

"Look at her!" Jule kicked the empty gasoline can. "Look at us."

"Trust me," Baz said.

She did not. But . . . the doctor was with the government, and the government was the one sealing off the town, trapping Jule in the last place she wanted to be. Driving her to do things that she never would have done. No wonder the woman apologized. She was responsible. And she somehow knew Jule's name. Why would she know that? What else did she know?

There was a certain satisfaction to ringing the mayor's doorbell at two in the morning, forcing the mayor to shake hands with a Prevette, shake hands and say thank you. She could tell it sickened him to touch her, to smile and pretend she was his equal. It pleased her more than it should have, nearly as much as the fire. There was shame in that, in the entire night. But shame was something she knew how to ignore.

The mayor called the deacon. Together, they summoned a doctor, one they could trust. The doctor tended to the stranger's wounds—old ones, he said, wounds caused by trauma, already healing up, poorly, dislocated shoulder, concussion, fever, and exhaustion—and laid her down. On a cot. In a cell. At the local jail. They locked her up and waited eagerly for her to wake.

"A government doctor," the deacon said to the mayor as they peered through the grating, watching her sleep. "If she knows anything, we'll make her tell us, one way or another."

"*If* she knows anything."

"If she doesn't, the colonel does. And will probably want her back. He wants us to give him something, he'll give us something."

"You want to hold her hostage?"

"I want to protect this town, whatever that takes."

"Funny, I thought you wanted to remake it in your own— excuse me, I meant the Lord's image."

"Same thing, *Mayor*." No word had ever conveyed less respect. "Same thing."


Baz insisted on walking her home. The streets were unsafe these days. You never knew what could happen.

She let him.

He was the perfect gentleman, until they veered into the deserted square between the church and the town hall, its uprooted bushes and downed trees a fort of green that hid them from the empty streets.

"I promised you trouble, remember?" He pressed her up against a tree. "Ready for some real fun?"

She had burned down a building; she had nearly let a stranger die in the flames. She was the kind of person who did such things. And so she let him mash his face against hers and pull her to the ground.

It wasn't a bad kiss.

But she gagged with his tongue in her mouth and his hands under her sweatshirt, digging at the waistband of her jeans. He stank of cheap beer and cigarettes, just like the parasite, and she tasted only bile, and pushed him away. He took the opportunity to undo his zipper and yank his pants down low on his hips, then extricated himself from his boxers. She was nearly on her feet when he grabbed her and pulled her down again. "Going somewhere?"

"Not going to happen," she said, but he was holding on too tight.

He always looked small, surrounded by his offensive line on and off the field, but he didn't look small now. He looked capable of doing his own tackling.

"Don't be nervous," he said. "It's all good." His hand shifted from her neck to the top of her head, pushing her down and down until her face was mashed against him, naked and fleshy and wrinkled and foul.

This was going to happen.

The realization—and the strength of his grip, the girth of his body, the smell of his sweat, slick against her face—was paralyzing. For a moment, she considered letting herself go limp, letting it happen, if it was bound to happen anyway. Let him do whatever he wanted to do. Play dead and wait for it to be over.

Instead, she took him in her mouth and bit down. Hard.

He was the one who screamed.

She scrambled to her feet and started to run, looking back only once to confirm that he was still curled in a fetal position, holding himself, gasping and cursing. "You're dead!" he shouted after her. *"Dead."* Jule had no doubt he meant it.

She ran all the way home, beaming in the moonlight, the wind crisp and sweet against her face, and when she got back to the house, she went straight through the front door and slammed it behind her, not caring who she woke.

Former police chief Richard Hayes, drunk and disgusted and a little high on something he'd confiscated from his nephew over the Fourth of July, drove his scuffed gray Ford down Route 72 at full speed, slowing for neither the signs nor the sirens nor the bullhorned warning. It was the tank parked in the center of the lane that finally forced him to stop.

"Get out of your car, sir," came the order, and a man of the law himself, he followed it.

"I'm the chief," he said, which was at least in the neighborhood of truth. "How about you let me through. We won't have to tell anyone." The handful of protesters had gotten bored and gone home for the night. They were alone.

"I'm going to have one of my men drive you back to your home, sir," a man in uniform said. "And I'm going to ask that you stay there."

"At least let me use the damn radio to call my daughter," he said. "She's up at school, probably doesn't know whether I'm dead or alive."

"The frequencies have all been jammed by storm damage," the man said. "You know that."

"Bullshit," he said. There was movement in the shadows. But that stuff he'd taken always made him a bit paranoid, so he dismissed it. "I'm getting out of here."

He turned back to his car, but a soldier stood before the door, hand on his sidearm, challenge implied.

"I'm the law," he said again. "This is my town. You have no standing here."

"Let us take you home, sir."

"Let me through," he said, and made a run for it, darting around the soldiers, giving the roadblock a wide berth, hooting with gleeful triumph as he made it clear to open road, nothing ahead of him but blacktop and horizon. He was shouting his daughter's name when the bullet entered the back of his head.

"Did I say fire?" the lead man shouted at the shooter.

"Thought better safe than sorry," he mumbled.

"You thought. Jesus. Do me a favor, don't do any more of that."

He cursed as his men cleaned up the mess. There would be paperwork now, and a headache he didn't need. But the idiot had been right. Better safe than sorry. And though he'd been told alive was better than dead, he knew the men in white coats were always pleased to get their hands on another body.

The former chief had few friends in town, thanks to the way he'd bungled things the year before. It was a long time before anyone noticed he was gone. And by the time they did, there wasn't anyone left who cared.

## 8

## THE DYING OF THE LIGHT

The reigning Miss Oleander, Laura Tanner, had, when choosing a life working with children, made one very important miscalculation. She had gone into elementary school teaching with her eyes wide open about the deficiencies of her young charges—the runny noses and "accidents," the dirty hands and discipline problems, the hyperactivity and unchecked aggression, the short attention spans and shorter fuses. She hadn't underestimated her tolerance for bureaucracy and tedium, or overestimated her willingness to wipe the snot and puke and tears from other people's children, to comfort them when they fell, to teach them to say please and thank you and ABC, to love them as much as school policy allowed. She'd anticipated all of it, except for one thing.

She'd forgotten to factor in the parents.

And oh, how she hated the parents.

She hated the ones who interfered; she hated even more the ones who couldn't be bothered. She hated the helicopter parents, slathering their kids with kisses and complexes. She hated the ones who let their kids get bullied and the ones who counseled their kids to fight back. She hated the ones who worked three jobs and left their kids sulking in the school parking lot till sundown; she hated the ones who had no jobs, whose kids brought in Oxy bottles and meth pipes for show-and-tell. She hated the ones who couldn't help it, and hated that she couldn't stop herself from doing so.

Lately, she'd lost the will to try.

In the church basement, Laura surveyed her kingdom: Jasper was playing a clumsy game of balance beam on one of the tables. Emily S. was playing chicken with a light socket. Emily K. had smeared chocolate pudding all over her face and was well on her way to Picassoing up the nearest wall. Henry and Max were pretending they were pro wrestlers, and at the knockdown stage of a knockdown, drag-out fight. Grace was reading comic books in a corner with the spooky preacher's son, and the high school cheerleader had her hands full, literally, with three mini blondes who were loudly demanding a French braid. Forty-three helpless little ones whose parents apparently had better things to do. Every day, Laura kept them safe; every night, their parents ferried them away to homes where Laura wasn't welcome, where Laura's protection wasn't desired.

Nights were hard for Laura, since the storm. When she closed her eyes in hopeless pursuit of sleep, she saw Henry's mother branding him with a hot iron or Emily K.'s father dragging her down to the basement, darkness in his heart. She saw herself, avenging and protecting her charges, smashing the iron in Henry's mother's face and laughing as the hot metal seared her flesh. Hanging Emily's father from his butcher's meat hook and carving him up from sternum to groin. The visions were as real as memories. She could almost feel the comforting weight of the carving knife in her hand, the delight of flaying flesh, laying bare pink muscle and pearly bone.

Some nights, she lay awake till dawn, stewing over these parents who thought they could do whatever they wanted, as if biology guaranteed ownership. As if creating something gave you the right to destroy it.

Not tonight, she decided.

Not ever again.

Her last boyfriend had given her a gun for her birthday. He'd also, before going back to his ex, given her a key to his house. Where he had an entire cabinet of guns, some for hunting, some for personal protection, some for fun—enough that it might be a while before he noticed that she'd slipped into his basement last night and claimed a rifle and a semiautomatic for herself. Just in case.

She clapped her hands over her head, twice, and the children fell silent. "Who wants to go on a little field trip?" she said, and when the kids cheered, she knew she was doing the right thing. They *wanted* to be rescued. They wanted her to save them. She would lead them out of this basement and into a world of her own making; she would keep them safe and raise them right.

And if anyone tried to stop her, she would make them sorry.


"Not for you, baby sis." That's what Scott always said, although he also said it was the best high he'd ever known, it was like snorting the solar system, it was like God and the devil playing a set with the Rolling Stones and you were the guitar, it was like life itself. But to Annie, he said only, "I'm doing you a favor."

Now Annie Prevette was going to do one for herself. Or, rather, her dear, depraved husband would do it for her. Unlike Scott, he wasn't in a position to refuse her much of anything. When you got caught pawing through your stepdaughter's underwear drawer, you tended to lose the upper hand.

She'd put on a good show at first, yelling and screaming about calling the cops, throwing him out, setting her brothers on him. It was that last that broke him. He dispensed with the bullshit excuses and begged for mercy, blaming it on Jule, as if she were some stealth Lolita in sweatshirts and combat boots.

"Just get me enough to last awhile," Annie had said. "At least a quarter pound."

"But that's everything I've got," he said. "More."

"Figure it out. Or I go to Scott." She whipped his cheek with the pair of black panties she'd caught him nuzzling. "He's *very* fond of his niece."

That night, Billy had dumped a ziplock bag of Nazi Cold on her mattress. It was swag crank, cheap and dirty, but it would do.

"So we have an agreement," he said.

"Jule's a grown woman. She can do what she wants."

*And so can you*, that was the real agreement. Jule *was* an adult, practically, Annie Prevette told herself. She never shut up about that. More to the point, there was *so much* meth, and Scott had been right about that, at least. It was good, and she wanted it, and surely Jule, whose arrival had ruined both her figure and her life, owed her that much. She took the deal.

She hadn't come up for air since.

\* \* \*

"I saw it on TV," Morgan said. "It'll be great."

"What show?" Clair asked. It was strange to be on the empty football field. She'd only ever been here at game time, cheering the team and occasionally handing out literature for the church. No one in Oleander doubted that God loved football—though after the Bulldogs finished out their third losing season in a row, there was some question as to whom he rooted for.

"I don't know," Morgan said. "It was a bunch of football players. And they did it to this loser. It was awesome."

"Yeah, but in real life . . ." Clair wasn't allowed to watch TV, which her mother thought was a tool of the devil. She did manage to catch the occasional glimpse on the library computer when the librarian took her afternoon nap. But cooking competitions and reality shows about wealthy divorcées hadn't offered her much insight into the mind of the average American teen, football-player variety. Not that she wanted insight into anything that disgusting.

"I asked Chuck Platch, and he said they totally do stuff like this all the time," Morgan said.

Clair scowled. "What were you doing talking to him?"

Morgan colored. There was a long pause while she searched for an acceptable answer. She seized upon the obvious one. "He had questions about the Lord."

There was skepticism in Clair's *mm-hmm*, but she didn't press it. There was no need. Everyone knew what Morgan did when she wasn't at church. It was one of the things they ever so politely didn't discuss, as neither of them acknowledged their raging jealousy that Ellie King, that stuck-up little deacon's pet, had practically ascended to sainthood. If this went as planned, Clair decided, maybe Ellie would be next.

*And then maybe Morgan herself,* Clair thought. Ten years was a long time to be best friends with someone you couldn't stand. Eventually something had to give.

"Think of it as striking a blow for feminism," Morgan said. "On TV, it may be a jock thing, but in real life, who's to say a couple of girls can't strike a blow for righteousness and show the devil where to shove it?"

The freshman on the ground between them whimpered something, but the duct tape over her mouth made it impossible to understand. Clair toed her in the stomach to shut her up. She was thinking.

"Okay," she said finally. "But only because we're doing it for Him."

"Of course," Morgan said. And it was true. The freshman had snuck out of church to smoke three Sundays in a row. She wore odd hippie dresses and chewed gum like a cow and had once, though she claimed it was an accident, knocked over Clair's tray in the cafeteria, spilling orange juice and tomato sauce all over her most slimming pair of jeans. She had also, rumor had it, given Chuck Platch a parking-lot blow job after the Memorial Day picnic.

As they stripped off her clothes and tied her to the flagpole in front of the school, the reasons no longer seemed to matter. It felt good to strip her bare; it felt good to squeeze her shoulders and wrists and thighs, to yank and stretch her into position, pressing hard enough to leave thumbprint-shaped bruises in her flesh; it felt good to watch her cry, and even better to rip off the duct tape in one swift, cruel tear and listen to her scream.

* * *

The house smelled of milk gone bad. The sink was heaped with paper plates and takeout containers, the trash having long since overflowed. Giuliana Larkin, still in the bathrobe she'd worn for three days straight, sat cross-legged in her son's bedroom, tearing up his comics collection one book at a time.

*Riiiiiip* went Batman.

*Riiiiip* went Superman.

*Riiiiip* went green guy with laser gun and robot with six arms.

Perhaps he was old enough to put away childish things, and this would help him become a man. But if so, she didn't much care.

She was due to pick him up at the church in a few minutes, and she didn't much care about that, either.

She'd wanted to be a good mother. Not at first, maybe. Not enough to stick around after the kid was born, but she'd come back for him. Was it her fault that it was too late, that he was already ruined? Maybe if she'd raised him, rather than leaving the job to trash, she could have found it in herself to love him. But she doubted it. She wasn't, as it turned out, the mothering kind. After she left her father's house, she'd vowed never to let anyone beat her again; after she had Milo, she'd vowed never to let anyone beat him, either. And the night before, when he'd knocked over his milk and she'd gone after him with the iron, its metal face still red-hot, she had stopped herself in time, before searing the flesh off his cheeks. But only just.

She'd promised herself the comics instead, and as soon as she'd gotten him out of the house, she'd taken a scissors to them. She soon discovered it was even more satisfying to tear them up with her own hands.

By the time he made it back, she would be gone.

"Whatever," Scott had said when she asked if she could stay with him for a while, nestled under his covers, her head against his scarred chest, her hand playing along the pipes and needles on the nightstand, already eager for night to come again, for their highs to mingle along with their bodies, for their skulls to open and joy to rush in.

It wasn't much of an invitation, but it was enough. When she finished with the comics, she walked out of the house, not bothering to pack a bag or lock the door behind her. That life had nothing she needed.

Jason didn't know how to punch or shoot. But he knew how to watch and wait and bide his time. He knew that he was smarter than Baz Demming, and he knew that he would not let Baz, or anyone else, hurt him again.

He knew that Baz was only human, and if Jason slammed into him with his mother's Jeep, Baz would bleed and break and die.

But that was how Nick had died, and so Jason could not do that.

It left plenty of options.

Poisoning. Drowning. Stabbing. Garroting. Strangling. Suffocating. Throat slitting. Jason's mother was a doctor, which meant Jason had access to any number of pills and potions that could drop a quarterback. It would be easy enough to get hold of a syringe. Or a scalpel.

Jason's mother liked to garden, and he was pretty sure even a confirmed weakling like him could swing a shovel hard enough to knock someone out—and an unconscious quarterback couldn't protect himself, no matter how many muscles he might have.

The world was full of weapons, when you cared to look.

Sometimes he thought it didn't even have to be Baz—it could be any of the football players, or anyone at all. As long as he finally got to hit back; as long as he got to be the one standing and laughing and deciding while someone else lay curled up on the ground, trying not to scream.

But it was Baz he wanted, and it was Baz that he followed, waiting for his opportunity. He stalked the quarterback from the shadows, and dreamed of poisons and knives and guns, and was too honest with himself to pretend this was still about justice or self-defense or even revenge. This was about two things: power and death. For the first time in his life, Jason would get one.

Baz would get the other.

There could be no more to clean; there was always more to clean. Twenty-four hours of scrubbing, vacuuming, dusting, laundering, Windexing, and washing had barely made a dent in the filth. After another twenty-four hours, high on cleaning fluid, hunger, and lack of sleep, Charlotte King had surveyed her work and deemed it inadequate. The house defied her. It was like living in a landfill, only a matter of time before the rats and maggots emerged from the walls to consume her.

Having turned her back on all the foul human needs like

food and sleep, she was well into her sixty-second hour—her daughter mercifully consumed by her mission to save the world—when the answer came to her. How could the surfaces be clean before the surfaces were bare?

The guiding truth of Charlotte King's life: cleanliness was next to godliness. And on this day, she ascended.

The clothes, the books, the flotsam and jetsam of two generations—photo albums and trophies and cookbooks and dishes—that was easy. Into the trash, first, until she got tired of tying the bags and discovered heaving them out the window was simpler. Her own clothes went as well, and it was better this way, with nothing to separate her from the deed. Clean mind, clean body, clean soul. The heap of discards grew, until, as the wedding china crashed to the driveway, she felt she would nearly explode with the radiance spilling out of her. The dog, which Ellie had dragged home one day and which her husband had insisted they keep, obviously had to go as well.

The furniture went next: Television. Computer. Chairs. Table.

Clutter.

Trash.

Filth.

It was not the first time she'd dragged her family out of the mud; it was not the first time she'd nearly acted too late. Surely the Lord could forgive her for not suspecting sooner that a fourteen-year-old could harbor so stained a soul. If she hadn't been vigilant, if she hadn't, in one of her periodic sweeps, found the diary, she might never have known, and Ellie might have followed her dark path to its inevitable end. Instead,

Charlotte had caught the animals in the act. A bucket of cold water hadn't been enough to wash away their sin, but it had been a start.

Of course, Ellie had never thanked her mother for the work done that day, for the gift Charlotte had bestowed on her, delivering her, still dripping with her shame, to the deacon's doorstep. But Charlotte had mothered three teenage girls. She knew better than to expect gratitude.

All these years later, Charlotte had allowed her vigilance to wane, and she saw now her mistake. She hadn't addressed the root of the problem. The taint remained. The dirt. The source of original sin. The seeds had been planted here, in this house, and as long as it remained, so would the danger.

The bare rooms were glorious, but the surfaces still screamed for purification. There was, in case of emergency, a stock of white paint in the garage, and Charlotte saw, as if by divine vision, that this would be next, and right. A home of lines and corners and nothing but unbroken stretches of white.

In an ecstasy of certitude, she began to paint.


Baz slammed his bruised shoulder into the tackling dummy, hard.

Again.

*Again.*

It wasn't working. The red was still there.

That's how he thought of it: the red.

It was both like and unlike living in a fog. Sometimes it was a mist so real he could touch it—was surprised that his hands weren't slick and wet with condensation. Sometimes he could even see it, his world tinged with red. Other times it was less tangible: the *feeling* of red. Neither fury nor lust nor fear, not exactly, but somehow all of them together, paired with something else: a *need*. The red wasn't content to just sit within him. He was its vessel, and when it woke, the only way to exorcise it was to let it feed.

The red had been with him since he was a child and, except for that time with the family cat, he'd managed to keep it under control. Football helped. So did tormenting the occasional loser at school. Always before, when it came over him, there was a simple supply-and-demand formula to banish it. The red demanded targets; Baz supplied them. Normally, a few runs at the tackling dummy or a misshapen face was enough to clear the mist for another few days or, if he was lucky, weeks.

Not anymore.

Not since the storm.

The red was with him all the time now. He would never be rid of it. He had never been in control. It had been toying with him all these years, and now it was tired of the game, and it was tired of waiting.

It was impatient, and it was hungry, and all the dummies in the world wouldn't shut it up.

He knew what would.

He ditched the field, changed out of his sweat-soaked jersey, and gave in to the magnetic pull of the Porter house (now the Prevette house) and *her*. The hedges around the perimeter were tall enough to hide him, so long as he was careful.

He was careful. From the edge of the backyard, he could see into her window. At night, when she stood before it with the blinds open, he could see her strip, a private show just for him. Almost as if she knew he was watching. Sometimes he sat there for hours, thinking about what he would do to her. Thinking didn't make the red go away. It only intensified it, to an almost painful degree, but there was pleasure in the pain. He could wait. At least until he was safe, from the Prevettes and anyone else who might want to nose into his business. Until they were alone.

The red was a gift, he understood that now. A reward for good behavior, and he intended to live up to it.

He was going to make it hurt.

Deacon Barnes thought he had prepared himself for the pain, but he never knew there could be pain like this. He screamed. And then, because his faith was stronger than his flesh, and his love for the Lord stronger than all, he brought the hammer down again. This time, the nail went all the way through his palm.

"Praise be," he managed to choke out, spots of black swimming across his vision and bile coating his tongue.

Praise be.

The Lord demanded sacrifice. A demonstration of fealty. Purification: all weakness, all temptation, all sin burned away. He would doubt himself no more, and no more would he doubt the Lord. Questions were for the weak. Envy, uncertainty, confusion, regret—these were the small concerns of small minds, impulses that stank of frail humanity. He had ascended beyond that. The pain would carry him to certainty.

This was the valley of darkness, but he would show no fear. He would be a beacon, and lead them to the light. Those who deserved to be led.

And so the nail, and so the palms, and so the pain.

It filled him up, and that was right. Satan would be left with nowhere to hide.

He smeared a finger through the blood and brought it to his tongue. This was the taste of salvation.

"Whatcha doing?" Milo asked.

Grace dropped another piece of paper into the burning waste bin. "Playing with matches," she said. It probably wasn't the best example to set for a bunch of small children, but the handful of kids who'd passed up the sudden field trip weren't paying attention to her. Even if they were, the high school cheerleader hadn't bothered to stick around after Ms. Tanner wandered off with the bulk of their charges, so who was left to complain?

"Can I?" Milo said.

"Why not?" She handed him a few of the crude wanted posters, each bearing a color photo of Cassandra Porter's smiling face. It looked like a prom picture. She wore a pastel green dress. "Just one at a time, though. That's important."

"Why?"

She could have made up some kind of fire safety reason. Or told him the truth, that it was more satisfying that way, that she liked to watch the flames eat away at Cass's face, singeing it into ash one perfect feature at a time, chin then lips then nose then eyes, curling in the heat and finally disappearing. She liked to imagine that she heard a tiny, paper-thin scream echoing up from the trash can. Cass was the one who'd told her about voodoo dolls one night, when they'd both gotten bored with whatever Disney trash her parents had planned they watch. Grace liked to imagine that each time she set the match to the photo, Cass, wherever she was, felt at least a tingle of heat across her scalp, along with a shiver of certainty that someone was out there, hunting. She could have told Milo that for some reason it seemed that if she set the whole stack on fire at once, it wouldn't have the same effect. But Milo was eight, and so it was easy enough to just say "Because."

He went with it.

"What do you think will happen if they find her?" he said, dropping a page into the fire. It wasn't as satisfying as when she did it herself, but it was good enough.

"I think she'll get what she deserves," Grace said.

Lately, it was all she could think about.

When her parents had been around, there'd been plenty of other things to distract her. The strain of smiling just the right amount, as if everything were normal. The tense pause, after every line, waiting to see if it would set off another unpredictable bout of paternal tears; the struggle of attending school every day and, when that became too tedious, the additional struggle of keeping her parents from finding out how many days she'd skipped. The puzzle of how to fill that time, hours that shuffled past with all the ardor of a retirement-home escapee.

Now, alone in the house since the storm, she had no one to pretend for and no one to catch her in her lies. She had nothing to do but sleep and read and come to the church basement faithfully every day and play with the children, Milo especially. The torture of being around him—of pretending to laugh at his dumb little-kid jokes and tolerating his dumb little-kid questions and suffering through the farce of a worshipful little brother—seemed like a reasonable penance. She hadn't managed to protect her own little brother—let her put up with someone else's.

It wasn't a terribly demanding schedule, and it offered plenty of time to focus on the only thing left that seemed to matter: Cassandra Porter. Where she would find Cassandra Porter. What she would do when she found her.

It had been her birthday, the night her parents announced that Owen was on the way. They'd served up the news along with the cake, like it was supposed to be the best present of all. And because parents, even the good ones, never really get it, they'd been surprised when she burst into tears and fled to her room. She'd stayed awake all that night, imagining what it would be like to have a baby in the house, sucking up all her parents' attention, all their love. A baby would be needy and cute and it would never talk back. It would lay claim to her parents, who were supposed to belong to her. Only to her.

Then the baby had come, and it had all come true . . . and she'd learned to deal. She'd even decided that the baby was cuter than expected, if not as cute as everyone else seemed to think. That, at least when her mother was tired and her father was busy and she had to hold Owen against her shoulder and rock him to sleep, she didn't actually mind having him around. But she never quite got used to the fact that her parents belonged to him, too. And now he was gone, and he'd taken them away with him. They weren't real anymore: they talked, they ate, they occasionally even smiled, but they were empty. It was all Cass's fault. Cass had stolen her family, and left Grace all alone.

She was *alone.*

Grace had promised herself, when Owen was still lying blue on the floor, that Cass would die. That Grace would do it herself. But she was a kid, and kids made idle promises all the time. *I promise not to lie. I promise to do my homework. I promise to be good forever if you let me have one last cookie.* A kid's promise didn't have to mean anything.

She didn't feel like a kid anymore. Lately, she'd felt like making another promise. A real one. She was old enough to know that real life wasn't anything like TV. Killing someone was probably harder than it looked. She had no idea whether she could actually pull a trigger or stab a knife or set a fire or do any of the hundred things that rushed into her mind whenever there was a vacant moment.

But she was starting to think maybe she could.

"What if she's not so bad?" Milo said.

"She is."

"Yeah, but what if she's not?"

"But she *is.*" Be nice, she reminded herself. Nice like she'd never been to Owen.

"You don't *know.*" Now he was whining.

"And you do?" She took the flyers back from him, dropped another one in the fire. Smoke was starting to billow. Soon some kind of fire alarm would probably go off and all hell would break loose. Let it. There was no one to punish her, and nothing to punish her with.

"So maybe I do," he said.

"Do you know what that girl did?"

"She says she didn't mean to," he said.

She stopped, forcing her gaze away from the flame. "What?"

"I don't think she's a bad guy," he said. "And I'm an expert."

"You know her? Cassandra?"

Milo pressed his hands to his mouth, a cartoonish tableau of someone who'd said too much.

"Milo?"

He shook his head.

She wanted to shake *him*.

"Do you know something, Milo? Something you're not supposed to?"

"It's a secret," he said. "I promised not to tell anyone."

"But I'm not 'anyone.' I'm Grace."

"That's true," he admitted.

"And you trust me, don't you?"

Milo nodded.

"We're friends, right?"

"You're my best friend," he said, too solemnly for his age. "But her, too."

"Cassandra. Who's not a bad guy."

He didn't say anything.

"Best friends trust each other, Milo," she said. Her hands were shaking. "And they really like to meet their friends' other best friends."

"You have to promise you won't tell."

"I promise."

"No, you *really* have to promise. Shake on it," he said.

They shook on it.

"You sure?" he asked. "You won't say anything? To anyone?"

She nodded. "Best friend's honor."

He bent his lips toward her ear and told her a secret.

When it happened, Cass thought it was a dream, because that was how it always happened in her dreams. The door blowing open, men in uniforms yanking her to her feet, wresting her hands behind her back, and dragging her away.

But it wasn't a dream, because in the dreams she fought back. Now she went willingly, bowing her head and offering her wrists for their handcuffs. She cooperated. At least, until the first blow landed. After that, she fought. It was of no use. Not with her hands chained. Not against three grown men with steel-tipped boots and metal batons. She screamed for Daniel, for anyone, even the Preacher with his guns. No one came. They got her on the ground and kicked her between them like a soccer ball, a rousing game of baby-killer-in-the-middle. When she hurt enough to cry uncontrollably but not enough to pass out, the shortest one said, "Save some for later," and they did.

There was no police car. Instead, they lashed something like a leash around her neck and waist and towed her the mile back to the station. Sometimes she stumbled on her bruised and bleeding legs, and they dragged her. That hurt worst of all. People massed on the street, and watched, and laughed. That hurt less than she'd expected.

They threw her into a cell. She waited, just in case, lying down on the filthy cot with her eyes wide open, willing it to happen, but she did not wake up.

* * *

When it happened, Daniel wasn't there, because of the dream. He was in the drugstore. Everyone dead was alive again, wide, knowing grins distending their faces, blood already starting to drip from the holes in their chests, shoulders, skulls. Bloody and oblivious, they went about their business, nodding and browsing and exchanging pleasantries about the chores that would be done that afternoon and the dinners that would be prepared and the fun that would be had, as if they wouldn't all soon be dead.

"You bringing someone pretty to the church picnic this weekend?" Daniel heard himself saying from the wrong side of the register as Mr. Gathers plunked down an ice cream sandwich and a comic book and a handful of crumpled bills.

"Not going to the picnic," Gathers said. "None of us are going, because we'll be in the ground, with the maggots and the worms and the blood. You'll be with us soon, Daniel. Should be a fine, fine day."

Daniel nodded, and toted up the purchases, and pulled the gun out from beneath the counter, and pulled the trigger, and pulled it again and again. Daniel laughed each time a body thumped to the ground, and then Daniel turned the gun on himself. He slid his lips around the cold barrel, and ran his tongue along its metal edge, then pulled back, gently, firmly, on the trigger, and it felt so good.

He woke to find himself behind the counter of the boarded-up drugstore, his hands cut up and bloody, apparently from breaking the window and climbing through the glass. He'd gone to sleep in his own bed, nearly a mile away.

In his hands was his father's shotgun.

# 9

## THE ANIMALS IN THEIR CAGES

Pain, she could handle. Locked doors, she could handle. But isolation, she could not. Not anymore, not after a year inside that cell and a week out of it, a week with the sky and the stars and human contact. Cass had lost the habit of solitude, and nothing terrified her like the thought of going back to it. She couldn't stand to lose the world again, nature and noise and words. And so, locked inside her dingy beige cell with its single cot and its malodorous toilet, she sat cross-legged on the cheap linoleum, and she listened.

They were careless about speaking near her, especially when it came to the prisoner housed in the cell next door. It didn't take Cass long to deduce her identity. She knew that voice as well as her own. The mayor came frequently to speak to the woman, as did the deacon, and when the doctor refused to offer them any new answers about why the town had been quarantined or how they might go about escaping it, and when, as always happened, the men gave up, they argued among themselves, in voices not nearly hushed enough. They argued about torture, and it was clear both wanted it to happen. Neither was willing to do it himself.

The mayor was the more hesitant of the two, especially

when the talk boiled down to fingernail pulling and water-boarding. "How long can we legally keep her if—"

"As long as you want," the deacon said. "Declare her a prisoner of war."

There was a pause, then a regretful "I'm not sure I have the power to do that."

"You would if you declared martial law."

"Can I do *that*?"

"I'd like to see anyone stop you."

This was how she learned that Oleander's era of democracy had drawn to a close.

This was how she learned of the town's rampant "disorderly conduct," law and order giving way to anarchy: people walking off their jobs, crimes committed in broad daylight, an armed pied piper herding packs of feral children into the woods, their parents not much seeming to care. This, too, was how she learned of the Prevettes' efforts to hasten chaos along, making bomb threats against various government-related organizations, setting small pipe bombs, even, allegedly, blowing up the offices of the local paper. The deacon suggested that they'd blow themselves up before they did any major damage, and the mayor laughed, and the subject was closed.

"Hey!" she called out, finally, as the mayor and the deacon retreated from yet another session with the doctor. This time, there had been very little conversation, at least that she could hear. But there had been some screams. That was what decided her. "I want a lawyer."

They were supposed to be the magic words. But the deacon only laughed. "The hubris of the sinner astounds."

"We're doing things differently now," the mayor said. "It's

time for this town to take justice into its own hands." The words had a stale quality to them, as if he'd rehearsed them one too many times. "It will be good for all of us."

"Even you," the deacon added. "You've never had a true chance to pay for your crimes. Everyone deserves the chance to meet their Maker with a clear conscience."

That was when Cass understood they weren't sending her away again. At least, not to a courthouse or a federal prison or another mental institution. She was too scared to cry.

That night, the doctor's voice floated through the dark. "They're going to kill you," she said. "Any day now."

This was Oleander, where she'd lived all her life. Deacon Barnes had taught her fourth-grade Sunday school class and given her a poster of a tiger cub in reward for winning a biblically themed spelling bee. Mayor Mouse had, before he was mayor, sold her family each of its cars. He always offered her a lollipop (even after she got too old for such things) while she waited for them to finish bickering over car-radio options and sign the paperwork. She had known both men since she was a toddler. But they were different now; Oleander was different. Even she could see that. So, unbelievable as it should have been, she believed it. They were going to kill her.

"I wouldn't sound so excited about it," Cass said. "You're probably next. Or first."

"I could have died in the accident. Or out there in the storm."

"Yeah, sorry about that." And she was, more than she sounded. Not least because she'd ended up here anyway.

"I need to get out of here," the doctor said. "Out of this whole town."

"Good luck with that."

"I want you to help me."

"Why didn't you say so?" Cass laughed sourly. "Hold on a sec, let me just grab the key and I'll let us both out."

"I know you've got no reason to trust me, Cassandra. You don't have to. But if I get the chance to get out of here, I'm taking you with me. I hope you'll do the same for me. These people are not our friends."

"'These people'? You mean the ones who just want to know what the hell is going on? The ones you won't tell anything to? *Those* people?"

"There are some things it doesn't help to know."

"You wouldn't say that if you had any idea . . ."

"What?"

"What it's like not to know."

"What if you did know?" the doctor asked. "What if I could tell you?"

"Tell me what?"

"What happened that night. Why you did what you did."

Cass sat up. "*You* know?"

There was no response.

Cass had to force herself to take several long, slow breaths. The doctor was infuriatingly silent.

"So tell me," Cass said. Still, no answer. She lost it. *"Tell me!"*

"Not here. It's not safe. But if we can get ourselves out, you'll get your answers. Hopefully, that will serve as an incentive."

Cass considered screaming for the cops and, when they arrived, volunteering to do their dirty work herself. She wouldn't mind some fingernail pulling at the moment, and forget water-boarding. She would happily plunge the doctor's head into the toilet bowl and hold it there for good.

"I was lying before. I'm glad I left you out there on the road."

"I am, too," the doctor said. "Because now I know you're capable of it, and I know better than to let it happen again. And it won't, will it?"

Cass didn't answer, but they both knew the answer was no. Because more than revenge, she wanted the truth.

She was allowed visitors, which only offered her the opportunity to think about all the people who didn't show. Her parents, of course: long gone. Her old friends: nonexistent. West: he'd already gone beyond what she could have expected of him, her fake boyfriend who didn't even trust her enough to confide his most obvious secret.

Ellie King showed up, more than once. Because of who she was, or what she purported to be, she was allowed into the cell with Cass, and, with a surreptitious brush at the dirty sheet, she sat on the cot beside her and asked if Cass had taken God into her heart. It was the kind of thing Cass would have laughed off easily—before. She'd embraced atheism at age twelve, not out of any serious conviction but simply for the aesthetics of it. Like reading glasses and her beat-up copy of *The Great Gatsby*, atheism seemed an appropriate accessory for the kind of person she aspired to be. Now she took the question seriously. Had she taken God into her heart? The answer was no. "What would it get me if I did?" she asked.

"It's not about what it *gets* you," Ellie said. "It's about *giving*. Giving yourself up to something greater."

"I don't think something greater would want me."

That was where they left it, the first day. The second day, Ellie quoted Bible verses, and Cass listened, waiting for something she could believe in. Ellie promised that if she gave herself to God, He would cleanse her soul. Sometimes, at night, she lay awake, searching herself for the conviction that there was a "something greater" up there beyond the ceiling. She experimented with talking to him, asking for favors small and large, praising him for killing the cockroach in the corner before she had to do it herself, and, finally, apologizing for what she'd done.

That was the end of the experiment. "I'm sorry," she said, and realized that it didn't matter whether there was some great omniscient entity weighing her words and choosing whether to forgive. What right did he even have to do so? He was the one who'd stood by and let her do it. They were all God's children, Ellie said, but what kind of a father let one kid kill another without intervening? And if it happened while he was looking away, what right had he to forgive the surviving child, or himself?

That was what she told Ellie, the third time that Oleander's saint appeared.

"It won't change anything," she said. "God forgiving me won't bring him back."

"God's not the one who has to forgive you," Ellie said.

Cass swallowed back a sob. "No one would forgive me. Not for that."

"Owen Tuck is dead," Ellie said. Even now, the words hurt. "You can't change that. But you're still here. You can fix you."

It sounded a little too self-helpy for Cass's taste, not to mention impossible, given the present circumstances.

"It's not about changing the past," Ellie said. "It's about making the present bearable. And the future. Because otherwise you look forward and . . ."

"There's nothing out there."

Ellie nodded.

"God is the light," she said. "That's how you see through the dark. Past it. How you keep going."

"And that's how it worked for you?" Cass asked. "What would someone like you know about the dark?"

Ellie stood up. "I should go."

"Why are you here, Ellie?" Cass asked. "We're not friends— we barely even know each other. What do you care?"

"Because I know what happened to you that night," Ellie said.

"What happened to *me*?"

"The devil claimed you," Ellie said, and Cass supposed she shouldn't have been surprised, but so far the girl had seemed so sane. "Possession is real," Ellie said. "I know. I've seen. Good people can do terrible things if they let the devil into their heart."

"You mean metaphorically."

Ellie shook her head. "The devil is real. I didn't want to believe it before, not until I saw it. And now I understand why . . ." She shook the rest of the thought away. "I understand a lot. He can make you do things you never imagined you would do. He made you do what you did. That's why I'm here."

"To banish the devil? Like an exorcism?"

"To tell you it was him," she said. "Not *you*."

"You really believe that?" Cass asked.

Ellie nodded. "Can you?"

Demonic possession: she supposed it was as good an answer as any and, conveniently, one that let her off the hook. After making such an effort to believe in an all-powerful entity who lived above, wouldn't it be churlish not to acknowledge the possibility of one that lived below?

"I'd like to," she said. "But no."

"The devil's not like God," Ellie said. "He doesn't want you to believe in evil. That makes it easier for him."

"I'll add it to my list of sins," Cass said. "Maybe you should go."

"I hope you know you're not alone," Ellie said before she left.

"I know, I know, God is always with me. Et cetera."

"No, I mean, what happened to you that night, the devil getting inside. You're not the only one."

Daniel came, too, of course. He'd sworn to anyone who asked that she had camped out in his shed without permission. The lie grew flimsier with every hour he spent outside her cell, blinking those puppy-dog eyes and fumbling for ways to help. "This is where I deserve to be," she reminded him more than once, at which he would make noises about due process and double jeopardy and the proper authorities. She was forced to agree that, yes, if someone opened the door, she'd be more than happy to walk through it, need for penance or not. It wasn't going to happen.

On the fourth day—after the doctor had put down her cards—he showed up wild-eyed and blotched with red, and pressed his face through the bars of her cell, whispering, "We have to get you out of here." But he wouldn't say why it had suddenly become so urgent, and when she pressed him, he started telling some inane story about a game they'd created when they were kids, an elaborate combination of tag, basketball, and TV wrestling. He was full of details like this, stories she only half remembered, reminiscences about kids who'd moved away and substitute teachers she'd long since forgotten, inside jokes she no longer understood, complaints about the food served in their elementary school cafeteria and the oafish pitcher on their third-grade softball team, conversations they'd apparently had during recess, swaying on the lower-playground swings, their legs pumping in sync, their heads tilted back, their feet kicking the clouds. He had nothing to say on the subject of his mother dying, or the way they'd all drifted apart after that, a pack of kids veering off in one direction, Daniel plodding off alone in the other. She wondered if she was supposed to feel guilty for ditching him along with the others—she couldn't even remember why she'd done it, any more than she could remember them being friends in the first place, but she assumed it was because he'd been sad and his father had gotten weird and she'd been a kid, ill equipped to deal.

She didn't let on about how little she remembered. And because he seemed to believe the stories would cheer her up—because he so desperately wanted to—she didn't let on how much it hurt to hear them. Why would she want to be reminded of a happy past, a past when there'd been nothing ahead of her but future? Why would she want to know that she'd sat on those swings and told him she was going to be a doctor, or maybe an astronaut, or, no, definitely an archaeologist, like Indiana Jones? It hurt to remember that girl, who didn't plan to grow up to be a prisoner, or a killer. And as he rambled, she was tempted to hurt him, too—tell him that his precious memories were her junk, that she'd long since packed them up and given them away to clear out some room. But it was a momentary impulse, and it passed.

The Cassandra he remembered wouldn't hurt him that way. And that was what she liked best about having Daniel around: the way he looked at her like she still was the old Cassandra, whoever that was.

When he reached for her hand through the bars, she let him take it.

She didn't need him to tell her why he was so panicked. She listened carefully. She heard things she wasn't supposed to hear. She knew it had been decided, that whatever the town chose to do to her, it would do tomorrow.

"This is so strange," he said, his fingers tight around hers. She could have held on to him forever. Like the squeeze of a hand could fix anything. Like the warmth of his palm in hers—even though she was on one side of the bars and he was on another, and they barely knew each other, and the next day she was probably going to die—actually meant she wasn't alone. "All of this," he added.

"Tell me about it."

\* \* \*

Grace came.

A cop escorted her down to the cell block, then, despite the fact that she was a kid, and probably shouldn't have been allowed there in the first place, left her alone.

When he did, she pulled out a gun.

"Gracie." Cass exhaled the name, shuddering. It wasn't the gun that scared her—or at least, it wasn't the gun that scared her the most. It was the girl holding it, same as she'd always been, if maybe a little taller, a little ganglier, but with something missing from her eyes.

She held the gun steady, trained on Cass. "Grace," she said. "Not Gracie."

"Please don't," Cass said. She had no right to ask.

She couldn't *not* ask.

She did not want to die.

"I don't know why I did it," Cass said, talking fast. "I don't remember anything. I never would have . . . I mean, I never meant to . . . I'm sorry. I know that's probably pointless to say, but I'm sorry. And I swear I don't know *why* I—"

"I don't care why," Grace said. Her voice was the same, too, thin and reedy with a hint of a child's whine. But it was so cold. "I don't need to know that."

"What do you need? Tell me. Just . . . please, the gun, put it down."

"I don't think I can do it," Grace said.

"You can. Just put it down, and we'll talk."

"I know I promised," Grace said. She was looking past Cass, into the wall, or maybe into the past, and Cass realized she was talking to herself. "But I don't think . . ." The barrel trembled, and Grace nibbled at the corner of her lip, and Cass let herself breathe again, remembering that whatever she called herself, this was a child, little Gracie Tuck. So she'd somehow gotten her hands on a gun, and dredged up the nerve to bring it into the police station and point it at the person who broke her world, but this was still kid stuff. Playacting. It didn't mean she'd become someone who could pull a trigger.

Then, visibly, the nervousness fell away, and she smiled.

And she fired.

## 10

## THE BAD AND THE UGLY

The bullet ricocheted off the toilet, setting off a spray of porcelain shrapnel. It embedded itself in the wall two feet to the left of where Cass had dropped to the floor and curled her head into her arms. She stayed that way, eyes squeezed shut, waiting. She could hear Grace's breathing, loud and slow. Her own breaths came quick and panicked, like her body was determined to get in as many as it could while it had the chance.

Blood pounded in her ears; her stomach hurt; she was angry, though she had no right to be.

She was terrified.

She heard a clicking sound, like some lever or mechanism on the gun had been shifted into place.

Though the shot must have echoed throughout the station, no one came.

"I'm sorry."

Cass was so muddled by fear that for a moment she thought she'd spoken the words herself. But then Grace repeated them and, with her parting words, made clear that she was sorry not for firing, but for missing. And perhaps for slipping the gun into her highlighter-yellow backpack and walking away.

"Next time," Grace said while Cass huddled on the ground, not willing to trust that it was over. "I promise."

West hadn't believed the rumors, not until he saw what they were building in front of the town hall, the heap fashioned from storm debris, the heap with the wooden stake speared through its center. It would—if the trial went as everyone assumed it would go—be Oleander's first public execution in more than a century. And there was no doubt the Watchdogs would be there. Which meant making nice with Baz. But when West arrived at the quarterback's house, a large Victorian just east of Main, he found he wasn't the day's first visitor.

Baz was in the driveway—on his stomach, licking the dirt. Jason stood over him, his back to West. He was holding a gun. Every window on the street offered a perfect view, but there was no movement, no adult intervention. Only the two of them, and West, and the gun.

"I'm going to kill you," Baz growled.

"In the next life, maybe." Jason laughed. The gun didn't waver. "Right now, I'm guessing, you'd take off my pants and blow me if that's what it took to stay alive."

West crept slowly toward Jason, cringing at each crunch of gravel beneath his sneakers. If this were the movies, it would have been a no-brainer to leap on the gunman and wrestle the weapon from his grasp, save the day. But in the movies, the bad guy always made a mistake and the hero never got shot. West was a pro when it came to good, clean tackles. He knew to bend his knees, keep his hips low to the ground, lead with his shoulder, and use his legs for power. But if the gun went off by mistake—or on purpose—what then?

"Whoever you are behind me, I can hear you," Jason said, without taking his eyes off Baz. "Come any closer, and this asshole dies. You're probably next."

"Jason," West said. "Put down the gun."

Jason sighed. "Walk away, Jeremiah. I already warned you to stay out of my way."

"What the hell is he talking about?" Baz shouted. "You two pricks in this together?"

"Shut up, Baz." West took a hesitant step toward Jason and then, when nothing happened, another.

"I'm warning you," Jason said.

"Of what? You going to shoot him and then shoot me? Really?"

"Don't tempt me."

"Get the gun, moron," Baz said. "Then we can shoot this guy together. Shove that gun up his ass and pull the trigger."

"Shut up, Baz."

"Don't be so hasty, Jeremiah. Everyone deserves their last words, right?"

"Come a little closer," Baz said. "I dare you. See what you can do when you're not standing ten feet away hiding behind that gun like a pussy."

"Says the guy belly-down licking dirt just because the man with the gun told him to."

"'Man'?" Baz laughed.

West was momentarily tempted to walk away and let events play out however they would.

"You don't want to do this," he said instead.

"Pretty sure I do." Jason cocked the gun. "I don't think I've ever wanted to do anything more."

"You can't just kill someone in the middle of the street. Even *him*."

"That was before," Jason said. "Haven't you noticed? These days you can do whatever the hell you want, even in the middle of the street. Just ask *him*. You always do what you want, don't you, Baz? Why shouldn't I get in on the fun?"

Someone who was better with words might have had more options.

West didn't have any. He tucked his head, bent his knees, and tackled him.

Jason tumbled to the ground, with West sprawled on top of him. Baz hooted with delight. Jason kept his hold on the gun. Trapped between them, it dug hard into West's gut. Baz was already running away. "You two crazy kids have fun together," he shouted in parting.

West tried to roll away, but Jason clung tight, both to him and to the gun. "I could kill you for that," he said. "I should. Pull the trigger. End it."

With a grunt, West shoved him away and scrambled to his feet, but couldn't get his hands on the gun. Jason stood, too.

"You want to be one of them, you should be punished like one of them."

"You're not a superhero," West said. "You don't get to run around punishing wrongdoers."

Jason grinned down at his weapon. "Thanks to this, I think I get to do whatever I want." He gestured with the gun. "Sit."

"No."

"Try again."

"You think I'm the reason Nick ditched you?" West snorted. "He must have figured out he was too good for you." It was probably unwise, but West was all out of fear.

"But not for *you*?" Jason looked ready to pull the trigger.

"He *was* too good for me. But you were supposedly his best friend. I figured you'd be . . . better."

Jason dropped his hands. Then sank to the ground, laying the gun down beside him.

"I was," he said. "I think I was."

West knew he should snatch the gun. Instead, he reached for Jason's hand and pulled him back to his feet. The gun lay on the ground between them.

"What is all this?" West asked. "What are you doing?"

"I don't know," Jason said, shaking his head as if to clear a fog. "It . . . it seemed like something I had to do."

"Shoot Baz?"

"I saw the girl toss the gun in the trash can—"

"What girl?"

"Who knows? Some little girl—she comes running out of the cop shop, tosses a gun in the Dumpster. Like a TV show. It seemed like a sign. Like it *wanted* me to take it. Use it. Then I'm walking home, and Baz comes along, and it just all . . . slid into place." He nudged the gun with his sneaker. "I'm a pacifist, you know. I led a protest against the war when I was in second grade. I think guns should be outlawed. But . . ."

"Yeah?"

"It felt *good*."

"I'm taking this," West said, and lifted the gun. It was

smaller than his father's hunting rifles, but seemed oddly heavier. This had not been designed for killing animals.

"I'll find another way," Jason said. His hair was standing on end and sweat matted his shirt. West tried not to notice how the damp cotton clung to his lean shoulders. "I don't want to, not right at this moment, but you've got to understand. I wake up in the morning and it's all I can think about. I go to sleep, it's all I can think about. I *dream* about killing this guy. Making him scream and cry and maybe suck himself off first, and then killing him dead. Right now, before you found us? That's the first time all week I haven't felt like throwing up. When I had that gun in my hand. That's the only thing that made it go away. And it's going to come back. It always comes back."

"I don't understand." That was a lie. Didn't he understand temptation, a need so intense it made you sick?

"Join the club. But I'm telling you. Take the gun, it won't matter. Something's wrong with me."

"You're angry. I get that." But it was more than that, wasn't it? There *was* something wrong with him—there was something wrong with everyone lately. Even at home, things got weirder by the day. The Thomases were gone, without explanation. Mr. Thomas had never made it back from his midnight "hunting trip," and Mrs. Thomas had, according to West's mother, gone to stay with some friends on the other side of town. Except her belongings were right where she'd left them, in the guest bedroom.

Except his mother had spent the last two nights in the kitchen, furiously baking Maddie Thomas's famous pumpkin pie.

Jason shook his head. "You don't get it. And that's good. Nick wouldn't get it, either, I don't think. Maybe you're right about me. Me and him, I mean."

"I don't know you well enough to be right or wrong about you." He hesitated. "I didn't really know him, either." West told himself he was just saying it to placate Jason—that the important thing was making sure Jason didn't find himself another gun.

Jason punched him in the shoulder.

"What the hell was that for?" West asked.

"Uh, hetero jock male bonding?" Jason laughed. "Think I saw it on TV."

"Oh, well, if you saw it on *TV.*"

"Can I ask you something?" Jason said.

"Guess we'll see."

"What was it with you two? What the hell did you even talk about? Or did you just . . ."

West could feel himself blushing. "No, we didn't 'just.' Not that it's any of your business. We . . ." He paused. They had talked about everything and nothing—that was the easy answer. Old football footage and new draft picks, teachers they hated, stupid jingles of commercials past that got stuck in their heads for days. But it was impossible to explain how any of that had added up to something more. How talking about nothing somehow mattered more when you could do it without lying—and before Nick, lying was all he'd known. "We talked a lot about football, I guess. He was into that."

Jason smiled, almost fondly. "You know he dragged me to every game. Before, I mean."

West shook his head. He and Nick hadn't happened until after the season, and Nick had never let on that he cared about the Bulldogs one way or another. They talked pro ball, college ball—but never anything that touched on real life, on the world West was set to rejoin in the fall.

"He liked to coach from the bleachers, you know? He was always convinced he knew better. That if he'd been down there . . ." Jason shrugged. "I can tell you, he loved watching *you*. Guess that's no surprise."

"I guess."

"He never said, but I always kind of thought he was so into it because he would have been down there himself if it wasn't for his leg. Like he wanted to *be* you, right?"

It had never occurred to West. The idea unsettled him.

"So much for my Psych 101 skills," Jason added. "Clearly he had . . . other motives."

West couldn't decide whether he wanted to get out of there and never see Jason again, or drag him home and hold him as a keepsake—a scrap of Nick, enshrined with the same care as the borrowed CDs and handwritten birthday limerick and ratty sweatshirt that still smelled of Nick's shampoo. "Can I ask you something now?"

"Guess we'll see."

"What was with his limp?"

"He never told you?"

"We didn't . . . talk about that kind of thing."

Jason hesitated.

"He's gone," West said. It hurt to say it out loud, more than it should have. "Whatever the big secret was, it can't matter now."

"No secret," Jason said finally. "Or if there is, I don't know it, either. There was an accident, when he was a kid. He was at his grandparents' place for the summer, and he fell off the tractor or something. Nothing too scandalous. It never stopped hurting him, though. He wouldn't admit it, but . . ."

"But you could tell." West had thought he was doing Nick a favor, not asking about it. He'd thought they both preferred pretending away the hard stuff. "Thank you. For telling me."

"You're welcome," Jason said, and leaned in. And kissed him.

Lips and tongue and breath and flesh and a brush of hair against his forehead and the pressure of fingers along his jawline: this was, for a moment, all that mattered.

This felt good.

And then West remembered himself and remembered Nick, who was gone but still held a claim over him. West wasn't about to betray him, allowing another set of lips and another pair of hands to make his disobedient body feel things it was no longer supposed to feel. He shoved Jason away, hard as he could. It didn't erase the fact that he'd let someone steal Nick's place. Or that he'd liked it.

"I'm sorry," Jason said, smearing a hand across his mouth as if to wipe away the kiss. "I don't know why I did that."

Too late, West thought to check the street, which was still mercifully empty, but there were plenty of houses with plenty of windows. Even with the phones down, news in this town traveled fast.

"Get out of here," West said. "Get away from me."

"I didn't . . . I wasn't trying to . . ." Jason sounded more afraid now than he had when they were scuffling for the gun.

"I wanted to see what the big deal was. You made him happy. Happier than I could make him. I wanted to know why."

All of the pain that West had buried, everything he'd stuffed inside himself and hidden away, Jason was wearing it across his face. West hated him for that, for being what West, what even Nick, could never be. Someone with no secrets. It made him angry, and the anger made it easy to be as mean as he needed to be.

"He picked me over you. Deal with it."

"I wasn't in love with him, you know."

"Could've fooled me."

"We were *friends*," Jason said. "Surely even a Neanderthal like you can comprehend the concept of—"

West snorted and turned away.

"Okay! Don't go. I'm sorry, it . . . slipped out?"

"Yeah, I'm always calling people Neanderthals by accident." But he stayed.

"We were just friends," Jason said. "And then we weren't. And yeah, that was because of you. I lost him. You got him."

"You waiting for an apology?"

"I'm not saying I blame you. I'm saying . . ."

*"What?"*

"I lost him," Jason said. "And now you lost him, too. We both did. I thought . . . I don't know. That made us the same, somehow. That it would be better, to have someone else who understands."

West was tempted. But what right had he to feel any better when Nick was in the ground?

"You should go," he told Jason. All at once, his anger drained away. "And promise me you'll stay away from Baz."

"I told you, I can't do that."

"Then at least promise you'll try."

"Honestly, what do you care what happens to that guy?"

"Honestly? I don't," West said. "Not about what happens to him."

"Oh." He seemed unsure of how to take that. So was West. "I'll do my best."

West felt better knowing he had the gun. "And you ever jump me in broad daylight like that again, you'll have bigger problems than Baz."

Jason saluted. "Understood, sir." He waited until he was halfway down the street to call back a jaunty "So it's all good, then, if I wait till dark?"

Somehow, West managed to hold down the smile until he was safely out of sight.

It was ten days after the storm when Jule woke beneath a heavy weight, with the parasite's callused palm over her mouth. He was straddling her; he was naked. She struggled beneath him, but, drunk and scrawny as he may have been, he still had several inches and at least fifty pounds on her, and he was unmovable.

She'd once, as a child, been in a minor car accident and woken to find herself stretched out on a morgue-like slab, trapped beneath a heavy lead apron that draped from her neck past her pelvis. There'd been a moment of sheer panic before the doctors' words had sunk in, *hospital* and *tests* and *don't move* (as if she could) and *don't worry* (as if she could stop). It had, as she'd been promised, been all right.

This would not.

His face was nearly pressed against hers, with only his hand separating their lips, the hand that was muzzling her scream. She sucked in air through her nose, but all she could smell was his beery breath. She wondered what would happen if she threw up while his hand was over her mouth, if the puke would spill back down her throat and into her lungs, if there could be a more humiliating way to die.

She pushed at him harder then, harder than she thought she could, fired by an irate refusal to let this disease of a man defeat her.

He didn't move.

It would be all right, she told herself. If she could simply survive this moment, and the next, cling to her life and her sanity until it was over, then it would be a memory. A memory couldn't hurt her. The past could be forgotten, like it had never happened.

It was only a matter of waiting for present to become past.

One moment.

Then the next.

"It's okay," he murmured, smoothing her hair back from her forehead with his free hand. She could feel his *thing* twitching against her thigh. "We don't have to pretend anymore. Your mother's given us her blessing."

Her scream came out as a muffled squeak.

Her mother had been holed up in her room for days. Sick, he'd said, and Jule hadn't questioned it. But now she did, and wondered what he'd done to her.

Because he must have done something, or she would be here, right?

That was what the small, panicked voice at her center said,

the child who had never grown up. *Mommy would save me*, that little girl screamed, and the parasite lay there, heavy and still.

"She wants us to be happy," he said. "Now we can be."

The little girl cried uselessly; the woman, who'd been grown up for too long, reached for the knife.

The knife that shouldn't have been there, because it was only there in her dreams.

She reached with the arm that wasn't pinned beneath his hairy chest, and tried to ignore what his hand was doing, as if it didn't have anything to do with her, wasn't her waistband he was probing beneath, wasn't her body, was just some other unfortunate person, or less than that, some unfortunate, mindless object, its violation a petty crime of trespassing and vandalism but nothing more. Her hand dug beneath her mattress for the thing that shouldn't have been there, and found its handle, and pulled it out, and stabbed it into his thigh.

Now he screamed, and rolled off her, and she pushed him onto the floor. He was flopping and thumping and bleeding like a gutted fish, cursing her, cursing her mother, and the knife wanted her to strike again. The hilt was warm beneath her fingertips, the blood gleamed in the glow of light from the hallway, and the parasite was no threat anymore, not tonight at least, but the knife whispered to her and wanted her to draw it across his throat. She wanted to do it. Oh, she wanted it so much. She maybe, almost, possibly would have given in, if her uncle Scott hadn't bounded into the room, pulled it gently from her fingers, and done the job for her, whispering, "I told you not to steal from me" as the carotid artery split open and the parasite's life spilled out.

"You killed him," she said stupidly.

"No, you did that, Jaybird. I just put him out of his misery."

She had never considered herself the kind of girl who would, like a delicate Victorian flower, faint in a moment of bloody crisis. But a tingle of pins and needles crept down her arms and legs and a film of gray passed across her vision. As a swell of nausea brought the contents of her stomach hurtling into her mouth, she lost the thread. Scott's voice, tinny and distant, warned of something she couldn't be bothered to understand, and then that faded, too. The floor was rising toward her, and then bloodstained arms were around her, and she was gone.

Somehow, she was in the shower, the pink-marble-tiled shower in Cassandra Porter's private bathroom, a cold spray blasting her face and her body, which was still in its clothes. The water pooling in the clogged tub was pink. It had all been real.

Uncle Scott was with her, holding her up. His fingers were stained with the parasite's blood.

She gagged, and staggered out of the shower, reaching the toilet just in time to heave a thin stream of bile into its bowl. Scott rubbed her back.

"First time's the toughest," he said.

She didn't know whether she was supposed to be grateful.

"Do I want to know how you got your hands on my knife?" he asked, and fortunately, she gagged again, saving both of them the answer.

He sat with her, and he waited until her hiccupy breathing smoothed and the dry heaving stopped. As she washed her hair and scrubbed her body and changed into fresh, unstained clothes, trying to ignore the body beside her bed, he washed off his knife in the sink, humming one of his country songs, as if he were doing the dishes. And when he decided she was ready, he informed her that they had work to do. Then pointed toward the body, with the knife.

She shook her head.

No.

*No.*

"We can't just leave him here, Jaybird. That'd be worse than leaving him alive."

"Self-defense," she whispered, a half-remembered excuse from a half-remembered crime show.

"I don't want to know what went on in here between the two of you. And I promise you, the cops don't, either. You're a Prevette. That's all that matters. Hey now, don't start that again."

She wasn't aware she was crying until he wiped the back of his hand across her cheek.

"He was stealing from me," Uncle Scott said. "Your mother always did like the dumb ones. I was going to get around to it sooner or later. You just got there sooner."

"My mother—"

"Your mother's ruined," Scott said. She didn't want to know what that meant. There was only so much one night could hold. "And that's another reason not to cry over this slug. Now take that sheet and help me wrap him up."

"I can't."

"Sure you can."

She shook her head, hard, harder, hard enough to knock the night out of her skull.

"He's not going to get rid of himself."

"Axe," she said, aware she sounded like a child trying to weasel out of her chores. "Or Teddy. They can do it."

"Yeah, they *can*. But you *will*. No more free ride, Jaybird. No more pretending you're anything but what you are. You're a grown-up now. Time to join the family."

She literally couldn't move. What would he do if she refused to help?

"You need a little fortification," he said. "I get it. Come with me."

"Where?"

"Come."

Anywhere had to be better than this room, with its ripening smell of blood and guts. So she followed Scott down the hallway, pausing only to peek in on her mother. Annie Prevette lay exactly where she had the last time Jule spotted her, sprawled in bed on a spreading pile of clutter and filth, her face pale and sweaty, her limbs thrashing in time with the punk metal blasting from the speakers. "Sick," maybe. Useless, definitely.

They ended up in Scott's room, where his newest woman lay naked in his bed, her eyelids fluttering and a watery smile on her face. Giuliana had shown up at the house a couple of days before and never left; she rarely came out of the bedroom. Scott ignored her, and retrieved a small collection of items from the nightstand:

A strip of tinfoil.

A lighter.

A small plastic bag of fractured crystals.

A pipe.

Jule shook her head again. This would not be her life. She'd vowed that a long time ago. She'd stuck to it.

He put his finger to his lips and nodded to the woman, then led Jule back out to the hallway. He took a seat at the top of the stairs and patted the carpet beside him, waiting for her to join.

She was afraid not to.

"It will help," he said. "Just this once."

"I don't need that. It's fine, let's just do this."

He squeezed her wrist, too hard. "Jule, you got a man in your room who bled like a stuck pig all over your pretty pink floor, and unless you want that room to start stinking like the back room of a butcher shop, we gotta get that body out of there, clean up all the blood. Then load the corpse into the truck. Drive out to the swamps and make sure no one ever finds it again. Come back here, burn our clothes. Then tell your mother, if she ever bothers to ask, that we got no idea where her precious husband is, and let her think that he just ran off. Then you got to go back to that room, where you killed that man, and go to sleep. You think you can do all that without a little fortification, you tell me now. But I'm telling you, this will help."

She didn't say anything.

"You got no one in this world who loves you like I do, Jule."

She had no one, period, she thought. If he loved her, he wouldn't make her do this.

It sounded nice, and maybe it was true for the kind of

people who lived in houses like this for real, who could afford to make pretty ultimatums and choose who was worthy of them. She wished Scott didn't love her, because then she wouldn't know that love looked like this. It was what she had; it was what it was.

And he was the one who had come for her.

She took the thin glass pipe and the foil from his large hand. "I don't know how."

So he showed her.

West took his time getting home. He'd found that a long, aimless walk, letting his feet go one way and his mind another, suited him nearly as much as those hours in the car. Things moved slower by foot, but he had nothing to outrun. Walking through the fields, the horizon drawing no closer no matter how many steps he took, was like being trapped in suspended animation, standing perfectly still despite the illusion of motion. It seemed fitting.

When he finally did make it back, his father was waiting for him on the front porch, two suitcases at his feet. His expression made the point perfectly clear: in Oleander, even with the phones down, bad news traveled faster than foot traffic. West wondered whether some nosy spy behind one of the windows on State Street had alerted his parents by semaphore. Or maybe carrier pigeon. Whatever it had been, the damage was done. West knew better than to expect a reprieve. Being a West meant honoring your promises and sticking by your choices. In doing neither, West had proved himself unworthy of the name. And if surviving this with his family intact required disavowing Nick, he wasn't sure he could.

He took a deep breath, preparing for his father's questions or accusations, trying to decide whether to deny or confess, and, lost in the labyrinth of options and consequences, he didn't notice his father's fist clenching and rearing back. It wasn't until the roundhouse punch had knocked him off the porch that it occurred to him this wasn't going to be a conversation.

"I really thought I could live with it," said his father, who suddenly had a rifle in his hand. "Then you go and shame us like that? In public?" He whacked West in the shin with the butt of the rifle. A bolt of pain shot through his leg. "You shamed your *mother*."

West raised himself from the ground enough to see his mother behind the parlor window, watching events play out. There was a distant, polite expression fixed to her face, as if she were watching someone else's child in a school play and making the minimal effort necessary to pretend she was paying attention. He found her tears unbearable, but he would have preferred them to this.

His father just looked . . . empty. Vacant behind the eyes. The rifle came down again, this time on his shoulder, and West cried out.

"Shut up!" his father roared. "There's only so much bullshit a man can swallow."

Now, it was his leg again, with a sickening crack. West's shinbone was on fire. His father's face was unrecognizable.

"Please stop." It was a whimper. It was humiliating. But he hurt so much, and now his father—his *father*—had dropped the rifle and was using his face for a punching bag, and cursing at him, and calling him disgusting, and West was big, maybe even bigger than his father, but he couldn't hit back. He couldn't do that.

And in the midst of it all, Nick's voice in his ear, with a reminder. *You still have the gun.*

He couldn't do that.

His mother was tapping on the window glass with her long fingernails, and now she was smiling.

"You had enough?" His father *laughed.* "That enough for you?"

Men didn't cry; his father had taught him that a long time ago. He was full of lessons. West blinked back tears.

"You think you hurt?" his father asked. "You don't know pain until you waste your life raising an animal. At least I can slaughter a cow and get something out of it. What good are you?"

This wasn't right. This wasn't him.

He spit in West's face.

"Don't come back here, Jeremiah. This rifle's not just for show."

Phlegm dripped down West's cheek; his nose bled; his leg throbbed. But he rose to his feet.

"Go ahead, Dad. Shoot me. If that's what you want."

It almost looked like it was.

"I'm tired of lying," West said. "You're not worth it. This family's not worth it."

"This family's not yours anymore. You saw to that. We won't bear your shame."

"No. Just yours."

The rifle leveled itself at him.

No. His *father* leveled the rifle. At him.

"This is my home," West said. "This is always going to belong to me."

"Go."

*You still have the gun,* the voice whispered.

He didn't take the suitcases; he didn't say goodbye. His parents were already gone. Soon, limping down the dirt road toward town, the sleeve of his sweatshirt blotting his bloody nose, the sky pinking up, so was he.

The deacon had taken Ellie that day to see the pyre, rising twelve feet into the sky, built from the wreckage of Oleander.

It was no wonder she couldn't sleep.

All she had to do, he'd explained, was stand there. Offer, via her presence and her silence, a divine stamp of approval. She hadn't asked what she was supposed to do if she didn't approve, and the thought never occurred to him. She hadn't asked any questions, because she'd been too shocked by the hastily stacked debris and the vision he painted for her, of scorching justice and righteous fire. Or because she was a coward.

That restless night, she gave up on sleep. She went to the church, to a small, secret room in the empty corridors; she knelt, and she prayed. *Tell me what to do,* she asked, *tell me what to ask and what to say and how to stop being so afraid.*

Instead, the voice told her she was a worthless joke, and what she should do was kill herself, and that was the only voice she heard.

She was crying when the lights came on and the deacon stepped inside.

"You're distressed," he said, and put his hands on her shoulders and raised her up.

She nodded, wiping away her tears.

"The time for doubts is over, Ellie," he said. "They only bring pain. I should know." He chuckled, rubbing his bandaged palms together. Some kind of accident with a hammer and nails, he'd said—a lesson for him to remember. "This is an age for certainty."

She couldn't look at him.

"Ellie," he said, then gently tilted her chin so she was forced to meet his gaze. "What is it? What do you need?"

*Someone to tell me what to do,* she almost said, *meant* to say, but the words wouldn't come out.

"It's the pyre," she said. "It's Cass. I can't do it." And then, so softly she couldn't even hear herself, "I can't let you do it."

"*I'm* not going to do anything. *The town* will judge her, and when the town finds her wanting, the town will seek its justice. Finally. And you'll see, Ellie, it will be as if a burden has been lifted from us. 'The Lord will wash away the filth of the women of Zion; he will cleanse the bloodstains from Jerusalem by a spirit of judgment and a spirit of fire.' Isaiah 4:4."

"It's not right," she said.

"I'll tell you what's not right. A murderer—a murderer of an *innocent baby*—not paying for her crimes. What else has our work been for, if not to guide this town to righteousness, to purge the sinners, and what better place to start than bringing the town's original sinner to justice?"

"It's *not right*."

He shook his head, sorrowful at her lapse of faith. "The Lord tell you that?"

"He didn't have to."

"Because if not, I don't see what makes you think you know right from wrong better than I do."

Was it true, what they said, that she had talked to God?

Was she talking to God still, as they believed? Did the filthy pronunciations on the state of her soul and the depths of her sin come from above, below, or merely within?

Ellie no longer knew.

There had been a brief flash of clarity once, she remembered that. In the darkness of the storm, light had shone through. It hadn't lasted. It never did.

Now there was only doubt, and the voice, and the deacon. He was sure, so she didn't have to be. At least, that was how it was meant to work.

"I'm not going to stand there while you set a girl on fire," she said.

"She's got the devil in her. You know what you have to do with the devil."

"The devil works by fire," Ellie said. "And you don't know what it's like when . . . someone burns."

He took her shoulders again and turned her to face him. His face was so bloated and red.

"You're fragile, Ellie. But the world is not. The world is hard, and it's full of hard choices. Someone like you shouldn't have to be troubled by making them."

"Let you make them for me, you mean."

"I wouldn't put it that way, but yes. I'm here to guide you," he said. "I'd like to think that the Lord brought us together so you wouldn't have to walk this path alone."

*But you* are *alone,* the voice said. *You will always be alone.*

*That is your fate.*

*That is your purpose.*

The deacon stood. "I worry about you, Ellie. We both know how far you've come. But every sin leaves its mark."

"I've been cleansed," she said. "Reborn."

"We all backslide. We all face temptations."

She shook her head.

"You need clarity, Ellie."

That was true.

"You need help remembering, and we can do that. Haven't I always helped you?"

She didn't need to ask what he was doing when he crossed the room and slipped into the private bathroom adjacent to his office. Soon she heard the water running. It would take some time to fill the tub, and then he would call for her.

She could leave right now.

She could walk away.

But he had always helped her; he had always known what she needed.

He summoned her.

Methamphetamine was first synthesized in 1893; it took fifty years for the drug to make it to the United States, where it was quickly embraced as a miracle cure. Within a few years, the drug had become the standard treatment for narcolepsy, weight gain, depression, anxiety, schizophrenia, hyperactivity, alcoholism, fatigue, impotence, and the common cold. Meth wove its way into the fabric of the nation, the quintessential American drug: a way for hardworking men and women to work even harder. Ads promised a dose would keep workers "peppy"; they showed housewives vacuuming euphorically, a little meth kick all that was needed to keep the little woman high on the drudgery of life. And its promise, in the short term, was no lie. For the uninitiated and the unravaged, meth offered a bump in concentration, energy, and focus—hence its appeal to factory workers, who could, until use turned to addiction turned to decay, pull eighteen-hour shifts without sleep and without complaint. It made the intolerable tolerable. It got you through.

That night, it did so for Jule.

There are five stages of a meth hit, even as small a one as Scott allowed her. As she helped him roll the body in expensive sheets, as she scrubbed at bloodstains on her hands and knees, as she loaded the corpse into the pickup, she luxuriated in stage one: euphoria. A rush of adrenaline and ecstasy floated her through the dark logistics, every swipe of the sponge against the bleached carpeting a blessed rhythm, a song that beat with the pulse of her heart, a happiness like she'd never known.

By the time the truck sped into the swamps, the mania had subsided into a smooth, easy high, a sense of well-being so rock solid she wasn't even troubled by the thought that this wasn't the first body Scott would have dumped in the water she'd so often used to bathe. Scott, who'd shot up a little crystal fortitude of his own, talked the entire way, increasing in volume and speed as they drew closer to the swamp. The body thumped about in the back of the pickup, so loudly that Jule had to stop herself from turning around to check that it hadn't returned to life in order to claim its revenge. The prospect only made her laugh.

"That's what the Man does, you know, you got to think about it from all the angles and you'll see he's got to fool us into keeping *ourselves* down. In this country we *volunteer* to get shit on. Military service? Voluntary. Giving up our hard-earned money to some government asshole with a shit-eating grin just because he mailed you a form and asked for it? Voluntary. You know Congress makes a hundred new laws per year? You know it's illegal here for a man to catch a fish with his own bare hands? Or to piss against the side of a building? They want *life* to be illegal, so they've always got an excuse to lock you up. They can lock you up for spitting on the sidewalk, but who's locking them up? That's what I want to know. They're the crooks. They're the terrorists. Who's locking *them* up?"

She was a pro at tuning him out. But this time, his words washed over her as if they were water, dripping down her body and slipping inside, and she found herself nodding. Yes, *yes*, it made sense, it felt *good* to have someone to blame for the mess of her life, someone who wasn't Uncle Scott, who rode beside her with his leg kicked up on the dash and his knee steering the truck and loved her like no one else would and killed so she wouldn't have to. There were soldiers in the town and the soldiers worked for the government and maybe the government *had* caused the storm and definitely the government was keeping them all locked up in this hellhole and if it weren't for that she could be on the road by now, she would have put miles between herself and the knife and she never would have jammed it into the parasite's puffy flesh and felt the blade work its way through gristle and meat as if it were tearing at a slab of steak. Though maybe it would have been a shame to miss that. All experience was good experience, yes? And perverts deserved to pay.

Yes, she thought. *Yes*. She felt like saying it to the universe, like her *life* should be one giant *yes*, like that was its entire point and, stupid as ever, she'd taken this long to figure it out. She didn't have to feel like her body was crawling with spiders just because some asshole wouldn't stop looking at her; she didn't have to lie in shit. She could take what she needed; she *should* take what she *wanted*. That's all Scott had ever done, and who had the right to knock him down for that? Who had the right to lock him up?

Jule was beaming as they unloaded the body from the trunk, a sarcophagus in seven-hundred-thread-count sheets. She couldn't stop a giggle from slipping out as they dragged it a short ways across the marsh and then, with two of Axe's barbells tied to its ankles, dropped it into the water. There were catfish in there, Scott said, fierce scavengers, and they'd make short work of him. It seemed unlikely that anything could live in those murky waters, but he'd been right about so many things so far, surely he was right about this, too, surely he knew all. Suddenly, overcome by this man who could take her up in his arms, lift her like a small child, and in one fell swoop make everything okay, she hugged him, and buried her head in his chest, which smelled like swamp and blood, and didn't know whether she was laughing or crying. The work was done; the night was finished; the parasite was gone forever.

And it was good.

When they arrived back at the house, all was dark and

silent. Scott put her back into her bed and brushed the hair off her forehead and told her not to let the bedbugs chomp on her innards, and when she said she couldn't do it, couldn't lie here where she would dream of the parasite and where the air was clogged with bleach and lemon-scented freshener and where she could wake up with him on top of her even though he was decaying at the bottom of a lake, Scott told her she could do it, and *yes*, with eye-opening surprise, she saw that she could.

"You never tell anyone what happened tonight," Scott said. "You even think about it, and I put *you* in the swamp. That would hurt me, but I'd do it. You get that?"

Yes, she did.

Afterward, most of the evening's events were left mercifully blurred in her memory, but she would always remember promising to keep her mouth shut. She would always remember saying thank you, and meaning it, because she didn't know then how hard it would be to forget, not just the smell of the body or the feel of the knife or the weight of the parasite and the twitch of his thing, but the glorious joy of the crystal coursing through her veins, the power and the clarity it gave her—and the hollow it left when it had gone.

Ellie knelt by the tub, with the deacon beside her. Steam rose from the water. She didn't need to dip a finger to know it would be scalding hot, but she did so anyway, hoping the pain might clear her mind. It didn't; it just hurt. It would hurt more if she disrobed and lowered herself into the water. She would scream, and thrash around a bit, and fear her skin was bubbling and burning, but in the end she would close her eyes and have faith and the Lord would guide her down.

At the beginning, it had been the deacon's arms that guided her, seizing her bare shoulders and forcing her deeper into the boil until her body was submerged. Afterward, her skin would be raw and painful for days, but his promise held true: there was no lasting damage.

"Your clothes," he said now. "You remember."

The day her mother had discovered her with Baz, there'd been no time to gather her clothes and cover herself. Charlotte King had forced her wayward fourteen-year-old daughter into the car, driven to the deacon's house, and dumped her on the doorstep, shivering, wet, and naked. The first bath had been curative, a warm, healing temperature to ease her shock and soak up her tears. It was only later, after the deacon had introduced her to the bedroom she would occupy until reformation was complete and her mother accepted her back into the fold, and to the daily schedule of chores and prayers, the ascetic, nunlike existence in which she would serve her penance, that he had introduced the cleansing ritual, the baptism of pain. He always carefully averted his eyes from her naked form.

That first day, he had taken her from her mother's arms and covered her nakedness with the closest thing to hand, a dusty white sheet. She would always be grateful for that. Her mother found her bare and put her out; the deacon covered her and took her in. He had given her shelter, understanding, and, eventually, the Lord.

Salvation hurts, he told her.

Pain helps us defy temptation, he told her.

Pain will not let us forget.

She skimmed her fingers across the water again.

Pain.

"You've let in the devil before, Ellie. If you begin to think you can trust your own mind over the word of God, well, we know where that leads, don't we?"

She could not go back to that.

But the water would burn, as Cassandra would burn, and she needed no one's word to tell her that was wrong. That had to be wrong. Didn't it?

The baths were their secret. She knew how people would talk if they knew. She knew what people would think.

They would be wrong.

It would be better if there were something indecent about the way his eyes passed over her naked body. If there were ulterior motives in his gaze, or in his touch. It would mark him as human—flawed as any of them, sympathetic to the desires of the flesh, victim to his own desires. But there was nothing in his gaze. There was no hint of impropriety, no thought of pleasure or trespass. He burned with righteousness, and nothing else. She'd never been a girl standing before him, naked and shivering. She'd been a sinner, with potential to be saved; she'd been a pawn in the devil's game.

*See me,* she wanted to insist. But she recognized the impulse as a symptom of her own sickness. To strip her clothes off, as he intended, then force him to see what he'd wrought, the skin that would blister in the water, the smooth flesh he was forbidden. *Touch me*—if it would remind him that she was a person, that *he* was a person, that there existed anything beyond law and judgment and God's wrath.

He clamped down on her hand. Not in the way of a man

reaching out for a girl, not like a father, or a lover. He held on because he needed her for his cause. Because he wanted her to burn bright.

She could see it in him now: he wanted everything to burn.

"Let me help you find your way back," he said.

She tried to pull her hand away. "I'm leaving."

He squeezed tighter. And she slapped him.

It was as if her arm had worked of its own accord. They both gaped at it, equally surprised.

"You're very disturbed," he said. "I can see we have a lot of work to do."

She slapped him again.

He snatched her wrists before she could go in for a third.

He would let go if she insisted. She knew that about him; she thought she knew that about him. All she had to do was follow through on her word and walk out.

*But you haven't.*

*You're waiting for him.*

"I won't stand by and let you kill someone tomorrow," she said. "I won't let you."

He laughed. "You won't 'let' me?"

"People listen to me now. You saw to that."

"Let me tell you what's going to happen if you go through that door, Eleanor King." This was not the honey-voiced peacock who fluffed his feathers for her at every opportunity. This was someone new, someone cold and honest and empty of illusion.

*The real Deacon Wally Barnes,* she thought, and was afraid.

"Let me paint you a picture of how this is going to go if

you leave here like this, much less if you try to stop me tomorrow, or anytime from here to eternity."

*You want him to make you scream.*

*If you wanted to stop him, you would make him scream.*

*You would slice him up.*

*Slice it off.*

There was a letter opener on his desk. She could see it over his shoulder, through the door, sharp and gleaming in the fluorescent light.

*You know who you are.*

*Soon everyone will know.*

*Give in to it.*

*Give in.*

It had to be the voice of God, she thought. It knew too much. It saw her too clearly.

"I will tell everyone in this godforsaken town how you tried to seduce me—"

"That's a lie!"

"—how I've put up with it for the sake of trying to guide you back to the way of righteousness, but I can put up with it no longer."

"No one would believe that."

But she could see that, already, he did.

"Silence, harlot. They will believe it because it's God's truth, and because you're stained in a way that will never wash away, and when I open their eyes, they will see."

"Then I'll tell them *you*—"

He held up a finger, and she fell silent. "Don't be so foolish as to believe you have the support of this town. You're an empty vessel for them. You're a tool. Without me speaking for you, you're nothing."

She shook her head. But, true to his word, she could not speak.

"I'll tell your parents you're a godless harlot, and they will believe it because they already know it to be true. And when I tell them it's best for them to put you out, when I tell them the only way you'll find your way back to the light is if we let you stumble into deepest darkness, they'll believe that, too. The town will know you to be a fraud. That you've never spoken to God, never heard His voice, that you've been lying all along, that you've made *fools* of them, and let me tell you, Ellie, no one likes to be made a fool of. No one likes that at *all*. You'll knock on doors, begging for a place to stay, for food and drink, for a single friend in all the world, and all will turn you away, because they'll take one look at you—pathetic and, soon enough, stinking of the streets—and know I speak the truth, that you're worse than nothing, you're a *pretender,* and they will shut their doors to you, and expel you into the wilderness. You will have nothing left, and nowhere to go, and naught to do but crawl into a hole and wait to die."

The bath awaited. She needed only strip herself bare for him and let him guide her down.

"Your choice."

*Slice it off.*

Her eyes betrayed her, straying to the bulge in his trousers.

*Watch the blood spurt.*

*An eye for an eye.*

*Justice served.*

The voice knew what she wanted, but she knew what was right.

She fled.

And all that he predicted would soon come to pass.

You didn't sleep. Not on meth. You got high, then you tweaked, then you went cold and dark and took some more so you could feel something other than empty. Then you started again.

So maybe she hadn't slept. She couldn't have. But somehow, lying in that bed, she lost herself for a time. When she found herself again, she found herself in Scott's doorway.

He was naked, tangled with the woman and the sheets.

Jule was holding his knife.

If he looked up and saw her there—

If it happened again, and the next time, she zoned out through not just the retrieval of the knife but its use—

If she had gotten a taste for it, and the knife had gotten a taste for her—

It was a silly thing to be afraid of. But she had no idea how she'd ended up there, or how the blade had ended up in her hand, or what might have happened next. In the dark, on that particular night, anything seemed possible.

In the dark, the drug leaching from her system, nothing seemed bearable. Not lying down in that bedroom, beside that bleached-out spot in the carpet, not with the Prevettes assembled down the hall, not with Scott knowing what she knew and worrying about what she would say. Not trusting herself to stay safe and stay hidden in her sleep.

She packed a small bag, tiptoed down the stairs, and fled.

She brought the knife.

* * *

Daniel couldn't sleep. Not knowing what was going to happen to Cass tomorrow; not until he found a way to stop it.

He'd exhausted the narrow range of legal options. Demanding she have a lawyer, an arraignment, contact with her parents or with anyone in the world outside the quarantine lines—none of it had done any good. Unable to get a straight answer from the cops, he'd gone to Deacon Barnes, thinking that a religious man might realize that things had gone too far and have the moral authority to rein them in. But he'd forgotten what his father had taught him about religious men. The only help Barnes had to offer was an explanation—in short sentences and small words, as if Daniel were slow—that Oleander was on the cusp of transformation. Step one would be remaking the criminal justice system in God's image, complete with final judgment. Even then, he hadn't quite believed it. Not even when he saw what was being built at the center of town, the tower of scrap wood that he recognized from his history textbook as a funeral pyre.

The town was angry, he got that. Crowds could be more violent than individuals—stampedes, riots, lynch mobs. People could go crazy, swept up in a storm of emotion. But he'd known the people of Oleander his whole life. They weren't the type to hang a girl from a tree or set her on fire.

That's what he thought when he went down to the station that last day to persuade someone sane to shut it down. Before he had the chance, Coach Hart, varsity football coach, Eisenhower High gym teacher, and all-around bane of Daniel's existence, had barreled past him, dragging his wife behind. Both were drenched in a massive amount of what looked like blood.

Only the wife was screaming. She was also naked. They were instantly surrounded by cops, all with weapons drawn. "Better let go of her, Sal," one of them said, but the coach held tight. She had her arms wrapped across her chest, but it did little to hide her ample bosom and nothing to shield the rest of her. Blood was everywhere.

"I have to confess to a murder," the coach said in a flat voice. "And my wife here has to confess to adultery."

He squeezed her shoulder, hard enough to make her wince. In a similarly flat voice, she said, "It's true. I'm an adulteress." And then, as if the admission had broken something in her, she started pounding at his chest and shrieking something incoherent. Daniel was pretty sure he caught the word *blowtorch.*

The chief pushed his way to the front of the cluster of cops. "Now, what's all this fuss about, Sal?" he asked, as if the man had wandered in to protest a parking ticket.

"Caught my wife in bed with George Stilton," Sal said, slapping her on the ass, hard, the way he did his players after a touchdown. George Stilton was the high school principal. He wore suspenders, had pubic-like hairs sprouting from his chin, and looked like the kind of guy who'd been carrying a briefcase around since he was six years old. Daniel couldn't imagine him in bed with anyone. "Spent the last couple days taking care of him. Put what's left out on the front stoop for you fellows to collect. But I'll tell you, I just don't have the heart to handle Amelia. A man shouldn't have to bring judgment down on his nearest and dearest, am I right?"

The chief sighed, sounding put-upon. What he did not do, to Daniel's horror, was slap the cuffs on Coach Hart and drag him away. Nor did he offer the coach's wife something to wear.

"What do you want us to do?" the chief asked, as if honestly curious.

The coach shrugged. "I always liked that part in church when they talk about stoning the wicked. Figured as long as we're changing things around here . . ."

"You don't think we have enough to deal with these days, Sal? You want us to start *stoning* people? For adultery?" He shook his head. "It's a man's job to tend to his wife, says so right there in the Bible—maybe you weren't listening to that part in church."

The coach looked suitably chastened.

"You want her stoned, you're going to have to do it yourself. And next time, don't come down here to bother my men unless you've got a real problem for us to handle."

"But, sir," one of the younger cops piped up. "We're just going to . . . send him home? That's it?"

The chief laughed. "You're right, Jackson. I almost forgot. Can't have people thinking we've gone soft around here. The new regime wouldn't like that much. Write him a ticket for . . . oh, let's say making a public nuisance of himself. And another for improper disposal of garbage. Pretty sure leaving a body sitting around on a porch can't be exactly hygienic. That sound all right to you, Sal?"

"Fair enough," Sal said. "I'll get out of your hair now, if these men will be so kind as to lower their weapons."

The men did. Coach Hart—grip on his wife never slipping—waited for them to scrawl out his tickets, then steered his wife out of the station and into the bright afternoon.

"What are you looking at, kid?" the chief asked, catching

Daniel gaping at the scene. "You here to visit your girlfriend again? Better hurry—you know what they say: act now, supplies running out!" The room broke into laughter. Daniel had a very difficult time suppressing his urge to run—not just out of the building, but all the way to the edge of town, to throw himself on the mercy of the soldiers who stood posted on the border, to drop to his knees and beg, if necessary, to let him the hell out.

He had not run away. He had descended into the basement, where they kept Cass locked up. The dark row of cells was familiar to him—he'd been there enough times to bail his father out of trouble—but no matter how many times he tramped down those stairs, his chest still seized when he hit the bottom. There was something about the place, the way sounds echoed off concrete, the stench of drying piss and puke, the scuttle of small creatures in the dark, the shadowed figures that peered out from other cells, shouting at him or at their god, or moaning, or crying, or arguing with the voices in their heads. Maybe it was the cells themselves, always so many of them empty, as if waiting for him. As if he belonged in one, and the jail was just biding its time, waiting until he crossed the wrong line and it could swallow him up. That day, after what he'd seen, it was harder than ever to walk down those stairs—hard to believe he'd be allowed back up. But he forced himself to go to her. He tried not to stare at her bruises—she didn't like that, had refused to answer his questions about what they'd done to her, about whether it hurt. Of course it hurt. Instead, as usual, he dug up something trivial to talk to her about, stories of a happier past. He couldn't even remember now what they had talked about, had barely been aware of it at the time, his mouth running on autopilot while his brain worked the problem, thinking through possible escape routes, none of them possible. He just wasn't the kind of person who planned jailbreaks.

He'd gotten out of there as quickly as he could without letting her know that anything was amiss and, half afraid it was a mistake, hiked out to Jeremiah West's place. The football player had helped Cass out once already, and as a potential ally, he came with some serious advantages, not least of them muscle bulk and a proximity to Baz, whose father surely had access to the cell keys. But West wasn't there, and his parents hadn't even let Daniel in the door. He'd met the Wests before, pushing pies at school bake sales and manning the dunk tank at the spring carnival, and they'd always been farm friendly, all too willing to offer a welcoming hug to anyone even tangentially related to their son. This time, Mrs. West would open the door only a crack, and as Daniel peered through, he caught a glimpse of Mr. West pacing in the background, holding what looked to be a rifle.

So he had gone home.

Only to find his father in the backyard, with Milo, teaching him how to shoot a semiautomatic.

It was the first time since Cass's capture that Daniel had seen Milo smile.

"Put down the gun," Daniel said.

*Calm,* he thought. *Careful.*

"You kidding?" Milo shook his head. "It's an *M16*. They use it in the *army*."

The Preacher ruffled his younger son's hair. "And now we'll use it in ours."

Milo grinned.

Daniel didn't know how he was going to keep his brother from finding out what the town had in store for her, or how he'd face Milo if he couldn't find a way to stop it. The kid had been inconsolable when they came for Cass. For some reason that he refused to explain, he blamed himself. He'd cried for two days straight, and even after Daniel bribed him out of his room with the promise of a junk-food binge, he hadn't managed a real smile. Not like this.

There was almost nothing he wouldn't do to cheer Milo up. Father-son gunplay, however, wasn't on the list.

*"Put down the gun and go in the house."*

"You don't want your little brother to burn in the hellfire, do you?" the Preacher said. "Now, Milo, it's important you aim for the head, because—"

"Milo!"

The boy flinched. The gun fired. Twenty feet away, bark exploded from a tree, and a bird squawked into the sky.

"You nuts?" the Preacher roared. "Shouting at a little boy holding a gun?"

"Milo, please," Daniel said to his brother, whose face had gone pale and pinched. He looked back and forth between his father and his brother, then solemnly placed the rifle into his father's hands.

"Permission for a pee break, sir," he said.

"Permission granted." The Preacher saluted, and Milo returned it with a shy smile, then ran into the house.

"You want to tell me what the hell that was all about?" the Preacher said. "You still grouchy about that girl they're going to light on fire?"

Daniel had never been this angry, or this terrified. "Stay away from him."

"My son? I think not."

"No more guns," Daniel said. "No more army talk."

"I'm his father. I think I know what's best for him a little better than you do."

The Preacher's eyes were clearer than usual. He was, against all odds, sober. For a long time, Daniel had harbored a secret hope, only allowing himself to creep toward it in the dark, when he was on the verge of sleep, and he could be trusted to forget it by morning. If, someday, the Preacher stopped drinking—if he cleaned himself up, finally moved on from the death of his wife, remembered he had children to care for, threw away the bottles, got himself to a meeting and then another one, if he went stone-cold sober—then he'd be himself again. He'd be the father Daniel could barely remember, gruff and occasionally cruel, but a *father* nonetheless, who'd hugged him and cooked him franks 'n' beans and told him bloody bedtime stories that made them both shudder and laugh. If darkness could fall, surely it could also lift—wasn't Cass proof of that?

But now the Preacher had gotten rid of the liquor, and it wasn't Daniel's father who'd been left behind. It was madness.

If it could happen to his father, surely it could happen to Daniel. Darkness could fall on anyone—Cass was proof of that, too. The whole town was proof of that.

Daniel had waited until night came. He couldn't persuade the Preacher back to rationality; he couldn't take Milo out of town; he couldn't let things continue, and leave Milo prey to the Preacher's delusions, and his guns. He waited until night, not because he was hoping a better solution would present itself, but because it would be easier in the dark.

There was a bottle of Vicodin in the bottom drawer of his nightstand, left over from when his father had had his wisdom teeth removed many years before. Saved for a rainy day. Daniel counted out four of the pills, ground them into powder, and poured them into a cup of tea. His father preferred that now to whiskey, and accepted Daniel's peace offering as if it were his due. He drank up.

It took a long time to lug the Preacher's limp body out to the shed. But once Daniel had made it, and caught his breath, and wiped off his sweat, it was easy enough to gather an armful of rope and bungee cord and truss up his father with the knots he'd recently helped Milo learn for a Cub Scout badge. He didn't let himself think about what he'd done, or what he was doing. He stretched a piece of duct tape across his father's mouth, so that in the morning, he couldn't wake Milo with his screams.

Topping the list of things he wouldn't let himself think about: Milo, and what would happen if he found out. What he would think of Daniel then.

What his father would do when Daniel set him free. If Daniel set him free.

They were just knots, Daniel told himself, concentrating on the ropes. They would hold for as long as they needed to, and then he would figure something out. Reef knot. Sheet knot. Double sheet bend. Clove hitch. He was good at knots.

His father was still breathing.

That was good.

\* \* \*

Jule had intended to throw rocks at his window, if she could figure out which one it was. Or maybe just throw caution to the wind and ring the doorbell, even if it meant waking his crazy father. But when she arrived at the Ghent house, Daniel was standing in his bedroom window, watching the night. Jule, one hand still clasped around the knife she had shoved in the wide pocket of her fleece, raised her other hand and waved. Moments later, he came to the door.

"You going to let me in, or what?" Jule said when he'd stood there dumbly for several seconds.

"It's five o'clock."

"Yes."

"In the morning."

"Were you in the middle of something?"

She didn't know how much longer she could keep from crying. She wondered if she looked upset; she wondered if she looked high, and if she still was. "I didn't have anywhere else to go," she said, breaking.

He took her bag and brought her inside. He didn't ask questions.

"Your father?" she said.

Daniel hesitated. "Upstairs. Out cold."

Could he smell it on her? Jule wondered. Could he see it in her darting eyes and widened pupils? The knife fit perfectly in the pocket of her fleece, like it belonged there. She wondered what Scott would think when he woke up to find it missing, along with his niece.

No one stole from Scott Prevette.

The room Daniel brought her into had no posters of punk

bands or swimsuit models and no pools of dirty socks or fraying T-shirts spreading on the floor. But there were enough clues—the neat stack of sci-fi paperbacks on the card-table desk, the framed photo of a very young Milo opening Christmas presents, the map of the world tacked over his bed with ANYWHERE BUT HERE scrawled in thick black letters across the entire American Midwest—to indicate ownership. Jule shook her head and started backing out. "I don't know what you thought, but—"

"Oh, this isn't a booty call?" Daniel pressed his hand to his chest. "How will my poor, broken heart ever survive?"

Under other circumstances, Jule might have observed that lack of sleep had made him feisty, and he should consider staying up all night more often. But she could say nothing; the night had been too hard, and too long. She was done.

"Hey, are you okay?"

She nodded furiously, lips clamped together until she could control what spilled out of them. Her face heated up with alarming speed, and her clothes were suddenly entirely too heavy and too tight. It was like one of those hot flashes that middle-aged women on TV were always complaining about, and it made her want to fling open the window and heave lungfuls of the night air—to climb out, if necessary, just to be out of this room and out from under Daniel's stare. She was done with being watched.

"Jule, you're shaking," Daniel said, approaching her, and she slipped her hand into her pocket and touched the knife. He stopped short of touching her. "What is it? What happened?"

"I . . ." She held her breath, cutting off a sob before it could slip out. That had been too soon. She took a deep, measured breath. She could hold off the tears, no problem. But the trembling was out of her control.

It was humiliating. But Daniel pretended it wasn't happening, which helped. "You can have my bed," he told her, in a voice that nearly approximated friendly, unconcerned chatter. "Sorry to disappoint you, but I'll stay in Milo's room. Sheets are . . . well, clean enough, I guess, and if you want to borrow a T-shirt or something, they're in the bottom drawer."

She shook her head, already undoing her boots and climbing into the bed fully clothed, pulling the covers up around her. The hot flash faded nearly as quickly as it had arrived, and now she was almost cold, but pleasurably so. The sheets were scratchy, but warm, and smelled like him.

"Or I guess you could just sleep in that," he said. "Bathroom's right next door, and Milo's is the second door down. If you need me, I mean. Not that you'll—well, you know what I mean."

"You don't have to go yet," she said quietly. Holding it together. "I mean, don't go. Yet. Okay?"

"Uh . . ."

"You can hang out for a while," she said. Then quickly added, "On the *floor*."

He smiled, and she found herself joining him.

"Of course," he said. "On the floor."

He flicked out the light and sat down beside the bed.

"You got your brother back," she said. Talking was easier in the dark.

"Yeah. Giuliana pulled a vanishing act. After all that. Can you believe it?"

She suddenly realized why the woman in bed with Scott had looked so familiar. "Kid's probably better off."

"Maybe." He didn't sound convinced.

"It's not the same thing," she said.

"As what?"

"As your mother. She's dead."

"Thanks for the reminder."

"So of course you think you'd be better off if she were still around, and sure, maybe you even would be."

"Not maybe," he said.

The Preacher hadn't always been the Preacher, she thought. Before there were disability checks and insurance settlements and oceans of whiskey, there'd just been Mr. Ghent, who she used to see dropping Daniel off at kindergarten, walking all the way there with him hand in hand. She remembered because she'd paid attention to things like that back then, trying to figure out exactly what it was that made her different from the other kids, and why they could all see it when, as much as she studied herself in the mirror, she was lost. Most days, that year and every other, she'd had to walk herself to school. By third grade, so did Daniel. She wasn't sure which of them was luckier: the one who didn't know what was missing or the one who did. "I'll give you that," she said. "Not maybe. . . . But Milo doesn't need that woman. He's got you."

"Why are you here, Jule?" he said. "What happened?"

In the dark, she could almost answer. She almost felt powerful again. Screw Scott—if he found out she'd told someone the truth of what happened, what could he do? What would she let him do? Answer: nothing. She wasn't afraid of him.

But she was afraid of Daniel, of what he would think. It was too dark to see his face, but she would hear it in his voice.

"Nothing happened," she said.

"Sure, that's obvious."

"Nothing happened that you need to know about."

"I'm not trying to get in your business. I just want to make sure you're okay."

"Like you care." It came out harsher than she'd intended.

"I should get out of here," he said. "I'll stop bothering you and leave you alone."

"Would you get out of my head and stop assuming you know what I'm thinking?" She hoped he couldn't tell she was thinking how desperately she didn't want to be alone. "Did I say I wanted you to go?"

"So . . . you want me to stay?"

"Well, *want* is a strong word."

For a moment, there was nothing but the sound of their breathing. *I could reach out my hand and he would take it,* she thought. *Take it and hold it and just* be, *if that's what I needed him to do.* That's how close he was; that's the kind of guy he was. But she wasn't that kind of girl. She couldn't ask. And he was the kind of guy who would wait to be asked.

"So what's the deal with you keeping Cass Porter in your shed?" she asked instead. "That's a bit kinkier than I would have expected."

"You know about that?"

"*Everyone* knows about that. Not to mention there was that day you came over and stole my underwear."

She could almost hear the whoosh of blood to his face.

"I thought it was hers. I would never have— I mean, I'm not— I was—"

She put him out of his misery. "It's fine. I get it. People do crazy things when they're keeping girls locked up in their shed."

"I wasn't . . ."

"Joke," she said. "Jesus."

"You know about what they're going to do to her tomorrow?"

"I've heard rumors."

"If you're going to say that kind of thing would never happen here, don't bother. People are different now. Something's . . . different."

"Kinkier than you look *and* dumber. No one's different, Daniel. Maybe they're being more obvious about it now, because they're tired of playing let's-pretend. But that kind of thing is always happening here. I thought you knew that."

"I don't think so. I don't believe that."

"You'll believe it when they light her on fire."

"No," he said. "I'm getting her out of there. Before they can do anything."

"Oh, really? How?"

He was silent.

"So you've got a rescuing complex. That's your deal?"

"It's not a deal. It's one person who needs me."

Either he was being polite, not mentioning the fact that he was currently in the process of rescuing Jule, or he didn't think of her that way, the kind of girl that needed a rescue.

Not that it mattered, since she resolutely did not care what he thought of her.

Not at all.

They were quiet for a long time.

"You asleep down there?" she finally asked.

"No."

"You know, when this is all over, and they open the borders, I'm getting out of here."

"Oleander?"

"Oleander. Kansas. Hell, I don't know, maybe the whole country. I hear Bali's lovely this time of year."

"They say Rio's nice," he said.

"There's always Antarctica. I could sacrifice temperature for distance."

"And isolation. No one to annoy us but the penguins."

"Oh, it's 'us' now, is it?"

"Like I'm letting you go to Hawaii and leave me here."

"Hawaii's in this country, Einstein. Off the table." She closed her eyes. "There's all these hotels in El Salvador. They built them in the eighties, all these giant resorts right on the beach, white sands and blue sea, the whole deal. To bring in the tourists, right? Except they're in the middle of a drug war, and getting decapitated really spoils a vacation, so the tourists never come, and the hotels just get abandoned, all of them. Sitting right there on the edge of the world, empty paradise. Just waiting for someone desperate enough to move in."

"How do you know so much about random stuff in South America?"

"Central."

"What?"

"You said *South*. El Salvador's in Central America."

"That's kind of my point. How would you know?"

She opened her eyes, looked at him, wondered whether to tell the truth.

"Oh," he said. "Right."

Like it was so stupidly obvious, like of course the Prevette girl would know all there was to know about Latin America, and anywhere else drug kingpins went to play.

"Not 'oh,'" she said. "Not what you're thinking."

"I didn't mean—"

"Mr. Sorenson told me."

Daniel's eyes widened. "The *Nazi*?"

Jule sighed. "He's not a Nazi." Kyle Sorenson lived in a decaying house on the edge of town, a house that in thirty years he'd almost never left. He was an Oleander legend, a story kids used to spook themselves on stormy nights, and one of the most persistent rumors swirling about him, the one that most delighted boys between the ages of seven and twelve, concerned his alleged Nazi past. War crimes, *Heil Hitler*s, and a desperate midnight escape to the American Midwest, where he could live out his days amid Christians and cornfields, longing for the moment when the Reich would rise again. Other rumors had him as a retired and potentially cannibalistic serial killer, with bodies frozen in the basement to remind him of his youth, or—this one was more popular with girls—a political prisoner, smuggled out of Siberia and into Kansas, so traumatized by years of isolation and torture that he could no longer bear human companionship. "He's just a lonely old man."

"And you actually *know* him?"

"He and my uncle . . . they had kind of an arrangement for a while." That had been when Scott became convinced the government was tapping his phones, and a cranky hermit with a shortwave radio collection came in handy. That had also been when Jule was still young enough—still cute enough and mute enough—that Scott towed her along with him when it suited him, and over the course of that year he'd towed her to Sorenson's once or twice a week. Sometimes he'd left her there, alone with the strange old man, who'd had no idea how to entertain an eight-year-old, and so told her stories. Exotic tales of exotic lands, places he'd touched only through his radios but could describe like he'd been there. He made her feel like *she'd* been there—for those brief afternoons, he made her feel like she'd already escaped.

"He knew a lot about other places," Jule told Daniel. "It was like . . . I don't know, like he wanted to get out as much as I did, but for some reason, he couldn't."

The Salvadoran hotels, those beached white elephants soaking in the sun, had always been her favorite story. She'd wanted to hear about them again and again, the sparkling waves, the endless tracts of sand, the lavish rooms, all of them abandoned. It would be so easy to be alone there, untouched and unseen. It would, she'd told herself, almost lulled to sleep by the slow rhythm of Kyle Sorenson's low voice, be easy to be happy.

It had been her secret dream that one day Scott would tire of towing her back and forth and would just leave her with Mr. Sorenson for good. That she would live with him in the big old house, perhaps wiping the spotted windows and washing the musty sheets, cleaning without complaint as she never did at home. She'd do whatever she needed to do to make herself indispensable. One day, she dreamed in these daylight fantasies, she would slip and call him Grandfather, and she would blush until he patted her shoulder and assured her it was all right. They would finally flee this place, together, and make a home in one of those faraway hotels on a deserted beach. They would be family, the only family either of them needed.

And then Scott went to prison, and she never went back.

But she never forgot about El Salvador, about her fairy tale. She'd never confided it to anyone else.

"They're probably not there anymore," she said, and didn't know why the thought made her so unbearably sad. "They probably never were."

He looked like he had a million questions, but he didn't ask any of them. Almost as if he understood that she'd already told him more than she intended.

"Tahiti, then," he said lightly. "You can't argue with Tahiti."

"Tahiti?"

"Tahiti."

"Sold."

"So it's a deal," he said. "When this is all over, we take off for paradise."

"It's a deal."

She reached out her hand. He took it.

They shook.

She didn't know if she could sleep. Daniel stayed with her, and she listened to his steady breathing in the dark, and thought about white sand beaches and storybook skies, and as dawn crept in, her hands stopped shaking and the sweat dried on her brow, and she could, in the gray light, almost imagine what it would be like to get away from all of it. To leave herself behind.

The deacon made good on his promise, and the response exceeded his expectations.

Ellie's mother nurtured a bit of a girlish crush on the good deacon herself, so was less than pleased at the reports of her slim, youthful daughter parading before him in her underwear. She told her daughter that she would be in her prayers but not, until she cast Satan from her heart, in her house. Ellie's father held little truck with all the Bible talk but believed the deacon to be a good, strong man who was steering the town in the right direction—and he'd always been uncomfortable with his daughter's newfound womanhood and the fact that when she emerged from the shower wet and glistening, he couldn't help noticing the swell of her breasts beneath the towel. He, too, thought that it would be best if she took some time away. "Your friend Moses wandered in the desert for forty years," he told her. "Seemed to do him some good."

"The deacon's lying," Ellie told them.

And, when that didn't work, "It's wrong, what he's doing to the town."

And, in desperation, "He's *wrong*."

But whatever he'd whispered in their ears had taken.

"You're the liar, Ellie," her mother said. "Leading us all to believe you're some kind of holy visionary."

"I never said—"

"I'm your mother, so I'm sure I can find it in my heart to forgive you, but the rest of the town? There's going to be anger out there."

"Be careful, sweetie," her father said before closing his door in her face.

She received similar treatment, if harsher, from Clair and Morgan, both of whom informed her, with little regret, that she was not welcome, and would not be until she repented her behavior and stopped spreading her lies. These were the days of God's wrath—she'd said that herself, hadn't she, more than once? The time of mercy had passed; this, Morgan said, was the time of justice, and there was something eager in her face, something *hungry*, that made Ellie leave hastily, and not try her luck with any more of her supposed friends.

She went to the jail. She'd lost her sway with the town; the deacon had seen to that. But he couldn't quiet her voice. And after all: *Whatever you did not do for the least among you, you did not do for Me.*

She went to the jail, and refused to answer any questions. She repeated only a simple request: "I want to see Cassandra." She could see it in their eyes: they were spooked. She'd never been very good at making people like her, but when it came to creeping people out, she was a pro, and there was a certain power in that, too.

When she arrived at the cell, Cass was asleep, or pretending to be. Ellie sat on the linoleum across from the locked door, ignoring the grime and the insects, and leaned her head against the wall. She would stand guard here tonight. In the morning, when they came to take Cass for judgment, Ellie would be with her, step by step, to avert her fate, or to share in it.

On the night before Jesus was to be arrested, he had called on his apostles in this time of darkest need. *Stay the night with me in Gethsemane,* he had begged. *Watch me safely through the dawn.* But in the end, even the most loyal among them had betrayed him, and fallen asleep.

Ellie did not.

West had a key to the locker room, so that was where he went. That was where he slept, or tried to, stretched out on one of the narrow wooden benches, resolved to ignore the fact that everything stank of pit sweat and feet. The walk through the dark had taken him more than an hour, and there had been nothing good or leisurely about it. Every step was pain.

West folded his hands on his stomach and listened to his breathing. His heart seemed to pound in time with the throbbing of his leg, and his thoughts beat with the same insistent rhythm.

They knew.

They hated him.

They hurt him.

They didn't want him.

They'd changed. Into something wrong, something diseased. Or maybe it was easier to think so.

*Now you know why I limp,* Nick said, reaching out of the dark to stroke West's bruised face, to kiss his wounded leg. *Now you understand.*

It wasn't real. He knew that. Nick was gone.

Probably he was going crazy.

*I can taste someone else on your lips,* Nick said, and West felt the ghost of a tongue tracing the line of his lips, the beads of sweat and the dried blood that smeared his jaw. *You've been bad.*

*You've been punished.*

*Was he better than me?*

"It wasn't like that." West stopped, aware he was talking to himself—or, worse, a voice in his head.

Another kiss on his leg.

*Does that hurt?*

The lips moved up his thigh.

*Or that?*

West closed his eyes.

*It never stops hurting. But at least we're the same now.*

"You were in an accident. It's not the same."

*There was no accident.*

*It was only an accident that he left a mark. That time.*

*It was only an accident that the damage was permanent.*

*You thought it was so easy for me.*

"No."

*You didn't understand pain.*

"No."

*There are ways to make it better. Ways to make* them *hurt.*

*You still have the gun.*

*There's a lot you can do, with a gun.*

"You're not Nick," West said aloud, if only to convince himself. "You're a voice in my head that's not even very good. Nick wasn't like this."

*You didn't know me.*

*Don't you get that by now?*

"Please stop," he said, for the second time that night, just as uselessly. The difference: this time, he didn't mean it.

He didn't want the voice silenced.

He didn't want the weight that settled atop him to fade away.

He didn't want to be alone, not tonight.

*It hurts?*

"It hurts."

*Let's make it better.*

In the dark, a body was a body, imaginary . . . or not. Comfort was comfort.

Joy was joy.

And sleep, when it finally came, was oblivion.

# 11

## LET HE WHO IS WITHOUT SIN

Daniel stayed awake till morning. He watched her, imagining that somehow, by marking each intake of breath, each flicker of her lids, he was protecting not just her, but Cass and Milo and even, in the most gruesome of ways, the Preacher—that standing vigil and ensuring nothing bad happened here, in this room, on his watch, would mean that for at least a few hours nothing bad happened anywhere. It was flawed logic, he knew that. Still, he did not sleep. And coincidence or not, the sun rose without incident, and they all survived the night.

Milo bounded out of bed shortly after dawn, eager to get started on that day's drill, a willing recruit determined to earn his stripes. Daniel had to lie. Daniel had to let him believe that their father had flaked on them yet again, had disregarded whatever promise he'd made to Milo and disappeared.

Daniel had to.

Milo accepted the news without much surprise, tromped back to his bedroom, and slammed the door. Like he'd expected as much. Daniel was tempted to follow him, if not to tell the truth, then to make up some elaborate lie about where their father had gone, something that would make the disappearance about a noble cause rather than an unlovable son. No eight-year-old should be that prepared for disappointment.

*But maybe better prepared than blindsided,* he thought, and let Milo sulk. If the only person Milo trusted to come through for him was his big brother, then that's what Daniel would have to do.

"So what's the plan?" Jule asked, slurping down a mug of watery instant coffee.

"What plan?"

"For this great rescue operation of yours. I assume you have a plan?"

The trial was scheduled for noon, with sentencing and punishment to presumably follow swiftly after. It was a few minutes after ten, which gave him two hours to come up with something brilliant and the nerve to carry it out.

His father could wait.

"Yeah, that's what I figured," Jule said.

She was significantly steadier than she'd been the night before, though Daniel thought he could detect a certain watchfulness about her. There was a tightness at the corners of her eyes and lips, a drawing back of her shoulders, a wary alertness to shadows and sudden movements that hadn't been there before. He didn't know her, he reminded himself. Not really. He couldn't begin to guess what had brought her to his door, and he knew better than to ask.

Five feet tall, nothing to her but a shock of purple hair and a sharp voice, and still, he was afraid of her. . . . What was he going to do when he had to go up against the cops? What hope did Cass have, if her only hope was him?

"I'll figure something out," he said. "I'm not letting them kill her in the street."

"Can I ask you something? Honestly?"

He waited for her to ask why he cared so much. It wasn't a question he liked looking at head-on. Did some dark part of him nurture the hope that, murderer or not, Cass would ride off with him into a happily ever after, that she would be so filled with gratitude she'd drag him to the shed on the spot and, as his father would have put it, make a man of him? It wasn't about that; it never had been, even when things were simple and Cass was nothing but a beautiful girl he used to know. He knew it was stupid, the way he clung to a childhood friendship that hadn't meant much at the time and meant less with every passing year. But it was all he had left of some other life, the life before everything had gone wrong. Jule had her fairy tale of white beaches and satin sheets; Daniel had Cass and the life he might have had if his mother had lived. That's what he'd clung to, these years, though he didn't like to admit it to himself, the idea that if he got Cass Porter to *see* him, the way she used to see him—the way he used to be—that he could resuscitate the past.

For him, Cass had always stood for what was good, and what could be good again. If he lost her, he'd lose that, too.

It seemed unbearably selfish, wanting to help someone only because it would help yourself.

"What if it were someone else?" Jule asked. "Would you still care? Would you still try to stop it?"

"Honestly?"

"Honestly."

Save someone, even a stranger, just for the sake of saving them? Risk himself only because it was right? He wondered what it said about him that the answer didn't come easily. "I don't know."

"Okay. Good enough."

"For what?"

"For me. I'm in."

"I don't think that's a good—"

"You want to give me some noble sexist bullshit about how this is a man's job and you don't want to put me in danger, or you want to hear my plan?"

"*You* have a plan?"

"You said the Preacher's preparing for war, right?" she said.

He nodded, suddenly nervous. It was one thing to resolve to do the impossible—it was another to team up with someone who seemed nuts enough to actually try it.

She smiled. "I assume that means he has an armory."

Daniel had, of course, held a gun before. His father had trained him to shoot nearly as soon as he'd learned to walk. But it had been a long time, and he'd never actually shot at anything other than soda cans. The first time his father had taken him out hunting, he'd gotten off one shot, about ten feet wide of a scrawny buck, and burst into tears. That had been the end of that hunting trip, and shortly after, his mother's death and father's drinking had put an end to the idea of taking any more.

The Preacher kept his arsenal in the dining room. In Kansas it was, as it turned out, surprisingly easy for even a drunken maniac to secure any kind of gun he liked. The Preacher had assembled quite the collection.

Daniel chose a shotgun, as it was the one that felt most comfortable in his hand, though that wasn't saying much. Jule took a 9 mm that would have fit in her purse had she carried one, but instead got tucked away in Milo's Spider-Man messenger bag. Daniel slung the shotgun over his shoulder, intending to tell anyone, if asked, that he was headed on a hunting trip, but he didn't expect anyone to ask—carrying a gun in plain sight in Oleander hadn't exactly been particularly noteworthy even before the storm.

"You don't have to do this," he told Jule as they approached the police station, thinking *I don't have to do this.*

Thinking: *This is crazy.*

But there was a pyre in front of the town hall, and Coach Hart was probably at that very moment stoning his wife, and the mayor had declared some kind of military theocracy, and his father was trussed up like a butchered pig. The whole town had gone crazy. There was no reason for Daniel to be an exception.

"I've got nothing better to do today," Jule said. "But are *you* sure? My uncle Scott always says never point a gun at someone unless you're a hundred and ten percent sure you can pull the trigger."

Daniel swallowed. The shotgun strap was digging uncomfortably into his shoulder. "He doesn't sound very good at math."

"Bad at math, good at shooting people. So . . . are you sure?"

The plan wasn't too complicated. They would storm the police station, Daniel grabbing the nearest body as a hostage while Jule covered him with the 9 mm. Ideally, this hostage would be weak and unarmed. If not, Jule would disarm him and Daniel would poke the gun into the small of his back and inform the room at large that either they release Cass or he would shoot.

He was pretty sure he would not shoot. So hopefully it wouldn't come to that.

Jule, after acquiring a hostage of her own, would accompany said hostage downstairs to release Cass from the cell while Daniel waited upstairs with the shotgun and a roomful of cops who no longer felt bound by any rules of legal conduct. Then, on the off chance all that went smoothly, they would flee on foot, around the corner to where Daniel had parked the Preacher's car. It still had enough gas to get them to the edge of town, where they would throw themselves on the mercy of the soldiers. Failing mercy, they would still have the guns. They would, somehow, get themselves across the border. Where Cass would, presumably, be taken into legal custody once again, at least this time by people who weren't intending to slaughter her in the street. Daniel and Jule would . . . well, there the plan went vague. But it was a good bet they wouldn't end up in Tahiti.

He'd kissed Milo's forehead before they left, a gesture of affection he rarely made. Milo had wiped it off with exaggerated disgust, and given him a punch on the arm for his trouble. "Tomorrow you're building me a fort," he reminded Daniel, who agreed: tomorrow. Then he'd distracted Milo with a dirty joke (one Milo would understand *just* enough to spend the entire day puzzling over the punch line) before they could shake on it.

He'd left Milo alone. It seemed criminal, but it was the only option. The day-care program had disbanded, half the town's children had disappeared with Laura Tanner, and word had it more went missing every day—something that seemed to alarm no one but Daniel, who no longer let Milo leave the house. There were no trustworthy neighbors; there was no one but his father, tied up in the shed. So Milo was alone, with a stack of comics and strict instructions to answer the door to no one but Daniel. Years before, their father had installed a small panic room beneath the kitchen—more of a cramped crawl space than a room, but complete with a steel door, a jug of water, and a week's supply of canned tuna. Milo rolled his eyes, but promised to lock himself inside at the first sign of trouble.

"Will you bring Cass home?" he'd asked Daniel.

"Only if you do what you're supposed to do and stay put," Daniel said, and would have to hope that was good enough. It probably would be, for the morning. Milo was a good kid, and a smart one.

But what was he supposed to do if Daniel never came back?

Part of him wanted to turn around, rejoin his brother, lock them both into the panic space until the craziness had passed. But what would he tell Milo if they lit Cass on fire and watched her burn? What would he tell Milo, who'd trusted him to be the all-powerful big brother who saved the day?

He'd tell him that he wasn't a superhero, and Milo couldn't expect him to act like one.

Who wanted to admit that to their little brother?

Jule was waiting for an answer.

"Definitely not sure," Daniel admitted. "But let's go."

He advanced to the front door of the police station. From his previous visits, he knew there were unlikely to be more than two cops and an unarmed and generally oblivious receptionist. Jule, as they'd planned, slipped in through the side entrance, ready to cover him should the cops not be as receptive to a hostage situation as they'd hoped.

*This is me, storming a police station with a shotgun,* he thought. *Daddy would be so proud.*

The shotgun, he suddenly realized, was the gun from his nightmares, the one he'd woken to find in his hands as he stood in the drugstore, dazed and confused. He'd chosen it without thinking, because it seemed to have the right size and heft—it had called out to him as the right gun for the job.

Or maybe called to him as the right boy for the gun. Maybe this was where he was supposed to be, not to do what was right or to carry out some nebulous vision of justice, but to fulfill a destiny of bullets and blood.

It was the kind of thought that really *would* make his father proud, and so Daniel shut it out of his head. He dropped the weapon to his side so that an unobservant receptionist might not notice until it was aimed at her head, and entered the station.

It was deserted.

Jule didn't know what she was doing. For seventeen years, she'd somehow managed to stay out of trouble, despite her family, despite her reputation, despite the multistate drug operation headquartered fifteen yards from where she pretended to sleep. And now, in one week, Jule had burned down a building, made out with a sociopath, stabbed a man, disposed of a body, and stormed a cop shop intending to take hostages and free a confessed murderer. So maybe it was fortunate someone else seemed to have done that last job for her.

The station was a ghost town. They moved through slowly, weapons drawn, both expecting a trap. The empty offices had the pregnant air of a surprise-party-in-waiting, with all the guests tucked into closets or under desks, tensed and ready to pounce.

"Maybe it's some kind of Bermuda Triangle thing," Daniel said. "Maybe the whole town's about to disappear."

"I don't have that kind of luck," Jule said, trying to shake the feeling that he could be right. "They probably all got food poisoning or something. Moldy donuts."

"Cops and donuts? That's the best you can do? It's beneath you."

"Kind of preoccupied right now, remember?" She waved the gun—carefully. When she was a kid, she'd always wanted Scott to teach her how to fire one. By the time he deemed her old enough, she'd figured out she didn't want her fingerprints anywhere near her uncles' weapons, nor did she want any of their "lessons" mucking up her brain. Those had been the years she'd declared herself a pacifist, a vegetarian, a Democrat—anything she could think of to ruffle the Prevette feathers. The night she'd suggested she might become a cop, her mother had slapped her face, but otherwise, no one had much cared. Eventually she'd given up trying to bother them, as she'd given up imagining she could be anything but what she was: a trailer-park Prevette. Still, she'd never touched a gun. Until now. It was heavier than she'd expected, and more awkward than they made it look in the movies. She didn't intend to fire it. The gun was for show. The knife, still tucked into her oversized pocket, was for use. It was strange, carrying it tucked against her stomach like that. It felt almost warm, almost alive—a strange and dangerous fetus, eager to greet the world. She could feel that, too. It was eager.

The stairwell to the basement was dark, and there was no switch. Slowly they descended. The lights were out in the cell block, too. In the quiet, it was all too easy to hear the scratching and scraping in the dark. The sound of insectile arms clawing at the shadows. Spiders, she thought she could handle. But not cockroaches. And definitely not flying cockroaches that dropped from above, tangled themselves in your hair, shivered down your neck, picked and chewed at your skin.

*Better cockroaches than cops,* Jule thought, and was sorry she did, because it was too possible. An ambush, cops streaming down the stairs, surrounding them, shoving them in a cell, locking the door, throwing away the key. Dying down here, medieval-dungeon-style, flesh falling off and rats nibbling their bones.

"Cass?" Daniel said softly. Jule wanted to slap him for disturbing the silence—and whatever might be lurking in it.

But she wasn't a child, afraid of the dark. "Cass!" she shouted.

There was no answer. "Hard to believe she rescued herself," Jule said. But then, Cass Porter was presumably no longer the anal rule follower she'd been the year before. Maybe she'd picked up lock picking and prison breaking somewhere along the way.

"She's gone," a woman's voice said from the cell beside Cass's. A moment later, a face appeared through the bars.

"The doctor," Daniel whispered.

As if Jule would ever forget the woman she'd almost burned alive.

"Dr. Cheryl Fiske," the woman said. "And sorry to tell you, but she's long gone. They took her over early, 'for her safety.'" The woman's laughter echoed through the dark.

"We've got to get to the gym," Daniel said. "Stop the trial."

Jule shook her head. Two of them against a stationful of cops? Those were underdog odds, which had a certain appeal. But two of them against every cop in town *and* a bloodthirsty mob? "That's not noble, it's suicidal."

"Whatever. Stay here. I'll go myself."

The stubborn ass; she was almost inclined to let him. "No, *we'll* go. But not like this, cowboy-style, guns blazing. There's got to be a better way."

"There is," the doctor said. "Take me with you."

"Why would we do that?" Jule said.

*This is my fault,* the woman had told her.

*I'm sorry.*

"Because you want to stop the trial, and I can do it," the doctor said. "If I tell the town what I know."

"And what's that?" Daniel asked.

"Not here. Get me out, then I tell you. And everyone. That's the deal."

"What, you can't say it twice?" Jule said.

"I tell you now, you might just leave me here."

"We might leave you here anyway."

"Then good luck with your angry mob."

Daniel blew a burst of air through his teeth. "Let's get out of here. She doesn't know anything and we're wasting time."

"You're smarter than that, Daniel," the doctor said.

Jule hesitated. "How does she know your name?"

"I've been here before," Daniel said.

"And I know *you're* smarter than that, Jule."

"Once and for all, how do you know my name, lady?"

"I know a lot about you, Juliet Prevette. Born to Annie Prevette, father unknown. Seventeen years old as of three weeks ago, and happy belated birthday, by the way. School records indicate attitude problems, difficulties with authority and anger management, inability to relate to peers, probably due to troubled home—"

"Shut up," Jule said. "Just shut up. How do you know any of that? Who *are* you?"

"Someone who's been paying very close attention to both of you for some time now. But not as close as I have to Cassandra. And I'm telling you that it's in all of our best interests to get her out of this town safely, and quickly. Get me out of here and I can make it happen. Or I can tell you more about yourselves. Daniel Ghent, age seventeen, who spends his days warring with child protective services and his nights cleaning up after a father who—"

"I'll go find keys," Jule said.

Daniel raised his father's shotgun. "Don't bother," he said, and shot the lock off the door.

\* \* \*

It was Monday morning, eleven days after the storm, and under other circumstances, it would have been the first day of school. The Eisenhower High School gymnasium, which drew students from all over the county, held eight hundred folding chairs. Every one was filled. Onstage were the mayor, the deacon, Grace Tuck, the disgraced Ellie King, and a handful of cops—the latter mostly there for show. It was the ring of Watchdogs, stationed backstage and at regular intervals around the perimeter, who had most of the firepower. A makeshift courtroom had been assembled onstage, with the mayor and deacon occupying a judge-like spot atop a riser, and a witness seat at stage right, all of them facing the audience. Cass, brought on surrounded by three armed guards, was greeted with a chair-rattling roar of disapproval. The villagers carried neither spears nor torches, but they had left their polite faces at home, along with their grudges and their closeted skeletons. This was a day for blood, and it had—as the storm and quarantine could not—united the town.

Ellie stood by her side, the designated "spiritual adviser," but knew she'd only been allowed to attend because the deacon was hoping she had come to her senses. If she recanted her accusations against the deacon, if she endorsed his verdict, he would draw her back into the bosom of the town and the church and all that was righteous and good. Her family would reopen their doors and their hearts. All would be as it was. If.

"We are the same," Ellie had told Cass when they rousted her at dawn and marched her out of the cell. "Whatever judgment comes, we'll bear it together."

Bold words could disguise the fear, but they couldn't erase it.

She watched her hands closely, searching for a tremble. Some telltale sign of indecision or weakness, evidence that her body knew she didn't have it in her. To rise before the crowd, to raise her voice over those who would shout her down, to plead. For judgment; for wrath; for mercy. Which, she didn't know—couldn't, until the witnesses testified, until Cass confessed her story, until Ellie figured out whether there were some things that could be neither excused nor forgiven.

What she did know: That she was afraid.

That it didn't matter.

West stood with Baz on one side and Chuck Platch on the other, searching the crowd for his parents, unsure whether he was hoping to see them or not. He didn't. Jason wasn't there, either, and for that, too, he couldn't decide whether he was grateful. There had been very little sleep the night before, stretched out on the wooden bench, wrestling with ghosts and nightmares. He'd woken that morning with two black eyes and a nose crusted with blood, his leg just barely able to support his weight. He wore his mustard-colored Eisenhower jacket, and in its left pocket, he carried Jason's gun.

He didn't notice Jason in the wings, watching Baz, resisting temptation, longing for blood.

Cass wanted to live. This is what she thought as they took her out of her cell. This is what she thought when they brought her to the high school, which she'd assumed she would never see again. This is what she thought when they paraded her onstage, where, in another life, she would have been standing as valedictorian. It was almost unreal, staring out at the crowd, drinking in hundreds of faces and voices, imagining herself into the crush of people. No matter how much they hated her, they were exhilarating—even the terror was exhilarating, after so many months of no one and nothing.

It only made her more determined. Screw justice, screw penance: she wanted to live.

Let them have their trial, if they were so eager. Let them get it all out, weep and moan and rend their clothes and berate her for her crime and themselves for letting her survive it.

Denial. Anger. Bargaining. Depression. Acceptance. Those were the stages, right? And she'd finally hit the last one. She was a killer: accepted. If she had to, if it meant getting out of this alive, she'd kill again.

She believed she could do it.

If she got the chance.

Grace had believed that *she* could do it. And maybe she hadn't missed on purpose. Maybe her reasons for setting the cops on Cass rather than handling it herself, in the shed, from the start, had been more logical than cowardly. She was, after all, thirteen, and it was the first time she'd fired a gun. Surely, it wasn't out of the question that she would miss, even at point-blank range. Surely, she couldn't be faulted for wanting to get the hell out of there before anyone showed up to arrest her, instead of trying again.

But no one had made her throw away her father's gun, and now she had nothing to use but words.

She settled into the witness chair, ready. Words would have to be enough.

* * *

"Do it now, before they get started," Daniel whispered, tugging his hood tighter around his face. The jail housed a collection of abandoned clothes, left behind by decades of drunk-tank deadbeats. He'd picked out the least foul of the hooded sweatshirts for himself and tossed another to Dr. Cheryl Fiske, who wanted nothing less than to allow the stained, lice-ridden rag anywhere near her body. But she had to admit he was right: Lice would be bearable. Being recognized and returned to her cell—or worse—would not.

Which made the prospect of climbing onstage and confessing her sins somewhat problematic.

She straightened in the chair, willing her legs to stand and carry her forward. It was no good. They weren't going to like it, the little hood rat and her scrawny champion. She didn't much like it, either—she'd never considered herself a coward. But then, she'd never needed to consider the subject one way or another, not until the tornado had blown everything to hell.

Trite but true: this wasn't what she'd signed up for.

She hadn't wanted to move to Kansas; she hadn't even wanted to *take* this job, not if it would mean relocating to the Midwest, cutting off all communication with friends and family, and experimenting on unwitting human subjects.

Though, if she was going to be honest with herself, that last one hadn't been high on her list of objections. Especially not once she'd gotten the salary offer.

It was all in the service of making the world a safer place. That was how she slept at night—that, and the assurance that she would never have to set foot in the town itself. She would never have to face any of her subjects, beyond the one safely enclosed in a padded room, behind a foolproof lock. She'd been promised she would never be put at risk—but here she was, trapped in this filthy, godforsaken excuse for a town, surrounded by people she wouldn't have trusted even under the best of circumstances.

She was trapped in the zoo, waiting for the animals to attack. Maybe it was karma.

She hadn't intentionally lied. She'd honestly meant to take the stage and tell the truth. Her words would set off an explosion, and the subsequent chaos could give them all cover to escape. Or it could get them killed. Specifically, it could get *her* killed. Eight hundred animals against her—the one to blame. And nothing between them but a couple of teenagers who, once they knew the truth, would have even less inclination to protect her than they did now. As if they could if they tried: there'd been security at the door, and Daniel had been forced to relinquish his gun.

Cheryl would never forget the things she had seen at the facility, after the containment breach: gutted bodies and steaming organs, beasts who looked human and flung themselves at death. She was a scientist, and she knew how to weigh facts, possibilities, cause and effect. For all she owed Cassandra Porter, she would not give the girl her life.

"If I got up there and told the truth, it would cause a riot," she whispered.

"Isn't that the point?" Daniel said.

"We can't risk it. You don't understand, these people . . ."

Daniel was nonplussed. "So you lied."

"I do want to help you," she whispered.

"What the hell good does that do us?"

"Right now? Very little. But when we get Cassandra back and it's time to get out of here—"

"And when hell freezes over, you'll be indispensable," Jule whispered. They were starting to draw looks from the people around them. "In the meantime, shut up."

Cheryl noted the scowl on Daniel's face and the way his hand twitched at an invisible trigger. She noted how everything in him loosened when Jule rested her hand on top of his. "Not till it's right," Jule whispered.

"It'll never be *right*." But his fingers curled around hers. Cheryl gripped the edges of her chair, which was not the same.

They held on, and awaited judgment.

"She never liked him, you could tell. I don't think she liked babies at all. There was always something in her eyes when she looked at him. Something . . . crazy." Grace had played an ear of corn in her first-grade class play, *The Bounty of Kansas*. The stage fright had been so bad she'd thrown up all over Jarrod Heinman, who'd been very proud of his Kiowa costume until it was covered in puke. The show had gone on; Grace had been called Corn Puke for the next two years (the name conveniently referencing both her costume and her stomach contents, and ending her acting career before it began). But now, despite the sea of faces in the audience, her gut was steady and her lies spilled out with more conviction than she'd ever been able to muster for the true facts of corn harvesting.

"We were supposed to watch a movie together, but she sent me to bed early, for no reason. She was always doing that. She *really* hated kids. I don't know why she was a babysitter. Maybe just so she could have a chance to . . ."

The events she was describing seemed to bear no relation to anything that had actually happened in her life. And not just because she was tweaking the truth a bit to serve her purposes. The facts themselves had been drained of their horror. As she spoke the words—describing the way a noise had woken her in the night, not Owen's cry, not his normal one at least, but something muffled and in pain, telling the rapt audience of her flight down the hallway, all at once consumed by a vague panic, as if the bond between her and her beloved little brother was such that she could sense his fear, share his pain, experience, even, the moment that his tiny soul departed the earthly plane—she felt nothing.

There was the rage, of course, but that was always with her now, and had somehow become unmoored from cause and context. It was the sole source of light in Grace's ever-present fog, a bright line connecting her to Cass, the only two remaining points in the universe. There was Grace, there was Cass, there was the unfulfilled promise that lay between them, and beyond that there was . . . nothing.

She didn't think about her parents anymore, except to consider the difficulties that might arise if they returned before she could do what needed to be done. She didn't think about Owen anymore, either. Not even now, when talking about him, and his little broken body. There was no remaining guilt or grief. The rage had blotted it all out.

There was probably something wrong with her, she thought on those late nights when she scraped at the last peanut butter jars and scrounged for a few remaining potato chip crumbs to quiet her gnawing hunger, and curled up under Owen's overturned crib, where she now habitually slept. But that didn't bother her much, either. That was the beauty of it. As long as she played dutiful servant to her master rage, nothing did.

"I saw her kill him," she told the town, and tried her best to look sad about it. She tried to look like a different person, young and sweet and broken. Like *Gracie.* "He wasn't even crying or making trouble or anything. She walked into that room for no reason, she murdered my brother, and then she jumped out the window. She *wanted* to die. But instead, they gave her some fancy lawyer and stuck her in the hospital and now here she is again, back in *our town,* like nothing ever happened. Like you can just kill someone and not pay for it. And I don't think that's right."

If she said anything after that, no one heard over the thunder of the crowd. Grace wiped her eyes. No one but the mayor and the deacon was close enough to notice she wasn't actually crying.

"I don't remember," Cass said.

"Nothing?" the deacon said. "Absolutely nothing?"

"Nothing."

"This is your claim."

"It's not a claim, it's true."

"It would give a great many people a great deal of peace to know why you did what you did."

"I'm one of them. But I don't know. I don't!"

"You stated that you're sorry for what you've done."

"Of course I am."

"And yet you claim you don't remember doing it."

"I *don't*."

"How can you be truly sorry for something you claim you don't remember doing? How can you repent?"

"I don't know," she said.

"I'm afraid I don't know, either."

The term for it, Ellie knew, was giving her enough rope with which to hang herself.

"Before a sentence is handed down, Ellie King would like to say something on behalf of the defendant," the deacon said, patting the air to quiet the angry crowd. They hated her, she could tell. Maybe as much as they'd loved her just a couple of days before. Somehow, the deacon had gotten the word out that they'd all been fooled, and seeing her reminded them of their gullibility. For a moment, Ellie was sympathetic to their obvious desire that she vanish.

"Remember, your choice," the deacon whispered as she stepped forward.

It was as if he'd even gone to the trouble of making the noose for her—all she had to do was slip her head through.

"I'm not saying that Cassandra Porter isn't guilty," she said. The judgment had been delivered by general acclamation. It was all over now, except the lynching. Somewhere, at the very back of the crowd, she thought she spotted Jule Prevette, and for some reason, focusing on that face loosened her lungs and her clenched stomach. "And I'm not saying we have no right to judge her sins. But . . ."

Was there a but?

A baby had died—surely that demanded payment.

A life for a life.

*I could tell them all,* she thought. *Open my mouth and say it. What I've done. Who I am.*

Unclean.

Unrepentant.

Unforgiven.

"We've all sinned." That was as close as she could bring herself to get. The crowd was rumbling again. Someone fired an apple at her with dead aim, hitting her solidly in the shoulder. "We're not perfect, any of us. We fight our temptations and sometimes we win. Sometimes . . ." She would not give in to the past. This wasn't about her. "Not everyone's strong enough to win. Should we hate them for being weak? Or should we help them? Shouldn't we lend them our strength, give them a *chance* to do better, to make up for their mistakes? People *can* change. People who do bad things can do good things, too. *Cass* can do good things. She can spend the rest of her life making up for what she did, if we let her. It won't erase what happened, not for us, not for her. I guess I think maybe it's still a punishment, maybe it's a *worse* punishment, to let her live. Let her remember what she did and have to choose what to do next. She took a life. That life is gone. But *her* life . . . what good does it do any of us to throw that away, too? When there's still good it could do? Sometimes mercy is justice, I really believe that. I believe that's what He would want."

"He tell you that himself?" someone shouted from the crowd.

"He told us all," she said. "In the Bible, in the Gospels, in church every Sunday. There's nothing special about me—I never said there was. God talks to all of us. We just have to listen."

The words flowed easily. They were true enough, but they weren't the *truth*, not the hard one. Not that it mattered. The town didn't want to hear. They hadn't stopped booing or shouting or throwing things since she'd begun, and now that she'd finished, the jumble of noise merged into a single desperate, pounding chant.

"Burn her."

"Burn her."

"Burn her."

The deacon had his men toss Ellie offstage and out of the gym. "You are no longer a part of this," he told her quietly, and whether he meant the trial, the church, or the town, she saw it to be true. Even when they closed the doors to her, she could hear them chanting. It began with words; soon it would be action.

The time for words was done.

"The defendant is sentenced to death," the deacon intoned. "Sentence to be carried out immediately."

And the crowd, as they say, went wild.

There was an Oleander tradition, at homecoming games, of rushing the field. Win or lose, the fans poured off the bleachers and into the dirt, swarming the Bulldogs' end zone, uprooting the goalpost, and, like an army of ants bearing bread crumbs three times their size, spiriting it away. In the unlikely event of a win, they charged with added frenzy.

This had been a big win.

The town scrambled onto the stage, shouting and spitting and pressing as close as they could to the baby killer, as if grabbing a tuft of her hair or landing a loogie on her cheek would be an achievement they could someday tell their grandchildren about. The Watchdogs formed a protective barrier around Cass. They'd been given strict orders that, no matter what, she was to make it to the pyre intact. The plan was to parade her down the street, in hopes of keeping the crowd at peak frenzy, before binding her to the stake and sending her screaming to hell. West positioned himself immediately beside her, doing his best to keep the vultures away, but could do nothing about Baz, who'd clamped down on her other side. The quarterback was, West knew, doggedly determined to keep Cass safe for as long as it took to make sure he got to watch her burn. Baz had once, in fifth grade, set a dog on fire, simply for the entertainment of his friends. They'd been suitably horrified to shame Baz into putting the fire out, and pretending the whole thing had been a joke that had accidentally gone too far. He'd even cried the next day, telling them how his father had put the dog out of its misery with a .20-caliber bullet, and then beat the living crap out of his psychopathic son. Even then, West suspected the tears were fake: Baz had been plainly exhilarated by the flames, and more so by the dog's agonized howls. He looked now, with his meaty hands on Cass, the way he'd looked then, holding that lighter: purely, recklessly happy.

As they inched toward the exit, West spotted a wild-eyed Daniel Ghent forcing his way into the heart of the crowd. West caught his eye and tried to give him a look that communicated they were on the same side—for whatever good that would do. Cass wasn't getting out of this alive. Anyone stupid enough to help her would probably suffer the same fate. But at this point, West wasn't sure that was a good enough reason not to try.

He was tired of being afraid.

Ellie had not broken the rules in three years, when the consequences of delinquency had finally proved too great to bear. But these were man-made rules, she reminded herself, and she served a higher power.

The voice told her she couldn't do it—would fail before she began. Had failed long ago. She ignored it. She prayed. She asked God to tell her whether this was right, but didn't wait for an answer, because the answer would be no use to her if it wasn't *yes.*

It wasn't faith that gave her the courage she needed, and it wasn't prayer that made her take a deep breath, shield her face, and kick in the glass door of the chem lab. It was the thought of Cass, on the stage, in her cell . . . in Owen Tuck's bedroom all alone, defenseless against the devil's incursion. It was the memory of a bloody Reverend Willet, approaching the cross with a lighter in hand, and the sound of screams as she'd run away.

Not this time. Cass needed her. Not her kind words or her sufferance or her assurances that life would be easier on the other side, but *her.* Ellie King. Who could do more than smile and nod along and let the town believe she was whoever they wanted her to be.

She couldn't know that this was the right thing, that the deacon was wrong and she knew better, that this was the path the Lord would have chosen. She couldn't know, not for sure. But she was good at faith.

So she did it anyway.

It was chaos. No longer a collection of rational individuals, but one beast with a thousand heads and a single thought: *Burn her.* Daniel cursed himself for not moving sooner, when he might have stormed the stage and swept Cass away before anyone had time to react. Now? To fight his way to the center of this, then fight his way out again? You might as well pull a gun on a tornado.

He was about to try it anyway—because it was that or follow the procession down the street and wait for the children of Oleander to toast marshmallows on her corpse—when the building rattled with a thunderous boom. Smoke billowed into the room, and someone let loose a piercing, stampede-inducing shriek: *"Boooooomb!"*

Statistics suggest that crowds panic far less frequently than most people believe. Usually, even in emergency situations, large masses of people will behave rationally, helping one another, working together to save themselves, looking out for the weakest among them. Even when they're trapped with no hope of escape, most people will accept their fate with some degree of calm. There are two exceptions to this: when people think they *might* be trapped, with one slim chance of escape, or when they have trouble breathing. Then all rationality burns away. Panic takes over.

The Eisenhower gym, with smoke pouring in, flames licking the walls, and one narrow exit at the back of the very large room, managed a two-for-one. Everyone went nuts. What had been chaos became pandemonium. The crowd reversed itself, pressing outward rather than in, flinging itself toward the back of the room. Apparently not trusting his safety to Providence, the deacon forced his way through and was one of the first out the door.

"Prevettes!" Daniel heard West shouting. "By the east side. I'll take the prisoner. You guys, go!"

Other than Jule, there were no Prevettes in the building, and surely if the explosion had been a bomb set by Scott's militants, they wouldn't have been dumb enough to stick around and watch. He'd interpreted West's strange look correctly, he realized. The football player was trying to help.

"Now!" he told Jule, who was already on the move, threading through the knots of shrieking people to where West and a couple of the other Watchdogs were pulling Cass back up onto the stage, into the wings.

By the time Daniel caught up with Jule, she had a gun trained on Baz Demming and two sophomore football players, while a dumbfounded Cass sagged in West's arms.

"You can't shoot us all, bitch," Baz said.

Out of nowhere, West pulled a gun of his own. "She won't have to."

Baz reared back. "What the hell are you doing?"

"Get out of here," Jule said, and the Watchdogs sprinted. Baz was left with no choice but to follow.

"I'll kill you," he screamed over his shoulder. "But first I'll fuck you. I'll fuck you to death!"

Daniel heard a madness in that voice that scared him far more than the flames.

Which were getting closer.

The cowardly doctor scuttled toward them, happy to re-join the rescue squad now that the rescue was done.

"What happened?" Cass murmured. "What's happening?"

West held her with one hand, and with the other, trained a gun on a figure lurking in the shadows. "You following me?" he asked.

Jason Green, a junior Daniel barely knew, stepped into the light. "Following him," he mumbled, jerking his head in the direction Baz had run. "Does it matter? The building's on fire."

"I know a place," Jule said, and they followed her, all of them somehow now in this—whatever it was—together. They ran away from the fire and away from the crowds, into the depths of the school, where they ran into a paper-white Ellie King, hysterically babbling something about having blown up the school. They absorbed her and ran faster, across the school, out the other end, past the overflow trailers, past the construction equipment that had collected dust since the expansion budget had run out, and ducked into a rusting construction trailer Daniel hadn't realized was there. Something about the possessive way Jule tapped the KEEP OUT sign as she climbed inside made him wonder if she'd made it herself.

They piled into the trailer and slammed the door shut behind them. It was a double-wide, with space for all seven of them: Daniel, West, Jule, Cass, the cowardly doctor, the sputtering saint, and the inexplicable junior. It was far from the fire; it was hidden; it was, for the moment, safe. Which meant, for the moment, so were they. Daniel drew in a long, shaky breath. Somehow, they'd actually done it.

"Take a breath," Jule told Ellie. "Then just say it. What did you do?"

Ellie took a deep breath. Then another. Then, in a wobbling voice, said, "I broke into the chem lab, I stole some fireworks and set them off, and then I came looking for Cass."

Daniel couldn't have been more surprised if she'd admitted to planting an actual bomb.

"I'm pretty sure there's a sin in there somewhere," Jule said.

A laugh spurted out of him as he realized the implications. "You set the school on fire, Ellie." Now he was laughing so hard he could barely catch his breath. Which, he was aware, probably had less to do with the humor of the situation than it did with his surging adrenaline and suppressed panic—but it felt good to laugh. And why not? A hundred yards away, their high school was burning down and their town was going nuts, and they'd just publicly aligned themselves with Oleander's Most Wanted. They were totally screwed. Why not enjoy victory while it lasted? "You blew up the freaking *school*!"

The hysteria was catching: Ellie giggled. "You're welcome."

Everyone laughed, except the doctor, who watched them suspiciously, as if wondering whether she'd be better off taking her chances with the mob and the fire—and except Cass, who looked blank. They settled in, Jule all too comfortably, pulling a cache of candy bars out from behind one of the steel cabinets and passing them around; Daniel didn't want to think about why she was so at home out here. He didn't like the idea of her spending days alone here, gnawing on Snickers and waiting out the final bell.

"We actually did it," she said, tossing him a bag of M&M's. "I thought you were insane, but we *did* it."

"Ellie did it." Daniel was slightly ashamed of himself. It wasn't that she was a girl, it was that she was *this* girl, this pale wraith who flinched from her own shadow.

Though she didn't look so pale now. She was still laughing.

Jule shrugged. "So she fixed the problem that she created in the first place. Are we supposed to say thanks?"

"That's not fair."

"It's fair," Ellie said. "It's true."

"It's done," West said. "So what do we do now?" Daniel wondered whether it was mad-dog Baz who'd given him those black eyes and the bruises peeking out from his shirt collar. Hard to imagine West letting it happen. Baz was a thug, but West was *big*. And—though West kept his eyes fixed on Jason, as if daring the guy to try something—he hadn't moved from Cass's side. His arm circled her shoulders, which looked all the narrower settled comfortably into his bulk. Daniel busied himself with the M&M's, and then with the view from the trailer door, peering through a gap to get a glimpse of the burning school. The flames hadn't crept past the gym yet, but they would. School was out for good. No senior year, no yearbook, no prom—no big loss.

It occurred to him that West and Cass had, at one point, seemed poised for the homecoming court, and he wondered whether they would just pick up where they'd left off. In the movies, that was always how it happened, the hero and heroine falling into each other's arms moments after they'd narrowly escaped mortal danger. Daniel should know, he'd imagined it himself enough times; it just hadn't occurred to him that he'd be in the background, snarky sidekick, comic relief.

"Cass?" West said, sounding less than besotted. "Cass, what are you doing?"

Daniel turned around.

Cass had somehow acquired a gun. And she was pointing it at the doctor.

"No more excuses," she said. "No more lies. Tell me what you did to me."

What did you have to do to accept that you were going to die? Daniel wondered. What inner switch did you have to flip that would allow you to walk calmly to a pile of lumber and kindling where you would be set on fire? Was it a question of turning off your ability to feel anything, or feeling so much you went insane?

Technically, she wasn't so sane to start out with, he reminded himself.

But she had never seemed quite this empty.

Cass held the gun with two hands. Neither shook. "It's now or never. Talk."

## 12

### THE GOOD GUYS LOSE

There was a lot of shouting. A lot of voices coming from what seemed to be very far away telling Cass things that didn't matter much, not compared with the things that the doctor had to say. But the doctor was silent. Even with a gun in her face.

There had come a point during the trial where Cass saw how the rest of her life was going to play out. She would fight back, and probably get in a few punches and maybe tear out a patch of hair, but she wouldn't win. She would die. Waiting for it to happen, she'd had ample opportunity to think about what she would miss. Not her parents, her home, her future—she'd already had a year to mourn them and move on. The basics, things that you figured death-row inmates craved in their final moments, the smell of a cloudless sky, the sweetness of buttered corn or a fresh-picked strawberry, the taste of a kiss, the sigh of a body breathing beneath you—these were things she thought she could do without.

But dying without ever remembering? Dying without knowing why? She couldn't. She wouldn't. And now, as if the God she'd given up trying to believe in had dropped a gift into her lap, she wouldn't have to.

"Shut up," she told the noise.

"Talk now," she told the doctor. "Tell me why I did it."

"Not with him here," the doctor said, pointing at Jason. "The rest of them are fine, but not him. He's dangerous."

"*I'm* dangerous," Cass said.

"You don't understand—"

"No, I don't. So you tell me. *Tell me why.*"

She felt better with the gun in her hand. There was comfort in knowing that she could pull the trigger. If she had to.

"There is no why," the doctor said. "No *reason* you killed Owen Tuck, because you didn't, not really."

Cass never let the gun waver. Focusing on that was the only thing that kept her upright.

"It was the drug," the doctor said. "The R8-G."

"I don't take drugs."

"You were given a dose of R8-G in your flu shot that afternoon. Five of you were, by random selection: Henry Gathers. Reverend James Willet. Gloria Birch. Paul Caster. Cassandra Porter."

"What, like some kind of experiment?" Daniel said.

"Exactly like."

*The gun*, Cass thought. *Focus on the gun.* The ground dropped out beneath her feet, the room spun around her, the words kept coming, making less and less sense, explaining everything and nothing at once; her ears buzzed and her eyes watered, but the gun was real. As long as the gun was steady, as long as her finger rested on the trigger, she was still in control.

"So you inject a bunch of people with some kind of experimental drug, it backfires, they murder some other people, and you just . . . sit back and watch?" Jule said.

"It didn't backfire," the doctor said. "R8-G did exactly what it was designed to do."

"Give me the gun," West said, suddenly beside Cass.

"No."

*"Give me the gun."* Cass risked a glance at him. Every muscle in his face was clenched. He was nearly vibrating with tension.

"R8-G turns people into killing machines," the doctor said, her voice rising in pitch and speed. It was like she thought if the words came quickly enough, no one would have a chance to take in their meaning. "They'll kill every living creature in sight, and when that's done, kill themselves."

West lunged at the doctor, bearing down on her with all his 243 pounds of muscle and ramming her into the back wall. From somewhere beneath his weight came a muffled but panicked squeak. Daniel and Jule were on him in seconds, tugging at his tree-trunk biceps, his thick waist, his immovable bulk, uselessly. It was like watching children try to shove an elephant. Ellie stood by with her arms hugged to her chest, her lips moving in what could have been a silent prayer. The junior, Jason, was hunched into a corner and seemed to be trying his best to disappear.

"West, stop," Cass said quietly.

"Only if you're going to shoot her." His hands pinned her to the cement wall. "Or you can shoot me. Because otherwise I wring her damn neck."

"That place you had me in. What was it?" Cass felt like she was moving underwater, trapped in one of those dreams where the world sped up and left her behind.

"Research base," the doctor gasped out. "Government."

"You mean military," Jule said. "Holy crap, Scott was right?"

Cass tried to wrap her mind around it. She wasn't a criminal or a mental patient. She was a *subject*. An *experiment*. There was no hidden reason—no why. There was just bad luck. Bad timing. Bad people. In AP psych, she'd learned about an experiment in which a rat, after being pumped with antidepressants for two weeks, had the drug yanked from its system. In the subsequent withdrawal, it went crazy and attacked any other creature unfortunate enough to share its cage. You couldn't blame the rat. Right?

She'd thought knowing would change everything.

But Owen Tuck was still dead.

In the silence that fell over the room, they could all hear it. West, his hands still at the doctor's throat, was crying.

"Jeremiah," Cass said.

"Don't call me that." It was more anger—more emotion, period—than she'd ever heard from him.

"Let her go, West."

"No."

She knelt to the ground and carefully laid the gun on the cement. Her fingers cramped and, for a moment, held their half curl around the weapon. Daniel stooped beside her and took her hands into his own, kneading the circulation back into them. She wondered if he felt better about himself, now that he had permission to feel sorry for her.

If it were a movie, he would take her into his arms and kiss her. Now that he had played savior and she had been redeemed, romance could bloom and the credits could roll. Events neatly tied up, lines of good and evil clearly drawn, hero and heroine on the right side of the border. Their shoulders pressed together, and for a moment, Cass toyed with the idea of kissing him, just to see what would happen. If she could magically convert her life from horror story to romantic comedy.

This time, at least, she managed to suppress the unseemly urge to laugh.

"She killed Nick. She killed them all." West's breath had gone ragged. "For the hell of it. For fun."

"For a weapon," Jule said. "That's it, isn't it? The weapon to end all weapons? R8-G. *Rage*, right? Cute." Her voice strained with the effort to sound flip, but couldn't quite make it.

"Do you know what you did?" West shouted. "Do you understand?"

"I'm sorry—"

"I don't care," West hissed, and something in it was more frightening than his roar.

Ellie chose that moment to rouse herself. "'Look around and see. Is any suffering like my suffering,'" she said quietly, "'that the Lord brought on me in the day of his fierce anger?'"

"What?" Jule said. "Does anyone know what the hell she's talking about?"

It was West who answered. "It's the Bible," he said, with a harsh laugh. "Lamentations of Jeremiah."

"'I am the man who has seen affliction by the rod of the Lord's wrath,'" Ellie continued. "'He has driven me away and made me walk in darkness rather than light.'"

West joined her in a whisper. "'Indeed, he has turned his hand against me again and again, all day long.'"

"It's all right," Ellie told him, in that maddeningly soft voice. "I understand."

"I doubt that," murmured Cass, who thought she actually did.

But West softened under her touch, and allowed Ellie to take first one arm and then the other off the doctor and back him away.

Daniel took the gun. He pulled Cass to her feet, and the five of them stood together, facing the woman who'd changed things for all of them.

"Drop a bomb of this crap on your enemy and they'd kill themselves off," Jule said. "Nice and neat and no army required. Is that about right?"

The doctor didn't answer. She rubbed her neck, where bruises in the shape of fingers had begun to bloom.

"And you're still here," Jule said. "Studying us. The lab rats are really that fascinating? Even when most of them are dead?"

"Some of us at the base were staffed to research, but most are there for . . . procurement." The doctor cleared her throat. Her fingers played nervously together, steeples rising and falling, thumbs warring and surrendering and warring again. "Here's where things get problematic."

Jule snorted. "Right. *Here.*"

"R8-G isn't a synthetic drug—it's a refined solution of a substance found in nature."

"What kind of substance?"

The doctor hesitated. "It's not a substance, not exactly, the way you'd think of it. It's got unusual qualities—unusual energy."

"Like radiation?" Daniel said.

"Like. But not like. This . . . substance seems to be excreted from the human body at the time of death—especially violent deaths, and especially when they happen in great numbers. The law of conservation: all that anger, fear, and rage has to go somewhere."

"And there just happens to be a big pool of it sitting under Oleander?" Jule asked.

"It seems to collect in certain pockets—some of us believe a pocket requires only a particularly brutal initiating incident, and then the substance tends to pool. It attracts more of itself, so to speak."

"Like an evil lint ball," Jule said.

"The Oleander pool is large and isolated. A perfect research site."

"Except for the thousand people living on top of it."

"We obviously took precautions," the doctor snapped. "Until . . ."

"The storm," Cass said. Remembering the explosion and the fire that had nearly killed her—and the massacre that had killed everyone else, all those bodies, piled on top of each other, bloody and whimpering and still clutching their spent machine guns. How much of this R8-G would it have taken to do that? And what else had it done? "Something went wrong."

"About twelve things went wrong—but all you need to know is that we had a leak."

"So why haven't we all turned into a bunch of murdering zombies?" Jule said.

"It's like radiation, remember?" the doctor said. Cass had

never seen her like this, vulnerable, defensive, and almost, if you squinted, afraid. "Nuclear material, when refined and assembled in a very specific way, can set off a concentrated blast of energy—a bomb. But if you were to release the unrefined raw material in a less controlled fashion . . . if you were to have, for example, a containment breach at a nuclear power plant, the result wouldn't have the destructive force of a bomb—"

"But people would still die," Daniel said. He balled up his fists. "Slowly. They'd get sick first, and without knowing why. And then they'd die. A bomb in slow motion."

"Except this crap wouldn't kill them," Jason said in a hoarse voice. "It would drive them nuts. Slowly. Until they couldn't stop themselves. And then *they'd* kill. That's right, isn't it? That's what's happening to me?"

She hesitated. Maybe trying to decide whether or not to lie. "The others are immune."

"But not me."

Everyone turned to look at him. Cass saw the fear in their eyes, and she saw Jason see it, too.

"It's already started, right?" Jason said, trembling. "It's happening right now?"

She nodded.

"So can you fix it?"

She shook her head.

"Then . . . then . . ." Jason backed away from her, from all of them, still staring at him, accusing him for what he hadn't yet done. He backed himself all the way to the door, and pushed through it.

"Jason . . . ," West started.

"She can't fix it," Jason said. "She can't stop it. *You* want me around? Knowing that?"

West didn't say anything. No one did. And so none of them should have been surprised when he ran away. Cass certainly wasn't. Cass understood. Finally, Cass understood.

Jule slammed her hand against the wall so hard the trailer wobbled.

Dr. Fiske sighed. "It's in the air, it's in the ground, it's in the water. It's been there since the storm, warping the entire town. Except for children, who for some reason don't seem to feel any effect—and except for you."

"Why?" Jule asked. "What are we, some kind of lucky mutants? Is this where you reveal our superpowers and our special destinies?"

"Cassandra's body has already been saturated by the R8-G. It can't do anything to her. The rest of you were each present at one of the killings; you each came into contact with a subject's blood while the R8-G was active. You've been inoculated. As . . . have I." She looked sick.

Contact with infected blood, Cass thought, and thought of gunfire and smoke, and stepping through broken bodies while a storm raged overhead. Of course the doctor was also immune.

Jule started. "But you said there's no cure."

"We're working on it." Her eyes rested on Cass.

That was the reason for all the needles, Cass realized, and all the tests. She'd been their weapon; now she was supposed to be their cure. Except she'd failed. And now people were dead.

"There's nothing we can synthesize for a large population. Not yet. And in the meantime, the whole town—"

"Milo," Daniel said abruptly. And then, before anyone could stop him, he was gone, too.

"Where the hell is he going?" Dr. Fiske said.

"You just told him his *eight-year-old brother* is out there with a bunch of people who are about to go hard-core nuts," Jule spit out. Cass thought that "about to" seemed generous. "Where do you think he's going?"

"Someone needs to go retrieve him," the doctor said. "None of you are safe here. We have to get to the border, and over it, as quickly as possible. They'll let you through on my word."

"You think he's going to just trot back here and forget about Milo? On *your* say-so?"

"Then we go without him."

"I take it back," Jule said. "West, feel free to rip her head off."

Jule crept along Sixth Street and Court, looping her way circuitously toward the Ghent house, crawling through bushes and hiding behind trees. She felt ridiculous. It was hard to take seriously the thought that if she bumped into Leo Fletcher, the local butcher, he'd take after her with his meat cleaver. Or that Barbara Boone, upon spotting her passing beneath her window, would raid her husband's Civil War gun collection and open fire. But humiliating or not, when she got the opportunity to crouch in a bush or duck behind a tree trunk, she took it. Jule knew, better than anyone, how a drug could wake the hidden monster. That there was always a monster.

This wasn't the smart move. They'd all agreed to wait a few hours, let the town's panic and fury die down before trying to make it to the border. The smart move would be to get to the swamps, hide out on her own territory until it was time to meet the others. Or maybe ditch the others altogether, and go it alone, as she always did. Instead, here she was, sneaking back into the lion's den with nothing but a gun she didn't know how to use and a knife she didn't want to. Here she was, because Daniel had been there when she needed him; because Daniel might need her, and no one ever did that; because Milo was a less irritating child than most. Because this was a good day to save someone.

She didn't have to apologize for what had happened to the parasite, or make amends, or repent, she assured herself. Surely even Ellie King would have to agree with that.

But saving someone—that would be good.

It was slow going, and she couldn't afford slow. Conveniently, the mayor's car lot was right on her way. So she picked out a likely-looking car—not so posh it would have cutting-edge security features, not so crappy it wouldn't run—and smashed the window with a rock. She cracked open the paneling under the steering column, stripped the two red wires, twisted them together, touched them to the brown ignition wire while revving the engine, said a silent thank-you for Scott's long-ago lessons, and was on her way. Too many of the roads were still impassable, and she had to drive several blocks out of her way, but she made it to Daniel's house before he did.

Staying true to his promise, Milo refused to let her in.

She'd always been crap at waiting, especially when wired with enough nervous energy to power a city. And sitting on the porch staring out at the empty road left her too open to the worries crowding in, to the thought of what would happen if Daniel ran into the wrong person on his way, and the question of what she would do if he never arrived. So she decided to distract herself by having a look around.

She started with the shed.

The girl had a halo.

Or it was just the sun.

Of many things, the Preacher was no longer sure.

"Come to save me, angel of mercy?" the Preacher said when she ripped off the duct tape. His fingers were numb, his stomach empty. More than anything, he wanted a drink. This was a long time to go without a drink.

The angel stared.

"Or maybe you come to kill me?" the Preacher said. "Same thing now, isn't it?"

The angel stared.

"You a mute?" the Preacher asked.

He'd given up on trying to get out of the knots himself. The rope was too thick, his son's work too sure.

He'd given up because of the things he wanted to do when he got loose. The things the devil wanted him to do, or maybe it was the Lord, or maybe the liquor.

"I'll kill them all," he said. "You let me out of here, and I'll bring down the wrath of God."

His own son had imprisoned him—his own son, doing the work of the devil.

Or his son was on the side of the angels, saving his father from himself, as was his duty and his way.

The Preacher was used to noise in his head, but now the noise was deafening. A man could drown in that noise. A man could lose himself.

He really wanted a drink.

The angel looked so sad, and in her sadness, she was beautiful, and he told her so. She reminded him of his wife, and he told her that, too, and that death would come for her and that death would soon come for them all and that maybe this was right and this was good.

He told her that he was rotting from the inside out, and of all things, of this he was most sure, because this was the truth at the heart of his life.

The noise in his head was calling for blood, and so he did what he always did when the noise got too loud, and fixed his mind on his wife, who was dead, and his sons, who still lived, and the man he once was, who would have died to save them.

"I'm sorry," the angel said, then closed the door and returned him to the dark.

When Daniel finally got there, Jule was waiting on the porch.

"Milo's safe," she said.

He didn't ask how she'd gotten there first or why she was there at all, just blew past her, into the house, and scooped his brother into his arms.

She watched him squeeze Milo unbearably tight and kiss the boy's forehead and try not to cry, and when the moment had passed, she filled them in on the plan, the laying low and the rendezvous point and the getting across the border. She didn't ask Daniel about what she'd seen in the shed. There was comfort in knowing that she wasn't the only one who'd done things this week, things she wouldn't want to admit. And there was comfort in knowing that Daniel was tougher than he looked. That he could do what needed to be done.

After looking in the Preacher's eyes and hearing the death in his voice, she had no doubt it had needed to be done.

They had two hours to wait. They locked Milo in the house, just in case, and they waited together on the porch, watching the road and the trees in case someone came for them, and wondering how a place that seemed so peaceful could be anything but.

"Do you believe her? The doctor?" he asked. "Is any of this possible?"

"Do I believe there's some magic crap in the ground that turns people evil? Of course not. Whatever it is, they brought it in. Or they made it. Whatever. But the rest of what she said? What she said it's doing to us . . . ?" She thought about her stepfather, her uncle, Baz. The townspeople crowded around Cass, begging for fire. "Yeah, I believe it."

"I don't know. The idea that a *drug* could make good people suddenly want to do terrible things . . ."

Spoken like someone who hadn't crossed paths with very many drugs, Jule thought. "Or it just gives them permission to do all the terrible things they've secretly always wanted to do," she said. Of course it would make the perfect weapon: Imagine the possibilities for stealth warfare, plausible deniability. Step back and watch the enemy destroy itself.

"People aren't like that. Not most of them."

"Not most of them. All of them."

"And what about the ones who are fighting it?" he said. "That Jason kid seemed okay."

"*Seemed.* You trust that?"

He didn't answer.

*You couldn't trust your own father,* she almost said. But she didn't.

"I don't even trust myself," he said finally. "This immunity thing—if she's wrong about that . . ."

It hurt to breathe, thinking about Milo inside the house waiting for them to save him. Trusting them. "I know."

Daniel examined her face. She forced herself not to fidget under his gaze. It wasn't that it made her uncomfortable— not the way she usually felt when men watched her, at least. Their gaze was a demand; Daniel's was a question. "Has something—" He stopped and course-corrected. "Do you feel like you're not immune? Like something's different?"

"You think *they* feel like something's different? I think the only difference is they're having fun."

"Then we're probably safe, since I don't think there's any danger of that. But . . ."

"Say it."

"If you were feeling weird, or if weird stuff was, I don't know . . . happening . . ."

She thought about the knife that she couldn't seem to let go of, and the way it kept finding its way into her hands. She thought about what she'd seen in the shed. Maybe she wasn't the only one who was going a little crazy.

Or maybe he'd conclude that she wasn't immune after all, and was a danger to him and his brother and all things good and wholesome, and would do what needed to be done.

"No weirder than usual."

Daniel shook his head. "This is crazy. All of it."

Before Jule knew it, she was laughing, and Daniel looked at her like she was the crazy one. Then he started laughing, too. They sat there on the porch, shoulders heaving with laughter, and so she didn't have to confess that laughing was just something that happened when she was too frightened to cry.

Eventually the laughter drained away, and so did their words. They sat together quietly, and waited, and then, finally, it was time.

Jule and the others had agreed to meet in the swamps by the trailer park. It was out of the way, off the town's radar, a mile from an isolated stretch of Route 8, and native ground for Jule, which would give her the advantage, if it came to that. It was pretty clear why the doctor was so determined to help them get out of town, and there was something unnerving about being so obviously used as currency. Jule allowed herself a moment to wonder whether life in a town full of burgeoning psychopaths would be better or worse than life as a lab rat, but even in the best of times, she lived by a simple motto: Anything's better than Oleander.

So she led the two brothers to the edge of the property, where she'd parked the stolen car.

Milo took in the smashed window and the wires poking out of the steering column. "You gonna hot-wire it?" he asked, like she'd just told him she could fly.

"Of course she's not," Daniel said. "It's not as easy as it looks in the—" He broke off as the engine roared to life. "Do I want to ask how you know how to do that?"

"Do you even have to ask? I'm a Prevette."

She hated reminding him, and proving that she was just like the rest of them after all.

But he grinned. "Lucky for us."

*This is crazy*, West thought as they snuck out of the trailer and crawled their way across town, like criminals, like rats. *This is crazy*, as they hiked out to the trailer park and then past it, forging through overgrown weeds and past culverts of sewage in search of the landmarks Jule had described, the scarred weeping willow and the lakelike thing in the shape of a comma. His ribs hurt more with every breath and his bruised face throbbed, but the pain in his leg drove out everything else, stabbing him with every step. It was all crazy: the idea that the town had gone mad; the thought that Cass had nearly been killed; the news that Cass was *innocent*; the fact that he was taking his cues from Jule Prevette, that he was in league with Oleander's fallen saint and son of a preacher man, that he was fleeing the only home he'd ever wanted. But there was the crimson cast to the sky; there were his parents. It explained too much not to be true. It explained everything, except . . .

"How would we know if we weren't immune?" he asked the doctor.

"You are."

"But if we weren't . . . I mean, would it cause, like, hallucinations? Or something?"

"Are you *having* hallucinations?"

"Of course not," he said quickly.

What he was having . . . whatever the thing that called himself Nick turned out to be . . . *hallucination* wasn't the word for it. He had no word for it.

He refused the word *ghost.* Better to be crazy than to start believing in that.

Unfortunately, you couldn't help what you believed in.

"But if we were?" Ellie put in. "Seeing things? Or hearing . . . voices?"

"Inoculation doesn't always confer *complete* immunity," the doctor admitted as they penetrated the woods. "Think of it like an allergy shot. You might not be deathly allergic anymore, but you might still have a light reaction . . . a rash, a scratchy throat. Nothing to worry about."

"Sure," West said. "Nothing at all to worry about."

It had seemed so real, speaking with Nick's voice, touching him with Nick's fingers.

Urging him to do things Nick would never want him to do.

Except he hadn't really known Nick at all, had he? So who was he to say?

The thought led him to Jason, who was, according to this woman, a lost cause. But Jason had only aimed the gun; he hadn't shot it. Was he still himself? West didn't know him well enough to make that call. But he seemed like someone Nick could have cared about. He seemed aware that something in him had broken, and like he was trying to piece it back together.

West slowed his pace to put some space between himself and the others, to give himself the space to think. But Cass dropped back with him, and brushed her fingers across his swollen cheek. "What happened to your face?" she asked quietly. "What happened to you?"

"Doesn't matter."

She let it go; that was their way. "I wanted to say thank you," she told him.

He looked at his feet. "You should thank Ellie."

"I will. But I should thank you, too. For today and . . . before. In the shed."

West shrugged.

"Why'd you do that?" she asked. "When you knew what I did."

"It wasn't your fault, Cass."

"Does that matter? I did it."

"Because you couldn't help yourself."

"How do you know?"

He couldn't; he didn't. "What about Grace?" he asked instead.

"What about her?"

"That stuff supposedly makes you kill everyone in sight, right? But you didn't touch Grace."

Cass shrugged. "Maybe she didn't get there in time."

"Or somehow maybe you managed to fight it—to stop yourself in time."

"But if I did . . . it wasn't in time," she said. "It wasn't soon enough."

He started to argue, but she shook her head, and made a face he recognized from before, the expression that had appeared when she was too polite to simply *ask* him to stop droning on about football or farming. The expression that said *Please. Spare me.*

He did.

"And you still haven't answered my question," she said. "Why did you help me before? Before you knew?"

West didn't know what to tell her. How was he supposed

to explain when he wasn't sure himself? "We were friends," he said. "Simple as that."

"Were we?"

"Of course we were. Are. Why would you even ask that?" But he knew why: because of all the things he'd never told her and the things she'd known better than to ask, because of the nights they'd spent not talking and not touching, because he'd liked her as much as he was able to, but no more.

"It's funny how we've all known each other since we were in diapers," she said. "But then sometimes it feels like no one knows anyone, not really."

"Cass, look, I'm sorry if—"

"I guess that's why I liked it. With you, I mean. It felt like we could know each other without really knowing each other, and that was okay, you know?" She laughed softly. "That doesn't make any sense. But I wanted to say it."

"It makes sense," he said. And even though they were tramping through a swamp on their way to face down armed military determined to pen them in with a town full of crazy, he smiled. "Sort of."

"And I wanted to say, I'm sorry about Nick."

He stopped cold. "What?"

She stopped beside him, and let the others continue ahead, disappearing into the overgrowth, and didn't speak until they were alone. "I didn't know you two were . . . friends," she said. "But I guess I figured that you . . ."

He couldn't breathe.

"Anyway. I'm glad you had him. And . . . I'm sorry you don't anymore."

"Yeah." His voice sounded ragged, unfamiliar even to him.

She chewed at her lip, then mouthed a silent swear. "I shouldn't have said anything. I knew I shouldn't have said anything."

"No. It's okay," he said, his face hot, his throat burning. "Thanks, I guess."

"Hey, West?"

"What?"

Instead of answering, she slipped her hand into his and held tight, and that was all she had to say.

They walked together through the woods, and held on to each other, and didn't let go until they reached the tree Jule had described and the swampy lake, and discovered they weren't the first to arrive.

The Watchdogs were waiting.

"Where is she?"

Jule froze at the sound of the quarterback's voice. Noises echoed strangely out here. He might still be some distance away—but not a safe distance. There was no such thing. Daniel had already pulled Milo down behind one of the trees. Jule dropped down to join them. The marsh grass waved in the breeze. It was nearly as tall as Milo in this patch, and she wished she could lose herself in it, lie down and let herself be claimed by the swampy earth.

"You think I don't know she's with you? Think I don't know where Prevettes go? Rats always go back to the nest."

She couldn't think about the fact that she'd steered everyone right into the waiting arms of the Watchdogs. She definitely wouldn't think about the fact that Baz knew this place, not just as a deserted swamp in which to park and drink and smoke and fuck, but as *her* place. Had he hidden in these woods as she was doing now, watching? How much of her had he seen?

"We have to get closer," Jule said.

Daniel looked at Milo.

She sighed. He was right. She wasn't used to having someone to take care of; her brain just didn't work that way. She pointed behind him, where the swamp shaded into dense forest, windblown and wild, its storm-damaged trees jutting at crazy angles. "There's a path about twenty yards that way—it winds around a bit, but it'll get you to the edge of the highway. I told West we'd catch up with them there if . . . things went wrong." She'd insisted on a backup plan, and no one had suggested she was being overcautious. The only thing that seemed unlikely at this point was anything going right.

"I can't just leave you here." Daniel said it like he knew he could.

"I'll find you there. I'll make sure we all do."

"But—"

"Trust me," she said.

It wasn't a question, but he answered anyway. "Yes."

"Then go."

Daniel sighed. "Come on," he told Milo. "And be really quiet, okay? Like the silent game."

"It's not a game," Milo said. Then, without warning, he wrapped Jule's legs in a tight hug. "I'm not stupid."

"No, you're not." She didn't want him to let go, but Daniel pried him away.

"Be careful," he told her.

"I'm not stupid, either."

But maybe that wasn't true, because as soon as the brothers were out of sight, she crept as close as she dared to where the Watchdogs had the others surrounded, pointed her gun at the sky, and fired.

It was all the distraction West needed, just a split second of split attention that let him tackle Baz and wrestle the gun from his hands. The linebackers rushed to defend their quarterback—allowing Cass, Ellie, and the doctor to slip away, running at full speed into the brush. Baz yelled at his lackeys to forget about him and chase the fugitive, as surely it should be evident to them that he could whip West's ass all on his own.

"You wanted my ass, all you had to do was ask for it," West said, and drove Baz's face into the dirt. Baz cursed and bucked hard enough to shrug him off. West stumbled backward and Baz lunged. His fist connected with West's black eye. Mistake. West bared his teeth, unleashed a beastly growl, hunched down, and made a hard tackle. The quarterback went down. They rolled and grunted in the mud, like wrestlers, like animals.

Jule could have run away, like the others. West was bigger and West was desperate. He could take care of himself.

Or she could have given in to the siren song of the knife she still carried, and plunged it into Baz's exposed back.

She compromised, waiting until Baz was on top, his eyes on the ground, his back exposed and defenseless. The gun made a satisfying thump as it cracked against Baz's skull. His body made another one as West dumped it to the ground.

They ran.

Sirens screamed in the distance, but not far enough so. It

looked like Baz had already summoned the cavalry. West headed east, while Jule peeled off north, thinking they'd make less of a target if they split up. After she'd reached the trees and the swamp was out of sight, she crouched in the weeds, trying to clear her mind enough to settle on a strategy. She could hear the others clomping around the woods, and the hoots of the Watchdogs as they gave chase. Her limited range of options: hide or run or—fight.

Jule hadn't spent much time hunting, but she knew that once a hunting dog scented its prey, it was unlikely to give up until it tasted blood. She ran, and Baz's dogs followed, crashing through branches and stomping leaves and shouting about what they would do when they caught up and how they would make it hurt. These woods were a second home to her, but everything was different in the wake of the storm: Familiar trees cracked in half, stripped of their bark. Paths blocked by torn branches, scorched trunks ripped from the ground. A smell of damp and earth and rot. All the comforting landmarks gone. These could have been any storm-ruined trees, anyone's safe haven—but no longer hers. They were getting closer, and Jule's legs were going wobbly, her lungs giving up. She'd cut too many gym classes and smoked too many cigarettes for a marathon. *You want to live, you keep going,* she informed her whining body, but she'd never been good at following orders.

A hand closed around her arm and yanked her into the bushes. She nearly screamed. But it was only Cass and, from the sound of the crashing branches, it was just in time.

They were coming. They were close.

"In here," Cass whispered, pulling her down a shallow incline. At its base, an enormous gnarled root had curled in on itself to form a natural crawl space just big enough for two. Jule nestled in beside her—and then the footsteps were upon them.

"How much longer we have to keep this up?" a husky voice asked, nearly on top of them.

Jule held her breath. Her head lay against Cass's chest. She could hear the girl's heart thumping. Or maybe it was her own.

"We keep it up until we find them," Baz said.

*I should have shot him,* Jule thought. *I should have let the knife have its way.*

The knife wanted her to show herself, so that she could slit his throat.

The knife promised her that if she did, it would protect her; she would be okay, and he would be dead.

Cass squeezed her fingers. Jule stayed put.

"Stick with me, and I'll let you have some fun with her before I take her out," Baz said. She hadn't hit him hard enough. She hadn't followed Scott's advice and done what she had to do.

"You promised the chief that you wouldn't touch her."

"Not the baby killer. The Prevette bitch."

What if he knew she was there? What if he was playing with her, cat-and-mouse-style, standing with one foot propped on the root she lay beneath, waiting? Making her promises— hoping to paralyze her with fear, so that when he finally struck, she would have nothing left in her to fight back.

"I'm going to tear her open," Baz said.

"Like a Thanksgiving turkey. Slice it up, get some of that stuffing, all them juices leaking out."

"You're twisted, man," Baz said. "I like it."

The other one laughed and laughed.

Jule listened to Baz describe what he would do if he found her, how he would tie her up and make her hurt, make her cry, make her *bleed*. And Jule remembered the way her teeth had ground against his flesh, and how good it had felt to hear him scream. She remembered that and tried to forget how it felt to be trapped, to lie beneath an immovable weight, to slip past fear and into inevitability. She tried to remember and tried to forget and tried not to breathe, and forced herself to wait.

Wait.

Wait.

"You take the west quadrant," Baz said.

"Which way's west?"

There was a thump, and then a grunt of pain, and then Baz said, "Stupid hurts, doesn't it?"

That was the last of them. The footsteps departed. But when Cass shifted her weight like she was about to show herself, Jule squeezed her hand.

*Wait.*

After all, stupid hurt.

Long minutes passed. Shouts echoed in the distance, but in their dark hollow, there was nothing but the birds, the wind, and their slow, soft breathing. The day was darkening, shadows deepening. They couldn't hide forever.

Jule climbed out first, her legs cramping.

"Do you think they gave up?" Cass whispered as she emerged.

"Definitely not," Baz said, jack-in-the-boxing up from the

weeds. He punched Cass in the side of the head. She dropped to the ground, hard, and he kicked her in the face, harder. Then twice in the stomach, for good measure.

"How about you?" he asked Jule. "*You* give up?"

Jule pulled the gun on him, and aimed it with a steady hand.

"You better shoot me," he said, and took a step toward her. "You better shoot me right now."

"Walk away, Baz."

He took another step. "Go ahead, I dare you."

"I'll do it."

Two steps this time. "What's the matter? Scared?"

She pulled the trigger.

There was an empty click. By then he was close enough to reach out and take the gun from her hands. He swung it at her, stopping just short of slamming it into her head. "Too easy," he chuckled. "Too fast."

He grabbed her left arm; her right arm went for the knife. "It won't be easy," she said, and lunged at him. "Or fast."

He jerked out of the way, not quickly enough. The knife sliced his bicep, just grazing the skin. He punched her in the stomach, and Jule doubled over, struggling to breathe. She took the knife with her and missed his groin but got his thigh, a good, deep cut. A dark stain blossomed across his jeans. He howled and grabbed her hair, yanking her backward, hard. Pain radiated from the roots, and she bit back a scream. It was like he'd taken a razor blade to her scalp. "You should do something about your pants," she gasped. Pain could be endured, she told herself, involuntary tears streaming down her face, her hair ripping from its roots, her hand on the knife, searching blindly for a limb, a chest, a neck to sink it into. "People will think you had an accident."

"People will think I took care of business."

His hand was over hers, prying her fingers from the hilt. He was stupid, he was an animal, but he was stronger. It seemed ludicrous that in the end that would be all that mattered. But in the end, she was on the ground beside Cass, who was breathing shallowly, her eyes open but glazed over, who was useless.

He was stronger, so she was on the ground, and he was on his feet.

He had her knife.

"You can't do this," she told him.

The blade drew a line of fire across her cheek. The blood tickled as it dripped down her face, and tasted of iron. She would not scream.

"Looks like I can."

It didn't feel surreal; it didn't feel like it was happening to someone else or that she was watching from a distance. It felt real. This was happening, and there was no way out. She was going to die here, alone in the woods. Gutted like a deer, her blood draining into the dirt. He'd do what he wanted, and when he was done, he'd leave her for the animals. She thought of the catfish, nibbling at the parasite's corpse, tearing off bits of skin and muscle until there was nothing left but bone.

"What about football?" It hurt to talk. It *hurt.* "What about your whole life? You're not this crazy."

"Everything has changed," he said in a faraway voice. "The red is here forever now. Everything is red. *I* am the red."

He was exactly that crazy.

"I'm going to slice you open. First with this." He tapped the blade of the knife against the crotch of his jeans. "And then . . ." He traced the blade of the knife lightly over her chest, up her neck, and across her bloody cheek, stopping at the corner of her lip with just enough pressure to draw a bead of blood. Gravel and twigs bit into her back, and she could feel something writhing against her neck. *Worms and maggots*, she thought, *getting a head start.*

"Don't worry," a familiar voice said from behind them. "He probably won't be able to get it up."

Jule wondered if adrenaline could make you hallucinate, because surely Ellie King hadn't just appeared out of nowhere to taunt Baz about an impotence problem. Baz looked like he was thinking the same thing. But Ellie's feet were real enough to make noise as they crunched against the leaves, her voice strong and unwavering. So not a wishful hallucination at all. For the second time that day: a savior.

"Nothing to be embarrassed about," Ellie said. "Just a little problem—a *very* little problem. And just because it happened almost every time we—"

"Shut up," Baz snapped.

"What's wrong? Don't like to remember those days?" Ellie taunted in a voice utterly unlike her own. It was like she'd been possessed. "It was so sweet, the way you had to call me a whore, just so you could get yourself in the mood."

"I said *shut up.*"

"And when it didn't work—which was often—he cried. Did he tell you about that?"

Baz let go of Jule and turned away from her. Toward Ellie. She was smiling fiercely, radiating a white-hot fury.

"Shut your mouth."

"Or you'll shut it for me?" Ellie laughed. "Still think you're the star of your own little S & M porn?"

Ellie wasn't armed, and was possibly the only person less equipped to take on a football player than Jule—taller, maybe, but so thin and reedy she'd blow over in a tough wind. Jule scrambled to her feet. "Don't," she said. "You don't have to do this."

"I think I do," Ellie said. "I think I should have a long time ago." Baz was coming toward her now, the knife dangling at his side, his grip deceptively loose. Jule considered leaping on him. Two against one—they weren't the worst odds. But it was two against one plus one knife.

"The Lord told me where to find you," Ellie said. "He told me to warn you about what you're going to find after this life. Salvation isn't for everyone."

"Stop talking, you crazy bitch." But he didn't do anything to *make* her stop. He seemed almost mesmerized, or maybe it was the shock of encountering a lunacy deep as his own.

"I used to wonder why you never told anyone about us," Ellie said. "But now I get it. You knew if you told anyone about me, I'd tell everyone about you. And the things you made me do. How you couldn't make it work unless I let you pretend to rape—"

"I said *stop*," Baz shouted, and laid his hands on her.

"Take Cassandra," Ellie told Jule, sounding unafraid. "Get her out of here." Then she started screaming. "The baby killer is here! Come and get her!"

Baz shook her, rag-doll hard. "Have you lost your fucking mind?"

"Baby killer! Baby killer!"

There was a series of answering cries, and then the crash of Watchdogs heeding her call.

"Get her out of here," Ellie said. "They'll get here before he can do anything to me."

"I wouldn't count on it." Baz punched her in the stomach. Ellie screamed and screamed and screamed.

They were coming. They were coming, and they were probably as crazy as Baz. There was no reason to think they'd stop Baz from doing whatever he wanted to do. But they were coming, and Cass was on the ground, and the pyre still stood at the center of town, and Jule told herself she was doing the right thing. She roused Cass from her stupor, slapping the girl once, then again, for good measure, dragging her to her feet, stumbling away into the brush. As the Watchdogs barked and Ellie screamed, she told herself this had everything to do with saving Cass and nothing to do with saving herself.

Once Cass was awake enough to make it on her own, at least to the point of putting one foot in front of the other, Jule turned back. The screams had fallen silent. She crept quietly and, because it couldn't hurt, she prayed.

She got close enough to hear the murmurs of the Watchdogs. Through the branches she caught a glimpse of Ellie's golden hair, and the stocky arm encircling it.

"It's all right, my child. You're safe now," the deacon's voice said. "You're with us now, child. All your sins will be forgiven."

There was a low complaint from one of the players, and the deacon boomed, "Not this one. Consider her under my protection. The Lord has plans for her."

Jule was caked in dirt, her hair matted with blood and sweat. Blood streamed from the wound on her cheek. It hurt to blink, it hurt to talk, it hurt to breathe. Baz would have killed her. She was sure of that, as sure as she'd been of anything. All those things he'd promised to do, make her scream, make her beg, make her hope and pray for death, he would have done, and then he would have slit her throat with her own knife. Baz would have killed her, but Ellie had rescued her, and now Jule was going to leave her behind.

Jule couldn't fight anymore. Not now, not while she was still bleeding, while Baz had her knife and her scent and the taste of her blood. She was too afraid to lose.

She peered through the branches. Ellie was smiling. Deacon Barnes was nuts in his own special way, but Ellie was like his wayward child. He wouldn't let the Watchdogs touch her. Not with the Lord watching. She was safe for the moment, Jule assured herself. Safe from Baz, safe with the deacon, who would keep her safe for his God. Jule could slip away with the semblance of a clear conscience. Ellie had saved her; the deacon had saved Ellie. Maybe this was how the day would continue, a chain reaction of unexpected gifts. A happy ending.

*None of you are safe here,* the doctor had said, and Jule believed it. So maybe she should have known better.

The shadows lengthened and the shouts quieted. Night was a bad time to search the woods and, as if one catch had satiated the hunger for the hunt, the Watchdogs faded away.

Daniel and Milo had made it safely to the edge of the highway hours before. They crouched in the bushes, Milo's pale moon of a face more pinched with worry than an eight-year-old's should be, watching the soldiers who stood before them and the acres of woods that lay behind. There were shouts in the distance, and, more than once, he thought he heard a scream. What if they'd all gotten caught, or worse?

What if he was the only one left?

"I'm tired," Milo whispered.

Daniel shushed him.

"But when can we go home?" Milo said.

"I told you, we're not going back."

"Ever?"

"Ever."

"But what about Dad?"

What *about* Dad, who—unless he managed to untie himself or, in his first brush with the kind of luck the universe had always denied him, attract the attention of someone willing to do the job for him—would languish in that shed indefinitely. But he'd be back before his father could starve to death, he told himself. If he made it back; if he made it out.

There was no alternative. Milo was the important one. And if it came to the worst, he'd have to forgive Daniel for saving his life.

Presumably, Daniel would find a way to forgive himself.

He brought his finger to his lips. "Remember, quiet."

Beyond the woods, a barbed-wire fence stretched across the deserted highway. Two tanks awaited anyone foolish enough to venture over it, and before them stood armed soldiers, gas masks hiding their faces. Daniel couldn't fight that. Not on his own, not with the others. If the doctor was wrong, if the soldiers wouldn't let them cross . . . Daniel clung to Milo and thought about going back. He wouldn't do it, not until he had to.

He would wait. For as long as it took, he would wait.

They trickled in one by one, first West, then the doctor, then Jule, half dragging a dazed-looking Cass. Daniel hugged the two girls, surprised by how relieved he was to see them. Milo hugged everyone.

"Let's do this thing," Jule said. She was bleeding from a nasty cut across her cheek, but wouldn't say what had happened. "I'm ready to get out of this hellhole."

"Shouldn't we wait for Ellie?" West asked.

"Ellie's not coming."

Daniel swallowed. "Is she . . . ?"

"The deacon showed up. He promised to protect her."

"And if he's lying?" West said. "We should go back." Daniel held Milo's hand, wanting to believe Jule. Wanting to go forward.

"She came for me," Cass said softly.

"And look where that got her," Jule snapped. There was something in her face, in her voice. It reminded Daniel a little too much of the Jule who'd shown up on his doorstep the night before, and he wondered what had happened in the woods.

"Enough," the doctor said. "I'm going now. You want to go, it's now or never."

They looked at each other, and Daniel wondered if the others were feeling it, the sense that the decision should be unanimous, as if they had somehow become part of a whole. Jule watched him, waiting—then, like a gift, nodded first. "I think we have to."

Daniel nodded, too, and Cass, her face bloodied and her eyes glazed, murmured something that sounded like agreement. West hung his head for a long moment, then, slowly, raised it. "We go," he said.

Daniel took Milo's hand and started toward the highway, but Jule clamped down on his arm. "No. Let *her* go. We'll watch from here. Where it's safe."

"You're safe with me," the doctor said. "Trust me, I—" The snarl on Jule's face stopped her cold. "Point taken."

This time, the doctor came through on her word. She strode out of the woods and faced the soldiers and the tanks, hands in the air.

"No one passes through, ma'am," the smallest soldier shouted to her. "You'll have to go back. It's for your own safety."

"I'm Dr. Cheryl Fiske. Access #78634. I'm inoculated. And I have Subject Four with me, along with four of the R8-G exposed carriers."

"That means nothing to me," the soldier said.

"I should hope not. Which is why you're going to radio back to your base and ask them to put through Colonel Franklin. You tell him who I have and what I can deliver, and he'll tell you what to do." She spoke like someone used to giving orders, and the soldier was apparently enough used to following them that he did so.

"Frying pan, meet fire," Jule murmured.

Lab rats, that's what lay in store for them. Daniel had no illusions. Not the best way to begin a new life. But *a* way. Beyond the borders of Oleander, away from his father, *away*. And

Milo had nothing scientists would care to study, which meant at least he would be safe.

From their perch in the tall grass, they could see the soldier speaking into some kind of headset, nodding at whatever he heard. His voice carried on the wind.

"Yes, sir. Dr. Fiske. Yes, sir." He put down the radio for a moment. "He wants to know whether you've apprised anyone in the quarantine zone of the situation."

"No," she said. The soldier relayed this to his superior. "But if I'm stuck in here any longer, I might have to."

"Understood," the soldier said, and repeated this into the radio as well. "He wants to know about the subjects?" he added. "Where are they?"

Daniel tensed.

"Somewhere safe," she said. "Waiting for my signal."

"And do they know about—"

"They know what they needed to know," she said. "Nothing more."

Daniel's mind boggled at the prospect of more. What was left?

The soldier put down the radio. "He says well done." Then, almost casually, like scratching an itch, he raised his weapon and shot her in the head.

Daniel's hand was across Milo's mouth before the shot's echoes faded away, just in time to muffle the boy's scream. Cass was out again, either from shock or concussion. West was cartoonishly slack-jawed, and Jule grabbed Daniel's forearm with a vise grip that seemed stronger and tighter than a girl her size should have been able to muster. He was glad of it, not just of the contact, but of the pain. It gave him something to focus on. Something other than the body on the ground with the hole in its head and the blood and . . . brain matter—was that what they called it on TV?—leaking away.

The soldiers had already started rolling the body in a tarp. "We taking her back with us?" one of them called.

"You heard her, she's inoculated," he said. "No use to us. Dump her in the woods."

They stayed very, very still. Daniel held Milo wrapped in his arms, trying to stop the boy's trembling and warm his clammy skin. The soldiers dragged the body to the edge of the woods and, on the count of three, slung it into the trees.

"Forty-eight hours on shift," one complained. "Even Uncle Sam doesn't make you do that kind of overtime."

"Uncle Sam doesn't pay you enough to retire in the Caribbean," the other said. "I'll stick with GMT."

"I'll tell you, though, I'm not going to miss this hellhole."

"Who would? These suckers would probably thank us if they knew. At least we're putting them out of their misery." They both laughed. "Two more days till final containment, and then it's mai tais and bikinis from here to the horizon."

"Your ass is kind of big for a bikini."

"How many times I got to tell you, stop staring at my ass."

No one spoke until the soldiers—who apparently weren't soldiers after all—had finished and retreated back to their side of the highway. No one spoke for a long time after that, not until they'd picked their way deep into the woods, away from the soldiers and the body already surrounded by flies. Not until they had come to terms with the fact that there was officially nowhere to go.

"Final containment," West said. Though his limp had gotten even worse, clearly paining him with every step, he'd insisted on carrying Cass. Daniel doubted unconsciousness and shallow breathing could be a good sign of anything, and vaguely remembered—again from TV—something about keeping concussion victims awake. But they couldn't exactly take her to a hospital, and there seemed little to do for her otherwise but make sure she didn't get left behind.

*One by one,* Daniel thought, thinking of Ellie, who he didn't know well enough to miss, but missed nonetheless. *That's how we'll go. Till there's nothing left.*

Milo had, somehow, fallen asleep in his arms.

Small favors.

"The whole town's a laboratory," Jule said. "An *embarrassing* one. You think GMT wants people to know what they did to us?"

"I knew it couldn't be the military," West said. "The government wouldn't do that."

"Yeah, big relief," Jule said. "Because we're much better off dealing with a massive defense contractor with all the money in the world and a huge incentive not to go to prison. You think they're not going to do whatever they can to shut us all up?"

"So they cut off the phone lines," Daniel said.

"Cut us off completely," West said.

"They wait," Daniel said. "They watch."

"And when they're done?" Jule mimed an explosion. "They put us out of our misery."

"They can't just erase an entire town," Daniel said. "That's crazy. Even if anyone *would* do something like that—you don't think people would *notice*?"

"Who'd notice if Oleander wasn't here?" Jule said.

"They could blame it on the storm," West said. "Maybe they already did. The whole world probably thinks we don't exist."

"We could try to turn ourselves in," Daniel said. "If we're immune—"

"If they cared, you don't think they would have tried to get their hands on us before they put a hole through her brain?" Jule said.

"We could go back," West said. "Tell people what's really happening."

"*You* want to try that?" Jule asked. "You want to go tell Mom and Dad they're maybe evil and definitely about to get blown up by the fake U.S. government?"

West didn't answer.

"Over at my place, that's just another day," she said. "But I still wouldn't count on them not to shoot the messenger."

"We could hide out here," West said, "but . . ."

But in the morning, the Watchdogs would be back. And even if they survived another day, there would inevitably come another night, and then another morning, and how long could they survive in the woods, getting chased, getting hungry, foraging for berries none of them were equipped to identify or squirrels none of them were willing to eat. Long enough to last until a bomb dropped and ended all their problems at once?

They hiked along the edge of the woods, searching for a weak spot, but the barbed wire stretched along the perimeter, dotted with what appeared to be motion detectors and cameras and nasty-looking wiring that suggested an electrified fence. If they were going to escape, it wouldn't be here, and it wouldn't be tonight.

"She's not breathing right." West lowered Cass to the ground. Her breaths were too shallow and too few, with alarmingly long pauses in between. Daniel shook her and called her name, but her eyes stayed closed. Her forehead was hot to the touch. West wasn't looking too good himself. And despite the sleeve she kept pressed to her wound, Jule was still bleeding.

"We have to get out of the woods," he said.

"We can't let them find us," Jule said, a hard edge to her voice. "I won't go back to . . . *that*."

"I think I know a place," he said. They would have to make it back through town without being seen, and once there, they'd be stuck in the heart of the town they were so desperate to escape. Which wasn't as daunting as the fact that they'd need to trust someone to keep their secret. Someone who was a child, and thus safe from the R8-G—but someone who was a child, who they had no reason to trust.

But then, they had no reason to trust each other.

"Somewhere no one would ever think to look for us," he said.

He didn't say: *Somewhere we'll be safe.*

That seemed too much to ask.

Grace was awake when the knock on the door came. She was nearly always awake these days. Sleep didn't seem like something she deserved, not until she succeeded where she had failed, twice now. Not until Cass was gone.

Her mistake, she decided, had been outsourcing the job to someone else, to a whole town of someone elses. That had been

the coward's way out. "If you want something done right . . . ,"
she murmured, from her makeshift bedroll beneath the crib.
*Do it yourself.* That was her father's voice echoing in her head,
her father before Owen's death, when he had talked too much,
embarrassingly much, always spouting his shopworn words
of wisdom, proud as if he'd coined the phrases himself.

*Do it yourself.*

When she was very small—older than Owen had been, but
not much—her father had briefly convinced her he had magi-
cal powers. It wasn't so much the coins he pulled from her ears
or the thoughts he managed to successfully "read" (most of
them about dessert) as it was her eagerness to believe that her
father had powers commensurate with his wisdom. He seemed
to know everything—so surely, if magic was possible in this
world, if you could control events with your mind and predict
the future and see through a face and into a soul, her father
knew how to do it. And she'd been so desperate to believe she
lived in that kind of world.

He had turned out not to be omnipotent, or particularly
potent at all.

He had turned out not to know everything.

But for a moment, when the knock came again and she
swung the door open to reveal a bunch of teenagers on the
doorstep, all of them smeared with dust and blood and fear,
she was inclined to believe once again. She barely heard them
explain what they were doing there, or beg for her mercy, or
promise they had answers to all her questions and could reveal
terrible things. It didn't matter why they thought they had arrived at her house, because she knew the real reason. They
had—she believed, she finally had to believe—been guided

there. Because the football one was cradling a limp body in his hands, a limp body that was still breathing. It would, as directed by Grace, be carried up to the guest room and laid out on a bed, where it would wait for her, like a present, unable to defend itself. Where it would sleep like a baby, one might say.

Grace swung the door wide and ushered them in, letting them babble, pretending to listen, trying not to smile. If her father wanted her to *do it yourself,* he could hardly have made it easier for her to try.

## 13

## THE WAGES OF SIN

They slept well that night, though none of them expected to. Grace felt the drowsiness take her while they were all still huddled in the living room, telling their confusing tale. Deciding that killing Cass would be all the sweeter once she'd opened her eyes and could see death on its way, Grace allowed the football player to carry her up to her bedroom, where she hadn't slept since the storm, but slept now, hard and deep, dreaming of blood.

Daniel fell asleep curled around Milo, lulled by the steady rise and fall of the boy's chest, and the way he smiled as his eyelids fluttered, as if he were dreaming them into a better day.

West dreamed of Nick, and though he told the phantom *You're not real,* he let the thin arms curl around him and the lips press to his bruised cheek and thought that maybe it would be all right to lose the fight, to die, if death would be like this.

Only Jule thought of Ellie as she closed her eyes and tucked her knees to her chest, wondering at the girl's transformation in the woods, at her history with Baz, at her determination not just to save Jule and Cass, but to put herself in their place. And she resolved, the next morning, to repay the favor. Maybe she couldn't save the town; maybe she couldn't even save herself.

But she could at least do what she had to do to find Ellie. *I don't believe in you,* Jule thought, *but she does. So watch out for her.* It was the decision about what she would do in the morning that finally let her give in to sleep. She dreamed of Baz, and her right hand twitched, reaching for an invisible knife.

They would not have slept, if they had known.

The deacon kept Ellie safe, as he'd promised. Long enough to spirit her away from Baz and his Watchdogs; long enough to get her back to the center of town; long enough to rally the people of Oleander, who'd had their hearts set on a burning, and would take what they could get.

They could not get the killer they'd been promised—not that day.

But they could get a fallen saint. A false prophet. Judged guilty, by public acclamation, of fraud and sacrilege, of making fools of the townspeople and dealing slanderous insults to the deacon. She had spoken so often of the need for cleansing, for purging the town of all sin before God struck again with His other fist. She had warned He would not hesitate to punish the many for the sins of the few. She was a liar, but in this, she spoke the truth. So said the deacon, so said the town.

"Your sins will be forgiven," Deacon Barnes had assured Ellie in the woods. He promised her so again under the moonlight, as the first stars cut through the dark, and she was bound to the pyre and delivered to her fate.

The deacon yanked her hands behind her head and tied them to the post. Clair and Morgan bound her feet and rued that they had ever been her friend. The wind screamed, and it was Oleander, crying for her blood. It was Ellie, crying.

She had always imagined there would be more dignity in martyrdom.

She was not Joan of Arc; she was not Jesus. She was not stoic, and she was neither silent nor brave. She was seventeen years old, and she was about to be set on fire, and she wanted someone to hold her and tell her it was going to be all right.

"The Lord will not abide false prophets," the deacon shouted to the crowd. "We will not abide!"

Ellie's mouth was too dry for words. *Please*, her lips said, and God had no answer.

"Oleander shall be purged of sin," the deacon shouted. "And the purging shall begin here and now."

He beckoned her mother to the stage.

No one knew the truth about Ellie King. Not her mother, who had read her diary; not Deacon Barnes, who had heard her confession, and promised to cleanse her sins. He could see her stain, but not its cause. Not the wound from which the tainted blood flowed.

Only God saw that.

God, and Ellie, every time she looked in the mirror.

There had been a baby.

In the time after Baz, after the night of the bucket and the bath, after she'd been cast out but before she'd been saved, there had been a baby. A month, first, of uncertainty and fear and secret vomiting in the deacon's guest bathroom—all of which, she'd told herself, could be ascribed to the stress of her situation. Things happened when your body was under duress. Things could happen, and they could be innocent: your breasts could tenderize, your stomach could lose its sea legs, your cycle could upend itself, and you could ignore it all. Especially if you could believe that you had been careful with your calendar and believe that Baz had pulled out in time and believe that things like that didn't happen to you.

A fourteen-year-old in Oleander, Kansas, couldn't easily acquire condoms without everyone knowing exactly what she was about to do, and a fourteen-year-old could, under no circumstances, acquire a home pregnancy test without everyone knowing exactly what she had become. Without a license, she couldn't drive to a town where no one knew her name.

She swiped a test from Gathers Drugs. She peed on the stick.

She locked herself in her room—a half storeroom, half office in which the deacon had shoved an air mattress and copies of *Prince Charming Is Worth the Wait* and *Protecting Your Purity: God's Handbook for the Christian Teen*. She stayed there for three days, and for three days, she fasted, and she cried. She dripped tears on the Bible, and found herself in Psalm 69: "When I weep and fast, I must endure scorn."

Abortion was out of the question.

Abortion, she knew, from school and from church, was murder.

She didn't know whether she believed that, or whether she believed Ms. Jacobs, the absurdly young gym teacher who'd been very fond of the word *choice*, as in "Abortion is a safe and valid _____."

It was not so in Oleander; it was not so for Ellie, who didn't need the Internet to tell her that in a state with only one abortion provider and a parental-consent requirement, her choice was only: tell her mother she was having a baby, or wait for her mother to figure it out.

She was having a baby.

The deacon had told her that if she prayed, she would be saved.

He told her that if she accepted Jesus into her heart, she would be saved.

And so she prayed. Every morning and every night, every spare minute, on her knees, in church, in the bedroom that wasn't her own, in the bathroom at school when no one was watching. *Please, Jesus. Make it go away.*

The deacon said Jesus knew what was in her soul, and so He knew what it meant. He heard her prayer as it was intended:

*Please, Jesus. Kill my baby.*

And one day, the blood came, and with it a wrenching pain, and a loosening, and with a soft whimper and a flush of the toilet, she was saved.

The deacon knew only that she'd given herself to the Lord, and he doused her in holy water, and celebrated, and she was welcomed back into her home with open arms. She dedicated herself to her new life. She scrubbed her soul. But the deacon had lied. Because all the soup kitchens and all the food drives in the world couldn't wash away the stain.

And now there was the voice, naming her sins.

*Filthy.*

*Lustful.*

*Baby killer.*

It knew her as no one else did, so how could she not believe it?

"I don't know if I can," Ellie's mother said as Ellie whimpered and screamed and begged her: "Please, no, Mommy, don't."

The deacon pressed the lighter into her hand. "You can, and you must. It's only right it be you. Her mother should save her."

Ellie's mother turned the lighter slowly in her hands, seeming hypnotized by it. "She's always made such a mess," she told the deacon. "Children can't help themselves, you know. Disgusting creatures."

The deacon patted her shoulder. "This is why they need us. To teach them."

"Yes," she said. "This way she'll learn."

Ellie closed her eyes. It couldn't be the last thing she saw: the deacon's eyes, her mother's smile. She closed her eyes, and the noise of the crowd dropped away, and she heard only the voice, except it was different now—no longer angry, no longer so gleefully knowing. It spoke not in her ears, but in her entire being, the words vibrating in her chest and head and heart. She knew it could be fear, or wishful thinking, or the drug, but it sounded like none of those. It sounded true.

*You have always been clean*, it said.

*You have always been saved.*

She had time to hear her mother's final goodbye—not *I love you*, not *I'm sorry*, but *It has to be.* She had time to wish that things had been otherwise, and she'd lived a different life. Or at least that she had lived this one with a friend. She found herself wishing, strangely, that Jule were by her side now, or Cassandra, or even the football player, Baz's friend, the strange one she barely knew. She had time for the voice to tell her:

*You are not alone.*

She believed that, too.

She had always believed less than people thought; she had believed less than she wanted to, though she had tried so hard. But she believed now. That He was here. That He was with her.

That she was good.

She took a deep breath, and believed that she was unstained and unbroken and deserved to live, and she had time to be happy before her mother's hand lit the pyre, and the flames swallowed her up.

# 14

## DEVIL TOWN

The execution of Eleanor King was an unqualified success. So much so that, as the deacon had predicted, the town found itself hungry for more righteous cleansing. By the next morning, the Watchdogs joined with the Oleander police force and a posse of citizen volunteers to round up what undesirables they could. In a town of this size, everyone knew the deviants—confirmed and suspected. The lesbian librarian, the gay hippie with the organic tea business and his tow-truck driver boyfriend, the outspoken atheists, the criminals, the drug addicts, and the alcoholics (at least the sloppy, unpopular ones), not to mention the unfortunates whose only crime was landing at the wrong end of a petty grudge or a bad business deal. Once the roundups began, it didn't take a genius to realize their efficacy in getting inconvenient colleagues out of the way.

Only those with known arsenals (and hair triggers) were spared. Which left the Prevettes and the Preacher unmolested, but everyone else was fair game. Baz and the Watchdogs contributed a list of younger residents who'd already showed signs of deviance and dissent. The primary sign, as it happened, was exhibiting disrespect for Baz and the Watchdogs and their sport of choice.

By midafternoon, the righteousness brigade had rounded up more than thirty people, ages fifteen through seventy-seven (the latter being James Priest, who, before retiring, had spent his career foreclosing on farms with just a little too much joy). They were dragged out of their homes, down their streets, and locked into an abandoned grocery store that would serve as a makeshift brig until something more suitable could be found. There was no consensus on what should be *done* with the deviants. The act of capture, the pleasure of taunting them once they'd been locked up, was enough for one day. Punishment could wait for the next.

The mood in town was joyous. All concern about the quarantine or fear of what lay behind it had burned away in the righteous flames. As if waking from a dream, they discovered that isolation was a gift: the opportunity to create an empire of their own. Every home was a potential kingdom; every man, every woman a dictator, finally empowered to reshape life according to desire and whim.

There were several homicides. Fights broke out on street corners at the slightest provocation. Those addicts who weren't swept up in the purge drowned in the depths of their poison of choice. Long-simmering sexual tension erupted regardless of circumstance or setting; long-simmering rivalries, grudges held for decades, presented themselves for immediate resolution. There were duels; there were ambushes. And that night there was more than one person who went to sleep and wouldn't wake up in the morning.

The children noticed; children always notice. Their parents had turned into creatures who lacked impulse control and ignored responsibility, who took what they wanted and did as they pleased, and there were children who ended up bruised, or broken. There were children who were turned out of their homes—or were wise enough to run—and they prowled the streets, enjoying the novelty of adventure until the moon rose and the night cooled and they had no bed to return to. When that happened, wherever it happened, Laura Tanner was waiting. The beloved Miss Oleander, with her weapons and her willingness to do what was necessary to keep her children safe, the children who now belonged to her.

This was the report that Grace brought back for her houseguests after a few hours of poking around the town. They heard very little after "the execution of Eleanor King."

They blamed themselves.

It was her house, but Grace knew when she wasn't wanted. They talked past her, as if she were a child—but then, that's what they believed she was. It was why they trusted her, and so she allowed it.

They barely noticed her, which meant no one thought anything of it when she slipped upstairs to sit in Cass's room and wait for her to wake. They probably thought it was touching, evidence that she'd accepted their story and forgiven Cass. The poor, helpless, unwitting victim of her own uncontrollable actions.

But Grace was, probably, under the control of this R8-G at that very moment, and she didn't feel very unwitting. Her desires were her own. The drug was not the reason she wanted Cass to die. If it was the reason she was willing to make it happen, then score one for the evil scientists.

Except that Cass was unconscious, and had been for

thirteen hours, and still she lived. Grace could bring herself to do nothing until the older girl woke.

She had to see it coming, Grace told herself. She had to know what was happening, and that Grace was the one responsible.

Maybe.

But the fact was, hours passed, Cass breathed, and Grace sat.

Waiting.

The safest time to leave was the middle of the night. But that wasn't saying much. Which was why West didn't tell anyone that he was going, or where. A day of sleep and talking in circles had brought them no closer to figuring out a plan for escape, other than risking another flight to the woods. If they made it that far, maybe they could scramble under the barbed wire and skirt the edges of the floodlights and somehow make it past the heavily guarded border and the twenty miles of prairie that lay beyond. It was a last-ditch, last-moment kind of plan, and they believed this to still be another day away.

Somehow, the others slept. But West couldn't close his eyes without seeing Ellie. He couldn't stop thinking about his parents and whether they would be exterminated before they could be returned to their right mind. And he was afraid that sleep meant Nick would come—and more afraid that he would not. So he walked the night.

The old grocery was under guard by twelve men, each carrying a rifle. Thanks to the boarded-up windows, there was no way of telling who lay inside. For all West knew, Jason was curled up comfortably in his own bed, dreaming of live music and dead bullies. But it seemed unlikely—and with Baz involved, it seemed impossible.

West couldn't get him out alone.

Maybe Jason would be better off inside. If the whole town was infected, then maybe being locked up was the safest place for anyone to be. Until the "final containment" began, that is.

If they could get out of town, if they could stop it, then everyone could be saved. If they couldn't . . . then the town was as much prison as the grocery, and did geography really matter if they were all going to die?

They were pretty rationalizations.

If he'd still been at home, West thought, then his parents would have delivered him here. This he did not doubt. Did that give him some obligation to play savior? If he'd been spared by the grace of his heavenly Father (and the madness of his earthly one), then should Jason and the rest be spared by the grace of West? In the morning, he promised himself. In the morning, if there was no better plan, no certain way to save the town or themselves, then he would rally these people who were somehow less and more than friends, and convince them to at least save someone. Or to try.

*Is that enough?* he whispered. *That's all I have.*

Nick was silent. That night, he did not come. He never came again.

"You sleeping?" Daniel asked, from his spot on the couch.

Jule opened her eyes to darkness. "Not a chance. You?"

The sofa was L-shaped. They lay head to head, their fingers nearly touching at the joint.

"Can't," he said. Then, because he didn't have to see her

face in the dark, because he wanted to tell someone and for some reason, he wanted the someone to be her, "I don't mind. When I sleep . . . I've been having these . . . dreams."

"Pretty sure that's natural in a growing boy," she said, her tone unable to match the joke in her words. "Testosterone and all."

"Dreams about that day in the drugstore," he said. "The shootings. Everyone dies. Again. Only this time . . ."

"This time you're the one holding the gun."

His breath caught. "How did you know?"

She hesitated. "It just figured. But, Daniel, it's only a dream. You know that, right? It's not like you're seeing the future or something."

There was nothing but to say it: "I wake up in the drugstore. I wake up in the drugstore holding a gun."

"You mean, in the dream?"

"I mean in real life. In the middle of the night. I wake up there, and my hands are bloody from broken glass, and I've got a gun, and I don't know how I got there, and . . ." He'd thought it would feel better to say it. But it didn't. "I thought I was going crazy. Maybe I am. Crazy."

She shifted on the couch, and when she settled back into place, her fingertips rested atop his palm. Without letting himself think whether it had been an accident, he closed his fingers over hers. She let him. Her hand was cold.

"For me it was a knife."

He held on to her fingers, afraid to speak and break the spell.

"My uncle's knife. First in my dreams, then—like you said.

I woke up, and there it was. In my hand. Somehow. And it was like it . . . this is going to sound stupid, but kind of like it . . ."

"Like it *wanted* you to use it?"

"You too?"

"Me too."

There was a sound: a ragged breath, or a choked sob. Some explosion of air and emotion.

"But it doesn't have to mean anything," he said. "It's like you said, it's not the future. If it's the R8-G, maybe knowing makes it better. We don't have to do what it wants."

"But what if . . . ?" The half-asked question hung between them. "Nothing," she said finally. "It doesn't matter anymore. It's over now."

"What is?"

"I told you, *nothing.* Anyway, maybe the dreams will stop now. I haven't had one since . . . well, not for a couple of days now."

Daniel realized that he hadn't, either. Not since the night Jule had shown up at his door.

"Not since we've all been together," he said. "It's like we're stronger now. Stronger than it."

"That's stupid," she said. "All we are now is screwed."

"I know that. But still . . . it doesn't feel that way. It feels better."

A shorter exhalation of air this time. Only a sigh, soft and defeated. "Maybe," she admitted. "It does."

"I was looking forward to Bali," he said.

"Tahiti."

"There, too."

"But now . . ."

"Stuck in Oleander for the rest of our days," Jule said. "Maybe we should be glad we don't have much longer to go. You think it'll be a bomb?"

"I don't know, Jule. We shouldn't think about—"

"That's too messy, I think. Too big. If it were the government, maybe. But a private company? They've got soldiers, they've got tanks—I think it'll be on-the-ground combat. Like in Iraq or something. A guy with a gun kicks in the door and sprays everyone inside with bullets, and next thing you know, we're all rotting in some mass grave."

"Please don't."

"Or some kind of toxic gas," she said. "That would be poetic, right? Less fun for them, maybe. If I had a tank, I'd want to use it."

"We'll get out," Daniel said. "And we'll tell people what's happening, and they'll stop it in time. We'll save everyone."

"Superheroes. You're just like Milo."

If only it were that easy. "I've never been like Milo."

"But you really believe it. That we're going to save the day."

It seemed suddenly important that *she* believe it. "Yes."

"At least, we know it's coming," she said quietly. "And when it does, we won't have to be alone."

He kept his hold on her fingers, and wrapped his other hand around hers. He tipped his head back, and met her eyes. The pupils were huge, drinking in the night. He could just make out the curves of her face, the whites of her eyes, the shock of purple slashing across her forehead, the bandage on her cheek. She went very still in his grasp and then, abruptly, sat up.

But she let him hold on.

Daniel sat, too. Their linked hands lay between them, carefully ignored by both, as if to acknowledge them would necessitate immediate release. Her skin was much softer than he had expected. Her fingers were so small.

"You better act now while you still have the chance," she said, a new sharpness in her voice cutting through the dreamlike intimacy of the night.

"What?" She couldn't have read his mind; he hadn't even made it up yet. This wasn't anything so clear-cut as want, or desire—those he understood, even if he'd never quite been able to act on them. This was . . . like standing at the edge of a diving board, or a cliff, gravity taunting him, eager to take its inevitable course. This was like the dream, like the gun, and he couldn't help thinking that if he closed his eyes and let himself fall, he would wake up to find himself in her arms.

"Sleeping Beauty up there," she said. "Little Miss Dream Come True."

"What?" he said again, now genuinely confused.

"Not that I encourage making out with the unconscious," she said. "Fairy tale or not. But she has to wake up sometime, and then I recommend you make your move before the whole food-for-worms thing."

"Are we talking about *Cass*?"

"Playing dumb probably isn't going to work for you. I don't get the sense she goes for stupid."

"You're not serious."

"I see the way you look at her," she said.

"And how's that?"

"Like you can't believe your luck. We're in the middle of the apocalypse here, but every time she's in the room, you act like you won the lottery. No, better, like some rock star in a bikini just parachuted into your living room and handed you a bottle of suntan lotion."

"That's . . . very specific. You really think that's how I look at her?"

"Really and specifically."

It was too embarrassing to consider that it might be true. And all the more embarrassing to explain that looking at Cass was like admiring a picture in a magazine, something glossy but flat, and more than a little unreal. He'd watched Cass from a distance, while Jule was *here*. Up close, too close, close enough to see the rough spots and touch the imperfections. Close enough to scare him. But he couldn't tell her that, any more than he could tell her that Cass made him wish he were someone else, while Jule just made him want to be brave.

"You always do this, you know," he said.

"I'm not sure you know me well enough to know I 'always' do anything."

"You get kind of mean. When you're nervous."

"I'm mean under almost all circumstances. It's my default."

He grinned—it took her a moment to get why.

"And I'm *not* nervous," she added quickly.

It was an obvious lie, which was surprising, but not nearly so much as the fact that *he* wasn't nervous. Nor, any longer, was he confused.

He was terrified—but somehow, that didn't seem to matter.

"I thought I was in love with her," he said. "Cass."

"Yes, we just covered that."

"But that was before I even knew her. The real her."

"The real her doesn't seem so bad. If you can overlook that whole brainwashed-murderer thing."

If he told her that maybe the problem was he hadn't known *himself*, she would laugh in his face.

"Okay, it was before I knew *you*," he said.

"And that's relevant how?"

*Show, don't tell*, their English teacher had drilled into them the year before. It wasn't until now that he understood her point.

He let go of Jule's hand, and cupped her face. Crossing the distance between seemed at once impossible and the easiest thing he'd ever done. It wasn't like stepping into an abyss; it wasn't like falling. It wasn't *like* anything. It was only what it was: Jule, soft in some places and prickly in others, tough all over, in his arms. Jule, the smell of Jule, sweat and clove cigarettes and leather. Jule, in the dark, a solid shadow, never afraid. Jule's eyelids, pale. Jule's cheeks, smooth. Jule's lips, soft.

It was kissing Jule. Not falling after all but, finally, landing on solid ground.

She didn't know she was going to push him away until she'd done it. As soon as she did, she wanted to take it back. But the space between them had opened up again. Daniel was on his feet, and she was shaking her head, and of course he took it as a no intended for him, because who would say no to themselves?

"Sorry," she said, unsure what she was apologizing for, unsure of everything. "I didn't mean . . ." She didn't want anyone to touch her.

She wanted him to touch her.

She could be bold. Move back toward him, close the space, take what she wanted—if she knew what she wanted, if her body hadn't gone rigid, if her lungs weren't so tight, if she could trust him enough to explain. If she could trust him.

She was afraid if he tried again, she would slap him or freeze up in his arms or, worst, cry; she was afraid he wouldn't try again.

Her lip throbbed where Baz had drawn blood.

Everything hurt.

"No, I'm sorry. I shouldn't have," he said, and so it was too late.

Because going back to sleep—or at least lying quietly together in the dark—seemed too intimate for the sudden awkwardness between them, they retreated to business. As if talking through their impossible circumstances yet again would change the fact that they were surrounded by concentric circles of enemies.

"If you think about it," Jule said, "we do have one weapon. The town itself. The people. If we aim them the right way . . ."

"If we start a war, you mean? Set them on the soldiers? Can you imagine how many people would end up dead?"

"They're not soldiers," she said. "And people are going to end up dead anyway, even if we don't do anything. You don't think they have a right to know what's coming, too?"

"They're not in their right mind."

"Or maybe they're just doing exactly what they want to do, for the first time in their lives. Maybe they're more themselves than they've ever been. Maybe the R8-G is doing them a favor."

"You can't believe that."

"Inhibitions aren't always good," she said, but that was getting too close, and they both edged away.

"We don't even know if this is curable. What if it's not, and we let them loose on the world?"

"Maybe the world deserves it."

"We'd be responsible for everything they did after that, Jule. Everyone they hurt."

She was sorry for him then, sorrier than for herself. Because he actually believed that; because it was how he had always lived. "You can't be responsible for everything, Daniel. You know that, right?"

"I'm going to sleep," he said, not unkindly, but with finality.

This time, without discussing it, they lay toe to toe, their heads pointed in opposite directions.

She did not sleep.

"You awake?" Jule asked.

For a moment, he wondered if maybe he had been sleeping after all, and had dreamed everything, their truth swapping, their kiss, his humiliation, and this was his chance to do it again, for the first time, right this time—or to be smart and not do it at all. Then, for another moment, he considered keeping his mouth shut. But, "What do you think?"

"I think I figured something out," she said. "A plan."

"For getting out?"

"What if we don't have to get out and get help?" she asked. "What if there were a way to make help come to us?"

Cass woke to Grace's dead eyes, and choked off a scream. Her head throbbed. Grace was fuzzy around the edges. She was in a strange room, but strangely familiar, on a soft bed, with no bars on the door and no guns—and Grace.

Maybe, she thought, she was still asleep.

As she puzzled it out, and the memories of the previous day trickled back, she remembered. The R8-G; the answer. At that, she couldn't help herself: she smiled.

Grace slapped her.

"It wasn't my fault," Cass said. It sounded feeble. "They drugged me. I didn't know what I was doing. I couldn't help myself."

"How do you know?"

"I know. If I could have stopped it, I would have."

"But you didn't. So Owen's dead."

"You tried to shoot me," Cass said. She was foggy and feverish and thought she might throw up. The light burned her eyes. "You actually pointed a gun at me and pulled the trigger."

"Yeah."

"Are you . . . do you feel weird at all, Grace? Like, different?"

"They told me everything," Grace said. She yanked the pillow out from beneath Cass's head. "Children are immune, remember?"

Cass tried to push herself up into a sitting position, but a wave of dizziness knocked her back to the mattress. The impact set off an explosion in her skull. "I don't feel well," she said. "Can we talk later? After I sleep?"

"You can close your eyes if you want," Grace said. "Maybe it's better that way. Poetic or something."

"What's better?"

"As long as you know it's coming. And why." The pillow descended, and her world went first white, then black.

Grace was small, but not too small to bear down. There was nothing for Cass to breathe; there was no breath, only a tightening, then a burning. Her skin tingled with panic. This was terror; this was her lungs swelling to fill her chest, to rise up her throat, to grasp and beg and hurt for the air that lay just beyond the soft cotton. This was floating away; this was death.

"That's what it felt like." The voice came from the other side, so far away. "That's what you did to him."

Her mouth opened, screaming, screaming noiselessly, tears soaking the cotton. She could feel Grace's hands through the pillow, pressing down, holding down, her lungs, her pain, her guilt.

*It would be poetic,* she thought, her arms spasming.

*It wasn't my fault,* she thought, her body forcing itself on, rebelling against all things final.

*It wasn't me,* she thought, and it still wasn't, neither her mind nor her will but her body, her heart pumping furiously, her blood rushing, her muscles flexing with such force that Grace flew backward and landed on the floor with a noisy clatter and cry. Cass's chest heaved with the sweet, fresh heaven of one full breath after another. It wasn't her, but she was the one who got to live.

It had taken all the strength she had, and she collapsed to the bed. There were footsteps in the hallway, murmurs of concern, a bursting through the door, a wait for explanations.

"Grace tripped," Cass said. Because this was between them. Because neither had had the chance to decide. "I woke up, and she was going to get me some water, and she tripped."

Jule helped the girl to her feet. Daniel rushed to Cass's side, rested a cool hand on her forehead. "You're covered in sweat," he said.

"A girl loves to hear that," Jule told him.

"Are you all right?" he asked. "How do you feel?"

"Alive," Cass said, and drew in another greedy breath, and another.

"Are *you* all right?" Jule asked Grace.

"I . . . tripped," she said. She would not look at Cass, at any of them.

"Cass, think you can get up?" Jule said. "We don't have much time, if we're going to make this work."

"Make what work?" Cass said.

Jule cast a strange look at Daniel, who turned from it. "Playing hero," she said. "We're going to save the day."

# 15

## THE DARK-EYED NIGHT

Milo wouldn't leave the room, wouldn't sleep, wouldn't stop weaving through Grace's legs and twining his fingers through Cass's hair and tugging at Grace's shirt and begging Cass to read comics with him. No matter how late it got or how much Grace growled, he stayed. And he stayed awake. It was as if he somehow sensed what might happen if he left them alone together. The others had taken off as soon as West came back. Upon determining that Cass was still woozy and Grace was still thirteen, Jule had decided that neither of them be told the details of this great and mighty plan. So they'd been left behind to mind the kid, and each other. It occurred to no one that it might be neither prudent nor kind to leave Grace behind with the girl who'd killed her brother.

Cass had said nothing, just let them leave. She watched Grace over Milo's bounding, sugar-crazed shoulders with that newly eerie stare of hers, watchful and, in some aggravating way, knowing. It was the kind of expression Grace longed to master herself. In a different time, with a different Cass, she might have spent the night taking surreptitious mental notes, trying to stretch the muscles of her face to match the baby-sitter's. She'd done it before.

"Wouldn't you like to take that puzzle back to your room?" Grace asked as Milo dumped out one of her old jigsaw boxes onto the carpet. Pieced together, it showed the entire Disney family, or at least it was supposed to. Over the years, Mickey's head, Cinderella's feet, and several other crucial pieces had dematerialized into the ether, leaving behind a family of ill-fitting pieces and jagged holes.

"It's not my room," Milo said.

It was Owen's room.

At least he'd confined himself to the corner and was amusing himself. Though Grace knew, because they'd already tried it, that if she and Cass dared slip away, Milo would follow. He was sticky.

"I know what you're thinking," Grace said, in a low voice.

Cass gave her a thin smile. "I doubt that."

"You think I'm infected." She glanced at Milo to make sure he hadn't heard. The kid seemed utterly absorbed by the chewed cardboard. "You think I've gone crazy, too."

"Not crazy."

"Off, then. Like spoiled milk."

"I think you're not yourself," Cass said.

"So why not tell the others?"

"I figured this was between us."

"If you told them, they'd probably lock me up," Grace said. "You'd be safe."

"Maybe."

"I hope you're not waiting for a thank-you."

Cass shook her head.

"So you're just counting on the fact that I won't do anything with Milo here? That seems kind of stupid, doesn't it?

What do I care what an eight-year-old thinks?" But she was sneaking constant glances at Milo; she was whispering. "If you're right about me, then I'm *bad* now. Maybe I'll just kill you both."

"I don't think you will."

"Imagine what Daniel would think if he knew about me. If he knew *you* knew, and let him leave Milo here anyway."

"What Daniel thinks isn't my priority right now," Cass said.

It was infuriating, how calm she was, how sure. So irritatingly certain that Grace wouldn't dash downstairs for one of her mother's butcher knives. Or maybe not certain, but serene about the possibility. Maybe there was a part of her that wanted to die. That was the most infuriating thing of all, because it couldn't be a true punishment if Cass wanted it. Then it would be a mercy.

"You know what I think? I think this has nothing to do with your stupid drug." It had to be the truth. It was the truest feeling, the deepest need, she'd ever had. If it wasn't real, nothing was. "This is just me. This is what I want. I'm a killer, too. You made me one."

"Prove it," Cass said.

Grace nodded at Milo. "Get him out of here, and I'm happy to."

"Prove it by waiting."

"For what?"

"Until this is all over—until you're *sure* it's got nothing to do with what's happening to the town. That it's just about your brother. Doesn't Owen deserve that?"

Cass thought she knew so much, but she didn't even know

that it wasn't about Owen. It was about her, Grace, and all the things Cass had taken away from her. Grace flexed her fingers, feeling strong enough to get it done right here, right now, just take a grip on her throat and squeeze.

"If you do it now, you'll never know," Cass said. "I think you'll always wonder. If it was the R8-G, or you."

Grace wasn't stupid. She wasn't a child anymore, easily tricked into an early bedtime by reverse psychology or a promise of extra dessert. She knew Cass would say anything to save her own life. But if the others came back to find Cass's dead body and Milo singing about the horrible thing Grace had done, Grace was finished. If they found a way to escape, they'd never take her with them. They'd leave her to the madness of Oleander, to these people with their infection, their *darkness*, and Grace didn't belong there. Grace wasn't one of them. If proving that meant waiting, then she would wait.

"If I am infected, and I manage not to kill you, then doesn't that prove that you could have stopped yourself?" Grace said. "That this whole 'don't blame me' thing is bullshit?"

"If we can find a way to cure you, and you don't want to kill anyone anymore, that would prove something, too," Cass said. "That it was just the R8-G. That it wasn't really *you*."

"I'll wait," Grace said. "But not because I care about proving anything to you."

Cass didn't argue.

"It won't matter," Grace said. "Now. Later. It's all the same. I am what you made me."

"Then I choose later."

Grace nodded. A deal with the devil.

As if he knew the danger had, for the moment, passed, Milo was finally asleep.

Nearly two weeks after the storm, most of the roads had been cleared, the downed trees, smashed cars, and shattered roofs pushed to the curb. Some streets now looked completely untouched, any windows repaired and broken glass swept away. But Daniel, Jule, and West kept mostly to the streets that had been flattened, streets like war zones, where the occasional leaning wall or overturned bathtub was the only sign that where there now lay an ocean of broken boards and bricks and trash, there had once been a town. It was already difficult to remember what things had been like when they were normal. When they'd all taken the sameness for granted, and prayed for it to end.

They passed a park, where feral children played on swings that miraculously rose from a field of rubble; they passed a license plate embedded in a tree trunk; they passed the tattered remains of American flags; they passed a waist-high brick wall, all that was left of a house, graffitied with the promise JESUS SAVES. Above the promise, a different hand had written WHEN?

Jule had no idea whether the house she needed was still standing. If it wasn't, they were screwed.

But it was.

"This is it," Jule said, peering up at the hulking ruin. The aging Victorian had weathered the storm, but two decades of disrepair had taken their toll. The peeling siding, boarded windows, and pitted beams were evident even in the dark. Jule hadn't been back in nearly ten years, and, judging from the weedy lawn, the overgrown bushes nearly blockading the front walk, the toppled mailbox, and the diseased poplars, entropy had run its course.

"You sure he still lives here?" Daniel asked.

"You don't think someone would have noticed if he'd moved?" West said. Kyle Sorenson rarely ventured out of his house and even more rarely made it into the heart of town, where he would be forced to interact with other human beings. Still, in the way of small towns and hermit-like old men, he managed to be a powerful presence, his fearsome scowl and wreck of a house fueling dares and nightmares for more than one generation of Oleander youth.

"I was thinking more like died," Daniel said.

"He still lives here," Jule confirmed. "Jack down at the Yellowbird makes regular liquor deliveries out here. He was whining about it last month."

"So, what?" Daniel said. "We just knock on the door, smile nicely, and ask if we can use his shortwave radio? Because of his reputation for being such a nice guy?"

"Just let me go first," Jule said. "He'll let me in."

"What's he *like*?" West asked, with the naked curiosity of one about to solve a major mystery of his childhood.

"Old," Jule said. "Older now, I guess. And . . . sad."

"Were there any swastikas?" West asked.

"Maybe he keeps those hidden behind all the photos of his dead wife," Jule snapped. "Why don't you ask him?"

"I was only *wondering*."

"He's just a lonely old man," Jule said. "That's it."

"No one's 'just' anything these days," Daniel said, and his trigger finger twitched.

Jule stepped gingerly onto the front steps. The rotting wood creaked beneath her weight. "If you men are scared, feel free to wait outside." She knocked.

She'd been afraid herself, the first time Scott had brought her here. She'd never bought the Nazi theory, even as a kid, but she'd caught enough glimpses of Kyle Sorenson shadowing his way through town in trench-coated gloom to form some theories of her own, foremost of which was that he possessed some kind of vampiric, youth-sucking powers and survived only by draining the life force of unwitting children. In fairness, she'd been eight years old, and had read her uncle James's copy of *Dracula* four times. She had not cried, waiting on the doorstep for the old man to reply to the sharp knock, nor had she begged Scott not to deliver her up to the monster. But she had prayed that he would suffer a heart attack on his way to the door.

His breath had been foul, his teeth false and yellow, his hands greased with some old-man slime, but he had not been a monster. Just an old man, with a bowl of candies that might well have been left over from World War II. If you ignored the fuzzy coating, they had a pleasant tang. The fearsome beast of Cherry Street turned out to be a lonely old man—whose only source of entertainment was a basement full of shortwave radios.

She couldn't believe it had taken her this long to think of the radios.

When Scott was finally busted and hauled off to the federal

pen, he hadn't accused Sorenson of turning him in. After all, the feds had been tapping the Prevette phone lines—Scott should have realized, he informed his family through the visiting-room glass, that the radio would be no safer. That the feds were always listening. Jule hoped he'd been right.

No one answered the door. Jule knocked louder.

"Maybe he's not home," Daniel said. He'd been in favor of sneaking into the basement without letting the old man know they were there. "Prudent," he'd called it, sounding—as Jule pointed out—like an old man himself.

"Maybe it's four a.m. and he's a hundred years old," West said, pounding on the door. "He's probably asleep. And deaf." He pressed a shoulder to the door and, before Jule could stop him, shoved it hard enough to crack the frame. The door crashed inward. "That should wake him."

"Or . . . not," Daniel said, in a muffled voice, his hands pressed to his nose and mouth.

Jule gagged. The smell was overwhelming. It was somehow *beyond* smell, a living thing with weight and texture that clawed its way up her nose and down her throat, coating her insides with some toxic mixture of bile and rot. The air itself felt solid, fuzzed like the decrepit candies, and her body rebelled. Everything in her screamed for escape. She somehow forced herself to stand still; she somehow, swallowing a sour mouthful of vomit that tasted of whatever lurked in the house, forced herself to breathe.

West pulled his shirt over his face. Daniel was hunched over, a puddle of puke at his feet.

"The radios are downstairs." Each word forced out cost more effort than she had. The smell would get better as they got used to it, she told herself. Smells always did. But this one seemed to get worse. She had a moment's panic at the thought that even if she fled the house, she wouldn't flee the stench of rot, that it lived inside her now, would hold on and never let go.

It smelled of freshly disemboweled deer, guts steaming in the fall air; it smelled of landfill, acres of garbage moldering under an August sun; it smelled of *wrong*. It smelled like it was coming from the kitchen, and to get to the basement, they had to go through it.

Daniel took Jule's hand. West nodded. She led the way.

Kyle Sorenson had ended his days at the kitchen table. The revolver was still lodged in what was left of his mouth. He'd left the light on, making it impossible to ignore the smear on the faded wallpaper behind him, or pretend it was anything other than a spatter of brain. The words I'M SORRY were painted across the table in his blood.

Now Jule did throw up, again and again, heaving until there was nothing left to expel, until she was hollow and could be entirely filled up by the noxious smell, the thought of which sent her heaving again.

*That's how a corpse smells,* she thought, and tried desperately hard not to think about Ellie, who she'd sent to her death.

*I'm sorry.*

For Sorenson, words hadn't been enough. She wondered whether he'd caught himself in time. When the storm came, and with it, the toxic cloud that unleashed a darkness, that made whatever wrong lived inside you seem right, how long had it taken before he'd found the gun, and the will to use it? What had the whispers in his head urged him to do?

"At least, we don't need his permission to use the radio," West said, sounding, amid all of this, somehow normal. Jule clung to the voice, and its implied sanity.

"Let's do this and get the hell out of here," she said. "Unless you want to check for swastikas."

"I'm good," West said.

No one suggested taking the gun.

They descended into the basement. The light switch on the stairs had no effect, and the narrow beam of West's useless cell phone cast more shadows than it did light. It only increased the sense that they were delivering themselves up to a dungeon. *I'm sorry.* Who knew what secrets were lurking underground? If not decaying skeletons chained to the wall or tables laid out with instruments of torture, then surely at the very least, families of rats summoned from far and wide by the ever-richening smell. But the dim light caught only what Jule remembered, a small space crammed with folding tables, each topped with old-fashioned radios in varying stages of dilapidation. Most were only for listening, but a few served as ham radios that would connect the Sorenson house to the outside world. Kyle Sorenson had been a man of organization and habit, laying the radios out from worst to best working order. Trying very hard not to think of the corpse upstairs or the stench, Jule crossed to the far corner, where, as she'd expected, she found the transceiver. It wasn't the best or most powerful in his collection, and lacked digital tuning, but it was the one he'd shown her how to use all those years ago, his hand covering hers as she inched across the dial.

She swallowed another mouthful of bile, and held out her open palm. "Phone," she said, and West handed over the light.

"You sure you can get this thing to work?" he asked.

"I'm sure."

"If we can't get a signal out—"

"We will."

"And if there's no one listening on the other end?"

"There will be," she said. "There always is."

A whole world of strangers without ever having to leave the house. She'd always wondered what Sorenson saw in these machines—why, if he was clever enough to crave the world beyond Oleander's limits, he didn't exercise his adult prerogative and join it. Why settle for voices, she'd wondered, when you could have the whole thing: new faces and new landscapes, oceans and mountains and canyons and anything but the endless flat? He'd always acted like this was his only option for expanding his small world. "I'm no good around people," he'd said whenever she asked, and she would think *You're good with me.*

Then Scott had gone to prison, and she'd never gone back. And now Sorenson was dead.

She took a few slow, deep breaths, trying to remember what she'd once known. She twisted the dial and tuned in the frequency Scott had used for his coded messages, in hopes the feds were still holding vigil.

"This is a distress call from Oleander, Kansas. People masquerading as soldiers have quarantined the town. There's been a leak of toxic material at the factory nearby, and people here are getting sick. People here are dying. They won't let us out, and soon they're going to kill us all. This is not a joke. My name is—" No one would believe a Prevette. "Eleanor King." She said another silent apology. "You can look me up. I live in

Oleander, Kansas, and if you can hear this, please send the authorities. Send help. Oleander, Kansas. I know this sounds crazy, but if you look into it, you'll see the town is completely cut off. We need your help. Please." Jule sent out the same message on another frequency, and then another. Someone a few miles down the road might tune in and hear her; someone in China might hear her. Someone from GMT might hear her, and do what was necessary to shut her up. There was no way of knowing. You just had to send your voice into the void, and believe someone was listening.

She broke off at the sound of footsteps overhead, seized by the impossible certainty that, stirred by the use of his shortwaves, Kyle Sorenson had woken from death and was on his way downstairs to show them exactly how it was done. But that was nightmare, and these days, reality was bound to be worse. Daniel raised a finger to his lips. Jule darkened the phone.

They held still in the dark, trying not to breathe. The radio crackled. Feet stomped overhead. There was a sound of porcelain crashing against tile, then a shout. "Smoke 'em out!"

The basement door eased open and something clattered down the stairs. Jule assumed it was a tear-gas canister—until it erupted in a ball of fire. She hit the ground. West and Daniel piled on top of her. Smoke billowed, and though the rational part of her brain tried to tell her that she still had time before the basement filled with smoke and fire, she could already feel her lungs tightening, her eyes watering, her heart thumping to the steady tune: *Get out get out get out get out.*

"We got the message out," Daniel murmured. "That's what counts."

They could die now, he meant, and maybe the town would live. The town that didn't mind cornering them in a basement, burning them alive.

"Just keep behind me," West said. Assuming a tackle position, head tucked, shoulders hunched, he charged through the smoke. Jule gave in to her body's panicked demands and followed, Daniel bringing up the rear, all of them bursting into the kitchen and drawing in great breaths of foul air. Six armed men were waiting.

"Told you I saw 'em go inside," Michael Louch crowed. He lived next door and, in a saner life, owned the gas station on State Street. Now he carried a rifle in one hand and a wine bottle stuffed with a dirty handkerchief in the other. Which explained the Molotov cocktail. Louch was notorious for playing with fire.

Six men: a gas-station owner, a shoe salesman, two drunks who spent most days in the drugstore alley, a football coach who by this time had probably killed his wife, and Jule's eighth-grade math teacher, who had, from the apparent goodness of his heart, passed her despite an 80 percent absence rate. He was the one who dragged her out of the house, while the shoe salesman grabbed Daniel. It took the coach and both of his drunk deputies to subdue a wild West.

*To hell with prudence,* Jule thought, struggling in Mr. Schubert's grasp. Exhilarated despite herself by the fresh air, she told the truth. "There's something in the air, in the water. It's making you crazy, but you can fight it." She had no idea whether that was true. "This isn't really you, Mr. Schubert." She had no idea whether that was true, either. "You're a math teacher. This is crazy!" The man showed no sign of hearing her.

When she stopped walking and started kicking, he simply hoisted her off her feet and carried her down the stone path, into the street. Behind her, she heard West grunt in what sounded like pain. Daniel was ominously silent. "They're going to kill us all," she tried again. "The soldiers. They're not really soldiers. They've been experimenting on us, and when the experiment's over, they're going to kill the lab rats. *They're* the enemy. You want to go crazy, go crazy on them."

"Seems like you're the crazy one," Mr. Schubert said. "But that's all right. We have a place for you now."

"You liked me," she said, twisting in his grip. "Remember? Please, remember."

"You were a little bitch," he said. "But you looked good in a tank top."

"You deserve what they're going to do to you," she shouted. "All of you. I hope they burn the place down. I hope you all burn."

The math teacher pinned Jule with the same disdainful stare he always gave the class when they mixed up sine and cosine. "You first."

West hadn't been inside the abandoned grocery store since he was fourteen, still young enough to think that breaking glass, scribbling on walls, and pretending to inhale the occasional joint marked him as daring. After that year, the pack of feral boys he'd run with divided: Half went straight, joining the football team and signing on to a new life of pep rallies and vaguely clean living. The other half graduated from pot to meth, from trespassing to vagrancy, and, in more than one case, from middle school to jail. West had joined the team. Thus saving his life—that's how the coach had put it. Now the coach was the one who shoved him through the door and slammed the padlock in place behind him. The building, abandoned since Clarkson's had gone under in the late nineties, had never been especially spick-and-span—there had always been discarded rags, used condoms, splashes of unidentifiable bodily fluids and heaps that might have been animal, vegetable, or mineral, a whiff of decay. But now the building warehoused nearly thirty of Oleander's undesirables, along with their assorted waste products. The smell of the place was part porta-potty, part charnel house.

The windows were boarded up, the cracks between rotting boards too narrow to let in more than a trickle of the dawn. Bodies cluttered the linoleum, most breathing heavily with sleep, a few suspiciously still. Couples hugged the corners, taking advantage of the darkness and the comfort of a warm body. A handful of solitary figures stood watch by the door, greeting the new arrivals with a hostile snarl that suggested they would find no friends here. So when the hand emerged from the shadows to grab West's shoulder, he seized it and flipped the body hard to the floor. A head cracked against tile. Jason blinked up at him, dazed.

"Nice to see you again, too."

West cursed. He pulled Jason off the ground, righted him, fussed over the bump on his head, apologized more than once and was shrugged off each time. It was stupid to sneak up on someone in here, Jason admitted. It was smart to stay on guard. It was right to strike first, ask questions later.

It was, all of it, worse than they'd thought.

Jason hugged him. West hugged back. Tightly. And didn't care who saw.

"Tell us," West said. "What happened. What's happening."

Jason told them it was no safer inside the makeshift prison than out. Arguments turned into fights turned into brawls, and some of the bloodied bodies fell without rising. No one tried to help. Every few hours the door opened, and either someone was pushed in or someone was yanked out. No one knew what happened to those who were taken away. But they all knew what had happened to Ellie King.

Everything was crazy, Jason told them. Everything impossible was possible; everyone was different. He'd once had a gun, Jason told them, and if he had it now, he'd cut to the last chapter and pull the trigger on himself. He said this without an abundance of emotion, as if standing in the rain expressing mild regret that he'd forgotten his umbrella. When West confided what they suspected about the "final containment," he barely seemed surprised. "Guess it sucks to be us."

Something had been extinguished in him, and West found that he missed it.

"We should check out the door," Jule said. "Maybe there's some way to break it open."

"There's not," Jason said.

"Doesn't hurt to look."

"Not as much as it'll hurt if you get through to the guys with the guns standing on the other side of it."

Jule stood. "Thanks for the input," she said, disgust plain in her voice. "Daniel?" She left. He followed. Leaving West and Jason relatively alone.

"Did they hurt you?" West asked quietly. "When they brought you here?"

Jason shrugged. "What's it matter?"

"It matters."

"I can't blame them," Jason said. "I bet it felt good."

"What are you talking about?"

"You want to know what it's like? To be 'infected,' as you call it? It's not like having some voice in your head telling you to do bad things. It's like . . . being yourself. But more than you ever were. It's like everything you want and everything you feel is suddenly *right*, as long as it's ugly. And everything you want is ugly. Everything you are is ugly." He raised his fist, slowly, bringing it into the beam of West's cell-phone light. The knuckles were scraped, the fingers stained with dried blood. "Yesterday I beat up some guy for his candy bar. I wasn't even that hungry, not then. But he had it, and I wanted it, and I was bigger than him, so . . . I took it. And then I bashed his head into the wall a few times, for good measure." He laughed. "Turned out to be an Almond Joy. And I hate coconut."

West cradled the fist in both hands, running his thumbs over the swollen knuckles. Jason winced. "I'm a pacifist, you know? Was a pacifist. And a vegetarian. Let no harm come to fish or fowl. Or any living thing. Until I decide I need a candy bar."

West had a strange impulse to press his lips to the knuckles.

"We got a message out," he said. "Someone's going to come and stop this and then . . ."

"Then what?" Jason said, in a choked voice. "They lock us all up somewhere? Do some superfun experiments?"

"Find a cure."

"You don't get it, do you?" He shook his head and pulled his hand out of West's. "I'm not sick. I'm *me*. These things I've done, these things I feel . . . even if you 'cured' me tomorrow, I'd still remember them. I'd still know how it felt to crush that kid's head into the wall, and how it felt to *want* to. The sound it made, his skull against the concrete, again. *Again*." Jason smiled faintly at the memory—then realized he was doing it, and shuddered. "I'm always going to be the person who did that."

West's father liked to say *You are the sum of your choices.*

"You don't have to be," West said. "A person can be whoever he wants."

"Funny, coming from you."

"Meaning?"

"It's just funny, that's all," Jason said. He looked very small, and very afraid.

"Jason . . ." West wanted to take his hand again, assure him that he was a good person, whatever he'd done. But he didn't want to lie, and he didn't know what was true.

"I miss Nick," Jason said.

"Me too."

Daniel hadn't owned a watch since he was ten. There was no way to measure how much time passed in the dark. It was, somewhere, daylight: he knew that much. Time was moving forward, too quickly. Running out. Once, the door creaked open. Daniel and Jule rushed it . . . along with most of the other prisoners. A crush of desperate flesh grabbed and pushed and stomped toward freedom. There was gunfire, and screams.

When it was over, there were more bruised and bloodied bodies on the ground, three additional prisoners, and a locked door, and no one was any closer to getting out.

He'd left Milo alone out there.

"He's not alone," Jule reminded him.

But he wasn't with anyone who could protect him. Or who would sacrifice their safety for his.

*Like I would?* he thought, and wondered.

"What are they waiting for?" Daniel asked, meaning the soldiers that weren't soldiers, and the "containment" of the problem they'd solved.

"You in some hurry to die?" Jule said.

"Maybe we're wrong about them. Maybe 'containment' just means they've got a cure."

"And then what? They march their soldiers in and give us all a happily ever after? Ask us nicely not to tell anyone what happened?"

He couldn't even smile. "It could happen."

"Have you thought about it?" Jule said. "What happens to all these people, even if they do get out? Get cured? What happens next?"

"Things go back to normal."

"How?"

He thought of Coach Hart and his naked wife, of the Watchdogs, of his math teacher holding a rifle, and of his father, tied up in the shed, left there to die. "I don't know."

Jule moved behind him, awkwardly, and put her hands on his shoulders. She kneaded them, for a moment, as if it were something she'd seen someone on television do in times of trouble, then gave up, and leaned against him, her forehead to his shoulder blades, her fingers still nestled into the grooves of his shoulders.

"You don't have to do that," he said.

"What?"

His face burned at the memory of what had happened at the Tuck house, or what hadn't. He pulled away from her and turned to face her, sparing himself the answer and her the act. He could feel the eyes in the dark, watching them, and wondered how it was that things had come to this: that there could be so many potential paths to death, and not one to survival.

She touched him again, again on the shoulder, again hesitantly. Her expression offered no hint of what she was thinking.

"You don't understand me at all, do you?" she said.

He had to agree.

"But sometimes . . . it feels like you could," she added.

She was close enough that when he nodded, their foreheads kissed.

"Ever since I met you, this keeps happening," she said. "The two of us, alone in the dark. Thinking we're about to die."

"I guess that makes me your bad-luck charm. Or you mine."

Maybe he had known from the beginning, in the storage closet in the back of the J&C, holding her and waiting for the end. Maybe they were still back there, stranded in the split second before the tornado swept them into nothingness, hallucinating a future because neither had a past worthy of flashing before their eyes.

"You thought you could somehow protect me," she said. "From a freaking tornado."

He laughed. "Don't worry, I wouldn't dare make that mistake again."

"All those times, you, me, certain death—you'd think I would be afraid, right? But I wasn't. Even now, I'm just . . . not."

"You're not the type," he said. "No fear. I may not understand much about you, but that part I got."

Now she was the one who laughed, and the sound was somehow purer, *lighter,* than anything he'd heard in days. "You don't understand anything."

She was still laughing when she kissed him.

Kissing him, in the dark. Reaching for him, touching him, in the dark. Everything simple, in the dark. Need—gratified. Want—have. Everything easy, everything warm and safe, salty and sweet, everything erased by the dark, everything but him. No Jule, in the dark. Only a girl, uncomplicated and unafraid. With no past and no future and no fears. No guilt. His hands on her, but not his eyes.

In the dark, no one watching.

Lips insistent, breaths fast, tongues searching out the dark inside the dark, skin slick and radiating heat.

No hesitation, in the dark.

No clock ticking away their lives; no consequences.

No fear.

A moment stretched like taffy, a word at his lips, stopped by the taste of hers. No talking, in the dark. No Jule, but still a Daniel, still sweet, still nervous, still skinny, still *good.* Daniel, kissing her, cradling her, wanting her, having her. Giving herself to him—taking him for herself—in the dark.

And then, beyond the two of them, in the world nonexistent, an explosion.

A flood of light.

Jule let go.

This time, it wasn't fireworks, either of the diversionary or metaphorically romantic variety. It was a true explosion, blowing the door off its hinges. A foot to the left and it would have knocked Daniel and Jule to the ground. He wasn't sure the shock would have been any greater. He wasn't sure the shock *could* have been any greater than the reality of Jule abruptly launching herself at him, then just as abruptly pushing him away as the door blew apart and their avenging angel appeared in the threshold, cast into shadow by the light streaming past. The shadow had a gun in each hand, a bullet-striped bandolier across his barrel chest, and a booming voice.

"Daniel Ghent! Hearken unto thy father that begat thee!"

# 16

## TO SUMMON UP THE BLOOD

Outside, it was daylight. Outside, in the sunshine, the ground was littered with bodies. Maybe those foolish enough not to run away when they saw the Preacher coming; maybe all of them—the Preacher had always been a good shot.

Outside, a still point in the river of fleeing prisoners, Cass and Grace waited.

Milo was nowhere.

Gunfire echoed in the distance.

"The war's upon us," the Preacher said, pulling Daniel into a rough embrace. "The soldiers of darkness are laying waste to the works of men."

So "containment" had begun.

"They're marching," Cass said. "Tanks, too. Heading for the center of town—shooting everything in their path. We heard they brought you here, and when we heard—"

Daniel shoved his father away, but the man was bigger and stronger and wouldn't let go. "Where's Milo?"

"We didn't tell him what was happening," Grace said. "But he must have overheard. I swear we were watching him, but . . ."

A sick certainty, birthed in his gut, spread like poison up

through his limbs. While he'd been holding Jule, while he'd been thinking of nothing but himself, believing that, for once, there could be joy without a price, Milo had paid. "Where is he?"

"He came for me," the Preacher said. "Through the circles of hell, through Satan's flames, crawling on his belly with the weight of Atlas on his shoulders, he searched for his father."

"Where is he *now*?"

But as soon as the question was out, Daniel willed his father's mouth to silence. As long as the words went unsaid, Milo could live, safe and healthy, in the space between question and answer.

*If I die right on this spot, he'll always be alive*, Daniel thought. Bring the curtain down before the final act and the doomed characters live forever.

"Young Milo is underground," his father intoned, "and there he will stay."

Daniel punched him. Daniel shouted and Daniel screamed and Daniel flailed in his father's tree-trunk arms as they held him tight and held him steady, and somehow, the words penetrated, not the Preacher's incantations or Jule's sharp rebuke or Cass's soothing, but Grace's voice, small and springwater clear.

"Safe," she said. "He's safe."

The crawl space under the kitchen, the stacks of tuna and the steel door—if Milo was in *that* underground, locked up with orders not to open the door until he ran out of food or Daniel assured him he was safe, then he might be. Grace promised him: She and Cass had stowed Milo behind a locked door.

They had soothed his fears. They had saved him, for the moment. Underground.

There was space for more people. Maybe not all of them, but space for Daniel and Jule, if they crowded in tight. If they could make it back to the house, they could ride out the apocalypse until all those infected were gunned down and containment was complete. They could hide beneath the earth and let the town die. Emerge when the smoke had cleared and hope for the best, a life as lab rats. A life for Milo.

Or they could revert to Plan A: Find a way out, somehow. Alert the authorities. Save whatever was left of the town.

Milo was safe.

With that guarantee, Daniel's fear lifted. Not just the fear of losing Milo, but all of it. It was background noise, buzzing dully in his ears, suddenly as easy to ignore as the mosquitoes and the wind. Milo was safe, and Daniel, and his friends, and the town, were screwed. But Milo was safe, and their father had saved him. Then, for good measure, he'd saved Daniel.

Grace was towing Milo's old red Radio Flyer wagon. It was piled high with weapons. Cass handed Daniel a gun. Jule had already taken hers.

"They'll have plenty to keep them busy," the Preacher said, fixing Daniel with a nearly lucid stare. "Town's going to put up a fight. Not a bad time to head for the woods."

"Come with us," he said, before thinking better of it.

But the Preacher shook his head. "I've got an army to command," he said. "'The mind is its own place, and in it self can make a Heav'n of Hell, a Hell of Heav'n.' I *will* make of this place a Heaven."

"Dad . . ." Daniel swallowed. He couldn't remember the

last time he'd said thank you to his father, much less had reason to. "I'm sorry. For the shed."

"You did what you had to do."

"But—"

"You did what I would do."

Daniel believed it was true—and was surprised that the thought brought him no shame.

"I'll always come for you," the Preacher said.

It wasn't, Daniel decided, that his father had gotten any less crazy. It was that the world had descended into madness around him. Now they were all together in the abyss.

There was another rough embrace, a bristle of stubble against his cheek, and then the Preacher hoisted his rifle and saluted his son. He marched west, toward the loudest gunfire, turned a corner, and was gone.

Jule cleared her throat. "He's right," she said, in a back-to-business tone that let Daniel off the emotional hook. *No time for any of this mushy crap,* her voice said, and the burning in his eyes faded away. His father had been gone for a long time. He'd already mourned the loss. No reason to do it all over again.

"We've got weapons now," she said, "and a head start, and if this town goes as nuts as I think it's about to, we've got one hell of a distraction."

"What about the radio message?" Cass asked. "Did you get it out? Is someone coming to help us?"

"Does it matter? They're not *here*. So we help ourselves."

Milo would be safer where he was, waiting for Daniel to call in the cavalry or die trying. He had to try. "I'm in," Daniel said.

They all were.

The other prisoners were gone, all but West and his unlikely friend, who were still hovering just inside the threshold of the grocery, their heads bent toward each other. Daniel waved them over.

"It's started," he said.

West seized a firearm from the pile. "So what are we waiting for?" he said. "Jason—"

"No sappy goodbyes, please. I'm a bit of a crier."

"I was going to say, come with us."

Jason tapped his chest. "Bad guy, remember? You can't trust me."

"Not true," West said, looking to the others for support. No one spoke. "Come with us."

"I can't trust me," Jason said, and curled his right hand into a fist. Daniel tensed, but West took the fist in his hands. The grip looked almost . . . tender.

Then he let go of the fist, and cupped Jason's face—again, and no mistake about it this time, tenderly. "I can," West said, and kissed him.

Daniel tried not to gape. He wasn't having much more luck at it than anyone else, except for Cass, who seemed utterly unsurprised.

"Did that just happen?" he murmured to Jule.

She rolled her eyes. "You really are dense, aren't you?"

But even Jason, when he broke from the kiss, seemed somewhat taken aback. West just grinned at the rubbernecking.

"You're coming," he said.

Jason shook his head no; West shook his head yes. Jason looked to the others, but no one objected. Daniel wondered if they were thinking the same thing he was: that this was a terrible idea, that Jason was infected, dangerous—he'd said so himself.

But: the Preacher had come to save him.

Daniel wasn't about to tell anyone, infected or not, that they had no chance of saving themselves.

Jason took West's hand, giving in. He gave the group a wry smile. "Just don't say I didn't warn you."

They decided not to give him a gun.

The quickest route to the woods took them straight past Cassandra's house, which suited Jule's needs perfectly.

"We don't really have time to stop and pick up your diary," West said, but there was no fire to the objection. Since the kiss outside the old grocery, everything about him was somehow lighter . . . looser. Which was fine with Jule, as long as he didn't get sloppy—or start imagining that she was some sentimental twit who couldn't survive without her precious bag of keepsakes. In fact, when they reached the house, which had the stillness and faint decay of a home abandoned, it was Cass who beelined for the stacks of photo albums and closets of shoes, pressed familiar items to her cheeks as if hoping some of her old self would rub off onto the new. There was no question: this house still belonged to her. Let her have it. The house had nothing Jule wanted; she'd come for what hid in the basement.

The Molotov cocktail had sparked an idea—the Preacher had set it afire.

Jule's uncles had done a good job of keeping her out of their lab, but they couldn't keep her off the Internet, where she'd educated herself on the substances with which she shared a home. Anhydrous ammonia, a necessary ingredient in basic batching, could burn straight through denim to melt off a testicle (as had happened to her uncle's clumsy delivery boy). The lithium strip of a battery could, when added to ammonia without caution, blow you up. Overheating red phosphorus could result in a cloud of phosphine gas, which would burn you from the inside out. Hydrochloric acid spoke for itself. Jule was uncomfortable around guns and didn't trust herself with knives, but chemicals? Those she understood. They were in her blood.

The basement door was unlocked. Her uncles Axe and Teddy lay at the foot of the stairs, both stained with blood. Both dead.

She shook it off. Told herself, however unconvincingly, that once you'd seen one dead body up close and personal, you'd seen them all. That it didn't matter that nearly everyone she'd counted as family was gone. That it had been a long time since Axe and Teddy had babysat her, keeping her up late with thrilling stories of outlaws and their pig-cop pursuers. That they were grown men with a choice, and they'd chosen a life destined to lead them to a pile at the bottom of a stairwell.

They were still her family, her only family. And now they were gone. Here was her will made manifest: She had finally escaped the Prevettes, and their fate. She was not one of them. She would not think about the body that had stained her bedroom carpet, or the glug and suck of the swamp that consumed it. That had been circumstance.

It did not define her.

Jule couldn't help noticing neither of the brothers seemed

to have an obvious weapon. They hadn't killed each other. But if it had been Scott . . . where was he? And who else did he now count as his enemy? She half expected him to pop up from behind the basement's makeshift lab table, wearing his stained apron and wielding an impossible knife. But the lab sat empty, a mad scientist's collection of plastic tubing and kitchen funnels, frying pans coated with a powdery white residue, stained coffee filters, bottles of Drano and antifreeze, towering stacks of batteries and empty blister packs, a smell like nail polish remover and urine. Finished stock sat on a shelf by the door, ready for distribution via a network that no longer existed. There was no one left to notice what she stole, or to care.

One foil, a few seconds with the pipe, and this would all cease to matter. She'd never understood that before, so never understood temptation. Now she saw: *temptation* was too small a word. Here was an answer to the unanswerable; here was an escape. Here was an ending, tidy and swift. Here was happiness, neatly sealed in a ziplock bag.

She began to gather supplies, packing them carefully into one of the Porter family's expensive leather satchels. Nothing that would explode in transit—everything that would cause damage when she needed it. She worked quickly, but not as quickly as she could have. As long as she stayed down there, the possibility stayed open: that she could allow herself to give in. Just this once. Become the person she'd been raised to be.

It had felt so good, in Daniel's arms, in the dark, letting go. She wrapped, she calculated, she packed, and she kept returning, out of the corner of her eye, to the stack by the door—the one-way ticket to the dark.

\* \* \*

They were supposed to be guarding the door, but West couldn't take his eyes off Jason.

West barely knew anything about him, and what he did know, he didn't much like.

West wanted to kiss him again.

Was this how it felt to be infected? Possessed by the temptation to do the last thing you should ever want to do?

Did it feel this good?

He gave in enough to let himself smile, and take Jason's hand.

"I shouldn't be here." Jason wasn't smiling.

"It's fine," West said. "You'll be fine."

"You don't know that. You don't even know *me*. Not really. And you don't know . . ." He was shivering. "I don't know what I'll do. You don't know what that's like."

"Hey, I get it."

"No you don't!" Jason snapped, and jerked his hand away. "All I want is . . . whatever I want. Anything, you get *that*? Doesn't matter what it is, or what else is going on. Right now? I want to tear your clothes off. Right here, in this stupid hallway, with all these people. Screw them, screw the town, screw everything. Just take what I want. Do you know what it's taking not to do that?"

"Who says that's the drug?"

Jason snorted. "You're cute. But not that cute."

West took Jason's face in his hands and kissed him, hard.

"They're right upstairs," Jason said. "They're coming back any minute."

"Don't care," West said, and ran his hands down Jason's neck, across his shoulders, down his biceps, and gripped tight.

"You think it's that stuff making you want this? Then fine. You focus on that. That's not hurting anyone. *You* won't hurt anyone."

"What if hurting someone is the point?"

"Who? Me?"

Jason pressed his face into West's shoulder, like he was trying to hold something in. "Not you," he mumbled. "Maybe you. I don't know. Maybe . . ." The rest was muffled.

"Jason?"

Jason raised his head. "Nick, okay? Nick. It's not about wanting you. It's about wanting to *hurt him.*"

"I don't believe that."

Jason shrugged.

"So, fine," West said. "Whatever. You may want to hurt him, but—" He swallowed. "You can't. He's dead."

"You're not," Jason said. "The others aren't. I'm not . . . safe."

"I'll make sure you are."

"You think you could stop me?"

"I think you can stop yourself," West said. And then, because he wasn't any more convinced of that than Jason was, "And yeah, if you can't, I can. But try this first. Next time you want to smash someone's head into the wall—"

"Picture you naked?" Jason said, his lips quirking into a smile. He looked like Nick then, and felt like Nick in West's arms, and it made West want to push him away and never let go, all at the same time. Instead, he kissed Jason one more time and told himself it didn't matter now, wouldn't matter until they were all safe. In the meantime . . .

"Whatever works."

* * *

*My house*, Cass thought, trying to believe it. *My bedroom.*

Very little had changed, at least up here. Her old stuffed animals still perched in the same corner of the closet, her photo collages still lined the mirror, her name, curlicued and neon, still blazed in lights. Cass felt like an anthropologist, studying a foreign environment for clues about the alien creature who might once have lived there. She ran her fingers across familiar spines. *My books.* She sat down on the bed. *My pillow, my sheets.* She lifted a framed photo. *My family.*

Grace watched from the doorway, betraying no sign of emotion.

Grace hadn't tried to kill her again. That was something.

They'd even worked together, once Milo had forced them to chase him to the Ghent house, and the Preacher—inexplicably trussed up in the old shed—had told them about the safe room. They'd plotted with the Preacher and with each other to save their friends, all the while watching each other carefully, Cass tensed to fend off another attack, Grace thinking her strange thoughts, frowning as Cass ushered Milo into the crawl space and locked the door. "This doesn't make up for anything," she'd said, and Cass had to agree.

"I always wanted to see this," Grace said now, nudging the doorjamb with her sneaker.

"If I knew that, I would have invited you over," Cass said, though they both knew that was a lie.

"It's different than I pictured."

Cass set down the photo. It had been taken at Thanksgiving dinner many years before, when she was still young enough to perch on her father's lap. In the picture, he rested his chin on her head. Her mother knelt beside them, planting a kiss on Cass's cheek. The image of domestic bliss. "Yeah. It is."

"You can barely tell the difference," Jule had said, peeking in on her drugged-out mother for the briefest of moments before going about her business. Daniel wasn't sure whether he didn't believe her, or simply didn't want to. He left her to her explosives raid and Cass to her short walk down memory lane, and he stayed here, in the bedroom, by Jule's mother's side. Downstairs, West and Jason guarded the door. Or at least, that's what they'd said they were doing. Daniel still couldn't quite wrap his mind around it. West, of all people? West, who he'd more than once imagined switching places with, just to have things simple and perfect and *easy*, to coast through life. But nothing was as easy as it seemed, not for anyone. That was what he'd learned from the storm and its aftermath. That, and everyone had their secrets.

Daniel knelt by the mattress and took the woman's clammy hand. She didn't stir. A meth high, he knew, kept you awake. Which meant this was something else, or this was an OD. Either way, there was nothing he could do.

Sometimes her lids fluttered open to reveal the whites of her eyes; sometimes she moaned in whatever was passing for sleep. She looked nothing like Jule, and was wearing far less clothing than Daniel would have preferred. He pulled the covers up over her nightgown, then, worrying about the beads of sweat on her forehead and collarbone, pulled them down again, hoping it didn't seem like he was just enjoying the view.

"Ms. Prevette?" he said, then repeated it louder, to no effect.

He'd never had much sympathy for his father's flight into the bottle. But the Preacher had never dived so far he couldn't make his way back.

"She deserved better," he told Jule's mother. But he stayed there until Jule called from below that she had what she needed, and they could go. It wasn't until he rose to his feet that he caught sight of the thing lying on the floor beside the bed, trapped in a tangle of sheets. At first, it looked like a blanket. But it had hair (brown with flecks of red, same as Milo's) and eyes (dark green, same as Milo's, but open and unseeing and with no hint of a spark) and fingers (half curled and, Daniel suspected, stiffened into place). He was caught off guard by the swell of sympathy. They'd hated each other, but they'd both loved Milo. He believed that now, in a way he hadn't let himself before, when she was alive.

They had all deserved better.

Only Cass seemed reluctant to leave.

"You sure you got what you needed?" she asked Jule.

"Did you?" Jule said, vaguely embarrassed, even under these circumstances, to share the house with the person who rightfully belonged in it.

Cass shrugged. "There's nothing left of me here." But as she opened the door to leave, she looked as if she'd rather not. Which might have been the right instinct, because rooted to the welcome mat stood Scott Prevette, his second-favorite hunting knife in one hand. Before any of them could move, he lunged forward and snatched hold of Grace with the other. He crooked an arm around her neck and pressed the blade to her throat. She fit all too neatly into the crevice of his chest.

Her face paled, but beyond that, she showed no fear.

Jule, on the other hand, was terrified. "Let go of her, Scott."

"She's a sweet one, this one. Sweet and young and sweet." He caressed her hair with his chin. "Too bad she has to grow up, isn't it? You were sweet once, but we always knew you'd grow up rotten, with that animal's blood in you. I tried my best, but you were tainted, girl, rotten from the start. Can't grow a straight tree from twisted roots, I know that much."

"Just let us past, Scott."

The others were frozen, all of them letting her take control, as if shared DNA would clue her in to the trick of defeating the giant. What she knew was that on a good day, Scott was about as dangerous as the town rumors would have him be. On a bad day, he edged toward monster.

"I know what you got in that bag," he said. His eyes were glittering. His face shone with sweat. The hand holding the knife was crusted brown with blood. "I know you stole from me, and you know what happens to people who steal from me. You know that real well."

"Then let them go," Jule said. "I'll stay here. You can punish me."

Somewhere behind her, Daniel whispered her name.

Scott laughed. It was an inhuman sound, too filled with sadistic joy. "I can punish *everyone*. You'll watch me do it. You'll be last, and then I'll gut you the way I'm gonna gut your little friends, and while I'm peeling your intestines, we can have a nice chat about family loyalty and how you don't tell the feds family business."

"I didn't tell anyone anything—"

"I know what you did!" he roared. "I know they've been

watching me, everywhere, they *know* things they shouldn't know, and how do you think that is, you little faithless bitch, unless you opened your dirty mouth? Do your friends all know where it's been, your dirty little mouth? Do they know you been whoring around with your wannabe daddy? Do they know how you stuck it in him, then stuck him in the ground?"

Jule swallowed her rage. The blade was at Grace's throat and she had seen enough bodies that day. She had enough blood on her hands.

Despite what she'd heard and what she knew, she couldn't quite believe that her uncle Scott would slash the throat of a child, and then murder her friends one by one before using his knife to gut the closest thing he'd had to a daughter. Not the girl he had swung onto his shoulders and instructed in the art of lock picking and rescued from more than one parasite. Every day, he disappeared a little deeper into the rabbit hole, the meth eating away at the boundary between Scott the man and Scott the monster. But she'd never doubted that her uncle loved her.

After carefully searching his face, the wolfish smile and the wild eyes, she realized her uncle was gone.

They had weapons, too. He couldn't kill five armed people with a single knife—but he could get a good start on it. He could kill Grace. He would kill Grace. As he had killed Axe and Teddy, and the parasite, and probably those other three men in whose disappearances he was an official "person of interest," and who knew how many more. Grace would be the last, because then there would be no reason not to aim guns and pull triggers and end him—but before that, the tough little girl who liked to pretend she wasn't would die.

And Jule was useless.

It was Cass who spoke.

"You're right," she said, and Jule wondered whether growing up rich left you irrevocably stupid, no matter how hard life later tried to smarten you up. "But it's not her. It's not any of them. It's me. I've been watching you. I've seen *everything*."

"You can't fool me," Scott snapped, too far gone to recognize her. "You're nobody."

"Maybe so, but I'm the one you want. I'm the one who's been spying on you. How else would I know about the creaky third step on the main staircase? Or the closet door in the master bedroom that's off its hinges? Or that there's something that looks like a giant bloodstain inside the fridge. I'm telling you, I've been watching, and I see everything. I even see you cursing in the shower when you forget that the hot and cold water taps are switched."

"I'll stab your eyes out!" Scott shouted. He let Grace drop to the ground and thumped toward Cass with the knife. Her bravado gone as quickly as it appeared, she shrieked and backed against the wall, arms over her face. As the knife bore down on her, a bullet tore open the air. Scott stumbled to the floor, clutching his leg. Blood oozed from a neat little hole just above his knee. Jason stared down at his hands, at the gun he'd plucked out of West's hands.

"I never shot someone before," he said, wonder in his voice. "I never thought . . ."

Don't point a gun at someone unless you're willing to pull the trigger, Scott had once told her. Jason was pointing the gun at her now. It swiveled slowly toward Daniel, then Cass, then back to Scott. A funny smile played across Jason's face.

*Not like this*, Jule thought. *Not because we trusted him.*

"I'm sorry, Jeremiah," Jason said haltingly. "I tried."

He dropped the gun.

"But I can't." He shouldered past West and ran out the door.

West watched him go. The others watched West. But Jule kept her eyes on Scott—and on the fallen gun.

"Pick it up, West," Jule said.

He wouldn't look at her. He kneaded his hands together and stared hard at the door, as if willing Jason to return. Scott writhed on the floor. Daniel had kicked away the knife. Scott was no threat to them now. Still, Jule wondered, remembering the lesson he'd taught her only a couple of days before. If you were going to shoot a wild animal in your own house, better shoot to kill.

"Pick it up," she said again, harder this time.

"I don't want to," West said. Shaking his head at her, at the gun, at the man on the ground with the hole in his leg and the blood running through his fingers. "I never wanted to."

"Welcome to my life," she said, and took the gun, and pressed it into his hands. He took it, and they walked through the door. This time, there was no monster lurking on the other side. There was only Oleander, the town turned beast, and the men with guns and tanks, tasked with putting it down.

# 17

## INTO THE DARKNESS WILD

Oleander was past the point of leadership. Which was for the best, as its leader had fled. Mayor Mickey Mouse chose the safest place he could think of to hide: the small, understaffed police station, which was the closest thing Oleander had to a barracks. Thanks to a generous federal grant dating back to the War on Meth, the local armory was significantly better stocked than the tiny department would seem to require. And as mayor, he had the key.

Mouse had always been a coward, and this seemed a fine, cowardly plan. Except that someone beat him to it. When he arrived, trembling, urine soaking his thighs and gunfire ringing in his ears, the deacon was already inside, splashing the canisters of bullets and shelves of assault weapons with a can of gasoline.

"You see how desperate they are to stop us from purifying the town," the deacon said. "But righteousness will prevail. And He said, 'When you walk through the fire, you will not be burned; the flames will not set you ablaze.'"

The mayor had always assumed that the deacon, like everyone else, had an angle. That though he would never admit it, the God stuff was just his way in. If that had ever been true—and Mouse hated to believe he could have so deeply misjudged a man—it clearly was no longer. Mouse was facing a true believer.

It was a good thing he'd already pissed himself dry.

"What are you doing, Deacon?" he asked, as if it weren't clear.

"'The Lord is coming with fire, and his chariots are like a whirlwind; he will bring down his anger with fury, and his rebuke with flames of fire. For with fire and with his sword the Lord will execute judgment on all people, and many will be those slain by the Lord.'"

"You're insane."

"'The blazing flame will not be quenched, and every face from south to north will be scorched by it. Everyone will see that I the Lord have kindled it; it will not be quenched.'"

"Stark raving mad."

The deacon dropped the empty can of gasoline and turned to face the mayor, arms out at his sides, palms facing up. *Crucify me,* he seemed to say. The lunatic would probably enjoy it.

The distant gunfire was no longer distant. The end was coming, and there was nowhere left to run. But there were many guns to choose from. As was his way, Mouse wanted the biggest but chose the easiest, the semiautomatic pistol closest to hand. Trembling, gibbering, he loaded it with stiff fingers while the deacon smiled calmly, waiting for something to happen. The room stank of gasoline.

"You should know I've always hated you." *Load magazine. Pull back slide. Release. Careful. Careful.* "I put up with you because the mental midgets who live in this shithole of a town think you've got a hotline to God."

The gunfire sounded like explosions. Men shouted to each other and stomped through the station, searching for signs of life. Mouse raised the gun. The federal grant had not covered infrastructure. The door to the armory wasn't bullet-resistant reinforced steel. It was just wood. It would stop no one who wanted to get through.

"I'll die," he said. "But you'll die first. At least, there's that."

Pulling the trigger felt ungodly good. The sheer physical release of the thing, like when he'd screwed Jessica Poblock thirty years ago in the back of her father's Honda. For those bare moments that slipped away almost as quickly as her wet, sticky body, he'd been possessed of a conviction that he was all-powerful, all-consuming, that he was, were he only to acknowledge it, a god. He'd spent his whole life chasing that high, which had never come again. Until now. You could live an entire life inside a moment that satisfying. For the mayor, time stopped. The cold metal in his hands, the spreading wound in the deacon's gut, the laughter burbling from his throat, the thunder of explosions behind the door, the smell of gasoline a reminder of long ago summer days on a steaming highway, the curve of the gun like the curve of Jessica's hip bone beneath his scrawny, grasping fingers—he was beyond thought, but he could still feel sure that it had all been worth it, if it had led here, to this end.

This end: a spark of gunpowder, a cloud of gasoline fumes, a wall of ammunition.

A ball of fire.

It consumed the men who had birthed this new Oleander,

and the men beyond the door, who had come to put an end to it. Then it spread.

And spread.

Daniel hated war movies. It wasn't the violence that bothered him, but the tedium of a narrative that expected him to invest in uniforms from a far-flung land or time, the trigger-happy men who chose to wear them, and the interchangeable conquest and pathos that ensued.

He now understood that it should have been the violence. And that maybe he should have paid better attention.

They moved across town slowly, clinging to the sides of buildings and the edges of wooded clusters, blending as best they could into the screaming mobs that occasionally surged past, trying not to see the stragglers who got left behind for the mercenaries to gun down. The uniformed men fanned across town in starched lines, kicking in doors, eradicating any signs of life. Daniel would never have believed a place could turn from a home into a war zone in less than two weeks, but here was proof, in fire and blood.

They saw no children.

A tank blocked half of Fourth Street, with two mercenaries astride it and a third on foot leading the way. From his safe and cowardly berth in an alley, Daniel recognized two of the girls running past, shrieking and falling as the bullets entered their spines: Hayley and Emily, no longer popular enough. (Kaitly, nowhere to be seen, still the odd man out.) At his shoulder, Cass moaned, and he remembered that they had been friends, of sorts.

There was no way out but through, and from where he hid, he had a perfect shot. He had, thanks to his father, excellent aim. But to aim a gun at an actual living person—to end a life that had a beginning and middle no less real than his, that had parents, nightmares, maybe a wife, maybe a child—that was different. He didn't shoot. His father would probably have called it fear, but fear would have made him pull the trigger. It was terrifying to do nothing, to watch the bodies fall and the tanks roll past. To wait until it was clear before venturing onto the killing fields and stepping over the body of a girl he'd once thought he hated.

In the movies, soldiers killed and killed and kept killing until battlefields were littered with bodies, and at the end, they got a medal, and a girl, and a sappy song over the closing credits. Daniel didn't want a medal. He just wanted out. His nightmares weren't prophecy; he didn't have to be the one to fire. Not this time; not yet. Jule took his hand, and he turned from the bodies and focused on getting to the next block, and the next one.

This wasn't his war.

Sometimes they huddled together and waited for the cleansing tide to pass; sometimes they were forced to split up, and for Jule, those were the worst times. She hadn't yet gotten used to the concept of together, but it was all too easy to wrap her mind around apart. Every time she found herself pressed into a doorway or curled up beneath a stone bench, every time she heard the sharp report of a bullet, she saw, playing in high-def on the screen of her mind, Cass cornered against a wall, justice rendered after all. Grace bloodied by the man Jule had allowed to live. West set on fire by a godly mob. Daniel cut down in midstep. Daniel falling.

A panicked mob was charging the intersection of Seventh and Garden. To avoid it, they ducked into separate corners. Jule crouched in a garbage alley on the west side of Garden, while the others tucked themselves away on the east side, somewhere equally out of sight. She hoped out of sight.

When someone penetrated her sanctuary from the President Street side, the flank she'd stupidly left unguarded, it was neither a mercenary nor a friend.

Baz Demming, red-faced and bloody-nosed but still possessed of his quarterback grace, flung himself into the alley and slid behind the Dumpster. His breath of relief cut sharply when he saw Jule. Or maybe when he saw that Jule had a gun. He brought a finger to his swollen, cracked lips. She leveled the weapon.

"Do it," he whispered. "Do me a favor."

"My pleasure—"

"Shut *up*," he hissed. Not so far away, girls called for him, a strange here-kitty-kitty note in their singsong voices.

"We'll *find* you," they chanted. "We've got a *treat* for you."

"Crazy bitches," Baz muttered.

"What'd you do to them?"

"Nothing."

Nothing different, he meant, sullenly, than he'd done to any other girl, than he'd been doing his whole life, than business as usual. Nothing that demanded consequence.

Garden Street had gone quiet. A patter of footsteps neared the alley, and the girls' catcalls swelled in volume.

"*Baz, Baz, Baz, Baz*"—like a swarm of bees, stingers at the ready.

"Take me with you," Baz pleaded. "Or shoot me now. Just don't . . ." He cast a terrified look back toward President. "They're *crazy*."

"What did you do to them?" Jule asked again.

"Nothing."

The gun came closer.

"Nothing but what they deserved."

"There's a lot of that going around."

He'd crafted a makeshift holster out of his belt and tucked her knife into it, like a trophy. She took the knife—and then, after a moment of thought, made him hand over the belt.

Terrified, Baz was nearly unrecognizable. He couldn't even muster up a filthy suggestion as he unfastened the buckle. Without his normal surly confidence, he looked defenseless, childlike. Almost redeemable.

She stood up, careful to keep the gun trained on him, and began to back away. "Follow me, and I'll shoot you," she said.

"They'll kill me!" Baz whimpered, scrambling to his feet. "You can't just leave me here!"

"It's just a bunch of *girls*, Baz. You can't be afraid of that."

"Please. *Please*."

The girls were close. They were infected, and if they found him, they'd be compelled to tear him to pieces. They had no more choice. By a quirk of luck, Jule did. She could choose to help; she could choose to walk away; she could choose to shoot him in the head. She suddenly got it: She hadn't been spared because she was superior. She had no iron cord of moral fiber that let her hold out while the weaker fell prey to their impulses. She'd just had some luck that, for the first time in her life, turned out to be good.

She'd had his weight on top of her, suffocating her, his hands holding her down, his sour breath on her mouth, his thick tongue, his body, his need. She had the slash on her cheek, which would heal and scar and always remind her.

She had impulses, too.

Bad ones.

She wasn't better, only freer. She could choose.

She fired the gun.

The bullet ricocheted off the Dumpster, several feet wide of Baz. As she'd intended. But the sound of the shot—it might as well have been a siren. It might as well have been an arrow.

"Come and get him," Jule said, just loudly enough.

His face had regressed past childhood now, straight into infancy, the animal fear of a baby left to shriek in its crib, defenseless against the wolves of hunger or loneliness or dark.

Or vengeance.

They moved like wolves, stealing into the alley. They were the God groupies, who'd probably scored front-row seats to Ellie's burning. They, too, had knives.

Jule left them to their work.

They always found each other again. And eventually they made it to the trees, somehow, all five of them whole and safe. Ahead of them lay the woods, and beyond that the highway, with its barbed wire and mercenaries. Behind them, more than one hundred were already dead, and the fighting continued. Behind them, the Preacher made his last stand atop the roof of the pawnshop, an assault rifle in his hands, clip nearly emptied,

Satan's army drawing near. Behind them, Scott Prevette bled to death, screaming at invisible IRS agents in the curtains and CIA drones dropping from the sky. Behind them, the fire spread, consuming the cop shop, the town hall, and the burned-out remains of Eisenhower High, still a mile from the Ghent house, where Milo cowered underground, far but closing in. Behind them, Oleander was dying.

They moved forward. The woods closed around them, dark and deep.

There was relief in the woods, in the quiet and the rich greens and browns of leaves and bark.

"Too bad we can't just stay here," Grace said, giving voice to Jule's thought. "Wait it out."

That was exhaustion talking, and fear—but then, Grace was a child. She was allowed to be both tired and afraid.

"If we wait it out, there'll be nothing left to save," Jule said.

And again, Grace dared to say out loud what Jule had been thinking—what maybe all of them had thought. "So?"

"They didn't deserve this," West said, and didn't have to say the name Jason. "None of them."

*Some of them,* Jule thought.

"We can't just hide out here and leave them to die," he said. "Not if we can stop it."

"Big if," Jule said.

"Maybe there won't even be anyone left at the guard posts," Daniel said. "We could just walk right through."

Jule did him the favor of not laughing in his face.

It took nearly an hour to penetrate the forest and make it through to the other side. They moved slowly, reassuring each other that it was good to be cautious, but they could all feel the emptiness of the woods, its stillness broken only by the wind and the insects and their footsteps crunching through the brush. The woods were safe, and they couldn't bring themselves to hurry. Jule knew the way, and could only get lost if she let it happen. There were stories of people who had slipped into the woods never to leave, lost to the forest sprites or—depending on the type of story—devoured by hidden beasts. But those were stories for children. These woods were less than a mile wide. Setting off in any direction meant that, before long, civilization would intrude.

Jule chose a different point this time, a few hundred yards south of where they'd tried before. There were no soldiers in sight, only electrified fencing that rose a few feet over their heads. Without consulting the others, Jule fired at the generator-type box wedged into a joint in the fence, emptying her clip. The box unleashed a hail of sparks, the fence sizzled madly, and then silence fell again. She stepped forward.

"Don't," Daniel said, too late. She'd already taken hold of the metal lattice.

Nothing happened.

"Not dead yet," she said, almost cheerful. Maybe the impossible was possible, and Daniel was right that the massacre of Oleander meant that they would go free. Guilt could wait. "Who's ready to climb?" She hoisted herself onto the fence.

An alarm sounded, Klaxons shattering the still of the wood, and mercenaries flooded toward them out of nowhere, firing at will. "Run!" Cass screamed, unnecessarily. They were already in motion, retreating to the safety of the woods.

Retreating.

Maybe they wouldn't be followed. There was nowhere to flee but back into town and its certain death. Why hunt when, eventually, the prey will come to you?

But they could all hear the hunters approach.

Jule swore, loudly, furiously.

"It's not your fault," Daniel said, already panting.

"Of course it's not my fucking fault." Though she'd been the one to test the fence without asking if anyone had any better ideas, without it occurring to her that a multi-billion-dollar corporation might be equipped with a Plan B. Stupid of her to think of herself as someone free, someone with a choice. All she could choose was the prettiest clearing, the perfect tree under which to make one last, pathetic stand.

She ran faster. They all did. Daniel took her hand; she couldn't scare him anymore. It was hard to run that way, matching her steps to his, weaving through the narrow pathways of the forest, but she hung on.

"Now what?" Grace asked, sounding not bored, exactly, but sullenly vindicated, a child asking *Are we there yet?* in the middle of a traffic jam.

Jule stopped. The rest of them fell into place around her. "Now we stop running. We hit back."

"How big an explosion are we talking here, Jule?" West asked.

She still had the satchel and, inside, the chemicals she'd stolen from the basement lab. To be saved for a rainy day.

It was pouring.

"Big enough to light the damn forest on fire," she said.

"We'd have to get as close to the highway as we could," Daniel said.

"Another possibility: I might accidentally blow us all up."

"You said you knew what you were doing," Daniel said.

"I know what I said."

"I'm not letting *them* kill me," West said. "Not after every-thing. Even if this doesn't work—"

"Which it almost definitely won't," Jule said.

"—at least it's on our own terms."

"At least we'll have tried everything," Daniel said.

"This time *we* choose," Cass said. "Not them."

West nodded. After a moment, so did Daniel.

"You're all morons," Jule said. But: "Okay, we loop around, back toward the highway, and I'll be ready when I have to be."

"I think it's a horrible idea, in case anyone cares," Grace muttered, but they had already started to run.

They ran their pursuers around in circles, gradually losing their lead, gradually drawing closer and closer to the edge of the woods, and as they ran, Jule carefully spilled out the bottle of hydrochloric acid in their wake, a trail of poisoned bread crumbs they could never follow home. When the ribbon of highway came into sight, Jule was, as she'd promised, ready. All it took was a little aluminum foil and a lighter. "Close your eyes and get down," she suggested, just before the world exploded.

## 18

## STREAMS OF MERCY NEVER CEASING

White light. White noise.

An ocean roar that was like the other side of silence.

Cass blinked the fire from her eyes, the white-blue glow that had consumed the world. Rubbed her ears. Stood. Breathed.

The air smelled like death.

There were men on fire, zigzagging through the trees.

Flaming monsters in the shape of men, mouths distorted by screams.

She heard only the roar.

The sky, through the trees, was so blue. Painfully blue.

Pain.

He was upside down, pain shooting up his back, down his shoulder, pain like fire but not fire.

He was upside down.

His head beat in time with his heart.

*Thump. Thump. Thump.*

He gazed at the blue; he could live in the blue.

He was upside down, for no reason, with no cause. He was

nobody, and there was good in that. Nobody was safe; nobody was easy.

A girl spoke a name that could have been his, or not. Just a word, just a noise.

The real name, the secret name, came as a whisper on the wind. It came from a distance, was meant only for him. It woke him up.

*Jeremiah.*

*You are Jeremiah.*

It brought him back.

In the dark behind his eyes, Daniel smelled smoke, and heard Milo scream, and knew the fire was coming, the fire was eating everything in its path, the fire was snaking its way toward home and would dig its flaming fingers into the earth and find the treasure hidden underneath. *Come out of there!* Daniel screamed in the silent space, and Milo's voice was so calm and sure: *Not until my brother tells me it's safe. Not until my brother saves me.*

Jule shook him and screamed, "Get up! Get up! Get up!" and hated herself for fooling him into believing her, hated him for letting her light the fuse. Not burned, not bleeding, but so pale and still, and limp in her feeble arms. She had done this. She had let herself believe she could choose, not just for herself, but for him and for all of them. She had let herself forget where she belonged, and who she really was. Prevettes never escape. Prevettes only destroy.

The body made a noise. The lips smiled. "You did it," Daniel murmured, and opened his eyes.

* * *

Grace lived and wanted to die. The end would come; the end was taking forever. She wished it would hurry.

Just not fire, she pleaded with whatever would listen. Bullets, fine. Toxic gases, tank missiles, deranged ministers. Just not fire.

She'd always been afraid of fire.

Time slowed down and then, as if to compensate, abruptly sped up, hastened by the crackle of flame eating through the trees. They dusted themselves off and stood and looked at what they had wrought: flaming soldiers, flaming corpses, flaming trees. A dancing ribbon of fire that, even as they watched, leapt across the highway, reaching hungrily toward the mercenaries who scattered from its grasp, toward the tank that exploded at its touch, and on to the plains of the prairie, and on to the horizon.

The wind was blowing south, out of the forest, blowing the fire in the direction of escape. It crept through the trees behind them, swallowing the dry bark and fading leaves, spreading.

"Well . . . it was worth a try?" Daniel offered as they maneuvered, in a clump, out of the woods and onto the road, backing away from the fire that now closed in from both sides. "At least we won't get shot?"

Jule couldn't stop shaking her head. Everything was shaking. "I did this. I did it. I—"

Daniel took her by the shoulders and held her until she went still. "You tried. You kept us alive a little longer. *You* did that."

West hugged his arms to his chest and laughed. "No one

ever actually completes a Hail Mary pass. Only in the movies."

Cass and Grace stood side by side, not touching. Both their faces were glossy with tears.

The flames licked at the trees. Branches fell. There was little time left. Daniel closed his hands over Jule's. "End of the world, again," he said. "You still not scared?"

She leaned against him. "I'm fearless, remember?" But when she pressed her lips to his, he could feel them trembling.

There should have been more time.

"It's not fair," Grace said.

Daniel was too old to believe in fair. But he agreed: it wasn't.

"What if the drug does nothing?" Jule said quietly, just for him. "What if they were wrong?"

Daniel didn't get it. "But everything that happened—"

"What if it was just people?" she said. "Just the way they are."

"Then what about us?"

"What *about* us? Maybe they've got the right idea with this containment thing. Maybe everyone's better off this way."

He put his arms around her and held on, tight. "No."

She fit so perfectly in his arms, and he cursed himself for not figuring it out sooner. He cursed everything. "People are better than this. We're better than this."

"It sounds nice in your world," she said. "Nicer than mine."

"There's room for two."

She laughed, and while he wasn't ready to die, would

never be ready, it would be easier now, with her laughter the last sound he ever heard. Jule, in his arms, softer than she seemed but tougher than anyone else, made everything easier.

The fire closed in.

The mercenaries were gone, dead or fled.

There was nowhere left to run.

They waited.

Some of them prayed.

It sounded like thunder at first, a low rumble in the distance, then another, a rippling wave of sky-splitting booms. After the thunder, a great wind. They turned their faces to the sky to meet their fate, expecting another tornado or a mushroom cloud or even—Ellie King vindicated after all this time—the fist of God.

God's voice was tinny and mechanical; God's fist was shaped like a helicopter.

*This is the United States Army,* the voice boomed. *Lay your weapons down.*

There were more helicopters, a fleet of them, but this first one sank lower and lower, a rope ladder hanging from its side, the words U.S. ARMY blazoned across its torso.

"The radio message," Jule whispered, unable to believe it had gotten out. That anyone had heard. That the cavalry had come.

"It's over," Cass said, raising her hands to the sky, waving and screaming and not caring what happened next, what they would do with the girl who was killer and fugitive and victim all in one. She wouldn't die in this town, at the hands of these people. That was more than could be expected. That was almost enough.

"It's over," Grace said, "and I'm sorry." They hadn't let her, a child, carry a gun. But they would not have left her, a child, unprotected, and so Jule had let her carry the knife. It was easy enough, when the rest of them turned their heads to the sky, to raise the blade and slip it into Cass's chest.

She hadn't expected she'd have to push so hard; she hadn't expect to actually *be* sorry. She'd promised to wait because she knew Cass was wrong. The things she felt, the things she needed—blood, vengeance, justice—they weren't because of the drug. Her desires were her own. She knew that to be true.

But what if she was the one who was wrong?

On the other end of that rope ladder were doctors and hospitals and the chance that she would go to sleep one person and wake up another, more forgiving, less sure. She couldn't afford to wait and see. She'd waited long enough.

There was a lot of screaming, but none of it was Cass's. She opened her mouth. Nothing emerged but a trickle of blood. Grace jerked the knife out of her chest and raised it over her head, preparing to strike a second time. It was harder, knowing how it was going to feel, knowing she would have to force the point past muscle and bone, and so she paused to breathe and to remember why, and that was when the bullet struck the back of her head.

The others would hesitate to hurt a child, even a child with a knife. She'd counted on that.

She hadn't counted on the men in the helicopter, too far away to mark her as a child, too far to see anything but flames, and a victim, and her attacker, holding a knife.

They were professional marksmen; she was dead before she hit the ground.

It took Cass a little longer. She lay beside Grace, staring into her eyes, the dead eyes she saw in her nightmares, and felt no satisfaction at having outlived her killer, if only by a few seconds. A blurry face bent toward her, shouting something she was too tired to hear. Her lips moved, but it was only to gasp out a last bubble of blood. Her last words were only for herself, and for Grace, because this was between the two of them.

*This is not what we deserved,* she thought, but was too tired to be sure. If she could only hold on, just a little longer, long enough to make sure, once and for all, to *know* . . .

She couldn't. She wasn't strong enough. She couldn't hold on to life; she couldn't even hold on to that final plea, and in those last few seconds, the need to know slipped away. There was no more question of judgment or mercy. There was only what she had meant, and who she had loved, and what was left to her now, the grit of dirt against her cheek and the press of skin on her forehead, and Gracie, who was no longer a child, who could no longer be protected, who had to be forgiven. Cass was beyond pain; her body was no longer her own. But somehow, she managed to move her arm. Somehow, her hand reached Grace's outstretched fingers. Somehow, as the world drained away, she held on.

\* \* \*

They watched it happen. But they couldn't believe it really had. Not when the knife slipped in, not when the bullet made its neat, tidy hole, not when the two bodies lay at their feet, sightless and pulseless and a testament to their failure. They couldn't believe it, and so they had failed to stop it, and now it was done. The soldiers—real soldiers, *good-guy* soldiers, as Milo would have said—bundled them into the helicopter, gave them water and blankets and blood pressure cuffs, and thought they were in shock. Maybe they were in shock. Couldn't believe they had been saved. Had saved what was left of the town. Couldn't believe this was how it felt to save and be saved. That this was to be their happy ending.

# 19

## THE BURIED CHILD

Of the three-quarters of town that had survived the tornado, half was consumed by the deacon's holy fire. This included all municipal buildings on State Street and most of the businesses on Main, along with twenty blocks of housing, mostly on the better side of town. The Church of the Word still stood, as did Asylum Bridge and the stone monument to victims of the Bleeding Kansas raids of the 1850s. The fire line had held at Green Street, and so the West homestead was intact, as was the land that stretched past the ruined trailer park. Prevette country, had there been any Prevettes left to claim it.

The cemetery was untouched. Even all these months later, there were no gravestones for those who had died in the fire, or the purge, or the madness before it. Those bodies had been zipped into bags and carted off in trucks bearing military markings, which caravanned down the highway behind buses bearing the survivors.

There had been a lot of doctors, and a lot of tests. Weeks at the facility where they were held without any clear timetable but with clear locks on the doors—held until a cure could be synthesized. None of the faceless agents in charge seemed particularly disappointed that this took its time. The longer it took, the longer they had to study the effects of the R8-G; the experiment had, after all, been a success. A weapon was a weapon, whoever had built it, and how.

Jule, Daniel, and West were sequestered in a separate wing and—their blood as useless to the scientists as their states of mind to the shrinks—left pretty much to themselves. That was how they liked it. West stayed in his room, watching old football games and listening for the voices of the dead. Jule and Daniel sat together and talked about the future, and the places they would go. Jule bitched at her guards and Daniel fussed at Milo and they circled each other, warily waiting for the thing between them to break. Sometimes they held each other in the dark, wondering if they would stay in this place forever, and then Jule would kiss Daniel or Daniel would kiss Jule and they would remind each other that they had survived.

It was Cass's blood that saved the day, after all, just as the GMT doctors had theorized. Cass's blood, from Cass's corpse, drained and analyzed and synthesized and injected into the people who had tried to burn her alive. A simple needle stick, painless as a flu shot, and they were cured. And still the doors were locked, and the people of Oleander waited as the government and the media wags argued their fate. The shortwave radio message, beamed to the four corners of the earth, had ensured that whatever the military's natural inclinations toward secrecy, this dirty laundry would be aired in public. No one from Oleander believed they would ever have been allowed to leave the "secure location" were it not for this built-in insurance policy.

Even so, there were those who suggested eradicating the lot of them, and blaming it on aftereffects of the R8-G, defying the public to challenge the story.

They'd lost the argument, but it had been close.

It was a useful time, politically, for the military to play the role of good guy, for the Justice Department to throw a corporate board in prison, for the president to make a stirring speech, for heroes to be valorized and medals handed around. So after the passage of months and the certification of nontoxicity, the people of Oleander were released.

Released, as opposed to sent home.

Home was gone.

The population of Oleander was not what it once was. The Preacher had been picked off by a sniper within minutes of taking a position on the pawnshop roof, and fell two stories to his heavenly reward. Scott Prevette bled out on the floor of his borrowed house, wasting his last breaths raging at the corpses of the brothers he'd murdered and the women he'd left to die. Thanks to Laura Tanner, most of the town's children survived, but more than two hundred of their parents and neighbors died, on that last of the dark days, some at the hands of the mercenaries, some at the hands of one another. At least that number chose not to return to their decimated town and face the neighbors who knew what they'd done. They took their government hush money and ran away.

But hundreds went back: Because they wanted to, or because there was nowhere else they could think to go. Because at least in Oleander they would not be alone in their shame and their memories. Because this was their home and these were their neighbors, and the devil you knew was no devil at all. In a strange new place, they would have to live a lie, but here, they would know, even if it was never spoken aloud, that they were not the only ones.

It had been decided that the crimes of Oleander couldn't be prosecuted in a court of law, and so they were set free. But that didn't change what they'd done.

Laura Tanner expected a hero's welcome, but no one could look at her: not the parents, who remembered her succeeding where she had failed, and not the children, who still had nightmares of the wild days and the witch that had enchanted them into the woods. She got a job at D'Angelo's, which needed waitresses, and when a family with children sat down in her section, she passed their table to someone else.

Coach Hart survived the battle, but lost a leg and most of his team. He settled back into the house he shared with his wife, and married life continued apace. He no longer worried about his wife cheating on him, and if she missed her dead lover, she had the large rust-colored stain on the porch to remember him by. Every night, the coach kissed his wife good night and told her he loved her. Every night, she considered killing him in his sleep.

The high school would never reopen. Instead, a new one was hastily built in the next town over. Any remaining Oleander students would be bused in and do their best to ignore the stares. Clair Grafton and Morgan Deets would be home-schooled. The former best friends no longer spoke; they didn't miss each other. Nor did they regret what they'd done. Clair still liked to imagine it sometimes, before she fell asleep, the sounds he'd made when they fell upon him. In the secret, secure government facility, she'd gone to services in the chapel every Sunday, and every Sunday she prayed to God with gratitude for the opportunity he'd afforded her. The nightmares that had plagued her for years were gone. Morgan abandoned the church and hooked up with Chuck Platch. They both wore a lot of black and read depressing poetry together, which came as a surprise to everyone who'd assumed Chuck couldn't read.

Kaitly Connor, always an also-ran, had finally reaped a benefit from being the odd girl out. Hayley and Emily had run one way, she'd run the other, and now no one remained to challenge Kaitly's reign. She had survivor's cachet, the whiff of danger, the romantically sorrowful aura of a girl who grieved her best friends, and it was of no concern that the girls at school gave her strange looks and whispered as she passed. She would mold them into shape, flatter and ignore them until they'd been trained to perform for her favor. She had learned from the best.

Ellie King's father died defending the menagerie of strays he'd packed into his lonely apartment—twelve cats, three dogs, and seven pigeons by the end, none of them enough to fill the hole his family had left behind. Ellie's mother, who seemed not to remember lighting the match that had sent her daughter to her Maker, was institutionalized. She would live the rest of her days in a featureless white padded room. All visitors reported that she seemed quite happy.

Cassandra Porter's parents were surprised to discover their daughter had been imprisoned so close to town, and even more surprised she thought they'd abandoned her. Under the guise of an anonymous benefactor, GMT had shuffled them out of town, paying the utilities on their old house and the rent on their new one. They had written weekly devoted letters to their daughter and received regular replies from someone purporting to be Cassandra, claiming to be well taken care of and occasionally happy. Now they were told that their daughter died a hero, and hoped that this time it was the truth. The Tucks, too, were told their daughter died a hero, and didn't question the claim. It didn't help.

Rosemary Wooden returned to her house, which had not burned, and continued her life of solitude. Eventually the town would come to life again, and inevitably, they would come, the boys who thought her a harmless old lady, ripe for the tormenting. She kept the pearl-handled revolver in her lap while she worked on her knitting, enjoying its weight on her thigh. She probably shouldn't have shot that large, nasty boy, she thought sometimes.

But it had felt so good.

Many people stayed indoors, at least at first, and those who ventured out rarely met their neighbors' eyes. But there were strangers here, too, construction crews and charitable volunteers and curiosity seekers, and a trickle of fortune hunters who saw, in the wreckage of the old town, more than a few opportunities for a new one. A third Oleander, built on the ruins of the second, as that had been founded on the ruins of the first.

It was considered taboo to speak of what had happened, but the old men who gathered every day for coffee at the rebuilt Elmo's Luncheonette weren't bound by convention. All the surviving members of this coffee klatch had returned to Oleander, and all were unfazed by what had transpired. They'd been around for a long time, and they'd seen stranger; they had seen worse. So they told themselves. They argued, over cold cups of coffee served to them by a stranger—because Elmo was dead and his two waitresses were never coming back—about what the drug had done to the people of the town. Whether it had driven them to do crazy things they would never, under other circumstances, have had it in them to do, or whether it had simply peeled away people's fancy exteriors to reveal their ugly truth. Henry Wallace was in the latter camp, arguing that when he'd taken that hammer to his son-in-law's head, it was nothing more than what he'd wanted to do for years. "A goddamned dream come true," he said, smashing the flat of his palm against the counter and grinning at the memory. But Paul Corey disagreed.

"If that drug did what you say it did, then how come I still got this headache that I've had for forty years? How come Mary's still sitting in the living room waiting for me to get home so she can yell at me some more?" Mary was his wife, and forty years was the duration of their happy union. Paul gulped down the rest of his coffee, spitting the last mouthful back into his cup. "No, I'd say if that drug did what you say it did, and made people do what they *really* wanted to do? Mary'd be chopped up in pieces in the backyard." At this point in the argument that he ventured nearly every day, he liked to karate-chop the counter with the side of his hand, even harder than Henry had whacked it, once, twice, three times, each time barking, "Chop! Chop! Chop!"

The other men laughed, and then they all went back to their coffee and discussed the weather or the football season or the hideously ugly brick face some idiot had designed for the new town hall. Because maybe it was true that Paul Corey wanted to hack up his wife, and maybe it wasn't. That was the thing about Oleander now, the thing that made it tolerable again: You weren't forced to know the truth one way or another. A person could choose for himself who he pretended to be, and you could choose for yourself whether to believe him.

Jeremiah sat cross-legged in the cemetery with Jason beside him. Before them was stretched a picnic blanket and a feast: homemade bread, farm-fresh cheese, jam preserves rescued from the West family cellar. After an unusually tenacious winter, spring was finally starting to bloom. A breeze stirred the willows, but it was nearly warm even where they sat, in the shadow of the trees, and the shadow of Nick's grave.

The Wests had chosen to return, because they were Wests, and Oleander was in their blood, as their blood was in its soil. But they would not lay claim to the house. That was for Jeremiah. They stayed in the new motel at the center of town, and could not look at their son, the hero, even when he finally persuaded them to come to the house for dinner. Jason cooked while Jeremiah sat on the couch across from his parents, waiting for one of them to meet his eye. He told himself they were embarrassed by what they'd done. His bruises had long since healed. But the doctor said he might always have the limp.

At least they had accepted the invitation: it was a beginning. They had—after a long pause and a pointedly loud throat clearing by their hero son—shaken Jason's hand. His father had shaken Jeremiah's hand, too, and his mother gave him a stiff, tentative hug. They'd managed to endure through two courses and dessert.

His mother brought a pie.

Once Jeremiah had been given his freedom, he could have gone anywhere. But Oleander was the only place he'd ever wanted to be. He and Jason had returned to the house together, and stayed together. In Oleander now, it was better not to be alone. Too many ghosts.

They talked of Nick, often.

Often, they didn't talk.

"He hated it here," Jason said now. He didn't have to say who. Jeremiah wondered, sometimes, whether it was natural, the thing growing between them. Whether it was healthy, this strange three-sided bond between two living people and a grave. Over the months, they'd discovered the occasional thing in common, but nothing that came close to matching that primary, fundamental thing, the loss. That after everything that had happened and all the people who had died, they could still feel this loss above everything, they both marveled. They both felt a small measure of shame, and this was another thing they could talk about only with each other, another thing that bound them together.

"I know," Jeremiah said.

Sometimes, in the dark, Jason's bare body in his arms, the down comforter a shield between them and the night, Jeremiah let Nick slip away, until it was only the two of them, and their need. On those nights, he held Jason close, and traced his lips across the thin arms and knobby shoulders and didn't think about how they curved and bent at the wrong angles, how the body beneath him was not the body it should have been. He let Jason fill him up; he let Jason be all he needed. Sometimes, when the light streamed in the next morning, he didn't even feel guilty.

He had waited for the ghost to return; part of him was still waiting, hoping that it had not been the drug. That it had been Nick.

Nick was gone.

Jason was a substitute for something he could no longer have; but Jason was also Jason, and Jeremiah needed him for himself. They were at a tipping point, and he didn't know which way things would go. For now, with Jason's warm body leaning against his and Nick's memory as close as a stone you could trace with your finger, following the granite curls and loops of his name, things felt right.

"He couldn't wait to leave, after high school," Jason said. "Sometimes we talked about dropping out, just running away in the middle of the night, finding a better place."

"But you never did."

"We ran out of time," Jason said. *Because then he met you*, he didn't have to.

"I didn't force him to stay. I didn't even know he was thinking about going."

"You didn't have to force him. You just gave him a reason."

Jeremiah didn't want to say *And you? Am I your reason?* He didn't want that responsibility—didn't want to be the reason another person stayed. He didn't want the blame for whatever happened next. But he equally didn't want to remind Jason that he had a choice. Because then Jason might leave.

"I never hated it like he did," Jason said. "I just didn't want him to go without me."

"He wouldn't have. He didn't like being alone."

Jeremiah took his hand. It was bandaged with a layer of

white gauze. Jason refused to talk about the things he'd done on that last day—what he'd done because he needed to survive, what he'd done because he wanted, and because it felt good. He'd been found in a gutter with a bullet hole in his leg, two corpses by his side, and a gun. The leg was still unsteady. But his battered hands, his bruised and slashed knuckles, they'd quickly healed. As soon as they did, Jason punched his fist through a window. Once that healed up, it had been a mirror. The next time, a car window. He always found something to break. "I like the reminder," he said when Jeremiah begged him to stop. "Of what I was."

"It wasn't really you." Jeremiah believed it. The drug had created monsters, not revealed them. He loved the town too much to believe the darkness had lived there all along. If he believed that, he couldn't have come home. And he had to come home. "It *wasn't*."

Jason let it pass.

It didn't matter what he'd been, or what he'd done. Jeremiah believed that, too. As it didn't matter what the town had become, now that it was something other—now that it was bare ground and ruins and possibility.

It hadn't been the town he'd believed it to be. But next time, maybe it could be. That was why he'd come back. That was why he would stay. It would be different this time. He would be different. Jeremiah kissed the bandaged knuckles. "We'll make it better," he said, and knew Jason would understand. Not just the hand, but the boy, the man, it belonged to. Not just him, but both of them, together, and the thing between them that either would or wouldn't be. And his family, someday. And his town, one house at a time, nails and beams and solid foundations. With his own hands, with his own will, he would reshape his world: different this time, and better. And whole.

YOU ARE NOW LEAVING THE STATE OF KANSAS.

Jule bit off the cheer just in time. It had taken hours to get Milo to fall asleep, and she wasn't about to wake him up. Three hours of license-plate bingo, geography, spell-offs, and super-hero factoid recitals was more than enough. She supposed she should be grateful that Milo had at least exhausted his desire to rehash the siege of Oleander again and again, never ceasing to complain about having missed out on all the action. Let him sleep. She could cheer all she wanted inside her head. She hadn't stopped since they'd gotten into the car, loaded up with junk food, and set off.

They were chasing the sun. Speeding west, until they hit the ocean, and if that didn't suit, they'd turn south, or north, or take on the ocean and go west some more. They had their please-don't-sue-us settlement money. They had, in their newly purchased duffel bags, two shiny medals, which, among other things, had given Daniel the pull to get official guardian-ship of his brother. A lot of rules had been bent, in the last few months. Enough that Jule started getting the sense a few would soon be bending back, which was all the signal she needed to get out of Dodge. She hadn't expected Daniel to suggest he come along. She hadn't expected to be so relieved.

"You know we only get along during times of crisis," she'd said. "We have no evidence that once life gets boring, we won't start hating each other."

"I'll risk it." Then he had kissed her, which seemed

appropriate, since they were half dressed at the time, and tangled together in a storeroom at the "secure facility" while their minders helpfully looked the other way, another rule bent, more than once. "And I'm not expecting boring."

"We'll crash and burn by Nevada," she'd predicted, but they were driving aimlessly, stopping on a whim at any roadside attraction or culinary wonder that caught their eye, and Nevada was a long way away.

"You think you'll miss it?" Daniel asked.

It seemed like she was always trying not to laugh at him.

This time, he did it for her. "Stupid question," he said. "Sorry."

"Will you? Miss it?"

"The town, or the people?"

"Both," she said. "Either."

She had one hand on the gearshift, and he covered it with his own. She was always surprised by how warm he was. How alive.

That day in the woods, he'd felt so cold in her arms. And then, even awake again, alive and apparently unscathed, he'd still been cold, shivering against her in the helicopter, teeth clattering like she'd never seen outside cartoons, even his tears cold, and she hadn't known what to do to stop him shuddering but kiss him. She'd done so, and he'd kissed her back, and she'd closed her eyes and seen the dead bodies in the grass and smelled the fire and the burned skin, and the tears against her cheek were no longer cold, but maybe they didn't belong to him.

He didn't have to say that he did and didn't miss the

Preacher, because she understood, in the same way she did and didn't miss Uncle Scott. They had been fixtures, they had made sacrifices and made mistakes, they had caused pain and they had stopped it, and now they were gone. "I miss Cass," he said. "I'll never . . ." He swallowed. "I would have liked to know her better."

"And Ellie. Whoever she really was." It was still hard to say the name. Jule touched the scar on her cheek. There was too much she had to forget. But it was either forget, or find a way to forgive herself. Right now both seemed impossible.

Neither of them mentioned Grace. It was an unspoken rule between them. The name invited thoughts of what she'd done, what they should have seen coming, and what they could have stopped. It was too big.

Daniel twisted in his seat, confirming that Milo slept peacefully amid the empty takeout containers and half-drunk sodas. Jule wondered what would have happened if there'd been no Milo, and no reason for Daniel to want to save anyone, or put up any kind of fight. If there'd been no one to believe in superheroes, and force them all to don their capes.

"It feels wrong, leaving like this," he said finally. She stopped breathing. It had never occurred to her that once they left, he would lose his nerve and suggest turning back. If he insisted on it, she would lose him. She couldn't tell herself that it didn't matter, but nothing was intolerable, she knew that now. Nothing but going back.

She realized the car was speeding up—she'd been bearing down on the accelerator without realizing it. Now that she did, she pressed harder. "I'm never going back there. I can't."

"I meant, I would never have wanted to leave like this. It's not how I thought it would be." He squeezed her hand. "But this is how it is. And this is all I ever wanted—to leave."

"It's not how I thought it would be, either." But it wasn't the destruction in their wake she was referring to. It wasn't anything behind them. It was the warm hand on top of hers; it was the child curled up in the backseat.

She'd thought she would be leaving alone.

The prairie was as flat as ever, and Jule hated its endless sameness as much as she always had, more now, in the twilight, with the sunset casting its red light across the corn and making her think of fire. But a gray mist hung on the horizon, where the line of highway disappeared over the curve of the earth. This far east, it was probably nothing but an illusion, or a cloud, or a hope, but Jule chose to believe it was the faint outline of the mountains, the promise of a place where the earth erupted to meet the sky, and nothing stretched on forever except the weight of hands, the warmth of skin, and the highway that would carry them away. She drove faster, racing the sun, swallowing the miles that lay between her and a new life, where she could be Jule Whoever, where she could even, if she dared, be Juliet, where she could be anyone. You couldn't run away from your troubles, her uncle had once told her, any more than you could run away from your family, or your fate, or yourself.

But you could try.

## ACKNOWLEDGMENTS

It's terrifying to write a book. I imagine it would be even more terrifying to do so alone. Fortunately, I'll never know, as this book—like everything I've written—survived its birth thanks only to the careful nurturing of people far wiser than me. Basically, it took a village.

For that care and nurturing—and for reading drafts and scribbling notes, smoothing rough edges and navigating thorny plots, plying me with caffeine and ego-boosting compliments, offering me soft couches and extra-long power cords, baking me brownies and talking me off ledges and even forcing on me the occasional hug—I thank Holly Black, Libba Bray, Sarah Rees Brennan, Cassandra Clare, Erin Downing, Maureen Johnson, Jo Knowles, E. Lockhart, Sarah Mlynowski, Dan Poblocki, and Marie Rutkoski. (True, they all refused to actually write the book *for* me, but I forgive them.)

Thank you also and always to my editor/cheerleader/therapist/guru Erin Clarke, for making the words right—and to designer Kate Gartner, for making them beautiful. I'm grateful to everyone at Knopf for their tireless support of my writing, and for making my dream of this book a reality. And speaking of dreams, I'm also deeply grateful to my agent Barry

Goldblatt, who strongly suggested I should stop dithering about what to write and follow mine.

Finally, though Stephen King technically had nothing to do with the writing of this book, I'm thanking him anyway, for making me the person who could write it.